# Fortunate
## Friends

Louise Guy

ISBN: 978-0-6480144-6-1

Edited by Alexandra Nahlous

*For Judy (Mum)*
*Your strength, independence and generosity are*
*truly inspirational. Thank you for always being so*
*supportive, interested and encouraging.*

# CHAPTER ONE

## *Shauna*

Shauna's breath streamed white into the night air as she tried to warm her fingers. Her watch confirmed it was 2.45 a.m., and instead of being fast asleep, she stood with at least two hundred others in a park across from the hotel.

The fire alarms had gone off twenty minutes earlier, yet hotel guests still peered out from the upper levels. Were they deaf? If the alarm hadn't been enough to shock them out of their sleep, surely the loud, recorded voice ordering to evacuate would?

The temperature had dropped to six degrees, and while some guests had grabbed blankets from their rooms, others stood in skimpy pyjamas, and a few had nothing more than a towel wrapped around them. Shauna now appreciated the extra thirty seconds she had taken to throw on a pair of jeans and her long wool-lined jacket, before grabbing her computer bag and dashing down the stairs.

The alarm continued and the noise level increased as two fire engines arrived. Six firefighters jumped out and raced into the building. Shauna was not in the mood to wait and watch. With an important meeting at nine o'clock, she'd stayed up until midnight to put the finishing touches on her presentation. Now cold, tired and annoyed, she was grateful for the flashing neon sign of an all-night cafe a few doors down from the hotel.

Shauna pushed open the door and was greeted by a buzz of music and chatter. The majority of the patrons were in their pyjamas, laughing and ordering drinks, definitely making the most of the situation. She slid into a booth. As much as she'd prefer to be sleeping, she might as well use the time to go over her presentation once more. She pulled out her laptop and clicked through the PowerPoint slides. Her pitch to Tonacoal, a large mining company, was one she intended to win. Since she had joined I-People in the role of business development manager twelve months earlier, she had predominantly worked with hospitality clients. Tonacoal would allow her to expand her portfolio.

'You're keen.'

Shauna jerked her head up. A guy in his late thirties, dressed in a singlet and Mickey Mouse boxer shorts, stood next to her booth. She suppressed a smile. 'Sorry, are you talking to me?'

He smiled, dimples creasing his cheeks. 'You're dedicated to be working at this hour.'

'Figure I might as well fill in the time somehow.' She raised her eyebrows and looked him up and down. 'Interesting outfit, by the way.'

The guy stared down at his pyjamas and laughed. 'You never know when you'll want to impress some crazy workaholic in the middle of the night. I like to be prepared.'

Shauna felt her smile slip. God, he sounded just like Simon. He'd always called her a workaholic, and then used it as his excuse to cheat on her. 'I'm not a workaholic.'

The guy put up his hands, his blue eyes piercing hers. 'Hey, no need to get defensive. It was a joke, a bad one obviously. It's not a normal night for any of us. At least you had enough sense to grab your computer. I've left mine in the hotel. If it burns down I'm in huge trouble. I started a new job this week and I'm supposed to be wowing a client in a few hours, plus I'm meeting a colleague I've heard is a complete pain in the arse. If I turn up like this,' he indicated to his clothing, 'I'm not sure I'll make the finest first impression.'

'No, probably not. The hotel will reopen soon so it probably won't be an issue.' Shauna's eyes flicked back to her screen. She was no longer in the mood to make small talk. This guy would be like the rest of them. Underneath the smile and charm he'd have another agenda, just like Simon had. She continued reading through the presentation, conscious that he hadn't moved. Why was he still standing there? She looked up, noting that his smile no longer reached his eyes. His eyebrows were raised. She didn't owe him an explanation. He clearly couldn't take a hint so she'd need to spell it out. She pointed at her screen. 'Sorry, but I need to go over this. So, if you don't mind.'

He continued to stare. 'Evacuations don't bring out your empathetic side, do they?'

'What?' Why was he still talking? Hadn't he got the hint that she would like him to go away? Shauna gripped the edge of her seat. Was he planning to insult her again?

He folded his arms. 'You're not exactly friendly. I thought emergency situations were supposed to be a bonding experience.'

'Are you for real?' Shauna glanced at the clock on the cafe wall. 'Three in the morning and you expect me to be delighted that some loser in his underwear is hitting on me? Considering half of the hotel guests came down in the lifts, rather than the stairs, I don't think this is an emergency situation.'

He shook his head. 'Loser? Really? That hurts. Cute, adorable, smart – they're all names I'm used to. But "loser"? Never been called that before.' He didn't wait for a reply, instead turned and retreated to the counter. The guy serving laughed at something he said.

Shauna averted her eyes. She knew it wasn't his fault that she was constantly on edge when it came to men. Even though twelve months had passed, trusting anyone after Simon was going to be hard. So far, unless it was for work, she found even talking to men difficult. She didn't know if she'd ever want to put herself in a position to be hurt so badly again. It wasn't just the cheating, it was the way he had tried to undermine her, taking credit for her work and suggesting to clients they request him as their account manager rather than her. She pushed it out of her mind and spent the next thirty minutes engrossed in her presentation. The cafe was empty when she'd finally finished.

'Hotel's open.' A girl wiping down the counter called over to her. 'False alarm.'

Shauna smiled. 'Thanks.' She packed up her computer and dropped some coins into the tip jar on the way out, conscious that she hadn't ordered anything. It was nearly four already. Hopefully, she would be able to get another hour or two sleep before her alarm sounded.

❊

'Graham and Michael will just be a minute.' The receptionist held up a piece of paper. 'Also, this phone message is for you. Why don't you take a seat while you wait?'

'Thank you.' Shauna took the message and walked over to the waiting area. She couldn't help being impressed by the spectacular views Tonacoal enjoyed of Sydney Harbour. She unfolded and read the message. It was from a Josh Richardson, who, according to the note, was running late.

Shauna went back to the front desk. She smiled at the receptionist. 'I'm afraid this message isn't for me. I've never heard of this guy.'

'He definitely asked for you, Ms Jones. I do apologise if I got the name wrong.'

'I'm not meeting anyone. I think you'll find it's for someone else.'

Confusion clouded the receptionist's face. 'I'm sorry for the error. I'll sort out the mistake when he turns up.'

Shauna returned to her seat, closed her eyes and took a calming breath. This was a big contract and an important client for I-People to obtain. Their elaborate office space and million-dollar views confirmed Tonacoal were doing well. She picked up a magazine from the coffee table and flicked through it. She barely looked up when the lift opened and a man carrying an overnight bag and briefcase walked out. Shauna's interest sparked when the receptionist spoke.

'She's in the waiting area, but I'm afraid she didn't seem to know who you are.'

4

'Oh, my interesting morning continues.' He smiled at the receptionist, and came over to Shauna.

She was already on her feet. What the hell was going on?

'Josh Richardson.' He stuck out his hand. He was tall, at least six foot. His beautifully cut charcoal suit sat snugly across his broad shoulders. Freshly shaven, he smelled clean, musky. This was a man who knew how to present himself. Looking at Shauna, his smile extended from his lips to the furthest depths of his eyes.

Had he not recognised her? Shauna's arms remained crossed. 'I believe you already know me as *a complete pain in the arse*.'

Josh's smile was replaced with a frown. He stared at her. 'Oh no.' He shook his head. 'Sorry, I didn't recognise you. You look a lot more professional during the day. Your hair wasn't that straight last night, was it? I kind of remember it being all messed up.'

Shauna's hand flew up to her shoulder-length bob. Hair? He was asking about her hair? She dropped her hand. 'Aside from standing around in your underwear in the middle of the night, who are you?'

The furrows in Josh's forehead deepened. 'Are you kidding?'

'No, other than being amused by the boxer shorts you choose to wear to bed, I don't know anything about you. Should I?'

'Craig didn't bother to mention I'm the new national marketing manager for I-People, and I'd be joining you for the meeting this morning?'

Shauna stared at him. 'Hold on, you can't turn up unannounced and join me at the last minute for a sales presentation. Do you have any idea how important this client is?'

Josh nodded. 'Yes, and that's exactly why I'm here. Craig wants me to accompany all pitches where the potential revenue is over a million dollars.'

'We're supposed to work together on the pitch if you're going to be part of the team. What the fuck is Craig thinking?' Shauna walked over to the full-length office windows. A large cruise ship was preparing to depart from Circular Quay. Why on earth hadn't someone contacted her? She couldn't have this guy messing up her first opportunity to present to Tonacoal.

Josh followed her. 'Don't stress, I'm here to observe this meeting, nothing more. I'll make that clear from the start.'

Shauna pulled out her phone.

'Now, what are you doing?'

'I'm calling Craig. This is ridiculous.'

Josh leaned towards Shauna, his voice lowered. 'No time. The client's here. Go with it. Show me how good you are. Rumour has it you're a remarkable salesperson.'

Shauna took a deep breath. She needed to put the entire morning out of her mind and refocus. 'Really? A remarkable salesperson? That's a step up from *complete pain in the arse.*'

'Pain in the arse is obviously true, so prove to me you can live up to both reputations.' Josh winked and turned to greet the clients.

❖

'See, all went well.' Josh clicked his seatbelt on as the taxi drove out into the traffic towards Sydney Airport.

'It would have gone a lot better if you hadn't thrown me off at the start,' Shauna said.

'What – by turning up?'

'Yes, your only contribution to the entire day is pissing me off at 3 a.m., and then throwing me off minutes before a huge presentation this morning.' She did her best to suppress a smile. Shauna had in fact been quietly impressed by Josh; not that she was going to tell him. He'd listened attentively throughout the presentation, adding value with some comments about additional marketing programs that would be undertaken for the direct benefit of Tonacoal.

Josh grinned. 'If I just witnessed you presenting when you were thrown off, I'd love to experience you at your best. You were bloody good. You'll win the contract.'

Shauna didn't respond. He was saying all the right things, but so had Simon. Both personally and professionally. Always stroking her ego to ultimately get what he wanted. She wouldn't let it happen again.

'Are you always this quick to decide you hate someone, or do you not like anyone? I'm just wondering if I should be offended.'

Shauna opened her mouth, ready to launch another sarcastic response, but closed it when she saw his face. His smile had been replaced with a frown. She was being a bitch. It seemed she couldn't help herself these days. A man just had to look at her the wrong way and she felt her jaw clench. 'I'm sorry, okay? Lack of sleep and pressure to get Tonacoal aren't helping. Craig's heard talk of them absorbing LJR Mining's contracts. It could be worth millions. I wanted to be on my best game today, and with middle-of-the-night evacuations, and surprise marketing managers turning up, I wasn't. I apologise if I've been rude.'

Josh nodded and they lapsed into silence.

After a while he turned to Shauna. 'How about we start again?'

'How do you mean?'

'We've never met. Today I'm some annoying guy you happen to be sharing a taxi with. Tomorrow, however, you'll be introduced to the new marketing manager of I-People. Not only will you like and respect him, you'll find him funny and charming. You'll be delighted when he turns out to be one of the best assets you've ever had on your team. Sounds like a dream man, doesn't he?'

Shauna felt the corners of her mouth twitching. 'Dream man? I'd say he probably only exists in *your* dreams. I'm not saying don't try. If nothing else you might give me a good laugh.'

'Anything would beat the look of contempt I've been receiving.'

The reproval in Josh's voice was obvious. Shauna had been unfair, she knew that. 'Prove yourself to be as brilliant as you say and my expression might change.'

Josh laughed. 'I can't wait to see the respectful, awed version of Ms Shauna Jones.'

'Neither can I. Good luck is all I'll say.' As the taxi raced towards the domestic terminal, Shauna turned to the window in an effort to hide her smile.

# CHAPTER TWO

## *Frankie*

Frankie caught her toe in a crack in the footpath and stumbled. She righted herself just in time to hear Hope groan.

'Mum, you really don't need to come with us. We're not babies.' Hope's eyes avoided Frankie's and remained firmly fixed on the street ahead as they walked towards the school.

Frankie's gaze followed the direction of her daughter's. The street ahead was empty. What, or who, was she looking for? A tightness developed in Frankie's chest as she refocused her attention on Hope. Her ash-blonde hair was pulled into a tight ponytail, her face pinched and tired. Where had her gorgeous, fun-loving fifteen-year-old disappeared to? Only a few weeks ago they were laughing together, acting more like friends than mother and daughter. Now, Hope was a stranger; a sullen, moody stranger. Had teenage hormones finally got the better of her? Frankie knew she'd been lucky to this point to have had very close relationships with both of her girls. She'd spent so much time nurturing, supporting and encouraging them. She hoped that this new attitude of Hope's would be short-lived.

'You look tired, sweetheart, another late night?'

'What?'

'I said did you have a late night?'

Hope shrugged. 'No later than usual. Would you stop telling me I look tired all the time? I know I look like crap, I don't need to hear it from you, too. The next lot of exams are important and I have to

9

be ready. Anyway, I'm going ahead. Walk with Fern if you think a thirteen-year-old needs a bodyguard. I'll see you later.'

Frankie watched as Hope stalked off down the street, her long, lean legs speeding up with every step. It was uncanny at times to realise how similar they were. Her height, her looks, even her stride mirrored Frankie's. Tom's dark hair, brown eyes and olive complexion had hardly got a look-in with Hope. Whereas her youngest, Fern, other than Frankie's green eyes, was all Tom.

She turned to face her younger daughter. 'I don't need to walk with you if you'd rather go on your own.'

Fern took Frankie's hand and squeezed it. 'Don't worry, I'm not embarrassed to be seen with you ... yet.'

Frankie laughed, giving Fern a quick cuddle. 'That's good to hear. Give you another couple of years and you'll probably feel the same.'

'Maybe.' Fern stepped out of her mother's embrace and they continued walking. 'Hope's just trying to be cool. I don't need to try. I already am and everyone likes me. They're not nasty to me like they are to her. It's weird, isn't it? She's the pretty one, and everyone used to love her.'

'You're not just pretty, you're gorgeous,' Frankie said. 'But what do you mean, used to love her?'

'You know she was really popular, but this year it's all changed.'

'Why do you say that?'

''Cause it's true. She used to hang out with the cool kids, but now she hides in the library all the time.'

'Hides? Are you sure? She's probably studying. She's taking the exams pretty seriously.'

'Nah, she hides. Her only friend these days seems to be that weirdo, Hailey. You know, the one who dresses like a Goth.'

Frankie nodded. Fern was right. Hope used to be out after school a lot, either at friends' houses or at the park with her crowd. Now most nights she was either at the library or home straight after school, head in a book, studying.

They arrived at school a few minutes before the bell was due to ring. Frankie gave Fern a last hug. 'Have a great day, chickie.'

Fern hugged her back. 'Thanks, I'll see you later.' She turned and walked slowly across the courtyard towards the school building.

Frankie watched until she disappeared through the front entrance. She looked for Hope but saw no sign of her. She wondered if there was something other than exams worrying her eldest daughter. She sighed, knowing she'd have a better chance of winning a Nobel Prize than getting Hope to open up.

Frankie retraced her steps through the neighbourhood, taking in the character of the old houses that lined the streets. The majority were run-down, in need of repainting and repairs, but she delighted in imagining the houses when they were first built, freshly painted with proud owners. She rounded the street corner, her own house now in sight. The muscles in her neck tensed. A familiar figure sat on the pillar by the front gate. What the hell was he doing here? She was tempted to turn and walk the other way. Unfortunately, it was too late; he'd seen her. By the time Frankie reached the gate, her mouth was dry.

'Dash, why are you here?' There was no warmth identifiable in his cold, grey eyes. His pointed chin and permanent scowl sent a chill down Frankie's spine.

He spat on the ground in front of her. 'Is that any way to talk to your brother-in-law? What would Tom say if he knew his wife was so rude?'

Frankie crossed her arms. 'What do you want?'

Dash forced a smile. 'How about we go inside and chat.'

Frankie shook her head. Why on earth had she let this go on for so long? She should have told Tom when it had first happened. She had no reason to feel guilty, she'd done nothing wrong. 'No, we'll chat here. Tell me what today's blackmail threat is and then we can both get on with our day.'

'Fine, I'm here to give you a heads-up. Rod and I have a business proposition for Tom.'

'What is it?'

'Don't you worry your sweet little self about it for now. Just be aware, sometime in the next few days I'll be talking to Tom. When he discusses the idea with you, make sure you think it's fantastic. Okay?'

'I'm not promising you anything,' Frankie said.

'Really?' Dash raised an eyebrow. 'Do you think that's a good idea? Are you happy for me to finally share our little secret?'

Frankie's stomach churned. She was a grown woman, supposedly setting a good example for her daughters. Why did she continue to let him intimidate her? She needed to be strong, and this needed to stop. She pushed open the front gate. 'Do whatever you want. You'll ruin your relationship with Tom; make sure you realise that.'

Dash snorted. 'You reckon? Willing to risk it? Don't forget my mate Justin walked in on us, saw you on top of me, saw me saying no. He'll be happy to tell Tom every detail.'

Heat coursed through Frankie's body. Would he really have his friend lie for him? How could he? It was bad enough he'd tried to force himself on her. She clenched her fists. How she'd like to smash that smirk off his face. 'You wouldn't dare.'

Dash's lips curled up at the corners, the smirk replaced with what a stranger may have mistaken for a genuine smile. 'No, you're right, of course I wouldn't. Look I'm sorry, okay? That night should never have happened. I was drunk and I was stupid. I'm glad you stopped me before we really did have something to hide from Tom. How about we agree to never discuss it again?'

Frankie stared at him. From bastard to charming in less than twenty seconds. It could flip back the other way just as quickly. 'Fine. Now, can you go? I've got heaps to do.'

Dash slipped off the pillar. 'Sure, but please listen when Tom tells you about the business idea and see it as the great opportunity it is. He'll listen to you. I don't think it's much to ask.' He flashed Frankie another insincere smile, shoved his hands into his pockets and began whistling as he walked back down the street.

Frankie blew out a breath. Her stomach was in knots. How Tom's beautiful parents had produced a manipulative, lying, self-obsessed dirtbag like Dash, she would never understand. The only positive to come from the tragic accident that had claimed their lives was they weren't here to witness any of his behaviour. How she loathed him.

※

Frankie felt herself blush as the old ladies fussed around her. For goodness sakes, she'd only written some emails. You'd think she'd invented the internet the way they were going on. She'd never been appreciated or encouraged as much as she had in the four years she'd worked as a volunteer at the Birkdale Retirement Village. Expecting to do a bit of sewing for some of the residents, Frankie had been surprised and delighted to meet the wonderfully entertaining duo of Mavis and Betty. They seemed to run the social side of the village, ensuring the residents were provided with plenty of outings and entertainment. 'We're not here to die,' Mavis had told Frankie on the first day she'd volunteered. 'We're here to live, and live well.'

'Or at least go out with a big bang,' Betty had added.

Now Betty looked at Frankie, her eyes full of admiration. 'Where would we be without you, dear? You should start up your own computer business.'

Frankie laughed as she switched off the screen. If only her high school computer teacher could hear these old ladies talk. Perhaps he wouldn't have been quite so keen to tell her that switching on a television was probably as far as she should push herself when it came to understanding and using technology. 'My knowledge is pretty much limited to writing emails, so perhaps not the best idea.'

'You know more than emails,' Mavis tutted. 'What about that Google program? You're an expert.'

Frankie clamped her lips together. She couldn't wait to relay this latest stream of compliments to Tom. If she ever needed a self-esteem boost, these were the ladies to visit. 'Just because I can type words into a search engine doesn't mean I can run a business.'

'Search engine,' Mavis said. 'Listen to her would you, Betty? She's got the lingo down pat, operates the computer like a whiz. You must think about it, dear. We'd pay you, wouldn't we, Betty?'

'Of course,' Betty said. 'With the amount of emails I send, I almost want someone's help full-time. Don't forget Twitterbook. I need a profile set up so I can friend my grandkids. They're dying for me to tweet apparently. You could show me how to do that.'

Frankie touched Betty on the arm and smiled. 'If anyone could conquer Twitterbook it would be you, but I think you might be talking about Facebook or maybe Twitter. You seem to be forgetting that I am here to help you, and for free. Why would you want to pay me?'

The old ladies exchanged a guilty glance.

Frankie sighed. 'Listen, I appreciate you looking out for me, but we're doing fine. I'm busy enough with everything I do now. I'm out every day delivering leaflets and that's a perfect job around the girls' school hours.'

'You're a wealth of knowledge, dear. You need to use it to help yourself,' Betty said.

'I understand you mean well, but other than email, using the internet and basic word processing, my skills are fairly limited. I'm not even employable. Believe me, I've tried.' Frankie cringed as she thought of the last job interview she'd attended. A nineteen-year-old had looked down her nose at her and informed Frankie that she did not have the skills for the position. A position that could be summed up as general dogsbody. 'Helping you send emails is a change from mending your clothes.'

'Maybe you should start a clothing-repair business,' Mavis said. 'There are so many people here who would pay for that service.'

Betty nodded in agreement.

Frankie closed down the computer. 'What is it with you two today? You seem very keen for me to turn you all into customers and charge you, instead of allowing me to do the volunteer work I happily signed up for.'

'A young girl like you deserves more,' Mavis said.

'Why? I'm blessed with a gorgeous husband and two beautiful girls. What else would I want?' Frankie was beginning to regret sharing information from her personal life with these two. Ever since she had mentioned that they lived from week to week, the ladies had grilled her about Tom's job and presented her with money-making ideas. Yes, it would be nice to have more money, but jobs weren't growing on trees and they were in a good place right now. The old ladies didn't seem able to appreciate this. Frankie shuddered as she thought back to eight years earlier. Tom had been laid off and was unable to get work for nine months. Providing for a young family had been incredibly stressful. Tom's wage might not be a lot, but he had a full-time position which gave them security and a regular income.

'Forget we said anything.' Mavis patted Frankie's hand. 'Your business is not ours to meddle in.'

A smile played on Frankie's lips. 'I think you ladies should concentrate on something more important, like afternoon tea.' She directed them towards the door.

'Will you stay for a cuppa, dear?'

Frankie checked her watch. It was nearly two o'clock. Tom and the girls would still be at the botanical gardens. 'I won't today. My family are having a picnic and I promised I'd be there.'

Mavis sighed. 'Sounds lovely. You enjoy your afternoon and call or email if you need anything at all.'

Frankie chuckled as the two ladies made their way into the dining room, wondering what business ideas they would come up with between now and her next visit. She collected her belongings and walked quickly out of the retirement village towards the train station.

※

Frankie's delight at the vibrant explosion of red and yellow leaves that engulfed the gardens' magnificent elm and oak trees quickly disappeared when she spotted her family. Anger instantly replaced her joyous mood. What was *he* doing here?

Fern was the first to notice her approaching. She nearly knocked Frankie down when she rushed over to hug her. Frankie pushed her anger aside and managed a laugh before hugging her close. She linked arms with her daughter and walked to the little group. Hope glanced up and gave Frankie a brief smile before returning to the book she was engrossed in. A smile, that was progress. Hope had adopted a permanent glare when Frankie tried to question her about school and whether anything was wrong.

Tom's face flooded with relief when Frankie arrived. His dark hair was a mess, as if he'd been continually running his fingers through it, the way he did when he was stressed. He managed a smile. 'Hi, babe, oldies happy?'

'Yep, fixed them up for another week or so.' Frankie turned her attention to Dash. 'I wasn't expecting you here today.'

'Good to see you.' Dash made motions to get up and hug Frankie, but she waved him back down. He would never touch her again. 'No need, relax,' she told him. 'So, what's been happening?'

'I was just telling Tom about a fantastic business opportunity that's come my way. Rod's too, actually.'

Tom gave Frankie a tight smile. 'Yeah, my brothers are looking for investors, and Dash is the spokesperson.'

Frankie laughed, sitting down on the picnic rug to join the conversation. 'I can't imagine we're on the top of your list of potential investors. I'm assuming you need people who actually have money. What's the business?'

'Charter fishing. A mate of mine is moving up north so he wants to sell up. It does pretty well already and Rod and me reckon we could improve things heaps. We'd own two boats; one needs a bit of work but the other is in great nick. The deal includes everything – the gear, clients, future bookings. It's a once in a life time opportunity.' Dash hardly drew a breath as he described the business.

'Sounds wonderful,' Frankie said. 'I hope you find some investors. Can the bank help?'

'They'll give us most of the capital, but there's a shortfall of a hundred and fifty grand.'

'That's where we come in,' Tom said.

Frankie laughed again. 'Dash, take a look at our beat-up rental house, our invisible car and our handmade and op-shop clothes. Doesn't it give you some idea of our financial situation?'

Dash nodded. 'Yeah, but the manager said if you had an income, loaning you the money should be no problem.'

'Did you want Tom to be a partner, too?'

Dash averted his gaze. 'No. We didn't think it was up his alley and he'd probably need to stay in his job to guarantee the loan repayments.'

*Guarantee the loan repayments.* Did Dash honestly believe his bullying techniques the other day would have her agree to this? He must be out of his mind. They could hardly afford to feed themselves, let alone make loan repayments when Dash fell behind.

'Babe, they want us to go into bloody debt for them so they can run a business together that we have nothing to do with. Not up my alley? I've only loved fishing since I was three.' Tom's eyes flashed with a mixture of anger and pain.

Frankie tensed. Why did Dash always do this? She couldn't remember a catch-up with him when he didn't ask for something, causing anger and disappointment for Tom in the process.

'Don't be such a bloody drama queen,' Dash said. 'It'd only be a loan on paper. Me and Rod would pay you back.'

Frankie forced herself to look at Dash. 'If you can't make the repayment, are we responsible?'

'Well, yes, technically I suppose, but not with our plan. Blue Water Charters will only be profitable. We'd give you a percentage of the profit of course.'

'Most small businesses take a while to make a profit,' Frankie said. 'I've even read that a lot fail within the first few years. What if this happens?'

Dash didn't get a chance to answer.

'No.' Tom crossed his arms.

Dash scowled. 'What? You and Frankie need to discuss things.'

Tom glanced at Frankie. 'We already have an answer, don't we?'

Frankie nodded.

'We're not going into debt on your behalf, not when we can't pay it back,' Tom said.

'Oh, for fuck's sake, you wouldn't be paying anything. You aren't listening to me.'

'Don't talk like that in front of the girls.' Tom's voice was sharp. 'Why don't you go and hassle someone else for the money? We're trying to enjoy our afternoon, not be harassed by you. You still owe me five hundred dollars from Rob's twenty-first. That was eight years ago. As if I'm going to trust you with a hundred and fifty grand.'

Dash stood up. He looked as if steam would come out of his nostrils at any second. 'Fine, well, be an arsehole,' he said. 'Rod told me I'd be wasting my time talking to you. He obviously knows you better than I do. And for the record, Frankie, the deal's off.'

They sat in silence as Dash stormed off, hands shoved deep into his pockets.

Tom finally spoke. 'What a nerve. My brothers are a piece of work. We only ever hear from them when they want something, yet they give nothing in return. I didn't see any presents at Christmas for the girls, did you?'

'Be fair,' Frankie said. 'Rod always makes an effort. Dash doesn't, but he's only twenty-five and doesn't appreciate family life. Let it go. There's no point getting worked up about it.'

'I'm not.'

'The vein in your forehead is bulging. It's a bit of a giveaway.'

Fern nodded. 'Be careful, Dad, I think you might explode.'

Tom sighed. 'Sorry. He constantly disappoints me. Last time I heard from him was when he moved and wanted me to lift all the heavy stuff. Before that it was bailing him out after the bar brawl. He's never offered to help us. My parents would be doing somersaults in their graves if they knew. Anyway, what was he talking about, the deal being off?'

Frankie's gut twisted. 'Who knows? I have no idea what he's talking about half the time. I don't think he does either.' She hated lying to Tom. But she'd made a promise, a promise to a dying woman. A promise that she would look after her boys and make sure they remained a family. She could hardly go back on this promise, especially after all her mother-in-law had done for her.

She moved closer to Tom and put her arms around him. 'Try to forget about him. He's self-absorbed and probably doesn't realise how much we struggle. We've got each other; that's the main thing.'

'Yeah, Dad,' Fern joined in. 'We love you. Ignore him.'

'Second that,' Hope said, not looking up from her book.

Tom smiled. 'Where would I be without you lot?'

'Alone, like Mr Duck in the lake.' Fern broke up a biscuit and walked over to the water.

'They're good kids, aren't they?'

Frankie nodded. 'We're lucky.'

'Thank God they're not like Dash.'

'Yes, thank God.' Not only would Frankie ensure they were not like Dash, but they would never spend time alone with their uncle again. 'Come on, lie down and forget about him.'

Tom allowed Frankie to pull him down next to her. They lay together watching as Fern coaxed the duck closer.

A short time later Frankie shivered. The sun had sunk behind the buildings and the temperature had dropped. She got to her feet. 'As much as I'd love to keep lazing around, we'd better head home before we freeze. I'm pretty sure a train leaves in about fifteen minutes. We should be able to catch it if we hurry.'

Frankie was right, and it was not long before they were all sitting on the four-o'clock express. The buildings flashed by as they moved further away from Melbourne's centre. The terraced houses quickly gave way to larger, more expensive homes. Frankie wondered how often the people left their sanctuaries to enjoy time at the gardens. Did they need to escape like her and Tom? Frankie let her mind wander, conjuring up stories about the inhabitants of these houses. The stories changed as they sped away from the inner-city suburbs and the neighbourhoods began to take on a tired, neglected feel. The beautifully manicured gardens were replaced with a mishmash of overgrown and even concrete allotments. At last they reached their station and all piled out, ready to walk the short distance home. Frankie squeezed Tom's arm as Hope and Fern chatted companionably. She cherished the family time they spent together. The old Hope, the smiling, happy fifteen-year-old, seemed to have joined them for the afternoon.

As they walked down Lincoln Street, Hope moved away from Fern and picked up the pace. Two boys were standing at the corner ahead of them. They looked about the same age as Hope, who was now a good twenty metres in front of her family, her eyes firmly on the ground as she passed the boys. They said something to her and burst out laughing. Hope walked faster.

Frankie looked sharply at Tom. 'What was that about?'

'No idea, they're probably at school together.'

The boys sniggered again as Fern passed them, trying to catch up to Hope. She stopped, and for a moment Frankie thought she was going to say something, but decided against it and kept walking.

Frankie's heart rate quickened. 'They'd better not be being mean.'

'Why would they?'

Frankie didn't respond. They were now level with the boys. She stopped. 'Afternoon.'

They exchanged a look and laughed harder.

'Something funny? Or are you being deliberately rude?' Tom asked.

'No, sir,' the taller of the two said. 'Only having a bit of fun.'

'Okay, you make sure that's all it is.' He turned to Frankie. 'I'm going on ahead to check on the girls.'

Laughter spilled from the boys as Tom ran on. 'He can run. Not a complete no-hoper, then.'

'Oh, I don't know,' the other said. 'I'd say, looking at those losers, Hope's probably got no hope at all, what do you reckon?'

Frankie jabbed a finger at the boys. She was furious. 'Like to repeat that?'

The shorter boy looked Frankie up and down. 'Was talking to my mate. None of your business.'

Frankie stepped closer. She couldn't believe the cheek of this kid. 'You made it my business.'

'So what? You gonna run us down with your car? Oh sorry, I forgot, you don't have one. Bike maybe? Oops, silly me, you probably haven't got one of those either.'

Frankie shook her head, turned and started walking towards home. There was no point talking to this kid. The arrogance that spewed from him was putrid. Luckily, the others were out of sight and hearing. She ignored the increasing volume of a single voice chanting 'no-hopers' behind her. It wasn't hard to guess which of the two boys that was. She clenched her fists. Was this why Hope hid in the school library?

Frankie stopped in front of their gate and took a deep, calming breath. She sighed as she looked ahead to the rented house. It was badly in need of repainting. Peeling paint and broken boards took away any charm it may once have had. The rusted iron panels on the roof were in desperate need of replacement, but as their leaks were minimal the owner refused to spend money on them. Frankie was sure that the removal of the wire fencing that separated them from the next-door neighbour would improve the aesthetics, but it was required to keep the neighbour's yapping dog in. She bent down and yanked at a weed that poked out through the front wall. She did her best to keep the garden tidy and the house as clean as possible, but overall the house, which at best would be described as a demolisher's delight, was virtually impossible to present nicely. The boys had touched a nerve. True, they didn't have a lot of money, but she'd never considered that they looked poor. Bloody kids. She pushed open the broken gate and walked up to the house. Tom and Hope were talking as she came in.

'They're idiots, Dad.'

'What else do they say?'

'Oh nothing, honestly. They tease everyone in the class and we all ignore them.'

'They called me "Mini-No-Hope",' Fern said. 'I hate them.'

Frankie came into the kitchen and embraced Fern. 'I think Hope's got things sorted. Don't waste any more energy on them.'

'They're just stupid boys,' Hope said. 'Now, I've got homework to finish. I'll be in my room.' Frankie untied herself from Fern and followed Hope.

'Are you sure you're alright, sweetheart?'

'I'm fine.'

'Are they the only ones being horrible? Is it because we don't have much money?'

'No, they use anything they can to be mean. The tall one, Hamish, he's not too bad. It's the other one who causes most of the trouble, the short, nasty one. I can't imagine why they're friends. They think they're hilarious calling me "No-Hope".'

Frankie walked over to where Hope lay on the bed and sat down next to her. 'You keep ignoring him. If he gets worse, or upsets you, come to me and I'll talk to the school.'

'It's fine,' Hope said. 'Don't worry about me. I'm not five. I don't need my mummy sticking up for me.' She moved over to the small table she used as a desk. 'Gotta get this essay finished.'

Frankie knew when she'd been dismissed. She got up from the bed and stopped in Hope's doorway. 'If something else happens tell me, won't you?'

Hope rolled her eyes.

'I mean it. You don't need to put up with that kind of behaviour.'

Hope said nothing, her eyes now focused on her books.

Unease settled over Frankie as she hesitated in the doorway. The likelihood of this sullen, sulky version of her daughter discussing the problem with her was zero.

# CHAPTER THREE

## *Bec*

Bec attached the last ribbon and sat back. A mountain of brightly wrapped presents covered the kitchen bench. Now all they needed to do was move them to the lounge ready for the morning. She heard a clunk above her. Paul was doing something in the bedroom. Fat lot of help he'd been tonight. She gritted her teeth. He was probably sulking after the argument they'd had earlier. Another argument. It was time for the fighting to stop. She'd promised herself to keep things as normal as possible for the boys until after Alex's birthday; then she and Paul needed to sit down and decide what was best for the future. She couldn't go on like this.

Bec slipped off the stool and went in search of Paul. He could help her move the presents and blow up some balloons. She made her way up the stairs to their bedroom and stopped in the doorway. Paul's back was to her, his t-shirt pulling tight across his broad shoulders, the sleeves hugging his well-defined biceps. Six months ago you would have called him pudgy. The transformation to lean and muscly was astounding. He was clearing clothes out of his drawers. Bec was sure he'd told her he wasn't going to Sydney this week. 'What are you doing?'

Paul didn't turn around. 'What does it look like I'm doing? I'm moving out.'

Bec stared at Paul's back. Surely he wouldn't ruin Alex's birthday? 'You've got to be kidding. You're leaving now?'

24

Paul continued stuffing clothes into his sports bag. 'Yep, leaving now.'

'So, let me get this straight, after months of lying and cheating, you pick tonight, *of all nights*, to leave.'

Paul forced the zip shut. 'What do you expect? I can't stand another minute living with you. Your nagging and bitching are why I'm leaving tonight, *of all nights*.'

'Are you from another planet? Complaining about you having an affair is hardly unreasonable.'

The lines around Paul's eyes were tight as he turned to face Bec. 'Oh sorry, I forgot, you're the queen of reasonable, aren't you?'

Bec clenched her fists. When had he become such a sarcastic prick? 'Alex is turning seven. He won't understand you not being here!'

'Fine, tell him I'll be back tomorrow afternoon for his party.'

'What about the morning and giving him his presents?' Bec felt her stomach contract. Alex would be gutted if Paul wasn't there.

'Oh, for God's sake, I'll ring him in the morning. Feel free to tell him whatever you want. How about Daddy's a lying, cheating bastard?'

Bec stared at the stranger in front of her. There was no point trying to reason with him. 'You're a real piece of work.' She picked up his aftershave and threw it, narrowly missing his head. 'Don't forget this. You'll probably want to cover up the smell of arsehole.'

Paul grabbed his bag and stormed out of the room, kicking the door on his way.

'Of course.' Bec sighed. 'Wake the kids as well.' She heard the screech of tyres on the driveway a couple of minutes later.

Bec sank back on the bed, nausea replacing the cramping sensation in her stomach. After nine years, how had their marriage been reduced to this? If not for Alex and Will, she would have walked out two months ago, when she had become suspicious. Late nights at the office, constant interstate trips, the sudden need to get fit and buy new clothes. Was he having a midlife crisis? Initially, Bec had joked about this, but she was no longer joking. Why does an advertising executive suddenly need to work until midnight? Why were overnight trips to Sydney essential every week? Paul's explanation – that his promotion came with more responsibility – didn't cut it.

Bec wiped her eyes with her sleeve. She would not allow herself to cry. She had a mountain of things to organise for Alex's party and needed to push all thoughts of her bastard husband far, far away. She sprang off the bed and headed downstairs.

❅

A little after six Bec woke to high-pitched squeals as Alex ran into her bedroom. She sat up and smiled. His excitement was contagious.

'Mum, Mum! I'm seven! Where's Daddy?'

Bec laughed, ruffling Alex's hair. 'My goodness, you're so big I can hardly fit my arms around you. How can you be seven already?' She planted a kiss on his cheek before he wriggled away.

Alex's eyes darted to each side of the room. 'Is Dad in the shower? I'll go and tell him to hurry up.'

A lump rose in Bec's throat. Of all days to disappoint Alex, her gentle, sensitive boy. What on earth was she going to tell him? 'Hold on, darling. Daddy's not in the bathroom.'

'Where is he? He has to come downstairs and see me open my presents.'

'So, you've been and checked?'

Alex's face lit up. 'Yep. There are hundreds, even more than last year.'

'Hundreds. Wow, that's fantastic, but I have to tell you something about Daddy.'

'What?'

Bec swallowed. 'I'm sorry, honey, but he's been called into work early. He did say to give you this.' She gave Alex a cuddle and kiss. 'And he said to let you know he's bringing a special present with him this afternoon.'

Alex's lip started to tremble. 'But we all need to be here.'

Damn Paul. Couldn't he have waited one more day? 'How about we wake up Will and then go and poke some of the parcels? If you like I'll make pancakes for breakfast. Sound good?' The lump in her throat expanded as Alex struggled not to cry. She put an arm around him. 'Come on, it's still your birthday, still the best day in the whole year. Let's not allow anything to spoil today, okay?'

'I guess so.' Alex hung his head but allowed Bec to steer him out of her room and towards Will's. They woke him and he bounced straight out of bed. He jumped on Alex, giving him a big slobbery kiss. 'Come on, Lexie,' Will said. 'Guess what present I chose? You're going to love it.'

Alex hesitated for a split second before chasing after Will. A slow smile spread across Bec's face. Alex's birthday excitement was back again.

The phone rang as Bec followed the boys downstairs.

'Let me answer,' Alex yelled. 'It might be Daddy.'

'Bloody better be,' Bec muttered.

Alex's delighted squeals confirmed it was Paul. After speaking for a few minutes, he handed Bec the phone. She watched as Alex rushed back to the present pile and started ripping off the paper. She'd spent half the night thinking of all the things she'd like to say to Paul, but not with Alex and Will within earshot.

'Well, whatever you told him worked,' Bec said. 'At least he now wants to open his presents. Ten minutes ago, when he discovered you had better things to do on his birthday, he didn't.'

'Hello to you, too.'

Bec didn't respond.

Paul cleared his throat. 'Fine, so what's the special present I'm supposed to buy?'

'What?'

'Alex said he couldn't wait to unwrap the special present from me this afternoon. I thought we'd already got everything.'

'I figured with you otherwise engaged this morning, the least you could do was go out and find him a special present.'

The phone went quiet. Bec rolled her head from side to side, trying to relieve the tension in her neck. After a few moments Paul spoke.

'Is this how things are going to be? Punishment's started already?'

'Call it what you want. I've gotta go. You might be happy to miss the fun but I'm not.'

'Wait, before you hang up. Would you take some photos?'

Bec slammed down the phone. She took a deep breath before turning her attention to Alex and the frantic present opening.

❄

'He did what?'

'Left. The bastard stormed out at ten o'clock last night.'

Jess dropped the tea towel onto Bec's kitchen bench. 'He left? You didn't kick him out?'

'I didn't get the chance. I told you I was going to get things sorted out one way or the other after Alex's birthday, but he beat me to it.' Bec's lip started to quiver. 'I'm a gullible idiot. I should have kicked him out two months ago when Maria first contacted me. Pass me the piping bag, would you?'

Jess handed it across to Bec. 'Maria? The one who sent the shirt?'

'Yep, the one he convinced me was psycho, angry at him for rejecting her advances. Stole his shirt out of his overnight bag, smeared it with her lipstick and then mailed it to me claiming they were having an affair. She was supposedly fired for sexually harassing clients and lying to their wives. She included a letter with the shirt that said he was looking for the thrill of an affair, whether it was her or someone else.' Bec started piping black lines onto Alex's soccer-ball cake.

'You're not gullible. He was pretty convincing. I believed him; so did Max. You said that guy Robert he works with, the one who's a pretty good guy, confirmed his story, too. Why would he lie?'

28

Bec dropped the piping bag on the bench and looked at Jess. 'As Robert's moved to London, I'll probably never find out. And you wanted to believe him. He's an advertising expert for God's sake. He could sell shit to a sewerage farm.'

Jess laughed, quickly covering her mouth with her hand. 'Sorry, I know I shouldn't be laughing.'

Bec smiled. 'If I can't laugh my only option is to fall in a heap and start blubbering. I've done enough of that in the past few weeks to last a lifetime.'

'Oh, Bec.'

Tears stung Bec's eyes. Jess's tone and face were full of concern; the same genuine concern she'd shown Bec a few years earlier, when on the first day of kindergarten Alex had fallen out of a tree and broken his arm. Jess had taken Will home to look after him so Bec could go in the ambulance with Alex. When Bec, exhausted from hours spent at the hospital, had arrived to pick up Will, Jess had opened the front door with a bottle of wine in one hand and a gorgeous toy dog for Alex in the other. They'd been best friends ever since.

'Is Paul still denying he cheated?'

Bec nodded, blinking away the tears. 'Still the same old story. He's never cheated. Nothing ever happened with Maria and the late nights he now spends working with Chris Jenkins are to make the most of the time she's in Melbourne each week. Their dinners in Sydney are of course purely business.'

'She's the woman you spoke to?'

'Yep, the one he let me assume was a man, until I saw a photo and *he* turned out to be a gorgeous woman. That certainly explained all the late nights.' Bec had been kidding herself when she'd rung Chris Jenkins. She'd assumed Chris would become defensive, deny the affair. Instead, she'd just laughed before dismissing Bec. Her exact words had been: '*Ask your husband. This is a place of work, Bec. I don't have time for your insecurities.*' And then she'd hung up. Paul had been furious when he'd arrived home that night – concerned more about being made to look like a fool at work than the impact his actions were having on their marriage.

'I still can't believe he would do this to you,' Jess said. 'He's convinced Max he's done nothing wrong.'

Bec rolled her eyes. 'No offence, but your husband is far too nice. Of course Paul would lie to him. You guys are our best friends. He's not going to admit he's at fault, that he's wrecked everything. There have been too many lies. Too many arguments. Anyway, let's not talk about him anymore. It's bad enough that he'll be here later for Alex's party. I'll have to be civil towards him for Alex's sake.'

Jess squeezed Bec's arm. 'We still have a couple of hours before we need to pick up the other kids from school and get the party underway. Tell me what you need me to do.'

'You're a lifesaver, you know that, don't you?'

'You'd do the same for me. In fact, you did when I went down with gastro two hours before Katie's fifth birthday party.'

Bec laughed. 'And everyone else came down with it a day later.'

Jess's face screwed up in horror at the memory. 'Best forgotten. Now, I'll check on Oscar and Will and make sure they aren't destroying your playroom. I'll be back in a minute to help.'

Bec forced her body to relax as she stood at the front door and watched Alex run down the driveway and launch himself into Paul's arms. After last night she wasn't sure how Paul would act towards her. At least he'd turned up before the other guests. The party wasn't due to start for another fifteen minutes.

Alex came running back as Paul opened the boot of the car. 'Daddy said I have to go inside and wait so he can bring in the special present.'

'Come on, then,' Bec said with a smile. 'Where's Will? He'll want to see you unwrap it.' Bec called Will down from upstairs and the three of them went into the lounge.

Paul winked at the boys but avoided Bec's gaze as he walked into the room holding a large, towel-covered box. His arms were outstretched so the box didn't touch his shirt.

Another body-hugging shirt. How many more clothes was he going to buy?

'Now, it's not wrapped, but there's a reason for that. You'll see when you remove the towel.' Paul sat the box down next to Alex. 'Go on – take it off.'

Alex flung off the towel, his face breaking into a huge smile. 'Oh wow! Will, Mum, it's a kitten.' He turned to face Bec. 'This is the best birthday ever. You said we could never have a cat. I'm going to call him Earl.'

Bec forced a smile as she watched Alex pull the grey-and-white kitten from the box. He and Will laughed as it started to explore and climbed straight up one of the curtains.

Bec shook her head. She caught Paul's eye and pointed towards the kitchen. 'A word, perhaps.' Heat flooded Bec's face as she moved out of the room. She turned to face Paul. 'How could you?'

Paul folded his arms. 'What? You're the one who told me to get him a special present, so I did.'

'A cat? We agreed we wouldn't get a cat or a dog. You know cats freak me out. How could you be so insensitive?'

Paul shrugged.

'That's it?'

'Yep.'

Bec clenched and unclenched her fists. She took a deep breath and picked up a plate of party food. She needed to keep busy or she would explode. 'The kids will be here in five minutes. Let's start moving some of the food to the tables outside.'

'Um, okay.' Paul dropped his arms and moved to help Bec. 'You're being remarkably mature.'

Bec stared at her husband. 'You're hoping I'll go ballistic, aren't you? I don't even know who you are anymore. You're not the man I married. You've achieved your aim, I'm pissed off. Now, let's get ready for the party.'

Bec took the plate of food outside, conscious of Paul behind her. Even though she didn't want to know the answer, she couldn't help herself asking. 'So, where did you go last night? Chris's hotel?'

Paul placed the food on the table. 'Jesus, you're not going to let this affair stuff go, are you? No, I didn't go to her hotel.'

Bec hesitated. She wanted to ask more, but knew it wouldn't get them anywhere. The majority of their arguments the last two months had started with her questioning his whereabouts and him lying. 'Okay, so we need to work out what we're going to tell the boys.'

Paul nodded. 'Not today. Let's not ruin Alex's birthday. I'll call you tomorrow.'

'Fine,' Bec said. 'Now, I can hear car doors slamming. Finish bringing the food out, would you? And I'll go and let them in.'

Bec flopped down beside Jess on the couch and handed her a glass of wine. 'Thank God, that's over.'

Jess clinked her glass with Bec's and took a sip. 'Birthday parties are exhausting. Still, Alex looked like he had a wonderful time, and so did the other kids. The jumping castle was a real hit. You were lucky to get it for free.'

'I know. The perks of having a friend whose husband runs an inflatables business. They're busy on the weekends, but rarely booked midweek. Perfect for an after-school party. Celeste offered, which was really lovely of her.'

'So, how did it go with Paul? You looked completely normal around each other. No one would have guessed anything was going on.'

Bec sipped her wine. 'Good, I don't want anyone knowing just yet. I didn't feel normal around him. Honestly, the moment I saw that bloody cat I just wanted to punch him. You'd think ruining our marriage would be enough, but apparently not. I'm beginning to really hate him.'

Jess gave a sad smile. 'You're angry. It's understandable.'

'Do you think it's my fault that he went looking elsewhere?'

'Your fault? Why would it be your fault?'

'I let myself go a bit once the boys were born. Put on weight, stopped caring so much about my appearance.' Bec ran her hand through her ash-brown hair. 'I can't even think when I last had my highlights done.'

'You don't need to lose weight. You're skinny enough. I work out three times a week and still can't get my stomach to shrink to the size of yours.'

Bec looked down at her stomach. Jess was right. The stress of the last two months had seen her lose weight.

'You're juggling two young kids, a part-time job and a husband who is away half the week. Your appearance has nothing to do with what he's done. And for the record, I think you look great.'

Bec smiled. 'Thanks. He says it's all my nagging and bitching that's driven him away. I'm only nagging and bitching because he's constantly lying. I wish he could be honest for five minutes. It must be the lawyer in me. I can't leave things alone until I know why he cheated.'

A shriek came from outside, followed by lots of laughter.

'That jumping castle is certainly getting a workout,' Jess said. 'You know it's not just the lawyer in you. I can't imagine there's anyone who's been cheated on who doesn't need, and deserve, an answer to why it happened. So, what are you going to do now?'

'Get some advice. I'll see if Celeste's available at work tomorrow and have a chat to her. She specialises in divorce.'

Jess sucked in a breath. 'Divorce?'

Bec sighed. 'I don't see a whole lot of other options right now, do you?'

'It's just so final.'

'Yep.' Bec poured herself another glass of wine and held the bottle out to Jess. It would be final. She dreaded having to tell the boys.

'No thanks.' Jess put her empty wineglass on the coffee table and got up. 'I'd better get my lot together and head home. Max is probably wondering where his dinner is.'

'Take some leftovers, we've got heaps.'

Jess went into the kitchen and filled a container, before going in search of her three tired children.

'Thanks so much for your help.' Bec hugged Jess as the kids ran down the driveway.

Jess returned the hug with an extra-tight squeeze. 'You're welcome. Now, promise you'll ring me if I can help. Anything at all. Babysitting, shoulder to cry on, wine-delivery service, anything. Max and I are here for you.'

Tears filled Bec's eyes as she hugged Jess again.

Bec looked out of the window, the quietness of her office a stark contrast to the vibrancy of St Kilda Road below. Trams zipped through the central median, while cars crawled along the congested side lanes. Leaves were beginning to turn orange in the park across the road, a sure sign that the beautiful summer days were now behind them. She sighed, turning back to the contracts on her desk. As much as she loved being a lawyer, today was not the right day to review contracts. She was having difficulty concentrating on anything other than the situation with Paul. The last thing Bec needed was to make a mistake with a client's intellectual property. She put the contracts aside, deciding to go in search of Celeste and tackle them later. She still hadn't had a chance to thank her for the loan of the jumping castle.

She stuck her head around Celeste's door and found her on the phone. Celeste waved her in and pointed to the couch. Bec sank down, admiring – as she always did – the beautiful furnishings.

'Sorry.' Celeste hung up the phone. 'Another angry husband having his lawyer object to the wife receiving a fair share of their worldly goods. What's up?'

'I came to offer to take you out for lunch to say thanks for the castle. Please pass on my thanks to Ross; it was the star of the party.'

Celeste smiled. 'I'm glad. So, how old was the birthday boy?'

'Alex turned seven, and they all had a ball. I gave out as many business cards as possible, so hopefully the freebie will pay off.'

'Great. I'd love to come for lunch but I'm flat out. Next week perhaps?'

Bec got up, surprised by the quick dismissal. Normally, she and Celeste would sit and have a good laugh together. She stopped at the door. 'Everything okay?'

Celeste looked up from her computer. 'Sorry, I'm having one of those days. Too many people wanting to get divorced. Sometimes I wonder why I went into divorce law. I should have done something less emotional, like you.'

Bec laughed. 'Financial law is hardly unemotional.'

'Of course not, I meant the stuff you do with intellectual property. I forget sometimes you wear two hats.'

'You'd be surprised at how emotional people get over the ownership of their song, poem or computer program.'

'At least they're trying to protect something, rather than rip its head off in a bitter fight to prove they're right.'

*Rip its head off.* That's exactly what she'd like to do to Paul right now. Oh God. Bitter and resentful were not words she'd ever imagined using to describe herself. Bec swallowed, trying to push down the rising lump in her throat. 'Mmm, speaking of ripping heads off, when you've got some spare time I might book an appointment for some advice.'

'Sure, who for? Not you?'

'Afraid so. Paul's walked out and I'm going to need a good lawyer.' Hot tears filled Bec's eyes as she bit her bottom lip. Hearing her words out loud made everything sound real. Celeste's shocked expression didn't help.

Handing Bec a tissue, Celeste led Bec back into the office. 'Come and sit down.'

Bec wiped her eyes and blew her nose. 'Sorry, I thought I was handling everything.' She cleared her throat, embarrassed.

Celeste leaned towards her. 'Don't worry, you're not expected to be able to handle everything. You'd be amazed at how many tissues I go through in here. So, what's happened?'

Bec told Celeste about Paul's behaviour, the affair, the fights and arguments.

'Look, you need to speak to Paul, clarify you both want to end the marriage, and go from that point. In the meantime, I'd suggest the two of you try to work out something amicable over having access to the kids. The more you can sort out yourselves, the easier it will be.' Celeste handed Bec another tissue. 'However, if he starts to cancel meetings on you, we'll get things rolling immediately. One bit of advice. Make sure that a separation or divorce is definitely what you want. Clients often come in here and spend a fortune working out the details of a divorce, and at the last minute get back together. Of course I witness more of the opposite, but it does happen.' Celeste tilted her head to one side. 'Has Paul admitted to having an affair?'

Bec shook her head.

'But you're sure?'

Bec nodded.

'Midlife crisis perhaps?'

Bec wiped her eyes again. 'That's what I thought. He started going to the gym, which he hasn't done for years, lost weight and went out and bought a truckload of new clothes. The woman he's been seeing is gorgeous. I guess he felt he needed to get in shape to keep her interest.'

Celeste nodded. 'It happens too often. The man hits forty and his own ageing is brought into focus. To make himself feel younger he does things that include some or all of the following.' She ticked them off her fingers. 'Working out five times a week, having surgery, buying a sports car, and jumping into an affair with someone at least ten, if not fifteen, years younger than him. Who is she?'

'A woman he works with, and we're both still two years away from forty, so he's jumped the gun a bit.'

'You know what I mean, though. A lot of women in their late thirties, especially with the demands of small children, aren't able to put their appearance first. Things start to sag and the men freak out.'

Bec could only imagine her face was beetroot red it felt so hot.

Celeste put her arm on Bec's. 'I didn't mean you. You're fantastic. I'm only saying that guys are stupid when it comes to ageing, and cheating is often the result. There's no excuse for an affair, so don't for one moment blame yourself.'

The intercom beeped on Celeste's phone. 'Celeste, your one o'clock is here. What do you want me to do with her?'

'Offer her a coffee and I'll be out in a minute.' Celeste sighed. 'Sorry, I have to go. This woman is a friend of the big boss so I can't have her waiting. Come and talk to me anytime you need to. I can definitely give you advice and handle any legal work.'

Bec thanked Celeste and made her way towards her own office, stopping at the ladies' on the way. She peered at her face in the mirror. Her skilfully applied makeup did its best to hide her blotchy skin, but she could see she didn't look healthy. Her recent weight loss suited her waistline but not her face. It looked pinched and drawn. Being able to blame the bags under her eyes on last night's lack of sleep would be nice, but she wasn't kidding herself. They had been there for weeks.

A tear rolled down Bec's cheek. She must be tired. She was never this emotional. She blinked away more tears, aware that the red-eyed reflection staring back at her looked more like a woman in her fifties, not her late thirties. No wonder Paul had strayed.

# CHAPTER FOUR

## *Shauna*

Shauna leaned back in her chair as Josh continued his presentation to Craig and the department heads. She was impressed. He'd had them eating out of his hands the moment he'd started speaking. Two weeks had passed since they'd returned from Sydney and Josh had shown he was keen to prove that he was an asset to the company. This was the second marketing meeting Shauna had sat in on and the amount of work he had achieved in such a short time was phenomenal. A new radio commercial would be airing the next day and an outdoor advertising campaign was under discussion now. Josh had mock-ups of the ads on display and Shauna could see from the directors' faces that they were captivated. So was she. He certainly knew his stuff. His passion and enthusiasm were contagious. A small smile played on Shauna's lips as she thought back to their middle-of-the-night encounter in Sydney. He probably wouldn't be thrilled if he knew she was picturing him in his Mickey Mouse boxers right at this moment.

'So, I would like a show of hands for your preferred ad,' Josh said. 'Once we've confirmed our choice with the agency, it will appear on the side of Kings' buses starting Friday next week.' He held up the artwork from the first version of the ad.

After a decision had been made – a clear majority in favour of the third choice – Josh wrapped up the meeting. Shauna stayed behind as the other department heads retreated to their offices. She clapped her hands together. 'Clever, very clever.'

'What, the one they chose?'

'No, not the ad, I meant the way you manipulated them. I was told they would be deciding on the concept of outdoor advertising, a decision you helped them bypass altogether by focusing on the actual advertisement.'

Josh finished collecting his papers and winked. 'I hoped nobody would notice. I'm not waiting for a bunch of directors to make those kinds of decisions. That's my job. They approved the ad I wanted them to.'

'The other three weren't brilliant.'

Josh laughed. 'They were as dull as they needed to be. I made my choice yesterday and unfortunately the set-up here is I need to kiss everyone's arse and make them think they approved it. So, I give them one good one and three mediocre, and guess what? I get my ad.'

'What if they'd chosen one of the reject ones?'

'Wouldn't happen. Now, moving on to more important matters, are you coming for a drink with us tonight?'

'Us?'

'Yes, the staff, you know, those other weird-looking people who hang around the office.'

Shauna rolled her eyes. 'Very funny. How on earth do you make friends so quickly?'

'Told you in Sydney. Funny, charming, adorable. Surely you remember?'

'You left out conceited. Seriously, you've connected with more of the staff in two weeks than I've managed in over twelve months.'

Josh shrugged. 'I make the effort to get to know people.'

'And I don't?'

'You tell me.'

Shauna laughed. 'No, I suppose I don't. I learned my lesson in my last job. I'm trying to keep my social and professional lives as separate as possible.'

'So, I can't twist your arm to come for one drink?'

'No, not this time. I'm having dinner at my mother's. Another night perhaps.'

Josh tapped his fingers on the table, not bothering to respond.

Shauna folded her arms in front of her. 'What?'

'What do you think? This is the second or third rejected invitation. I think I should be taking the hint. It'll save you coming up with any more excuses.'

'They're not excuses. I'm just busy. I've been putting off this dinner for about three weeks. She'll kill me if I cancel again.' Shauna knew it would be quicker to just get dinner over with than have to listen to her mother complaining that Shauna didn't care about her.

'Not close with your mum?'

'It's a bit hard to be.' Shauna hesitated. She didn't usually discuss her mother with other people but something about the way Josh was looking at her made her feel like she wanted to tell him more. 'She has a few issues which makes it difficult to have a close relationship with her.'

'Oh,' Josh said. 'I'm sorry to hear that. What sort of issues?'

Shauna sighed. 'Mood swings, anxiety issues, impulsive behaviour. She can swing from being paranoid to being manipulative quite quickly. She's very self-centred. She's one of those people who likes a huge fuss made of her but doesn't reciprocate. Forgets my birthday most of the time.' Shauna gave a weak smile. 'Actually I should be fair. She did remember last week, although I'm not sure if the three seconds it took to shove a lotto ticket into a card really counts."

'She doesn't sound like much fun,' Josh said. 'Has she been diagnosed with an actual problem?'

Shauna shook her head. 'No, in her opinion she doesn't have a problem. If she's upset with me it's because of what I've done, there's no other reason. The same with her other relationships. She's never at fault if things go wrong. She doesn't believe her mood swings and behaviour are abnormal. I've tried to get her to talk to her GP to see if there is anything that could help her but she won't.'

Josh's eyes were filled with sympathy.

Shauna cleared her throat. She shouldn't have spoken about her mother; it was better to keep that problem to herself. As much as she knew she should give up hoping things might change, there was a small part of her that just couldn't. Since her father had abandoned them when she was four, she'd craved a close relationship with her mother. She wanted her mother to show an interest in her, be supportive and proud. Even though she believed her mother had undiagnosed issues, it was difficult to constantly overlook her behaviour because of them. Thirty years after her father had walked out she continued to find herself disappointed.

'Sounds like hard work,' Josh said.

Shauna nodded. 'I won't bore you with any more details.' She stood, collected her notepad and pen and walked towards the door. Letting her guard down with Josh was out of character and left her feeling a little unsettled. 'I'll join you all for a drink another night.'

Josh smiled. 'Not sure I should believe you, but I'll hold you to it anyway.'

Shauna followed her mother out to the kitchen, her hands stacked with dirty glasses and dishes. It had been an effort to enjoy the succulent roast-lamb dinner with the conversation initially friendly then turning argumentative. 'I don't know why you invited me. He obviously can't stand me.'

Shauna's delight to find her mother in a cheerful and friendly mood when she'd arrived at the townhouse had been short-lived. When Bob, Lorraine's latest boyfriend, emerged from the lounge room, Shauna's own good mood had instantly dampened. It was not going to be a night of enjoying her mother's unusually upbeat mood by herself. As the meal progressed, Lorraine's mood had changed to one of anger and accusation.

Plates clattered on the bench as Lorraine turned to face her daughter. The thick makeup she insisted on caking on each day did nothing to disguise her contempt. 'Always have to stir things up, don't you? You're the one causing trouble.'

Shauna moved to the dishwasher and began loading the dishes. 'Me? You're kidding? He hasn't stopped since I walked in. Sneering every time I try to say something. What's his problem, other than being drunk?'

Lorraine passed Shauna the glasses. 'His problem is you pointing out you earn at least three times what he earned at any time during his career. It's disrespectful. You and your horrible attitude are why he's drunk more than usual.'

Shauna gasped. How could her mother misinterpret the conversation to such an extreme? 'Hold on a minute. He pestered me for over fifteen minutes to find out my salary and you encouraged him. I only asked if he ever aspired to being an engineer when he was working as a draftsperson. Showing an interest is not suggesting he was a failure.'

'Interest?' Bob stood in the doorway of the kitchen. He used the doorframe to steady himself. 'Yeah, right.'

Shauna turned to face him. 'Do you need to be rude every time we meet? What's that about?'

Bob waggled his finger at Shauna. 'You're a troublemaker. In your mother's ear to get rid of me. Won't work, I love her and she loves me.'

Lorraine moved over to Bob's side. 'Come on, darl, go and sit back down. It's not worth wasting your breath.'

Shauna shook her head as her mother guided Bob back to the lounge room. Three would always be a crowd for Lorraine. She didn't seem to be able to handle more than one relationship at a time. If there was a man in her life she took out every frustration on her daughter. Shauna took a deep breath, collected her bag from the kitchen bench, and made her way down the hallway towards the front door. She stopped briefly as she caught Lorraine's words coming from the lounge room.

'Even as a child she was incredibly jealous, hated having to share me with anyone.' Lorraine gave a bitter laugh. 'Didn't exactly help me with relationships. They often ended because of Shauna's outbursts. I sometimes wonder if that was the real reason her father left.'

A lump formed in Shauna's throat. She'd heard her mother say similar to this on other occasions and did her best to ignore the comments. Her mother was notorious for not taking responsibility for her own actions. As a result Shauna would never really know why her father left them. Still, even if it wasn't true, the words still hurt. She couldn't listen to any more. She slipped out of the front door and hurried down the driveway, blinking away the tears that threatened to fall.

# CHAPTER FIVE

## *Frankie*

Frankie swung the leaflet-filled tote bag over her shoulder and walked away from the house towards the gate. 'Come on, girls. Time to get to school.'

Hope and Fern came out of the front door, bags casually slung over their shoulders.

Frankie raised an eyebrow at her youngest daughter. 'Fern, darling, as lovely as they are, you can't wear those shoes.'

Fern dropped her bag on the path. 'Why not?'

'Converse aren't part of the school uniform. And I know you love them, but they're too big. Erica was very kind to hand them down to you, but she should have checked your shoe size first. Quickly, go and change.'

'They're not too big.'

Frankie shrugged. 'Irrelevant. They're not part of the school uniform, so go and take them off.'

Shoulders slumped, Fern turned and dragged her feet back into the house.

Moments later Frankie nodded as Fern reappeared in her school shoes. She held out a pile of advertising leaflets to each girl.

Hope didn't reach out for hers. 'Really, Mum? Do I have to do this? It's embarrassing.'

Frankie stared at her daughter. 'Embarrassing? The job that puts food on the table is embarrassing? Well, I'm sorry you feel like that.'

Hope had the good grace to flush red. She said nothing more and took the leaflets from Frankie. They set off, posting them into every letterbox on the way to school. Twenty-five minutes later they reached the school gate and said their goodbyes.

A friendly voice spoke from behind Frankie. 'I'm surprised she'll still help you.'

Frankie turned around to see a mum she recognised from Hope's class. 'Sorry, what did you say?'

'That.' She pointed at the tote bag full of leaflets. 'Hope's fifteen, so I'm surprised she's helping. Logan's the same age and she won't even talk to me. I'm Sheila. Sheila Matheson.'

Frankie shook the hand Sheila offered and smiled. 'I'm lucky. They're great kids. They understand the need to work.' Frankie tried her best to forget the look Hope had given her earlier. 'I'm Frankie, by the way.'

Sheila's huge hoop earrings jangled as she nodded her head. 'I think my kids need a lesson in hard work. They've had it good for far too long. We aren't rich by any means, but we're not in your situation. Perhaps I should take things off them and make them earn some money. Even get them into second-hand clothes like yours are.'

Frankie blinked. 'I didn't realise we looked so poor.'

Sheila's hand flew up to her mouth. 'Oh gosh, please forgive me, my feet seem to be permanently planted down my throat. Logan happened to mention you struggle from time to time, that's all.'

Frankie decided to let her off the hook. She smiled. 'Logan's right, but we get by.'

'Of course you do. So, how long have you been delivering the leaflets?'

'Close to eight years I think. I started after Tom was laid off. Jobs I could do during school hours were pretty scarce so this one worked well for us.'

Sheila gasped. 'Eight years! But surely something else has come up in that time?'

Frankie laughed. 'Not that I've been suitable for. Jobs are still pretty scarce, especially those that require no skills and fit into school hours. As hard as this may be to believe, I enjoy my job. It keeps me fit, I'm outdoors and I explore the neighbourhood every day.'

The look of distaste on Sheila's face suggested she wasn't convinced. She forced a smile and patted Frankie on the arm. 'As long as you're happy. Now, as much as I'd love to stay and chat I'd better go.' She held up a hand. 'Nails are a mess. Time to get to the salon.'

Frankie watched as Sheila hurried towards the car park. Frankie had been honest, she did enjoy delivering leaflets. Over the years, she had seen babies grow into toddlers, toddlers grow into school-age children and school-age children drive off to start lives of their own. She'd seen houses sold and new residents arrive, houses knocked down and rebuilt, and she'd enjoyed working out whose house the weekly book club was being held at. So much was going on in the streets where they lived.

As she turned to leave Frankie saw a familiar face. The tall boy who'd been nasty to Hope on the weekend was talking to an older woman. She made a beeline for them. Before she reached him, the boy turned and ran towards the school building.

Frankie kicked the ground in front of her, stopping only a few metres from the woman. 'Little coward.'

'I beg your pardon.' The woman faced Frankie. 'Are you talking about my son?'

Frankie nodded, taking in the woman's appearance as she made eye contact. Her face seemed unable to show any expression it was so pumped full of something. 'Yes, I am. I wanted to talk to him, but he took off like a frightened rabbit the minute he saw me.'

The woman crossed her arms. 'And what is it that you've done that would cause my son to react that way?'

Frankie snorted. 'What I've done? That's a good one. He's been horrible to my daughter and I want it to stop.'

'Excuse me, Hamish is a decent, well-brought-up boy. Whatever your daughter's told you is lies.' The woman's voice and eyes were starting to show her anger, even though her facial expression remained unchanged.

Frankie hadn't finished. 'I witnessed your son and his mate harassing Hope on Sunday so I'm afraid you can't defend him. Her name is Hope and the constant teasing and calling her *No*-Hope needs to stop. It's disgusting to turn our situation into a weapon.'

'What are you implying? My son is calling your daughter names because you're poor?'

'Yes, and it's disgusting and hurtful.'

The woman put her hands on her hips, her eyes locking with Frankie's. 'Here's some advice for you. Get your lazy husband to go out and find a job and move yourself off Dole Street. Give your kids something to aspire to.'

Frankie gasped. How dare she? She knew nothing about their life. It was little wonder her son was a bully. Frankie opened her mouth to defend herself but was cut off.

'I haven't finished. Instead of giving me some pathetic excuse, stop thinking about yourself for just one second and think about how hard your laziness makes my life. I'm sick to death of watching my husband work himself into the ground to pay ridiculous amounts of tax so you can claim every bit of welfare under the sun. So, get off your high horse having a go at my son, who's only pointing out exactly what you are, and do something about it.'

'How dare you make assumptions about my family?' Frankie's body shook as she spat out the words. 'You know nothing about us.'

The woman shrugged. 'I know enough. Now, I'd better get on. Some of us contribute to the community. You should consider trying it.' Looking down her nose at Frankie one more time, she turned, the click-clack of her heels echoing as she crossed the schoolyard.

※

Tom arrived home after working an early shift to find Frankie sitting on the couch, eyes red-rimmed, with a box of tissues by her side.

'She said what?'

'That we're dole bludgers living off her husband's tax and her son was only being honest calling us no-hopers.'

'Bitch!' Tom paced around the lounge room. 'Who the hell does she think she is? We hardly get any help from the government and we pay tax.' He picked up a cushion and Frankie was worried he might rip it apart. She got up and took it off him.

'Come on, sit down. Us getting upset and angry isn't really going to help.'

Tom sighed, allowing Frankie to lead him to the couch. He took her hand. 'Stupid woman. First the kid upsets Hope and now us. We don't even know her name and she's managed to get us all worked up.'

Tom pulled Frankie close and kissed her. 'Let's ignore her. We've had a tough time, but we're working hard and doing everything possible for our family. She was probably born with a silver spoon shoved right up her surgically enhanced butt.'

Frankie managed a small laugh. 'I'm not sure her kids would be in public school if that was the case. I think she was actually going to work.' She frowned. 'You don't think other people believe we're living off welfare, do you?'

Tom shook his head. 'They better bloody not. We work hard and the few benefits we get, like rental assistance and family tax benefits, most of them are getting too.'

'I wish we didn't even have to accept those,' Frankie said.

Tom hugged Frankie closer to him. 'Forever independent, aren't you? Remember when we first had Hope? You wanted to pay back every cent the government gave us as assistance and the same when I was laid off too.'

'I hate the idea of handouts.'

'Mmm.' Tom stroked Frankie's leg. 'I can think of something we could do to make us both feel a whole lot better.' He got up from the couch and took Frankie's hand. 'Come on, there's nearly an hour before the girls get home from school.'

Frankie smiled and allowed herself to be tugged up and led to the bedroom. Hopefully, Tom's plans would help stop the awful words replaying in her mind.

❧

Frankie was calm and relaxed as she set about delivering her leaflets the next day. The girls had been in great form all morning. Even Hope had made an effort to act like a human being. She hugged a secret smile as she thought back to the afternoon before. After sixteen years the passion still existed between her and Tom.

Frankie wound her way around to Baar Street, with the pub on the corner and row of shops below. She stopped as usual outside the pub to chat to her beloved Pete. He was up on his feet, tail wagging, the moment he recognised her. 'How are you, my beautiful boy?' Frankie scratched Pete behind the ears. He watched her adoringly as she stroked and petted him. She dug into her bag and pulled out a package of tin foil. At least once a week Frankie would try to save a leftover to give Pete a treat. Today was a sausage and he wolfed it down appreciatively. One last pat and Frankie continued on her way.

She stopped, as she often did, to pick up some rubbish blowing along the street. She threw the paper in the bin and kept going. Before she reached her next letterbox she'd picked up a can, an empty chip packet and what she assumed was an old lottery ticket. About to throw the lot into a nearby bin, the word 'Mega Draw' caught her eye. She'd only just walked past the newsagency, which had signage spilling out of the door promoting a thirty-million-dollar mega draw. She checked the date and discovered the mega draw was being drawn the following week. Frankie made her way back to the store.

'What brings you in here today, Frankie?' Jim the owner gave her his big welcoming smile.

49

'I'm returning this.' Frankie put the ticket on the counter. 'Someone's dropped it outside.'

Jim picked up the ticket and ran it through his system. 'It's not registered to anyone, love.' He looked at the ticket again. 'It's a Quick Pick. Someone's just come in and bought it and probably dropped it on their way out. So, I've no way of telling whose it is. Why don't you keep it? Might be your lucky day.'

'But what if the owner comes in searching for their ticket?'

Jim looked carefully at the ticket. 'This was purchased last Wednesday, love. I'd say whoever dropped it is long gone.'

'I wouldn't feel right keeping something someone else paid for.'

Jim reached for a pen and paper. 'I'll tell you what, you leave me your details and if anyone comes in asking for a ticket I'll put them in touch with you. How's that sound?'

'Sounds good.' Frankie wrote down her phone number and handed the paper to Jim. 'Thanks, I'd better get moving and finish my deliveries.'

Two hours later Frankie arrived home and stuck the ticket on the fridge. After a quick bite to eat she grabbed the shirt she was sewing for Hope. She had made it as close to the one Hope had been admiring in the window of Just Jeans a few weeks earlier. Matching the exact stitch had been difficult, but Frankie thought she had managed to. She couldn't wait to see Hope's face when she gave it to her, it should guarantee a smile.

# CHAPTER SIX

## *Bec*

Bec laughed as Alex and Will flung themselves into her arms the minute she opened the front door. 'So, did you enjoy your day out?'

'Sure did,' Will said. 'We had McDonald's and ice-cream and went to the zoo. We even ate pizza for dinner. We had the best time ever.'

'Sounds wonderful.' Bec raised her eyes at Paul, who shrugged.

'I wish you'd come, Mum,' Alex said. 'Then the day would have been perfect.'

Bec gave Alex a hug and sent the boys upstairs to find Earl whom she'd last spied curled up in a sunny spot on the desk in Alex's room. She spun around to face Paul. 'Are you mad? McDonald's, ice-cream and pizza?'

'I wanted it to be a fun day. It seems like ages since I last saw them.'

'You're the one who was too busy last weekend to even ring them.'

'I was moving into the apartment.'

'Fine, but next time if you're going to feed them exclusively on junk, they can sleep at your place. You can be the one up in the night cleaning up vomit.'

Paul looked at his watch.

'Sorry, am I keeping you from something more important than your kids?'

Paul ignored her sarcasm. 'Yes, I'm running late for dinner, I'd better go. I'll drop around during the week to fetch the rest of my clothes and we can work out an arrangement for me seeing the boys.'

'Okay, but make it soon and when I'm home. We've got to sit down and talk properly about everything. We have to let them know if we're splitting up. I can't keep saying you're away for work.'

'You don't need to. I told them today.'

Bec was overcome by a wave of nausea. This was the type of announcement they needed to discuss and make together. How could he? 'Told them what exactly?'

'Alex asked why I hadn't been home, so I explained how I needed some time to myself and would be living somewhere else for a little while.'

'A little while?'

'They know I'll be living at the apartment for the next few months and I'm not sure at this stage when I'll move back.'

'When you'll move back? That's not going to be an option.' Did he really think she was going to forgive and forget? Was he mad?

Paul hesitated. 'Fine. I figured as we haven't worked things out ourselves it was better to be vague. I really need to go.' He jangled his car keys. 'People are waiting for me.' He turned, walking away from the front door. Halfway down the driveway he looked back over his shoulder. 'I'll phone you on Monday and work out a time to get my stuff. We can chat about it then.'

Bec kicked the front door shut. *People are waiting.* What people? Bloody Chris Jenkins didn't he mean. She wasn't sure what was making her the angriest, the fact that Paul had been unfaithful and left them, or his casual indifference to the situation.

Bec glanced around the coffee shop. Her shoulders relaxed as she realised she didn't recognise any of the other customers. Other than Jess, she hadn't talked to any of her friends or acquaintances about the split with Paul, and for now she would like it to remain that way.

'What? He told the kids?'

'Yep, on Saturday. They asked why he hadn't been home so he said he'd moved out for a few months.'

Jess spooned some sugar into her coffee. 'He seems extremely casual about everything.'

'That's what's getting to me the most. He's ridiculously calm. Acts like our marriage breaking apart is an inconvenience and nothing more. Our family is disposable. I'm the idiot for not realising this.'

'Has Paul given any indication of what he wants?'

'He rang me on Monday to discuss things, or rather dictate his terms. Suggested we start alternating weekends with the kids and he would try to take them one night through the week, depending on work. That's all we've discussed.'

Jess gave Bec's hand a squeeze. 'What about the two of you? Has he made any suggestion for you to get together?'

'No, you'd think we were already divorced the way he's acting. He's very practical and appears emotionless, whereas I'm probably coming off as a total bitch.'

'Would you talk to Paul if he wanted to?'

'What? About us?'

'Yes, could he do anything to fix this?'

Bec twisted her wedding ring around her finger. 'No. What's he going to say? Sorry, but sleeping with someone else suited me? I couldn't ever trust him again. I just hate everything being unfinished. I guess divorce will solve that. Once we split up with proper arrangements in place, the situation might feel final.'

'How are the kids taking it all?'

'Will's fine. He thinks the idea of staying at Daddy's apartment is *awesome*. Alex is having a hard time, though. He's heard of divorce and keeps asking if we're getting one. What on earth do you tell a seven-year-old? Hopefully Paul will be vague over the next two days.'

'So, this will be their first weekend staying with him.'

'Yes, he'll pick them up from school this afternoon and drop them back on Sunday.'

'Do you have plans?'

'Not yet. Any other time two child-free days would have been heaven, but not under these circumstances. What if he introduces them to *her*?'

Jess's mouth dropped open. 'He wouldn't, would he?'

'Who knows? He acts like a complete stranger. When I asked him about Chris, and whether he planned to introduce her to the kids, he got angry and told me it was no longer any of my business.' Bec watched as Jess pulled out her phone. 'Who are you calling?'

Jess grinned. 'You'll see. I'm making plans. You need a distraction this weekend and I'm going to create one.'

Four hours of pampering later, and Bec could only stare at her reflection in the South Yarra salon mirror; the transformation was unbelievable. Her hair had been changed from lifeless, dull strands to frothy ringlets. How Bernardo had managed to add a wave and a curl astounded her. The deep chestnut colour complemented her hazel eyes, and for the first time in weeks she found herself smiling. Even her skin looked ten years younger, the bags under her eyes having mysteriously disappeared. She couldn't wait to thank Jess for organising all of this. She had been treated to the works.

Bernardo swept over to Bec with a glass of sparkling wine. 'From dull to dazzling, my darling. Now, drink up and celebrate the new you.'

Bec laughed and accepted the drink. 'What an unexpected treat. Thanks to you I won't need to complain about my first weekend without the kids.'

'We're not finished. What's next? Shopping?' Bernardo surveyed Bec. 'Your outfit is all wrong. You're not some frumpy old hag and you shouldn't dress like one.' He put his hand out to Bec. 'Come with me, we'll make you beautiful.'

Bec raised her hands in front of her. 'Oh no, you need to work, and anyway my budget is spent after the morning you've indulged me in.'

'Nonsense. Today's session was a gift, so we have plenty of budget to spend.'

Bec's cheeks grew hot. 'What? You can't. I'm touched and extremely grateful, but you don't even know me.'

Bernardo tapped his nose. 'You'd be surprised at who and what I know. The gift is not from me, it's from Jess. I owe her a favour, which she called in today, at my greatest pleasure. No arguments. Let's go and get you frocked up.'

Before Bec could argue any further, Bernardo whisked her out of the salon and down Chapel Street.

Two hours later she loaded shopping bags into her car, stunned by the wonderful day she'd experienced. Bernardo had easily replaced most of Bec's wardrobe with stylish clothes. The beautiful cocktail dress he'd convinced her to buy had completely blown her budget, but considering she had walked away with casual weekend outfits, suits for work and two pairs of shoes, she was delighted.

Bernardo had insisted she wear the dress that night. Jess was taking her out and while Bec had no idea where they were going, he did. A makeover, new clothes and a day spent with someone so motivating had done Bec's self-confidence the world of good. She decided to stop on the way home at the newsagency to buy thankyou cards for Jess and Bernardo.

❋

A loud crash from the back of the newsagency made Bec jump. She grabbed the cards she'd been looking at and hurried over to find an old lady staring at the stationery display, which was now scattered across the floor.

'Are you okay? Do you need some help?'

'Oh, thank you, dearie, so silly of me.' The older woman pointed to the destroyed display. 'That's what happens when you get old and doddery. All I came to do was buy my Oz Lotto ticket and for some reason I can't even find where to do that. Have they moved everything around this week do you think?'

Bec doubted the shop had been changed in the past five years, let alone that week. A sales assistant came over to clear up the mess. 'Why don't I help you?' Bec took the older woman's arm and guided her over to the large display of lotto tickets. 'Do you want me to fill in the form or would you prefer to do it yourself?'

'You are so kind. My hand is a bit shaky after knocking everything down. I'd love your help.'

The older woman reeled off her numbers to Bec. 'Memorised these for sixty years, play them every week I do.' She chuckled. 'Try to come in at the same time every Saturday to buy my ticket. It's my good-luck ritual.'

'Sixty years? I didn't know lotto went back so far.'

'State lotto goes back even further. Bill and I bought tickets in Hobart the first week we met and we've used the same numbers ever since. Of course we've added some lines for our wedding date and all the kids' birthdays since we started.'

'Have you ever won anything?'

The older woman's face lit up. 'Yes, we had a big win in eighty-six. Won almost four hundred dollars. Life changing, as you can imagine.'

Bec smiled, instantly loving this woman. Even in 1986 four hundred dollars wasn't much money. She'd spent more on one outfit earlier today. 'Would you like help with anything else?'

'No, thank you, dearie. What a lifesaver you are. Don't forget to get your own ticket now, will you. You do buy tickets, don't you?'

Something about the older woman's face stopped Bec from saying no without explanation. 'Normally I do, but I haven't the last few weeks. I'm going through, um, I guess you might say an upheaval.'

'Nothing could be so terrible you need to give up your lotto dream. Imagine if your numbers came up the one time you didn't buy one, then things would be bad, awfully bad.' She placed her wrinkled hand on Bec's. 'You can afford it can't you, dearie? I'd be happy to help you if money's tight.'

Bec smiled. 'Thank you, you're very kind, but the problem isn't about being able to afford the ticket. My situation is rather complicated.' Bec wasn't going to tell a complete stranger that she'd stopped buying tickets in a competition she'd entered every week religiously for the past eleven years, because they included her bastard husband's birth date. It sounded stupid, even to her.

The older woman patted her arm. 'Take my advice, buy your ticket. If things aren't going well it'll give you something to hope for.'

Bec nodded. Maybe she'd win enough money to hire a hit man. That was something to hope for. 'Okay, you've convinced me.' Under the older woman's watchful eye, she carefully chose her usual four lines of numbers.

After they'd paid for their tickets, and Bec the cards, the older woman gave Bec a quick hug. 'Good luck and thank you, dearie.'

Bec caught a glimpse of her own reflection smiling back at her from a shop window as she watched the old lady slowly walk towards the bus stop. The old girl had a real spark, one she hoped was contagious.

The taxi pulled up outside Bec's at seven-thirty. Jess opened the door and whistled. 'Wow, what a transformation! Bernardo didn't exaggerate.'

Bec was wearing the burnt-orange cocktail dress Bernardo had convinced her to buy only hours before. She smiled as she rubbed her hand over the silky material. With her new metallic gold strappy sandals, and tan Fendi bag slung casually over her shoulder, she felt like a new woman. 'All thanks to you, and Bernardo of course.' She gave Jess a hug and climbed into the taxi.

'I love your hair. The colour suits you, as do the curls. Bec, you're stunning.'

Bec grinned, delighted with Jess's appraisal. 'It's been far too long since I made any effort, so today gave me the big shove I needed. I've had the best day. So, why did Bernardo owe you such a favour?'

'I'll tell you in a minute, but first where did you get the bag? Did Bernardo actually manage to talk you into buying a Fendi?'

Bec laughed. 'No, but thanks for assuming it's real. I bought it off eBay about a year ago and never used it. Shows what a hermit I am.'

'Ahem.' The driver cleared his throat, waiting for an address.

'Oh sorry,' Jess said. 'To Dunstin's please.'

'Dunstin's?' Bec had always wanted to go to Dunstin's. 'But you need to book months ahead.'

Jess winked. 'Lucky you're with me.'

'Wow, I'm liking this side of you. First Bernardo and his favours, and now Dunstin's. How come I never knew you had a secret network?'

Jess laughed as the taxi sped towards the restaurant. 'Don't let the full-time-mum facade fool you. I'm more mysterious than I let on. I'll tell you about Bernardo over drinks.'

They arrived at the restaurant and Jess paid the driver. She linked arms with Bec and led her into the lobby. 'Come on, let's go and celebrate.'

A waitress showed them to their table. She took their drink order and headed towards the busy bar area, leaving them to chat.

Jess pushed her dark fringe from her eyes. 'So, Bernardo. I helped him out of a sticky situation a few years ago. Let's just say a certain male stalker thinks I'm his wife and Leo, Katie and Oscar are his kids. We pulled off a very convincing family picnic at the botanical gardens, knowing this guy would be watching him. He's not a bad kisser by the way.'

'What, you kissed Bernardo? Was Max okay with this, and the kids?' Bec couldn't begin to imagine how Paul or her kids would react if they saw her kissing another man.

'Max was in on everything. He watched us and the stalker from behind a tree. He went as far as going over to the guy and questioning him, telling him he'd better not be stalking me because that was what he was doing.'

Bec started to laugh. 'How did the guy react?'

'Told Max he wasn't interested in women and denied watching us. Max threatened him and he ran off. Bernardo never laid eyes on him again. So, after our help, Bernardo owed me a favour, which I cashed in today.'

'You should have kept it for yourself.'

'No, Bernardo always takes care of me. He was delighted to repay the favour. He rang me this afternoon to tell me what a wonderful day he'd had. We can wipe the slate clean now, which is good.'

The waitress reappeared with a bottle of champagne and two glasses. 'With compliments from the gentleman at the end of the bar.'

Bec stole a glance towards the bar. 'Looks like George Clooney.'

The waitress laughed. 'George Clooney? Maybe a little bit. Handsome definitely, I certainly wouldn't be saying no to him.' She winked at Bec as she finished filling their champagne flutes. She put the remainder of the bottle into an ice bucket before returning to the bar.

'That's unexpected,' Bec said.

'That he sent it to you?' Jess said. 'How could he not? You're glowing.'

'Lucky he didn't meet me yesterday.' Bec lifted her glass. 'To my beautiful friend, thank you.' She also tilted her glass in the direction of the Clooney look-alike. He met her eyes with his and raised his own glass. Bec felt her breath quicken and she swiftly averted her eyes. God, he was gorgeous. Why was it that a smattering of grey through a guy's hair gave him a distinguished air, whereas a woman did everything possible to cover it up? Although with that bone structure and those gorgeous chocolate-brown eyes, this guy could be bald and he'd still be incredible. Why on earth was he sending her drinks? There must be something wrong with him.

A few minutes later Bec stole a glance in the direction of the bar.

'Oh, he's gone.'

Jess raised an eyebrow. 'You sound disappointed. Hoping for something more?'

'No, of course not, just wanted to say thanks, that's all.'

Jess leaned across the table and lowered her voice. 'Get ready because you're about to have the opportunity.'

George Clooney had come up behind Bec and was now standing beside her, a friendly smile on his face. 'Good evening, ladies, I'm sorry to disturb you.'

Jess smiled at him. 'Not at all. Thank you for the champagne.'

'It's my pleasure.' He turned his full attention to Bec. His lips parted in a sexy smile.

Bec's stomach fluttered uncontrollably. She couldn't think of the last time a good-looking stranger had bought her a drink.

'The chance to speak to you beautiful ladies tonight is thanks enough. However, I don't want to disturb your evening.' He reached into his suit jacket and removed a business card. He handed it to Bec. 'I'd very much like to meet you again. Please think about giving me a call.' His eyes locked with hers. 'Enjoy your evening.' Flashing a last smile, he turned and left the restaurant.

'Wow,' Jess said. 'I think he likes you. He's pretty intense.'

And incredibly sexy, Bec thought. 'Definitely intense. He didn't ask me my name. How would he know who I was if I did ring?'

'Will you?'

'Probably not. I'm not sure whether I'm properly separated yet.' Bec glanced at the card she was holding and smiled.

'What?'

'His name is George.'

'You're kidding! George who? Clooney?'

Bec laughed. 'No, Fletcher.'

'Mmm, Fletcher, sexy. Suits him.' Jess pushed out her chair. 'I'm going to find the ladies', pour me some more champagne while I'm gone, would you?'

Bec heard her phone beep as Jess walked away from the table. She checked it. Fifteen missed calls and two text messages from Paul. Bec's lip began to tremble. What if there'd been an accident? She got up from the table and quickly walked through to the restaurant's courtyard, hoping it would be quieter out there. She was relieved to find it empty, closed for renovations.

Paul answered on the first ring. 'Where the hell are you? I've been trying your mobile and the home phone for ages. You didn't tell me you were going out.'

Bec ignored him. 'Are the boys okay?'

'Yes, except Will had to cry himself to sleep as he couldn't say goodnight to his missing mother.'

Bec took a deep breath, attempting to calm her heart rate. She wanted to scream at Paul. If he'd been in front of her she would have strangled him. She made every effort to control her voice. 'Are you for real? You've rung my phone fifteen times and sent me texts because the kids wanted to say goodnight? Didn't you give any thought to what I'd be thinking when I saw those missed calls? Is there a brain in your head?'

'I'm sorry you don't think reassuring them on their first night here was important. I wanted things to be as normal as possible. I promised them they could talk to you. You never go out. Where are you anyway?'

'None of your business. This is your night with the boys. Don't make promises to them on my behalf. The situation we're in right now is your choice so don't turn me into the bad guy.' Bec's fist was clenched so tightly her nails were digging into her palms. 'I'll see you tomorrow. Have them back by five.' She ended the call, wishing she could slam down the phone. She had to be content with turning it off and slipping it into her bag.

'Everything okay?' Jess asked as Bec sat back down. 'I wasn't sure where you'd gone.'

'Outside to call Paul, the dickhead. I need another drink.'

Jess refilled their glasses.

Bec took a quick sip before filling Jess in on the conversation.

Jess's face filled with concern. 'Don't let him ruin the night. He's probably dying to know who you're with. Sounds like a more likely reason for why he kept calling. He's used to you being available for him.'

'And taking me for granted. He needs to realise he no longer has any say or hold over me whatsoever.'

Jess patted her arm. 'Good girl. Now, let's drink these and forget all about him. I think I'd rather talk about Mr Fletcher.'

Bec agreed, glad of the change of subject. Paul may have wrecked their marriage but he wasn't going to wreck her night.

❖

Paul's headlights shone into the lounge room as he turned into the driveway. It was a little after six. Bec had been looking out of the window since five, expecting them at any moment. She shook herself, determined not to show how mad she was.

Alex and Will ran into her arms the moment she opened the front door. They hugged her as if they hadn't seen her for six months. She laughed, revelling in their warmth. 'How are you guys?'

'Good,' Alex scooped up Earl who was rubbing around his legs. 'It was too long, though. Maybe we could just see Dad for a day next time, not a whole weekend.'

'Oh, I thought you couldn't wait for the weekend, to be with Dad?'

'We want to be here. We missed you and Earl and all our stuff.' He stroked the kitten whose purr increased in volume.

'You're home now,' Bec said. 'Why don't you go upstairs and wash up for dinner?'

'What's for dinner?' Alex asked.

'A roast.'

'Yippee,' Will cried, and raced up the stairs with Alex who was still holding onto a now squirming Earl.

Paul brought the boys' bags up to the front porch, his eyes fixed on Bec. His lips parted as he drank in her appearance.

Bec's plastered-on smile wavered. He had the look she'd come to know as his 'seeking sex' look. What was he playing at? She decided to ignore it. 'Happy about a roast? What did you feed them?'

Paul shrugged. 'I haven't had time to set things up so they ended up with a lot of hot chips. I thought they loved them.'

'They love them as a treat, not as their staple diet,' Bec said. 'Anyway, I need to feed them so give me their bags and you can enjoy your night.'

Paul hesitated at the door. 'You look gorgeous. What have you done?'

Bec's hand flew up to her hair. 'Nothing, a haircut, that's all.' The muscles in her face tightened. He had a nerve. He'd walked out on them for God's sake. He had no right to look at her like that. To imply he still desired her. Bernardo must be a miracle makeover worker. First George Fletcher and now Paul.

Paul continued to stare at Bec in a way she hadn't seen in months. 'I'm in no hurry. Would you like to chat? I'm pretty hungry, too.' Roast was his favourite.

Bec crossed her arms, her body blocking the front door. 'If you'd arrived at five like we agreed then yes, but as you've turned up an hour late with no explanation or apology, no.'

The smile quickly left Paul's face. 'God, you can be such a bitch.'

Bec reached out for the bags. 'Are their bears in these? You know they won't sleep without them.'

'Yes, of course.'

'Goodnight.' Bec closed the door.

Alex and Will chatted nonstop during dinner. They had enjoyed being with Paul for the first few hours, but then it had become boring.

'He did too much work,' Will complained. 'There were no toys or anything for us to do.'

'You'd better take some things with you next time,' Bec said.

'Next time?' Will said. 'Can't Dad just come home?'

'Yeah, I'm never going again, especially if the woman keeps turning up. She was a pain,' Alex said.

Bec's stomach contracted. She tried to keep her voice as casual as possible. 'Which woman?'

'CJ Meanie Pants.' Will stuck out his tongue. 'Daddy was supposed to be playing with us but he said he had to help her with some work so couldn't play. It wasn't fair.'

A wave of nausea overcame Bec. CJ. Chris bloody Jenkins. How could Paul invite her there on the boys' first weekend? Bastard.

'Are you okay, Mum?' Alex asked, his face scrunching up with concern. 'You look all weird.'

Bec slowly exhaled, forcing a smile onto her face. 'Of course. I'm fine, darling. Now, tell me what fun things you did. You must have enjoyed something about staying with Daddy. Where did you sleep?'

An hour later, with the boys tucked up in bed, and Earl shut into the laundry for the night, Bec sat down in the lounge with a glass of wine. The wine had a soothing effect on her stomach; she no longer felt as though she'd been punched. She contemplated ringing Jess, but decided to leave Jess to her own family for the night. She hadn't told her parents about Paul moving out so was reluctant to call her mum. Luckily, they were away travelling for a year, so the regular phone calls and drop-ins had stopped, meaning no explanation was required.

Sipping her wine, Bec thought about the weekend. Saturday had been so much fun being made over and then having a wonderful night with Jess. She smiled as she remembered George and his sexy smile. It was exhilarating to be wanted after months of rejection. She found her train of thought wandering back to Paul and CJ Meanie Pants. At least the boys hadn't liked her. God, she needed to stop thinking about Paul. She reached for her Fendi bag. In the bottom she found the card

George had given her. She ran her fingers around the edges, a smile playing on her lips, a welcome distraction. The sensible part of her said it was too early to get involved with someone, but on impulse she picked up her phone and typed a text message. She pressed 'send' and sat back sipping her wine. It couldn't hurt. Saying thank you for the champagne was only being polite.

Exiting the meeting room, Bec walked down the corridor towards her office, thankful the day was nearly over. It was only Monday, yet she was wishing it was the weekend already. Back-to-back meetings left little time to get any work done. She pushed open her office door and stopped. An enormous arrangement of long-stemmed pink roses sat in the middle of her desk.

What was Paul thinking? He hadn't sent her flowers for over twelve months. Was this an apology? An attempt to fix things? She moved closer to her desk, reaching for the card. George! The flowers were from George. Her text the night before had resulted in numerous texts going back and forth between them. He'd obviously taken note of where she worked. A nervous flutter erupted in her stomach. What would Paul say? She shook her head and dismissed the thought as quickly as she'd had it. Who cared what Paul said? He'd already well and truly moved on. She bent down and breathed in the brilliant perfume of the roses. They were beautiful.

Tuesday proved to be as hectic as the day before. Bec let out a long breath when the boys were finally settled in bed. She sank down on the couch, a glass of wine in hand, and flicked through the TV channels. There never seemed to be anything good on. She inhaled. The lounge smelled delicious; the perfume of the roses wafted throughout the house. She'd debated between leaving them at the office and bringing them home, deciding fewer questions would be asked at home. The boys happily bought her story that they were a gift from a pleased client.

Settling on this week's Oz Lotto draw, Bec relaxed into the couch, enjoying the first sip of her wine. She thought back to the old lady in the newsagency. What a wonderful woman. She deserved a bigger win than the one she'd enjoyed in 1986. Bec watched as the first number dropped. It was one of hers. So were numbers two and three. She didn't need to check her ticket. The numbers had been etched in her memory for years. Bec put her glass of wine on the coffee table and moved forward to the edge of the couch. The presenter kept talking as Bec waited for the fourth number. Twenty-two, Will's birthday. Four in a row. Bec's mouth felt dry. They'd never had four in a row before. Twenty-eight, their wedding anniversary. That made five. Bec wrung her hands together. Five numbers was division five. One more, or even one of the supplementary numbers could be worth a lot. The sixth number dropped. Bec stared at the screen. She had six numbers. She only needed one more. The seventh dropped. Forty-five, the number they'd chosen by adding together the boys' birth dates. Seven numbers. Bec stood up, her stomach churning. This couldn't be happening. The supplementary numbers dropped, but she didn't even need these. She already had the seven winning numbers.

Bec's legs buckled under her and she grabbed the coffee table for support. Adrenaline pumped through her body, sending her heart rate out of control. She'd just won lotto and was probably going to have a heart attack. She fumbled for the remote and paused the screen. The numbers were still displayed. She had seven numbers, first division. Oh no, the ticket! A weird noise escaped Bec's lips as she steadied herself and raced into the kitchen. Where was her handbag? She'd bought the ticket without registering it. What if she'd lost it? The bag sat on the kitchen bench. She ripped it open and removed her purse. The ticket should be in the note compartment. Please, God, let it still be there. She pushed her fingers into the wallet, feeling the folded piece of paper. She pulled it out and opened it. She checked. Line three of the ticket showed the seven winning numbers.

�֎

Bec's hands trembled so violently she had to put the phone on speaker and place it on the kitchen bench to ensure she didn't drop it. Words were spewing out of her mouth that even she couldn't make sense of. Neither could Jess.

'Bec, calm down, would you. What happened? What old lady?'

Bec tried her best to talk slower. 'The numbers, my numbers, they came up.'

'What numbers?'

'Oz Lotto numbers. All seven. My seven numbers. All of them. First division.' Bec could hear Jess breathing but nothing else. 'Jess?'

'I'm here. Are you sure?'

'Sure? I checked at least ten times.'

'Don't move, I'll be right over.'

The phone went dead and ten minutes later Jess hammered on the front door. Bec rushed to open it. They looked at each other, screamed and started hugging and dancing. Bec calmed down when she noticed that the neighbour's light had come on. She giggled and dragged Jess inside.

'This is ridiculous,' Jess whispered. 'How can you have won lotto?'

'The old lady,' Bec whispered. 'I have to find her.'

'What old lady?'

'Why are we whispering?'

Jess raised an eyebrow. 'No idea.'

They both collapsed with laugher.

'Come and see.' Bec led Jess to the lounge room. The ticket was still clenched between her fingers. She handed it to Jess and pointed to the TV screen. 'Line three is the winning one.'

Jess looked from the ticket to the TV and back again. Bec watched as she repeated this for each number. Her face broke into a huge grin as she looked up at Bec. 'This is unbelievable.'

'I know. I think I'm drunk.' Bec took the ticket back from Jess. 'I'm going to sober up and you'll tell me it was all a weird dream. Speaking of being drunk, there's wine in the fridge. Come on.' The ticket shook in Bec's hands as they made their way into the kitchen. 'Where should I put this? What if I lose it or someone breaks in and steals it?'

Jess stared at her for a moment. 'Shit, I don't know. Hide it in a container in the cupboard or somewhere like that. Shame you haven't got a safe.'

'I know. I don't want to put it down. My tickets are usually registered, so it wouldn't matter if I lost it, but this isn't.' Bec pulled a small black container out of the cupboard. She put the ticket in it and placed it in the pantry behind the pasta jars. 'No one would think to look there.'

Jess laughed. 'We might need to sleep in the kitchen with a huge knife just in case. Now, come on, let's get out the wine. This is way too surreal.'

Bec took the bottle from the fridge, and held it out for Jess. 'You open it. My hands are a mess.'

Jess rescued the bottle from Bec's trembling hands and poured the drinks. She handed a glass to Bec. 'I didn't even realise you played lotto.'

'Paul and I bought tickets every week, but when he left I stopped. Then this old lady at the newsagency said she and Bill had been buying them for sixty years, so she made me buy one.'

'Who's Bill?'

Bec explained what had happened on Saturday.

'Thank God for the old lady. Imagine if you hadn't put the ticket in and then found out your numbers had come up?'

Bec suddenly clapped her hands together. 'Not just the old lady. I went into the shop to get you and Bernardo cards to say thank you for the day of pampering. I've won because of you.'

Jess laughed. 'No, you forked out the money and chose the right numbers. Absolutely nothing to do with me.'

Bec grabbed Jess's arm, a wide grin on her face. 'You gave me a day I needed and you will be sharing in this.'

'Don't worry about me for now, I don't expect any. What about Paul?'

Bec stared at Jess. 'I'm not sure, I suppose, I mean no. Oh, I don't know, what do you think?'

'He'll probably find out and if they were numbers the two of you had chosen he'll expect his share. Worry about that later, for now, we should concentrate on celebrating.'

Bec nodded. Bloody Paul. These were their numbers. It was time to celebrate, not file for divorce. If only this had happened before he'd cheated. Bec downed her glass in one hit. She wouldn't let thoughts of Paul ruin this moment. 'I wonder how much first division is worth?'

Jess pulled out her iPhone and was keying something in. 'Let's check, the website should tell us. Tatts Lotto or Oz Lotto?'

'Oz.'

Jess waited for the page to come up. 'Holy crap, the prize pool is thirty million, a mega draw. Is this the right one?'

'No idea. I didn't pay any attention. Let me see the winning numbers.' Jess handed her the phone.

'They're my numbers. Does it say how many winners?'

'No, imagine if you are the only winner?'

'There'll be heaps.'

'How do you know?'

'Just a feeling. When do they publish the full result?'

Jess took the phone back from Bec and scanned the page. 'It says by nine p.m. on the day of the draw.'

Bec checked her watch. It was almost nine. Thirty million dollars. Jess was right. Imagine if she was the only winner. What on earth would she do with thirty million? One million would be enough to pay off the mortgage, pay the kids' school fees for their entire schooling and still leave some over. Any more than a million would be unbelievable.

Jess held up her empty glass. 'We've got about three minutes before we find out. Another drink please, I think we're both going to need it.'

Bec's hands shook as she poured them both another glass. She giggled as she spilt some on the bench. 'I'm a nervous wreck.'

Jess's glass wobbled as she brought it to her lips. 'I don't think I'm any better than you are.' She glanced at the kitchen clock. 'It's nine. Shall we check?'

Bec handed Jess her phone. 'You check. Refresh the page, the result should be up.'

Jess refreshed the web page. She scanned the information for a few seconds, before looking up at Bec. She couldn't speak. She handed the phone across the bench.

Bec took a deep breath. Her eyes were wide with disbelief when she raised them to meet Jess's. Her voice was barely audible. 'Three winners, only three. Jess, I've won ten million dollars.'

# CHAPTER SEVEN

## *Shauna*

Shauna looked up as Josh poked his head around the door of her office.

'Okay, I'm not taking no for an answer. You're coming for a drink.'

Shauna laughed. 'Bossy, aren't you?'

Josh came into the office and sat down across from her. 'Not much choice when I'm dealing with you or you'll think you're wearing the pants in this relationship.'

'Relationship?' Shauna hesitated. He wasn't serious was he? She'd come to realise there was a lot to like about Josh but he was a work colleague and therefore could never be considered as anything else. 'I didn't realise we were having a relationship?'

'By the pure nature that we work together and converse together, we are having a relationship.' Josh grinned. 'Don't worry though, when this turns into the type of relationship you're thinking of you'll be blown away.'

Shauna smiled, relieved he was joking. 'Cocky, too. Don't hold your breath on it turning into *that* type of relationship. Been there, done that, never again with a colleague.' She was aware that Josh was waiting for her to elaborate, but she didn't. Simon was not a topic she wanted to discuss. Instead, she tidied some papers on her desk before making eye contact. 'Now, I hate to disappoint you once again, but I can't come out tonight. How about I say yes to Friday night instead.'

'I think I'll need that in writing.' Josh handed Shauna a piece of paper and a pen. 'I'm not convinced you actually exist outside of work.'

'Fine.' Shauna scribbled on the paper. She handed it back to him.

He read her note and burst out laughing. 'Drinks slave? This is all it takes?' He stood and bowed. 'Madam, I'm happy to be your drinks slave for the evening. In fact, I'd be delighted to be any kind of slave you like.'

Shauna pointed to her office door. 'Go. You can prove to me on Friday how irresistible and charming you are, but right now I've got a presentation to finish and you're just annoying.'

'Who's the client?'

'Mifflins, in Adelaide. They're not big enough yet to need your expert marketing input.'

'Mifflins? I read something about them in *OzBuzz* the other day. Did you see it?'

Shauna shook her head.

'My copy's at home. You're welcome to come home with me.' He raised his eyebrows and attempted to flutter his eyelashes. 'There are other things I could show you at the same time.'

Shauna laughed and once again pointed towards the door. 'Go.'

'Mmm, you like it rough, my kind of woman.' Josh winked and disappeared.

A little after seven Shauna finalised her presentation. She packed up her computer and the files she needed for her trip to Adelaide. She had a quick look in reception for a copy of *OzBuzz* but was out of luck. She needed to stop at the supermarket on the way home so made a mental note to check if the newsagency was still open.

Shauna was relieved to discover the newsagency was not only open but still had copies of the magazine. She picked one up and rummaged through her bag for her purse as she took it to the counter. She opened her purse. The lotto ticket her mother had given her for her birthday was tucked into the note compartment. She took it out and checked the date of the draw. It was last night. She held it out to the salesgirl. 'Can you check if this won anything please?'

The girl ran the ticket through the machine, her eyes fixed on the screen. 'Oh!' The girl's hands shook as she checked the ticket.

'Are you okay?' Shauna asked.

'Yes … yes, of course. I might just need someone else to take a look at this.' She called over to another staff member.

An older woman smiled at Shauna as she entered the service area. She glanced at the computer screen. 'Holy crap, whose ticket is that?'

The salesgirl who'd served her was smiling and nodding but seemed unable to form words.

The older woman looked at Shauna. 'It's yours?'

Shauna nodded. 'Is everything okay?'

'Okay? It's won!'

Shauna smiled. 'Well, that's good news. How much?'

The woman's face broke into a huge smile. 'You might need to sit down. It's won first division.'

A bead of sweat ran down Shauna's back. 'Is this a joke?' She looked around the shop. Perhaps there was a hidden camera waiting to catch her reaction and then make fun of her. But all she saw was a man flicking through a magazine and a woman looking at birthday cards.

The woman started to laugh. 'I'm sorry, but you should see your face. I'm not playing a cruel joke. This is real. I'll get the manager, maybe he can convince you.' Shauna's heart raced as the woman called out to her manager.

'Is everything okay over here?' The manager made his way to the counter.

The woman handed him the ticket. 'This lady has won, but I don't seem to be able to convince her it's true. I think she's in shock.'

The manager raised his eyebrows at the grinning saleswoman and then ran the ticket back through the machine. He gasped before looking up at Shauna. His face broke into a huge smile. 'First division, now that was a good investment.'

'It was a present.'

'Bloody good present, if you don't mind me saying. First division is worth ten million dollars.'

Shauna's legs started to tremble as she watched the grin expand on the manager's face.

'Ten million dollars? You're kidding?'

'I'm not kidding,' he said. 'You're one of three winners from the thirty-million-dollar prize pool.'

Shauna's mouth dropped open as she stared at both the manager and saleswoman. Thirty million dollars! She'd won a share of thirty million dollars?

Half an hour later Shauna slid back into her car. Her ticket had been registered by the store and she had been given all the information she required to claim her prize. She stared at the steering wheel and wondered what to do. Her original plan of an early night didn't feel right. She had to tell someone. Share the news. Her thoughts flicked to Josh, but she shook her head and dismissed the idea. What was she thinking, she hardly knew him. Her mum, of course; she was the one who bought the ticket. Shauna decided to get a bottle of champagne and surprise her. They hadn't spoken since the unpleasant dinner with Bob, but that suddenly seemed very trivial. Her announcement of a ten-million-dollar win was sure to clear the air between them.

Shauna danced from foot to foot, waiting for her mother to open the door. Come on, where was she? She knocked again.

The door flung open, her mother's scowl ageing her heavily lined face ten years. 'Geez, don't break the door down. Why are you here? I'm on my way out.'

Shauna grabbed Lorraine's hand and dragged her into the lounge.

'What on earth?'

'Sit down.' Shauna led her to the couch. 'You need to sit down.'

'Fine.' Lorraine glanced at her watch. 'Bob's expecting me in fifteen minutes. What's so urgent?'

'He can wait, I've got news.'

'Shauna, we've made plans. You can't turn up unannounced and expect me to drop everything.'

'Yes, I can.' Shauna held up her hands when she saw Lorraine about to object. 'You know the ticket you bought me for my birthday, the Oz Lotto ticket?'

'Did it win something?'

'Something? Yes, it won something. Mum, the ticket won ten million dollars.'

Lorraine's face paled. 'Ten million dollars? Is this a joke? Because if this is it's not funny and I'm going out.' She got up off the couch.

'Sit down. This is no joke. First division was thirty million and there were three winners. I'm one of them.'

They sat in silence staring at each other. Without warning Lorraine leaped up. 'We're rich, oh my God, we're rich!' She grabbed Shauna and hugged her so tightly Shauna thought she might stop breathing.

'Okay, okay.' She laughed, untangling herself from Lorraine's grip.

'Where did you put the money?' Lorraine looked at Shauna's bag.

Shauna followed her gaze and burst out laughing. 'They aren't going to have ten million dollars in the store. The woman in the newsagency said I take the ticket and claim form into Tattersall's and they'll pay me by cheque or direct deposit.'

Lorraine picked up her phone and started pressing buttons in a frenzy. 'This is so exciting, so exciting. I've got to tell Bob.'

Shauna grabbed the phone from her. 'You are not telling Bob. No way. This is nothing to do with him.'

'Oh, Shauna, don't be silly. I'm telling Bob, he'll be as thrilled as we are.'

'Mum, I don't want him to know. I don't want to listen to him

75

telling me why I should give him money. Why can't you just share this moment with me, not make it about someone else?' Shauna sat down, the pleasure she'd felt only moments earlier gone. It was always the same; her mother could never make it about the two of them, enjoy something together. There was always some guy on the scene, who usually lasted only a few months, but was always so much more important to Lorraine than she was.

Lorraine laughed. 'Oh, come on, Bob can share our excitement. And anyway, how am I supposed to explain our change in circumstances?'

'This is my money and I'm not giving any to Bob.'

'What do you mean, *your* money?'

'The ticket was mine. Of course I'll give you some, but tonight is about a celebration. I hoped you'd want to celebrate with me. Open the champagne, enjoy the moment.'

Lorraine faced Shauna, hands on her hips. 'Shauna, I'm going out. I'd love you to come, we can celebrate with Bob, but if you won't let me tell him, what's the point? Bob will be happy for you, too. I wish you'd stop being jealous for a moment. We're getting serious and you need to get used to him.'

Shauna rolled her eyes. 'Fine, whatever. You go out, enjoy yourself.' She picked up her bag. 'I'm off, thanks for the birthday present. It was one of your better ones. Makes up for all of the years you've forgotten I actually had a birthday.'

Shauna slammed the door on her way out. Why couldn't her mother act like a normal person just this once? This was the biggest night of her life. It needed to be remembered.

As she drove away from her mother's house, Shauna became acutely aware of how alone she was. She'd drifted away from the mutual friends she'd had with Simon and other than her girlfriend Kristin, there really wasn't anyone. Kristin had moved to New York twelve months earlier, and while they kept in touch via Facebook and Skype, it wasn't the same. She decided that joining Josh and the others from I-People would at least give her the chance to party.

The music throbbed as Shauna walked into the crowded bar. She waved to Josh when she spotted him at a table with a group of their work colleagues. He was listening intently to something someone was saying when he saw her. A smile spread across his face. His pleasure at seeing her was reassuring. Perhaps she wasn't as alone as she'd thought.

Josh jumped up and wove his way through the crowd towards her. 'I thought you weren't coming?'

Shauna put her mouth close to his ear so he'd hear her over the noise. 'I should be working, but I decided to come out. Felt like celebrating.'

'Celebrating? What are we celebrating?'

Shauna hesitated. 'Oh nothing, bit of unexpected luck. What are they all drinking? My shout.'

Arriving at the table with a tray full of drinks, Shauna was immediately welcomed by the group. She couldn't help noticing two of the girls from sales raise their eyes at each other. No doubt they were wondering why the Ice Queen had joined them. Months before she'd walked in on a meeting where she had heard herself referred to as the Ice Queen. Choosing not to socialise with the staff had earned her this label. Shauna smiled as the two girls happily accepted their free drinks and gushed unconvincingly at her generosity.

An hour later Josh stopped Shauna as she came back from the toilets. 'So, what's going on?'

'What do you mean?'

'Everyone says you never come out with work people and you hardly drink. You've got a huge day tomorrow and yet you're knocking back vodka like it's about to run out. What's happened?'

Shauna giggled.

'And I don't think you're the giggling type. Did you take something after I left you?'

Shauna laughed outright. 'What? Drugs?'

'Maybe? I don't know, you don't seem like you. If I had to fork out five or six hundred dollars on drinks I wouldn't be looking so happy.'

Shauna was silent for a moment. 'If I tell you something, will you promise to keep it to yourself?'

'Of course.'

'I won some money tonight and I want to share some of my good luck.'

Josh frowned. 'Hopefully your win was huge with the way these guys are drinking. We all appreciate you buying a few drinks, but it's getting a bit out of hand.' He turned towards the bar. 'They're doing shots now; you'll be up for close to a grand by the time this lot finish. Let me stop the tab. You want to keep some of your winnings for yourself.'

Shauna grabbed him by the arm. 'No, wait, don't stop them, they're having a good time.'

'At your expense.'

'I can afford it. Like I said, I won some money and yes, I won a huge amount.'

'How huge?'

Shauna started to giggle. 'Okay, but you can't tell anyone.'

Josh stood to attention, giving Shauna his best boy-scout salute. 'I solemnly swear all information will be retained only by myself.'

'Ten million dollars.'

Josh's hand dropped to his side. 'No way.'

'Yes way, Oz Lotto Mega Draw. I've been walking around with a winning ticket and didn't realise. Actually, it was because of you that I even remembered to get it checked. I couldn't find my copy of *OzBuzz* at the office so stopped at the newsagency to buy one on the way home. The ticket was in my purse. Now you can see why there's no need to worry about the tab.'

Josh's eyes searched Shauna's face. 'You're not bullshitting, are you?'

'Nope.' Shauna had surprised herself again by confiding in Josh. What was it about him that made her want to blurt out all sorts of things about her private life? She looked at him – it was those damned eyes. She was a sucker for beautiful eyes and his were trusting and sexy and she found herself drawn to him. Shauna shook herself; the money, or alcohol, was making her crazy. He would make a good friend, nothing else.

Josh stared at her in disbelief. 'Wow, I don't even know what to say. What are you going to do with ten million dollars?'

'I have no idea. I only found out a few hours ago. For now, I think we drink!'

Josh grabbed her hand. 'Come on, this calls for champagne.'

At a quarter to two, having had far too much to drink, Shauna called a taxi and went home.

Fully clothed, she set her alarm and passed out.

# CHAPTER EIGHT

## *Frankie*

Footsteps had Frankie look up as she packed the last of the cleaning supplies back into the kitchen cupboard. 'Morning, sleepyhead.'

Hope yawned and stretched her arms above her head. 'Morning. I can't believe it's so late. Why didn't you wake me?'

'It's Saturday. You're allowed to sleep in, you know.'

'I've got plans, though. I'd better hurry up and get ready.'

'Why don't you wear your new shirt?'

Hope opened the fridge, avoiding her mother's eyes. 'I'm keeping it for next weekend. Lisa's having a party and I want to wear something new.'

Frankie watched as her daughter shut the fridge empty-handed. 'Hon, if you don't like it, I understand. You won't hurt my feelings.'

Hope still refused to meet Frankie's eyes. 'I love it, don't be silly.'

Frankie wasn't convinced. 'I know it's not exactly the same as the shop one, but it's pretty close—'

Hope cut her off. 'It's perfect, okay? Like I said, I'm saving it for next week. Anyway, gotta go, I'll be at Hailey's until dinnertime. We've got an assignment due for English.'

Frankie gave her a hug. 'Okay, don't overdo the work and have some fun, won't you?'

Hope rolled her eyes and laughed. 'You're supposed to say the exact opposite. Tell me to study hard, not mess around.'

'I know you, you crazy, studious girl, and you'll spend the whole day with your head in a book and miss out on the glorious sunshine.' Frankie pointed out of the window. 'Look at those two.' Tom and Fern were outside sitting on the grass sharing an orange with a pile of newspapers on the ground between them.

'I'll try not to study too much, okay?'

'Perfect.'

Hope reached for her books, ready to go.

'Wait a minute. Is that boy still hassling you at school?'

'No, Mum, don't worry, everyone's fine. He stays right away from me.'

'Really?'

'Yes, really. Just leave it, okay. I'm a big girl. I can look after myself.'

Frankie nodded. 'Okay. Now, off you go, enjoy the day.'

Once Hope was gone Frankie surveyed the kitchen. She'd been cleaning before Hope came in. It was clean enough to allow her to take her own advice and escape into the sunshine. As she was about to walk out the back door the lotto ticket on the fridge caught her eye. The draw would have been earlier in the week; she had completely forgotten. She'd better check the numbers in case the person did contact her. She went outside to find Tom.

Frankie sat down next to Fern, picking up one of the papers. It was Thursday's. She put it back down again. 'What papers have you got? I need to check the lotto ticket I found.'

'What date do you need?' Tom asked. 'I've got at least two weeks' worth here.' Tom collected day-old papers at work, bringing them home each week to read through. He and Fern would often sit and read the comics together on a Saturday morning.

'I need Wednesday this week.' Frankie watched as Tom worked his way through the papers checking the dates. Finally, he pulled out the paper she needed and handed it to her.

'Perfect, the lotto result should be in it.' She flicked through the paper, found the page with the results and then handed it back to Tom. 'Can you read the numbers and I'll check the ticket?'

'Got a pen?'

'Yep. Now, there are eighteen lines, so go slow.'

'First number's four.' Tom waited while Frankie scanned the ticket, circling a few numbers. He read out the second and third numbers.

Fern checked what Frankie was doing. 'Ooh, three numbers.' She pointed to the fifth line of the ticket.

Frankie looked up at Tom. 'Does that win?'

Tom shook his head. 'No, I think it needs four. Fourth number is twenty-two.' Fern gave a squeal. 'Ooh, four numbers.'

'You're right, four in a row. What are the others?'

Tom read out the next three numbers.

Frankie froze, her hand shaking. 'You're kidding?'

Fern screamed. 'Seven, seven numbers, you've won!'

Frankie and Tom stared at each other.

Tom was the first to speak. 'Let's double-check, maybe we made a mistake?'

They pored over the ticket and newspaper, checking the numbers again – they had the seven numbers straight.

# CHAPTER NINE

## *Bec*

Celeste held her office door open for Bec. 'Come in and sit down. I'm so sorry you needed to make this appointment.' Celeste raised an eyebrow as Bec sat down. 'Although, you look gorgeous. You are still here to talk divorce aren't you? Or have you reconciled and this meeting is for something else?'

Bec laughed. 'No, definitely here to talk divorce.'

'Well, you're looking a hell of a lot better today than you did a few weeks ago. You're glowing and your hair colour is incredible.' Celeste paused, her finger on her lip. 'It's more than I'm seeing. A new man perhaps?'

The question took Bec by surprise. 'What makes you think there's someone new?'

Celeste waved her arm down the length of Bec's body. 'The clothes, the hair, the gleaming cheeks, they would be my clues.'

Bec smiled. 'Something pretty huge happened last week and I think what you're seeing is the version of me when I'm in shock.'

'Good shock by the looks of it.' Celeste sat at her desk across from Bec. 'So, what happened?'

Bec hesitated.

'This is a proper appointment. Anything you tell me during this time is confidential.'

'Yes, I know. I need answers to a lot of questions, so here goes.' Bec took a deep breath. 'I won ten million dollars.'

'What?'

Bec started to giggle. 'I won ten million dollars, and for some bizarre reason, every time I say the words, I laugh. It's too ridiculous.'

Celeste's mouth fell open, which made Bec snort with laughter.

'How did you win?'

'Oz Lotto.'

'Are you sure?'

'Yes, I'm sure. I took the ticket into Tattersall's. The money will be released to me next week.'

'This is fantastic! Wonderful!' Celeste's mouth opened and shut like a goldfish.

Bec laughed even harder. 'I don't think I've ever seen you lost for words.'

Celeste gave a little laugh. 'I am never lost for words. This isn't something that happens every day. I'm happy for you, don't get me wrong; it's just hard to believe.'

'Don't worry, I'm still expecting to wake up and find out it was all a dream.'

'Why are you here?' Celeste wore a puzzled look.

'I need to discuss my divorce.'

Celeste laughed. 'No, sorry, I meant why are you still at Milson Pierson? You just won ten million dollars. Why on earth are you turning up for work? I'd be out the door immediately.'

Bec cleared her throat. She hadn't even considered not going to work. 'Two reasons. First, I actually love my job. I think I'd go insane if I didn't have something more than just the kids to do each day. And second, I want to get things settled between Paul and I before I touch the money.'

'What, you aren't going to spend any of it?'

'No. Other than a gift, not for the moment.'

Celeste's mouth dropped open again.

Bec smiled. This side of Celeste was something she'd never seen before. She was usually so cool, so calm and confident.

Celeste did her best to pull herself together. 'Okay, ignore me, I've recovered. Let's get started. First, the divorce. Does Paul know you're getting advice?'

Bec shook her head. 'No, I'm so angry I can't talk to him. He's lost my respect and I want him to realise he can't treat me like this.'

'Good for you. The main hurdle at the moment is how long you've been separated. Did you consider your marriage over before Paul moved out?'

'To be honest I have no idea what I was thinking.'

'So, you never discussed the marriage being over?'

'No.'

'Okay, we can't file for a divorce yet. You need to be separated for a period of twelve months before we can fill in an Application for Divorce. In your circumstances, this would be twelve months from the date Paul left the family home.'

'Even though he's with someone else, I can't divorce him?'

'Afraid not. I suggest we send him a letter of intent to divorce. This way the separation date is clearly spelled out.'

'I suppose it'd be a starting point. What about everything else? The kids, the house, the money?'

'Two choices. You try to work out the details yourselves, or, if you prefer, we ask him to attend a mediation session.'

'Am I obligated to tell him about the money?'

'Yes. All assets acquired during the marriage are considered common property'

'He'd get five million dollars?'

'We could think about fighting for more, but we'll need some pretty good reasons. My guess is most judges will rule fifty-fifty on this amount of money. They would assume spite to be the reason you didn't want to give him a share.'

Bec sighed. 'They'd be right. Add in a healthy dose of resentment of course. I mainly object to the woman he's having the affair with getting her hands on the money.'

Celeste nodded, her eyes full of understanding. 'Divorce is never fun, Bec. More things than money will leave you bitter and resentful. Custody issues and the division of assets, for a start. Selling the family home is usually another item of contention, although this won't be an issue for you now. It comes down to the more personal items you will divide between you, things you bought together, things you may lose. Don't underestimate how hard the kids will find going between households, too. I'm afraid if you do go ahead you need to prepare yourself for a tough time.'

Bec slumped in the chair. The money had helped gloss over the reality of what was about to happen.

'Sorry to burst your bubble, but I like to get my clients prepared. Divorce can be overwhelming. Expectations need to be set at the right level.'

Bec nodded. 'I appreciate your honesty. I thought I'd leave here today having papers drawn up and the money was going to solve the rest. Not quite the case. Do I have to tell Paul about the money now?'

'No, it'll come up as a joint asset when we go through the finances with his lawyer. It's up to you whether you tell him any earlier. There's no point preparing divorce papers just yet, but we can put the letter of intent to divorce together now if you'd like. Alternatively, we can wait, give you some more time to work out what you want to do.'

Bec hesitated. Was there any reason to wait? There was nothing Paul could do now to undo the affair, even if he wanted to. 'No, I don't need any more time; let's get things moving. Do the letter please.'

Celeste went through a few details before Bec returned to her own office. Her phone rang as she sat down at her desk.

She answered it. 'Hello, Bec Hutton.'

'Ah, so at long last I have the pleasure of speaking to the lovely Ms Hutton. Are you still looking as beautiful as you did at Dunstin's?'

The deep, warm voice caused a flutter in Bec's stomach. She tried her best to ignore it and laughed. 'I hope this is George, or I'll assume you're a stalker and hang up.'

'Of course it's George, although no doubt many admirers are calling you. I'm sorry if I was presumptuous.'

'Not at all, and no admirers for some years.'

'That's impossible to believe. Let me guess, you've been locked away and only just released for a night out with your friend.'

This made Bec smile. 'If you consider marriage being locked away, then yes, I have been.'

'Oh, what a shame. I should have guessed that you'd be married. Kids, too, I suspect?'

'Suspicion correct. Two boys, five and seven.'

'Then I shall thank you for being so charming and leave you to your happy, married life.'

Bec hesitated. She should be saying goodbye. It was too early to be considering dating.

'Why aren't you hanging up?'

Bec cleared her throat. 'Well, I need to thank you for the flowers for a start, they're beautiful. And ...'

'And?'

'And ...' Bec hesitated. '... My husband and I recently separated so I'm not happily married, but it's rather soon to be moving on.'

George was silent for a moment. 'I'm sorry to hear you're going through that,' he said. 'It's hard to move on. I know, I've been there. I'm a good listener, though, if you feel like dinner one night. No strings, just friends.'

Bec cleared her throat. Paul's behaviour should have her swearing off men forever; instead, she'd felt an instant attraction to George when they'd met at Dunstin's. As much as she knew it was too early, her mouth spoke before common sense could. 'I'd love to.'

'Really?'

Bec could hear the smile in George's voice. 'Sure, why not?'

'Fantastic! How about tomorrow night? I'll pick you up at eight o'clock. Does that suit?'

With the plans confirmed, Bec hung up. She wondered what exactly had just happened. She was supposed to say goodbye when she found herself agreeing to dinner, a date. Should she ring back and cancel? What if Paul found out? Did she want him to know? She tried to push all thoughts of Paul out of her mind. It was a dinner, nothing more.

❧

Bec operated on nervous energy all afternoon waiting for her date with George. When Paul collected the boys for their sleepover she'd been fidgety and on edge. She'd had to keep reminding herself that she was under no obligation at this stage to tell Paul about the money, and she wasn't cheating on him. After numerous wardrobe checks, she'd settled on a little black dress she'd bought for the company Christmas party last year. Paul hadn't been able to keep his hands off her then. How quickly that had changed.

Now, she sat across from George listening to stories of his recent travels through Indonesia and Vietnam. She tried to pay attention, but the way his tongue rolled over his lips made her legs tremble. Her stomach had flip-flopped the moment she'd opened the door to him earlier in the evening. His calm, steady gaze had her stuttering and stumbling over her own words as she drank in his appearance. He was even better looking than she remembered from the bar. He oozed charm. He'd kissed her lightly on the cheek when he arrived and she'd found herself breathing in his freshly showered scent. She hadn't felt this level of attraction for a man in years.

'So, tell me more about the lovely Ms Hutton. Her hopes, her dreams, her fantasies?' George's voice broke into Bec's thoughts.

As the wine flowed, Bec found herself able to put all thoughts of Paul and the lotto money out of her mind and relax enough to enjoy the evening. George was not only sexy, but interesting, funny and attentive.

She learned he owned a furniture chain importing unique handmade pieces from Java and Bali. He travelled to Indonesia to discuss new

88

items of furniture and meet with his factory managers on a regular basis. It explained his golden tan. He did the same in Australia, with frequent visits to each of his ten stores. She loved how passionate he became as he spoke of his business.

After a delicious dinner, George suggested they have some coffee in the quieter lounge area of the restaurant. He took her hand and led her to an antique fireplace, which had a gentle fire flickering away.

'This is lovely.' Bec sank onto a couch.

'Lovely for a lovely lady.' George sat down next to her, his leg pressing into hers. He traced his finger along her thigh, letting his hand rest on her knee. Bec trembled.

'Is this okay?' His eyes searched hers as his fingers gently swirled over her skin. 'I know I said just friends and no strings and all that, but I can't help myself.'

'Yes,' she whispered. 'It's okay.' The attraction was mutual, there was no denying it.

George turned towards her. He used both hands to cup her chin and brought her face closer to his. He waited a moment, and when she didn't hesitate, kissed her lightly on the lips. He moved back and asked softly, 'Still okay?'

Bec nodded. A tingling sensation had started in the pit of her stomach and she needed to taste him again. George reacted to the desire in her eyes by pulling her close and this time parting her lips with his tongue, the kiss deep and passionate.

Bec was being swallowed up by the tingling sensations as they spread to every part of her body. She thought of nothing else but the kiss. The passion she felt took her by surprise – God, she wanted more. She pulled away after a few minutes, breaking the spell. 'Wow!'

George looked at her and laughed. 'You are beautiful.' He ran his finger along her lips. 'So, so beautiful. I'm having a wonderful time. Are you?' His forehead crinkled, his eyes anxious as he waited for Bec's response.

'I am, definitely.'

'But?'

Bec smiled. 'But, I'm beginning to feel a tiny bit guilty.'

He continued to stroke her face. 'You're doing nothing wrong.'

'I know, it's just strange after so many years with the same person. Give me some time, I'm sure that's all I need.'

George smiled and wiped his brow in mock relief. 'Phew, there will be another date. Thank goodness. I don't think we can ignore this. Our bodies are telling us we should be together.'

Bec nodded. Her body was definitely agreeing with George, but her mind was drifting to Paul, and whether she should really be doing this. George was right, she wasn't doing anything wrong, so why couldn't she put her cheating husband out of her mind?

George ran his fingers lightly down the inside of her arm, jolting her back to the present. She shivered in anticipation. The sexual attraction was undeniable. He kissed her again, a long, lingering kiss, then stood up and hauled Bec to her feet. 'Come on, Ms Hutton, time to take you home. To your house,' he clarified.

Bec smiled as she experienced mixed feelings. Her brain was telling her she wasn't ready for more, yet the throbbing between her legs told another story.

❖

'Come on, Zebras.' Bec jumped up and down, screaming from the sidelines of the under-eights' soccer match. Alex's team was down by two goals as the game approached half-time. The field was wet and the kids were covered in mud. Bec turned to Jess. 'Why doesn't he put Leo in the game? Is he an idiot? He's the best player by far and we're getting killed.'

Jess laughed. 'You're turning into a crazy soccer-mum freak. Don't forget this is supposed to be for fun.'

'Your son is sitting on the bench. Don't you care?'

'He'll go in during the second half. This coach rotates the players, he doesn't only play the good ones so we'll win every week.'

'Bloody stupid if you ask me,' Bec muttered.

The siren blared signalling half-time and Jess pulled Bec away. 'Coffee time.'

'But I need to have a chat to the coach.'

'No, you do not, come on.'

Bec gave in and let Jess steer her towards the refreshment stand.

'So, I went out with George the other night.' Bec kept her focus on the ground in front of her.

'What?' Jess demanded. 'When?'

'Thursday.'

'Today's Saturday, why am I only hearing this now?'

'Sorry, I meant to call you yesterday.'

'Well? What was he like?'

Bec felt her cheeks grow hot.

Jess's hand flew up to her mouth. 'You didn't?'

'Didn't what?'

'You're as guilty as hell. You slept with him.'

Bec laughed. 'No, of course not, although he kissed me.'

Jess whistled. 'Are you going out with him again?'

'Yes, one night next week when Paul has the kids.'

'Did you tell Paul?'

'No, and not Alex or Will either. They don't need to know unless this turns into something.'

Jess went quiet.

'What's wrong?' Bec asked.

'Nothing. I'm just surprised you're moving on so quickly. I'm pleased for you, but I guess part of me was hoping you would work things out with Paul.'

'Sorry lovely, not going to happen. We've hardly spoken other than working out a schedule for the boys. I could never forgive him for what he's done.'

'Okay, but don't look now, he's behind you.'

'You're kidding.' Bec turned around. Paul's face contorted with rage as he approached her.

'I think I'll leave you guys to chat.' Jess waved to Paul as she walked back to the soccer game.

Hands on hips, Bec waited for Paul to reach her. 'This is my time with the kids. Why are you here?'

'To talk to you, not the kids. What the hell is this?' Paul pushed a piece of paper into her hands.

Bec unfolded the paper and saw the Milson Pierson letterhead. It was the letter she had instructed Celeste to prepare. She thrust it back at Paul. 'Exactly what it says it is. Notification that I'll be filing for divorce twelve months from the date you chose to leave us.'

'Just like that? No attempt to sit down and talk? You can throw away nine years of marriage? No consideration for me or how the kids are affected?'

Bec narrowed her eyes. 'What are you talking about? *You* left *us*. You're shagging some bimbo and you have the audacity to question my motive to divorce you? You must be even dumber than I imagined. Now, I'm going to watch the match, so I suggest you leave. Get a lawyer if you don't understand the letter; they can spell out what lies in store for lying, cheating bastards.'

Bec turned on her heel and walked back to the game.

Bec added the boys' toothbrushes to their bags and placed them by the front door. She contemplated pouring herself a glass of wine, but her thoughts were interrupted by the squeal of tyres on the driveway.

Hearing the car door slam, Bec called up to the boys. 'Alex, Will, Daddy's here. Get anything else you need for tonight and come downstairs.' She opened the front door, wondering what level of anger she'd be dealing with from Paul today. Other than an email to confirm tonight's arrangements, she hadn't heard from him since their angry confrontation on the weekend at the soccer match.

'Oh.' Bec took a step backwards. Where was the permanent frown she'd grown accustomed to from Paul? Why was he smiling at her?

'Wow. You look stunning.' Paul's eyes wandered the length of the strapless, midnight-blue dress she was wearing.

'Um, thanks.'

'Night out with Jess?'

'No.'

'Who, then?'

Bec called out to Alex and Will to hurry up before turning to Paul. 'It's none of your business.'

Paul's face hardened. 'A guy?'

'Yes. We've split up, remember? I'm free to do whatever I choose.'

Paul continued to stare at Bec.

She folded her arms. 'What, you can date but I can't?'

'I'm not seeing anyone. How many times do you want me to tell you?'

'Fine. Now would you leave? I need to finish getting ready.'

Bec hugged the boys and went back inside. She poured herself a glass of wine. She'd spent her lunch hour getting her legs and bikini line waxed. She was pretty sure George's plans for the evening included more than dinner. The first mouthful of wine helped calm her nerves and Earl, spinning in circles as he chased his own tail, was a comforting distraction. She'd never admit it to Paul, but the kitten was growing on her. Paul . . . she needed to block all thoughts of him out of her head. She hadn't been with a man other than him in over eleven years. She wasn't cheating; he'd already moved on. As long as she could keep reminding herself of that she'd be fine.

The moment George arrived and drew Bec into a kiss, she knew she was a goner. Tingling from his touch, she was tempted to suggest they cancel their dinner plans and stay home. Instead, she composed herself and followed him out to his car.

'I've booked us a table at Donovan's. I hope that's okay?'

'Of course,' she murmured. 'Anything would be good as far as I'm concerned.'

George's eyes pierced hers. 'This is going to be some night.' He leaned over and kissed her again. He finally pulled away and turned the key in the ignition. 'Come on, we'd better go and get you fed. You're going to need your energy.'

Bec fidgeted in her seat as they drove towards Donovan's. Her stomach fluttered as she thought about the night ahead.

George's phone rang as they arrived in the restaurant car park. 'I'm sorry, it's my daughter.' He rested his hand on her leg as he answered the call.

After a few seconds he removed his hand, pushing it roughly through his hair. 'Oh shit, which hospital? Okay, I'll be about ten minutes.' He switched off the phone and turned to Bec. 'It's my son, Oliver. He's had an anaphylactic reaction and is being rushed to The Alfred. I'm so sorry, I need to go.'

'Oh God, of course, just drive.'

'What about you?'

'I'll get a taxi home from the hospital, or I'll get out here if you like?'

'No, come with me.' George turned into the main road. He explained to Bec how his son was allergic to seafood, pineapple and almonds. 'We found out when he was three and he reacted to a pizza. He almost died.'

'What did your daughter say? Will he be alright?'

'I think so. The paramedics gave him an adrenaline shot and he's on his way to hospital now.'

Five minutes later George was manoeuvring into the hospital car park.

Bec placed a hand on his thigh. 'Do you want me to come in with you?'

'I'd love you to.' George grabbed Bec's hand as they followed the signs to emergency. He dropped it the moment a young woman, her face tear-stained, came flying into his arms. George comforted her, and once she calmed down, asked what had happened. She explained how they had been out with friends at a Thai restaurant, when suddenly Oliver couldn't breathe. He didn't have an EpiPen with him so she had called an ambulance straightaway. 'I don't know what he ate, fish sauce in the curry maybe? They told me a doctor will be out soon.'

Bec stood silently as George processed this information. She squeezed his arm in support.

He turned to her, his eyes apologetic. 'Forgive me, I'm being so rude. This is my daughter, Natalie. Natalie, this is Bec.'

Natalie smiled through her tears. 'Sorry to have ruined your date, but our family likes to make our introductions as dramatic as possible.'

Bec smiled back. 'As long as Oliver's okay, nothing else matters tonight.'

Natalie's smile faded. 'Mum's here.'

Bec turned as the lift opened and a woman stepped out. Concern lined her face, only adding to her intensity and raw beauty. Her long, dark hair cascaded over her shoulders towards her tiny waist and long, toned legs. Bec swallowed. *This* was George's ex?

She reached them and grabbed George's arm. 'Georgie, what's happened? Is he okay?'

'I don't know, Marianne, we just arrived. We're waiting for the doctor to give us some news.'

Marianne collapsed against George.

Bec stepped back as the scene unfolded. George looked up from comforting his ex-wife, his eyes full of apology.

Bec smiled and pointed towards the lift. She held her hand up to her ear and mouthed 'Ring me' before moving away.

�֍

Bec sank into the comfort of Jess's couch, grateful for the glass of cab sav her friend passed her.

Jess picked up her own glass and sat down. 'So, you left?'

Bec nodded. 'I had to. I hardly know him and I'm standing there like an idiot while his sexy ex-wife throws herself at him. Not the best time to announce I was about to sleep with her ex-husband.'

Jess raised her eyebrows. 'Were you?'

'Possibly. The universe certainly had other ideas.'

'Oh, you poor thing.'

'Poor thing?' Bec laughed. 'I think his son deserves those words, not me.' She groaned and put her hand to her head. 'What am I doing? About to sleep with someone else. I'm not even divorced yet.'

'You are separated though. You're not doing anything wrong.'

'If that's true, why is part of me relieved we were stopped?'

'Give yourself some time. This relationship with George has happened pretty quickly. You met him before you even had a chance to get your head around ending your marriage.'

'I should probably end things. Sort everything out first. He's so damn sexy, though.' Bec leaned towards Jess and lowered her voice. 'Part of me wants to have sex with him so badly.'

'I'm sure I can oblige.' Max stood in the doorway, a huge grin on his face. 'You might need to convince Jess, however.'

Heat flooded Bec's face as Max walked into the room.

'Sorry, I know I'm banned from listening, but the boys are in bed, the footy's finished and this sounds juicy.'

Jess picked up a magazine and swatted him on the leg. 'This isn't for your big ears.'

Max sat down on the couch next to Bec. 'Okay, I'll leave you alone in a minute, but I did want to come and talk to you, to say thank you. A million dollars is unbelievably generous.'

'I tried to give Jess more, I hope she told you.'

'No way, it's your money,' Max said. 'We can pay off the mortgage, the kids' schooling is covered and we've still got three hundred grand left to play with. Thank you.'

'You're welcome.' Bec's smile wavered. 'Although, I'm trying to forget it exists until I tell Paul, so please don't say anything to him.'

'Sure, don't take too long though. He'll be wondering why his friends are suddenly rich. You know, you really should tell him. He'll be ecstatic. You might be able to work things out.'

Bec's jaw clenched. 'Ten million dollars doesn't change his behaviour. You're his friend so let's not get into a debate.'

'Okay, but can I say one thing?'

Bec nodded.

'Talk to him properly. I believe him when he says he's done nothing wrong. You've got your wires crossed somewhere. There's no other woman.'

'Not now, maybe. Whether it's still going on or is over is irrelevant. He cheated, he wrecked us.' Bec held up her hands to stop Max interrupting. 'I don't want to discuss Paul tonight. I appreciate you're trying to help, but please stop.'

Max nodded. 'Sorry, let's talk about something else instead.'

'No,' Jess said. 'Let's talk about you getting up and taking yourself somewhere while Bec and I chat.'

'Oh, you're so cruel. Here I am, being Mr Sensitive and you throw me out. It's discrimination. I can't help being a man.'

Jess rolled her eyes. 'That's for sure, a sane person would hardly make that choice. Now, go.' She pointed towards the door.

Max dragged himself out of the lounge, blowing Bec a kiss as he left.

'So, how are the kids taking everything?' Jess asked.

Bec thought back to earlier in the week. Alex had crawled into bed with her in the middle of the night, his eyes red from crying. He'd asked her why she wanted to get divorced. Why she wanted to destroy his family. She'd tried to explain to him there were a lot of problems that he was too young to understand, but his eyes had been full of accusation when he'd told her: *It's not that hard if you love Daddy like you're supposed to.* Bec had felt as if her heart would break as she had held him close. She'd managed to contain her tears until he'd fallen asleep.

'Not great,' she admitted. 'I think this limbo land we're currently in is probably the worst bit. Once we're divorced and have a proper routine in place, they'll come to accept the new arrangements. Everything's a bit raw at the moment, particularly for Alex.'

'Oh, Bec.'

Bec couldn't meet Jess's tear-filled eyes. Instead, she poured them both another drink. 'So, I'm thinking I should track down the old lady who convinced me to buy the ticket. I'd like to give her some money. She was so gorgeous.'

'How will you find her?'

'She said she tries to buy her ticket at the same time every Saturday. Assuming it's always from that newsagency, I guess I'll go down and wait.'

Jess smiled. 'Now, that's a meeting I'd love to be at. She'll probably have a heart attack.'

'God, I hope not. That's all I need. I'll be needing a lawyer to represent me for accidental murder. The divorce will pale in comparison.'

'Nothing like an extreme distraction.'

They both laughed.

Close to midnight Bec called a taxi. She'd received a text message from George telling her Oliver was okay. In a strange way the night had turned out to be a good one. She and Jess had drunk wine and laughed and she had switched off thoughts of Paul and the dramas that were likely to unfold over the coming weeks and months. At the start of the night all she could think about was having sex with George. Five hours later, she sank back into the taxi, thankful that she hadn't.

# CHAPTER TEN

## *Shauna*

Shauna checked her watch and continued to pace up and down outside her mother's house. Finally, the familiar blue car turned into the driveway.

'Where have you been?' Shauna's face was at Lorraine's window the moment it opened.

Her mother didn't smile. 'Hello to you, too, dearest daughter.'

'I've been waiting for ages. You're usually home by six on a Tuesday.'

'Not always. Next time ring if you want to come over, or let yourself in.' Lorraine opened the boot and took out some shopping bags. 'So, to what do I owe this special honour?' Her eyes shifted past Shauna and back out to the street. 'New car? Your latest purchase I assume?' Lorraine nodded towards the Mercedes E Cabriolet. 'Throwing around a bit of loose change, are we?'

Shauna ignored her mother's sarcasm. 'Yes, it's mine. Come on, let's go inside, I want to talk to you.'

Shauna followed Lorraine into the house and headed to the kitchen, while Lorraine took some bags into her bedroom.

'What are you doing?' Lorraine called as Shauna opened cupboards.

'Something we should have done weeks ago.' Shauna grabbed two champagne flutes and removed a bottle out of her bag.

Lorraine came into the kitchen and sat down on a bar stool across from Shauna. 'Mmm, Krug, I've always wanted to taste Krug. Fancy cars, expensive champagne. Nice for some.'

'Don't be bitchy. I wanted to celebrate the win and talk to you. There's a gift for you, by the way.'

Lorraine jumped up off the stool, her scowl replaced by a beaming smile as she flung her arms around Shauna. 'Well, why didn't you say so? Come into the lounge and tell me all about what's been happening. You must be on cloud nine. When did you receive the money?'

Shauna knew the mention of a gift would change her mother's attitude. She followed Lorraine into the lounge room and perched on one of the chairs. 'The money went into my account about a week ago.'

'You were quick to get the car.'

'I put in an order the day after I won the money.'

'How much was it?'

'None of your business. It's extravagant, I know, but what's the point of having millions of dollars if you don't spend some of them?'

'I couldn't agree more. Cheers.' Lorraine raised her glass. 'So, what else have you bought?'

'Nothing, just the car, but I'm thinking about apartments.'

'You had plans to buy even before you won the money. I guess you're looking at something a bit more luxurious now? You won't be comfortable coming over here soon, you know. I'm afraid this is all a bit basic.' Lorraine swept her hands around, motioning to her furniture.

Shauna rolled her eyes. 'Hardly basic, Mother. You're not exactly living in poverty.' She opened her bag and removed an envelope. 'Now, I've got this for you.' She passed it to Lorraine.

'What is it?'

'Open it and find out.' A flutter grew in the pit of Shauna's stomach as her mother slipped her finger into the back of the envelope. She'd been planning this moment for over a week now and couldn't wait to see her mother's face.

Lorraine pulled out a card, quickly dismissed the picture on the front and opened it. She sat staring at the contents.

Shauna took a deep breath, savouring the moment. Her mother speechless was not an everyday occurrence.

Finally Lorraine looked up. Her voice was low, practically a whisper. 'One-and-a-half-million dollars? You're giving me one and a half?'

Shauna got up and sat next to Lorraine on the couch. She put her arm around her mother. 'Yes, I wanted to surprise you.'

Lorraine shrugged her arm away and jumped up. This time she wasn't whispering, in fact she sounded almost hysterical. 'Of ten million, all you're giving me is a lousy one and a half?'

Shauna's mouth dropped open.

'Not only did I give you life, I raised you on my own and stupidly gave you that ticket for your birthday. This is the thanks I get?'

Shauna swallowed. From all of the scenarios she'd imagined when planning this moment, this reaction was certainly not one of them. 'One-and-a-half million is a huge amount of money! How much were you expecting?'

Lorraine didn't hesitate. 'Half.'

'Half? Why on earth would you need five million dollars?'

Lorraine stood with her hands on her hips. 'Why do you need ten?'

'I don't, no one does, but I'm not giving it all away either.'

'I didn't say all, I said half. I bought you the ticket and I deserve an equal share. Bob thinks so, too.'

Shauna put her champagne down and stood up. 'Unbelievable,' she muttered as she went to get her bag.

'Where do you think you're going?' Lorraine followed her into the kitchen.

Shauna turned to face her. 'Home. Your attitude stuns me.'

'What do you expect? I'm supposed to be grateful you can only spare fifteen percent?'

'Yes, Mother.' Shauna sighed. 'Most people would be pretty happy right now. They're not all as greedy as you.'

'I'm not being greedy. I bought the ticket and I think I'm entitled to a share. You owe me.'

'What's that supposed to mean?'

Lorraine's voice was verging on hysteria. 'I gave up everything for you. Protected you. I left my friends and family behind to make sure you were safe.'

'What the hell are you talking about?'

Lorraine hesitated. 'Nothing, forget it.'

'You told me you left Brisbane to be closer to friends in Melbourne after my father deserted us. Is that true?'

'Yes, of course it is.' She pushed her fingers into her forehead. 'I get muddled sometimes, that's all. It was a very hard time, one I'd prefer not to think about.'

'And family?' Shauna pushed. 'You've always said there was no other family. You had no siblings and your parents, my grandparents, are dead. What family?'

Lorraine sighed, her voice returning to a calmer state. 'There's no other family. Just the two of us. I guess I was referring to your father. He was our family. Until he took off, leaving me to raise you.' Her eyes hardened. 'You should show some gratitude. Try to understand the sacrifices I've made and do the right thing.'

Shauna stared at her mother. What sacrifices? Her mother had always done exactly what she'd wanted; put herself first and treated Shauna like an afterthought. Now suddenly she owed her?

She shook her head. 'If you don't want the money then return it. I'm not giving you any more. Now, I'm going home.' She walked down the hallway and let herself out the front door. She could hear her mother pressing the buttons on her phone as she pulled the door shut behind her.

❋

Shauna slammed the files down on her desk. Could the week get any worse? First Lorraine's lack of gratitude earlier in the week and now this.

Josh had seen Shauna storm out of the reception area and stopped in the doorway of her office. 'Anything wrong?'

She scowled at Josh. 'You tell me, you little shit. I thought you were trustworthy.'

Josh walked towards Shauna's desk. 'Little shit? What's going on?'

'How do all of the staff know I won ten million dollars?'

Josh frowned. 'I never said anything, I swear.'

'Who else would tell them?'

'No idea, but I promise I didn't say a word.'

'Yeah, well, I'm finding you hard to believe right now. People have been uncharacteristically nice to me this morning. And check this out.' She turned her computer screen around for Josh to see.

He sat down and read the email. 'No is the only answer to this.'

'How can I say no? Andrew's a colleague and I even met Ben, his brother. He'll die without help. How could I look Andrew in the eye if Ben died and I didn't try at least to help?'

'He's got cancer according to this message. We have top specialists here. Medicare would cover most of the expense. He doesn't need to go to America and pay hundreds of thousands for treatment.'

'Read it again, Josh, he's got a rare form of cancer and according to Andrew if they get to some clinic in Texas he has a small chance. The drugs he's already been exposed to are damaging his kidneys so he might need transplants. The guy's a mess and I can help.'

'He's asking for two hundred thousand dollars.'

'A bargain if it saves Ben's life.'

'Shauna, every man and his dog will be coming after you for money if you say yes.'

'No shit, Sherlock, that's why I wanted this kept as a secret.'

'Hey, drop the attitude and stop blaming me for something I have nothing to do with.'

Shauna scowled at Josh, her arms crossed in front of her. 'I've told one person about the win and I'm staring at him right now. What am I supposed to think?'

'You're supposed to know me well enough to trust me and believe me when I tell you something.'

'Obviously I don't know you well enough, then.'

Josh stood up. 'You can be a real piece of work. I'm not sure I should even bother, but I'll prove it wasn't me.'

'Yeah, right.' She sat back down and re-read Andrew's email once Josh left the room. She typed a message and suggested he contact her to make a time to catch up and discuss the situation. She spent the next hour returning client calls and emails. Her stomach rumbled, a reminder she hadn't eaten for hours. She contemplated asking one of the assistants to get her some lunch when Josh knocked on her door.

He waved a bag and juice container at her. 'Peace offering.'

'That's hardly going to earn you forgiveness, but my stomach will overlook that and accept the sandwich.'

Josh came in and put the food on Shauna's desk. 'Thank you would have been enough. Like I said earlier, it wasn't me. I've done a bit of nosing around and worked out who leaked the information.'

'Who?'

'Turns out Jenni at reception opened your mail, which included a letter from a law firm.'

'Law firm?'

'Check your in-tray.'

Shauna sorted through the contents of her in-tray and stopped at a letter printed on gold-embossed letterhead. She sat down to read it. She finished and looked up at Josh. 'Do you know if Jenni told anyone what this says, other than the ten million?'

Josh cleared his throat. 'Um, yeah, I'm pretty sure she mentioned all of the details.'

Shauna picked up the phone and dialled reception. 'Jenni, it's Shauna. Get in here, now.'

'Should I go?' Josh asked.

'No, stay.' She looked up at Josh and swallowed. 'Sorry about before. Calling you a little shit and all that.'

'You should be.' A hardness had replaced the usual warmth in Josh's eyes. 'You need to know I won't put up with you talking to me like that. Do it again and we're no longer friends. I mean it, okay?'

Shauna's face grew hot as she replayed what she'd said in her mind. 'I wasn't that bad, was I?'

Josh raised an eyebrow. 'I get it that you were upset and angry, but you don't treat me like that ever. Deal?'

Shauna blinked, surprised at how much it meant to her to keep Josh as a friend. 'Deal and thanks for lunch.'

Josh smiled, the smile reaching his eyes, and Shauna was relieved to know all was forgiven.

'So, what will you say to Jenni?'

'I'll be speaking to Craig to have her fired. This envelope is marked private and confidential. Not only did she read the letter, but she's gone and shared the details with everyone. Stay. I might kill her otherwise.'

Jenni poked her head around the door. 'You wanted to see me?'

'Come in.'

Jenni approached Shauna's desk. 'Is there a problem?'

Shauna held up the letter. 'Thanks to you, there is. Why are you opening my mail and discussing the contents with the other staff?'

Jenni's eyes widened in surprise. 'I open all of the mail.'

'Even if it's marked "private and confidential"?'

'Yes, Craig and Allan's instructions are for me to open the mail, everyone's.'

'Do they also tell you to share any information you think is interesting?'

Jenni's face flushed red. 'No, I don't usually discuss the letters.'

'So, why did you with mine? Surely you could work out this was confidential?'

Jenni's surprise was genuine. 'But why? It's marvellous. I'm so happy for you.'

'Happy that my mother is threatening to sue me?'

'No, of course not. I meant happy you've had such a windfall. I only mentioned it to Pam, and certainly didn't mention your mother. At least I helped clear up the stories about your car.'

'My car?'

Jenni's hand flew up to cover her mouth. 'Me and my big mouth again.'

'What do you mean stories about my car?'

Jenni glanced at Josh and then down at the floor. 'A few people suggested you might have received a gift from someone.'

'Like who?'

'Um, well, a rich man perhaps.'

Shauna wasn't sure whether to be angry or laugh. 'And now I've got a sugar daddy, too?'

'No, no, that's what I tried to explain to Pam. I only told her you'd bought the car yourself because I felt bad about the rumours going around. Dave reckons they cost a packet.'

'Thanks for the good intentions, but how did the staff learn about my mother?'

'No idea. I put the letter in your in-tray last night. I'm sorry, Shauna.'

Shauna sighed. 'Fine, go back to work.'

Relief flooded Jenni's face as she turned and left the office.

Josh winked. 'No threats to fire her?'

Shauna shook her head. 'She's too naive and innocent. She seemed convinced she was helping me. Did you hear any rumour?'

Josh laughed. 'Yeah, I'd been told something along those lines. Figured you wouldn't care; help keep them off the track of the lotto win.'

Shauna nodded. 'Okay, now enough about Jenni and the rumour mill. Can you believe this?' Shauna handed the letter to Josh.

'Outrageous.' He handed back the letter. 'You need to make an appointment with a lawyer. It's ridiculous. No way in the world could she be entitled to half the money. I'd be surprised if she was entitled to any at all. The money you've already given her is more than generous.'

'Yes, I'll ring someone this afternoon. This is crazy.' Shauna was still astounded that her mother had been to see a lawyer. This was low, even for her. But she also knew her well enough to realise she'd mean business. She'd push and push until she got what she wanted. Her chest tightened. Was it really too much to ask for a normal relationship with your own mother?

'Hey, don't let this get you down. Your win is an amazing thing. You just need to learn how to ride the problems that come with it. Now, why don't I take you out for a bite to eat tonight? We can talk more then.'

Shauna stiffened. 'What, a date?'

'No, two friends having dinner. Actually no. One friend taking the other out to apologise for accusing him of being a little shit.'

The muscles in Shauna's face relaxed. 'Okay, I think I owe you one. Meet me in reception at six and we'll go and get a drink first.'

Josh grinned. 'Six sounds good for our non-date. Now, I'm out of here before you change your mind.'

❧

The waitress placed drinks in front of Shauna and Josh before retreating to the busy bar area. Music and laughter floated through the restaurant as tables continued to fill. Spirits was an increasingly popular spot for after-work drinks and early dinners.

Josh raised his glass. 'Here's to you finally agreeing to dinner.'

'I hate to burst your bubble, but you did force me to as an apology. This isn't a date, I hope you realise.'

Josh put down his wine and grabbed his chest with both hands. 'Oh, the pain, my poor heart! How can you be so cruel?'

Shauna laughed. 'Idiot!' She opened her menu. 'Now, what do you suggest we order?'

'I think as you're paying, and you are officially a multimillionaire, I shall order the, ah, drumroll, the gnocchi.'

Shauna dropped her menu, the corners of her mouth breaking

into a huge smile. 'Gnocchi? Really, that's what you plan to order?'

'No need to laugh.'

Josh's mock offence made Shauna laugh harder. 'How about the lobster or even the eye fillet? Go all out.'

'Gnocchi's my favourite, especially with a gorgonzola sauce. Doesn't get much better than that.'

Shauna put her hands up. 'Okay, whatever you want. Don't let me stop you.'

The waiter came and took their order.

Shauna waited until they were alone again. 'So, what should I do about my mother?'

'First, explain to me why she would get a lawyer to contact you? Is your relationship that bad?'

Shauna took a sip of her wine, carefully considering her answer. 'It's a hard one. As I told you, my dad left when I was four. We never heard from him again. No explanation and no financial help at all. My mother's moods have always been irrational. Loving life one minute, in the depths of depression the next, and they got a lot worse once it was just the two of us. I've always been aware of an underlying resentment in her. We'd be having fun and suddenly something would remind her of him and she'd become angry. She'd take things off me, send me to bed or cancel plans we might have had. We've never been close. I'm sure she blamed me for him leaving. Apparently, before I came along they were completely in love and had a wonderful time together.'

Josh nodded. 'Perhaps, or it was her way of blaming someone else for her marriage failing?'

'Oh, who knows, this is the story she's always spun. She makes out he couldn't handle being a father, they started arguing and when things got worse he left. The fact that I've never seen him again suggests she's telling the truth.'

Josh looked like he had something to say, but changed his mind.

'You don't agree?'

Josh frowned. 'I'm thinking, that's all.'

'No. Come on, tell me.'

'I just hope your father doesn't suddenly appear if he finds out about the money.'

Shauna's mouth dropped open. 'How would he hear?'

'I'm only suggesting you be careful. The whole office knows, and you said you were thinking of giving Andrew money for his brother. Make sure you consider things carefully first.'

'Too late, I gave them the money.'

'What? Already?'

'Yes, I saw Andrew this afternoon. It might be crazy, but I can help someone, possibly give him back his life. It was an incredible feeling. In fact, I started thinking I should be giving more away to help people.'

Shauna had been overwhelmed when Andrew came into the office earlier. He had openly wept when she'd written a cheque for the full two hundred thousand dollars.

'It's a good idea to find worthy causes,' Josh said. 'You just need to make sure that you're the one finding them, not the other way around. Avoid the conmen who will be coming out of the woodwork.'

Shauna's cheeks burned. 'Andrew's not a conman. God, do you think I'm so stupid I'd give money away to anyone with a sob story?'

Josh put his hands up in defence. 'Whoa, calm down. I'm just saying the more people who find out you have money, the more who will come after it. I don't want you to get hurt.'

The waitress placed their meals down, interrupting their heated discussion.

Josh took the white cloth napkin off his lap and started waving it to and fro. It had the desired effect.

Shauna began to laugh. 'Sorry, this money is making me crazy. Let's eat. The food smells wonderful.'

'Phew, so you're not going to storm out?'

'Not this time.'

Josh smiled and took a bite of his gnocchi. 'Oh wow, this is delicious. How's your lobster?'

'Better than delicious.' Shauna attacked her meal. 'Told you to order one.'

'Lobster's not my thing, but try this.' Josh held out his fork.

Shauna leaned across the table, taking the gnocchi into her mouth. 'Mmm, okay, you win, sensational.'

'Told you. Getting back to your mum, why does she want so much money?'

Shauna shrugged. 'She's probably jealous and no doubt annoyed because she bought me the ticket. Her boyfriend is most likely also encouraging her, hoping he'll get something out of it.'

'Can you imagine before winning lotto someone coming up and giving you over a million dollars? Would you be complaining and asking for more?'

'Crazy, isn't it?'

'Did you contact a lawyer?'

Shauna nodded as she reached across and stole another piece of gnocchi from his plate. 'I made an appointment for next week.'

'Good. Now, what about you? What are your plans with the money? Why are you still working, for a start?'

'What do you mean?'

'Most people say the first thing they'd do if they won lotto is quit their job.'

Shauna laughed. 'Yes, but that's because they hate their job to begin with. I love what I do.'

'But you could do anything. Take a holiday, start your own business. Anything you want.'

Shauna continued eating, thinking about what Josh had said. 'All I've really thought about so far is getting a new car and buying a house or apartment. I was going to give some to charity and probably invest the rest. I've never bought lotto tickets so I haven't sat around dreaming about what I'd do if I won. What would you do?'

Josh thought for a moment. 'Probably very similar to you. Like you, I love what I do. I'd probably throw a bit around for the fun of it, a fast car and a boat perhaps. I'd enjoy planning some amazing holidays, but I'm not sure if I'd quit my job straightaway. I like the buzz it gives me. You could think about setting up your own business.'

'Mmm, maybe. I'm not sure if I'd want the responsibility that would come with it. I think I'll just enjoy a few luxuries for now. The money will be there if I want to do something different. One bit of advice I did read for lotto winners was not to make drastic changes in your life too quickly. Lotto winners are known to end up bankrupt and unhappy after a few years of bad decisions. I don't want to be one of them. So, there you go, turns out we're both sensible and boring.'

Josh raised an eyebrow. 'Not sure if I'd go as far as saying we're boring, but then again I don't know all that much about you. Tell me about your childhood. It'll help me judge your level of boringness.'

Shauna laughed. 'What do you want to know?'

'The usual stuff. Where you grew up, went to school, music you like.'

'All the things you'd talk about if you were on a date?' Shauna teased.

'No, all the things you'd talk about on a non-date.'

'Fine, I'll bore you.' Shauna started talking of her childhood, her days at university and previous jobs. 'Your turn,' she said when she'd finished.

'Ask me anything, I'm an open book.'

Close to midnight Shauna and Josh left the restaurant.

'You know,' Shauna said. 'Considering how many hours dinner went for, I hardly learned anything about you. Are you hiding something?'

'What do you mean?'

'You managed to turn nearly every question into a question about me. I didn't learn anything about your family or your upbringing.' She raised her eyebrows. 'You know, the usual stuff friends discuss.'

Josh laughed. 'That's because you're more interesting, and it gives us the perfect excuse to go out for another non-date.'

Shauna smiled. 'We'll see about that.'

Josh rubbed his hands together. 'Want to get a nightcap? I could consider sharing some of my story with you.' He pointed at a bar across the street.

Shauna checked her watch. 'I'd better say no tonight. It's getting late and I've got an early appointment with a treadmill.'

'No tonight? Does that mean yes to another night?'

Shauna smiled. 'If you shout next time. I can't afford to carry you with such expensive gnocchi tastes.'

'Okay, but at least let me get you home.' Josh waved to a taxi driving past on the other side of the road. It slowed and turned back towards them. 'I'll drop you first and keep going.'

'Don't be silly, you live in the opposite direction. There's another one coming.'

Josh hesitated. 'Are you sure? I'm happy to come home with you.'

Shauna raised an eyebrow.

'Not that. Take you home, to your door, not come in or anything.'

Shauna leaned towards Josh, lowering her voice. 'What if I wanted you to come in?'

Josh's eyes were bright. 'Um, I didn't think you would want me to.'

Shauna winked, opened the taxi door and jumped in. She wound down the window. 'Thanks for tonight, I've had a lovely time. I'll see you on Monday.'

Josh exhaled. 'Jesus, you had me going for a minute.'

'Scared you, did I?'

'No, aroused followed by frustrated would be a perfect description.'

Shauna laughed as the taxi slowly pulled away.

# CHAPTER ELEVEN

## *Frankie*

Frankie scrubbed the frying pan in an attempt to remove the heavily baked-on sauce. She silently willed Tom to leave the room before another argument unfolded. Every night this week had been a variation of the same theme. It was like a broken record.

'Frankie?'

She placed the pan on the sink to drain and turned to face Tom. 'What?'

Tom put his coffee cup down on the table. 'Come on, hon, we're sitting on millions of dollars. Why can't we spend some?'

'The money isn't ours. When will you get it?' Frankie cursed the day she had laid her hands on the lotto ticket.

'Don't be silly, the money is ours. You won it.'

'I didn't win it. Someone else bought the ticket and the winnings belong to them.'

'No, they never went back to the newsagency to say they'd lost it or contacted anyone. We would have heard. It was a Quick Pick. Random numbers they didn't select themselves.' Tom sighed. 'Why can't you accept something good happened to us? We're living in this hellhole, we can't afford the electricity bill, we can't afford anything. We literally have millions in the bank. Why don't we just spend some? I'm not talking about a lot. Enough to find us a decent place to live at least.'

'Do you realise how unhappy people end up after winning lotto?' Frankie had spent hours on the computer reading about lottery winners and how a win was more likely to ruin your life than improve it. 'There are so many stories of people who've ended up losing friends, becoming depressed and going bankrupt a few years down the track. Using the money will cause misery.'

Tom wrung his hands together. 'Misery? Hon, what do you think we live in now?'

'We aren't miserable. The money's already coming between us. Before the money we were so happy. Our problems never affected our happiness.'

Tom rubbed his face and sighed again. 'Do you honestly believe I'm not affected? The fact that I can't provide for my family, how do you think I feel? We're struggling to cover the essential expenses, let alone give the girls anything special. Rod and Dash think I'm a loser and my parents probably did, too. A total stranger told you she thinks we're dole bludgers. Who knows how many people see us the same way?'

'Oh, come on, neither your parents nor Rod ever thought anything of the sort and Dash isn't worth wasting energy on. The woman at school was one nasty person who we should ignore. The girls love our life. We spend more time as a family than any of their friends do. They don't ask for fancy clothes or new computers or iPhones, they need our attention, our love.'

'Fine, fine. I'm only saying our lives could be easier if we spent a little bit. Poor Hope's using that archaic computer for homework that hasn't got half the programs she should be using. It's crazy when we're in the position to buy exactly what she needs.' Tom yawned.

'Why don't you go to bed? You look done in.'

'I am. Think about the money would you, hon?'

Frankie stayed in the warmth of the kitchen after Tom went to bed. She made herself a cup of tea and sat down. As she ran her fingers over the cracks in the old wooden tabletop, she thought about Tom's words. He was exhausted trying to work as many hours as possible as a labourer and they were constantly going backwards with money.

Frankie sighed, taking in the room through fresh eyes. She had tried to make the house cosy, but the peeling paint, crumbling plaster, rotten floorboards and damp-soaked walls made it unachievable. Maybe Tom was right. Perhaps she should forget her concerns and start using the money. She finished her tea and put her cup in the sink. An uneasy feeling crept into the pit of her stomach as she flicked off the light and went to join Tom.

❧

Early the next morning Frankie crept out of the house, careful not to wake the rest of the family. The sun had only just begun to rise as she pulled her jacket around her, breathing in the crisp autumn air. She strode briskly in the direction of the newsagency.

Jim looked surprised to see her outside his shop so early. 'What are you doing out and about at this time? I thought your early-morning visits were a thing of the past?'

When Frankie had first discovered the lottery win, she had gone to see Jim every day, checking if anyone had been back for the ticket.

Frankie smiled at Jim. 'Yes, they are a thing of the past, but I'm doing one last check before I spend some of the money.'

Jim took a step back. 'What? You haven't spent any of it?'

Frankie blushed. 'I was worried someone might come forward and report the ticket missing.'

'No need now, is there, love. No one has and the draw was over two weeks ago. You can safely consider the money yours. Why don't you go and treat your lovely family to a special breakfast?' He pointed towards the bakery.

'I don't think—' Frankie stopped herself. She would have to change her mindset that they could now do things if they were going to use the money. She smiled at Jim. 'Fantastic idea, thank you.'

Tom and the girls woke up to the smell of warm croissants, muffins and fresh coffee. Fern squealed with delight.

'Does this mean what I think?' Tom grabbed Frankie by the waist and twirled her around the small kitchen.

Frankie laughed. 'Yes, but on one condition. I want us to visit a financial adviser so we don't end up in a mess like some people do.'

Tom stopped dancing, tugged Frankie towards him and kissed her firmly on the lips.

❊

Two days later Frankie found herself sitting opposite John Wilton, Financial Planner. A giggle rose up in her throat. The whole situation seemed surreal and quite ridiculous. She, Frankie York, a millionaire. John Wilton was seated comfortably behind his large mahogany desk, wearing an expensive suit, slicked-back hair and a large gold Rolex on his wrist. Frankie couldn't begin to imagine her reaction if Tom ever came home looking like this.

'Frankie, Tom.' John Wilton put a file to one side and looked at them. 'Congratulations. A ten-million-dollar lotto win; not something I see every day. With some clever investments, we can turn this into a lot more money for you.'

'What sort of investments?' Frankie asked.

'It depends on your level of comfort, but for starters I would be suggesting a mixed portfolio. Invest a percentage of the money in high-risk, high-return commodities, some in medium-risk and probably at least half in low-risk investments.'

'High risk? I don't want to lose any money,' Frankie said.

John laughed. 'Neither do we, let me assure you. It's in all of our best interests to turn this money into an even larger amount. We would recommend taking a large percentage of the overall sum to invest in low-risk funds. Funds that will pay more than a term deposit, though.' John pulled out a folder and handed it to Tom. 'Now, this should give you an idea of the sort of return on investments we've been having over the last few years.'

An hour later Frankie and Tom sat in a cafe across the road from John Wilton's office. 'Are you sure you don't want a cake?' Tom asked. 'Cake's affordable now, you realise.'

Frankie gave a tight smile. 'I know, but I still find eight dollars a slice excessive. I'm probably not cut out to be rich.'

Tom laughed. 'Don't be silly. Old habits will take a while to break. Let's start now. I'm going to get a piece of cake to share, not spend too much at once.'

Frankie tapped her fingers on the table as she watched Tom make his way over to the counter. The uneasy feeling in her stomach had returned. She'd tuned out halfway through John Wilton's explanation of stocks and bonds and whatever else he was going on about. Did they really need to invest the money and make more? Surely ten million was enough for anyone.

'So, what did you think of our Mr Wilton?' Tom asked through a mouthful of chocolate mudcake.

'I didn't understand much, how about you?'

'Neither did I, but that's why we get experts in to guide us. I believe we'd be best to invest half with them and invest the other half ourselves. We can decide how much to give away, work out how much to use to live off and put the rest in a term deposit. I'm not sure whether we're best to have one term deposit or split the money into a number of smaller deposits. I'll find out.'

Frankie raised an eyebrow. 'Listen to you talking like a financial planner. You've been giving this some thought.'

Tom's eyes widened. 'Thought? It's all I think about. We've been given a chance to change our lives. The money's bought us freedom we didn't have before. We should make the most of it, but without losing any either.'

Frankie smiled and picked up a spoon.

'What? Why are you smiling?'

'You're sounding pretty sexy, Mr York. Talk money a bit more.'

Tom laughed. 'Turning you on, am I?'

Frankie slowly licked the remains of the cake from her spoon. 'Mmm, might be. Don't stop, keep talking.'

Tom groaned and shifted in his seat. 'Bloody hell, stop licking that spoon like that. You'll get us both arrested in a minute with what I'm thinking.'

Frankie stood up. 'Hold that thought. Come on, let's go, we've got a few hours before the girls come home.'

Tom didn't need to be convinced. Jumping up, he grabbed Frankie's hand and led her out of the cafe.

※

Frankie's pleasure built the next afternoon as she watched the anticipation on the girls' faces as they waited in the driveway for Tom. He'd rung ten minutes earlier telling them he had a surprise. Fern pulled herself up onto the pillar by the front gate. She craned her neck to be the first to see Tom round the corner from Dorcas Street.

'If he comes that way, you idiot,' Hope said.

Fern stuck out her tongue. 'He always walks down Dorcas. Lionel, then Dorcas then into our street. You're the idiot.'

'Okay, girls, enough,' Frankie said. 'Call out when you see Dad and we'll walk down to meet him together.' She leaned down and tried to straighten a broken paver in the path. Another thing that needed fixing. They would have to start thinking about moving somewhere nicer. Frankie's thoughts were interrupted by the beeping of a car horn. A midnight-blue Honda CRV turned into the driveway. Tom waved from the driver's seat.

Fern jumped off the pillar, a shriek of delight escaping her lips as she ran towards the car. Hope followed closely. 'Is this ours, Dad?'

'Sure is. Jump in and we'll take a drive.' The girls climbed into the back. Tom got out of the car, making way for Frankie. 'Come on, babe, come and check out your new wheels. There's another surprise, too.'

Frankie was transported back to being a five-year-old on Christmas Day. The wonderful bubbles of excitement starting in her stomach days before and lasting for days after. 'It's lovely, Tom. What a surprise!'

'Are you sure? We can choose a different car if you prefer? This is for you.'

'Why for me? Won't you need to drive, too?'

'I think we could use one each, don't you?'

'Did you buy two?'

'No, I wanted to make sure you liked this one first before getting myself anything. We've been without a car for so long we're not in any hurry.' He handed Frankie the keys. 'Come on, jump in and take us for a drive.'

Frankie climbed into the driver's seat, admiring everything as she did. 'I've never had a new car before. In fact, I've never even had my own car. We had those old bombs you owned when we were first married, but we've used public transport for so many years now. I hope I remember how to drive.'

'Exactly why I got an automatic, easier to handle. It's an all-wheel drive too so we can go off-road. Nothing too extreme, but we can get to some places we couldn't in a regular car.'

Frankie thought of the national parks she had always dreamed of exploring.

Hope broke into her thoughts. 'Mum, the car's got sat nav and everything. I think you can even send text messages.' Hope was looking at the car manual.

Frankie laughed. 'Mmm, texting, useful.'

'Imagine if you moved into the twenty-first century and bought an iPhone,' Hope said.

'Good idea,' Tom said. 'Let's talk about phones later. We need to go.'

Fern stuck her head through the seats to the front. 'So, what's the other surprise? Something for me and Hope?'

'Kind of, a surprise you'll get a say in at least. We're meeting a real

119

estate agent in fifteen minutes. He's going to take us around a few nicer houses to rent.'

'Now?' Frankie asked.

'Yep, what do you think? Is this okay?'

'Of course. A house is the number-one thing on our list.'

'He can show us properties for sale, but you said you'd rather rent in an area first before we commit to buying.'

Frankie leaned across and hugged Tom. 'Thank you.' She lowered her voice and whispered in his ear. 'Remember what happened after the cake the other day?'

Tom nodded, his breathing becoming more rapid.

'Prepare for a repeat performance tonight.'

'Performance?' Fern said. 'What are you two talking about?'

Frankie pulled away from Tom and turned around to speak to Fern. 'Nothing, darling, just thanking him for being so thoughtful. I think your dad was right; having this money is only going to improve our lives.'

❊

Frankie moved around the kitchen island and looked outside to the leafy courtyard. Her family loved this house, but she still wasn't sure. They had been shown six properties, all a huge improvement on where they currently lived, and while she could have said yes to living in any of them, the expense was her concern.

She turned to face Tom, the eyes of the girls on her. 'I know we can afford the rent, but do we really want to be spending four times more than we pay now?'

'We need to rent the quality of house we want to buy,' Tom said. 'These would give us a feel for a bigger, nicer house and they're still close to school, but in a better neighbourhood. This is where you've always dreamed of buying.'

'You're going a bit fast for me. As much as I love the idea of

120

moving, shouldn't we sit down and work out what we need in a house?'

'We can work out the details when we buy or build our dream house. For now, our priority is getting out of the dump we're in. I don't even want to risk parking the new car in the driveway.'

Frankie smiled. 'The area's not that bad. Nothing's happened to us in the ten years we've lived there.'

'Only because there's nothing of value to wreck or steal.'

Fern interrupted their conversation. 'Can we choose our bedrooms now?'

Tom squeezed Frankie's hand.

Frankie turned to Hope. 'Do you like this one?'

Hope's eyes widened. 'Like? No. Love? Yes. You've seen the outdoor area. Imagine sitting out there for breakfast or lunch.' Her forehead creased. 'One problem though.'

'What?' Frankie asked.

'Furniture. In addition to the open-plan living space, separate lounge, dining and media rooms, there're four bedrooms and an office. The master suite is huge and even has a balcony. I'm worried our furniture won't be enough.'

Tom laughed. 'You might want to consider a career in real estate, Hope. You're doing a better sales job than the agent. You're right though. We'd need to go and do a bit of shopping before we move in.' He turned to Frankie. 'What do you think?'

Frankie had wandered from room to room, trying to imagine them living here. It was at least four, if not five times the size of their current house. 'You don't think this one is too big?'

She was met with three loud 'nos'.

Of course the girls would enjoy having their own space. She turned to her family and smiled. 'Let's vote, shall we? All in favour of moving, please raise your hand.'

Three hands shot up into the air.

Frankie nodded. 'Okay, decision made. Find the agent and we'll sign the lease.'

A week later, Frankie unpacked the last box for the kitchen before crushing it, ready to recycle. The thought of freshly brewed coffee convinced her to take a break. Frankie made herself a flat white and sat down on one of the new stools that lined the island bench. She found herself looking around the kitchen and open-plan living area, in awe that this was their new home.

'Hey, beautiful.' Tom came into the kitchen and went straight to the coffee machine. 'Coffee, definitely need coffee. I can't believe we survived this long without a coffee machine, can you?'

Frankie laughed. 'It wasn't really a choice before. Now, we have more appliances than I realised existed.' Frankie had spent two days shopping for furniture, new computers and appliances before moving in. Most of their old possessions were now at the Salvation Army.

Tom poured his coffee and plonked himself on a stool next to her. 'Did I tell you Rod's moving?'

'Is he? Where to?'

'A new apartment. There's a pool and gym so he's pretty happy. I think Dash is hoping another one will come up in the same complex.'

'How can he afford to move?'

Tom was unable to meet Frankie's eyes.

'You've given them money?'

Tom nodded. 'Sorry, I was excited. I couldn't wait and we did agree to give them some. You should have seen their faces.'

'You told them we won ten million?'

He nodded again.

Frankie groaned. 'Are you crazy? We said we would sit down and work out the best way to give your brothers money without them knowing how much we won. We agreed. We didn't agree for you to go off and tell them to help themselves to our ten million.'

'Of course I didn't say to help themselves, I'm not stupid. The money was a once-off gift.'

'How much did you give?'

'Two hundred and fifty thousand each, like we discussed.'

After their meeting with John Wilton, Tom and Frankie had sat down and worked out exactly who they would gift money to.

'We discussed two hundred and fifty thousand, but we also decided not to let on how much we'd won. We agreed not to tell anyone, remember?'

Tom stared at his cup.

'You just couldn't help boasting?'

'I'm sorry. I wanted to see their reactions.'

'How were their reactions when you told them they were only getting two hundred and fifty thousand of our ten million? Let me guess, pissed off?'

'Of course not. They're blown away we're giving them any money.'

Frankie rolled her eyes. 'Yeah, right. They'll want more.'

'No, you're wrong. Dash couldn't stop hugging me and Rod was crying. They didn't expect anything.'

'Okay, let's hope that's the case.'

Tom drew Frankie towards him. 'Don't worry, this will turn out for the best. I might finally have a decent relationship with my brothers.'

'Because you gave them money?'

Tom shook his head. 'Not because I gave them the money, but because we're all better off, which is a huge stress relief for everyone.'

'I guess. At least they should be able to go ahead with their boat business.'

'Mmm, probably.' Tom moved his gaze back to his coffee cup.

'What? What aren't you telling me?'

'Nothing, don't be silly.' He got up from the stool. 'It's almost three. I'll go and pick up the girls. Might even take them for a milkshake or something as an after-school treat. Coming?'

'Wait. First, tell me what else is going on with Rod and Dash?'

Tom continued to avoid Frankie's eyes. 'Nothing, okay. Now, do you want to come?'

123

'No,' she said. 'I'd better continue unpacking. But Tom, I need you to promise me something.'

'What?'

'If something's going on with your brothers, you'll tell me.'

Tom laughed. 'So suspicious. Nothing to tell. I promise you'll be the first to know when there is.'

# CHAPTER TWELVE

## *Bec*

Bec checked her watch; it was two-thirty. She was pretty sure it was around three o'clock when they'd met. She pulled her jacket tight, glad of its warmth as she sat down at an outside table. The cafe was two doors down from the newsagency, giving her a clear vantage point to see the old lady. Hopefully she would be buying her ticket today. Imagine scheduling the purchase of a lotto ticket for the same time every Saturday? Bec wasn't into rituals; however, the old lady's lotto ritual was one she would always be grateful for. She ordered a coffee and sat back and observed the goings-on around her. The strip mall was busy with people ducking in and out of shops, savouring the temporary warmth they offered.

A few minutes before three, a bus stopped across the road. Moments later it manoeuvred back into the traffic, leaving a small figure standing on the footpath.

Bec jumped up. Her stomach fluttered with nerves. It was her. She walked over to the curb and waited.

The old lady crossed the road, a smile lighting up her face. 'Oh, hello, dearie. Fancy seeing you again. How are you?' She patted Bec's arm. 'Things settled down for you, I hope?'

Bec smiled. 'I'm very well thank you. Actually, I hoped I might bump into you here today. Do you have time for a cup of tea?'

The old lady hesitated. 'Yes, I suppose that would be lovely. But I must buy my ticket first.'

125

'Of course. Would you like me to come with you or shall I go and order?' Bec pointed to the cafe she'd been waiting at.

'You order, dearie.' She winked. 'I'll try not to knock anything over this time. I'll be with you in a few minutes. Just a cup of Earl Grey for me, thank you.' The old lady reached into her bag and removed her purse. 'Now, you let me buy you a drink. I seem to remember things were a little tough the last time we met.'

Bec wanted to hug the old lady; she was every bit as lovely as she recalled. 'No, you put your money away, this one's on me. I'll meet you inside the cafe as soon as you're done here.' Bec didn't give her a chance to argue, she turned and walked towards the cafe. She'd played this moment over in her mind all morning. What she would say, how she would deliver the gift.

Bec sat down at a table near the window, placed her order and waited. About ten minutes later the bell on the cafe door chimed as the old lady came in.

She took off her coat and hung it over the back of the chair. 'Sorry, dearie, always takes longer than I expect.' She sat down just as a waitress brought their drinks. She smiled. 'Here you are buying me a cuppa and I don't even know your name. I'm Millicent by the way, but please call me Millie.'

'It's lovely to meet you properly, Millie, I'm Bec. I was actually looking for you today. I have some news I want to share with you.'

'Oh?' Millie spooned some sugar into her tea and slowly stirred it.

'You know the day we met, when you suggested I buy a lottery ticket?'

'Of course, dear, how could I forget? I practically destroyed the shop. I'm lucky they let me back in.'

Bec smiled. 'It was only a small spill. Anyway, I had some luck with that ticket.'

Millie stopped stirring her tea, her eyes sparkling. 'Oh, how wonderful, dearie, I'm so pleased for you. So pleased for you.'

'Yes, well, that's why I wanted to find you. I wouldn't have bought the ticket if you hadn't convinced me to, so I want you to share some of my winnings.' Bec slid a folded cheque across the table.

Millie pushed the paper back towards her without looking at it. 'Oh no, dearie, I couldn't accept this. They were your numbers. Meant to be, I'd say. I'm delighted to enjoy a cup of tea with you. You shouted my tea, let's call us even.'

Bec laughed. 'No, we're not even.' She lowered her voice. 'Millie, I won more than I could ever spend. Please accept my gift. Use it for yourself, or for your children or grandchildren. I want you to have it.' She pushed the cheque back across the table.

Millie hesitated. 'I don't know what to say, other than thank you. This is extremely kind of you.' Her mouth dropped open as she unfolded the cheque. 'Oh no, oh no, I can't accept this.' Her eyes remained fixed on the cheque. When she spoke her voice was low and strained. 'Dearie, how ever much did you win?'

'Ten million. So, this is only a small token to thank you.'

Millie's eyes filled with tears. 'Small token? My dear, you can't go around calling five hundred thousand dollars a small token. I can't accept this.'

Bec put her hand over Millie's and the cheque. 'Yes, you can. You changed my life. That ticket secured my family's future. I'll never be able to thank you enough.'

'I think you just did.' Millie's hands shook as she extracted a hankie from her bag and dabbed at the corner of her eyes.

'Are you okay? You look a bit pale.'

Millie gave a shaky laugh. 'Yes, dear, don't worry, I won't cark it on you.' She held up the cheque. 'I have too much to live for now. I'm still not sure what to say.'

'Don't say anything. How about you drink your tea and then I'll give you a lift home. We need to fill in your details on the cheque.'

Millie nodded, reaching for her teacup, her hands still shaking.

An hour later Bec drove away from Millie's house having safely delivered the older woman to her front door. Tears pricked her eyes.

Her heart was filled with happiness for the first time in months. What a lovely woman. They'd exchanged phone numbers, along with more tears, and promised to keep in touch.

❖

Bec's delight at the shock and surprise she'd delivered to Millie had stayed with her all weekend. She was still smiling when she stepped through the doors of Milson Pierson on Monday morning.

Celeste, coffee in hand, arrived in the foyer as she waited for the lift. She smiled. 'You look like you had a good weekend?'

Bec nodded. 'I did, thanks. You?'

'Not bad. Spent most of it working. Actually, I was thinking about you on the weekend, and the situation you're in.'

'What? With Paul?'

Celeste nodded. 'I'm sure your instincts are probably right, but I've just had another client discover that his wife, whom he was sure was cheating, in fact wasn't.' Celeste gave a little laugh. 'Guess I'm now hoping all my cases that involve cheating might have a happy ending like theirs.' The lift opened and the two women stepped in. Celeste turned to Bec. 'Are you a hundred percent certain that he cheated?'

Bec nodded.

'Even though he denies it?'

Bec hesitated this time. She was sure, wasn't she? Everything pointed to Paul having cheated. So, why were Celeste's questions planting a small seed of doubt? 'I'm as sure as I'll ever be without actually having him admit it,' Bec said.

Celeste smiled. 'Okay. I just wanted to check. I'm probably being silly. It's just that my last client touched a nerve.' She laughed. 'Maybe it's me that's having a midlife crisis, wishing all's well with the world. God, if everyone lives happily ever after, I'll be out of a job.'

Bec laughed as the doors opened to the fourth floor and the two women stepped out.

'Let's catch up for lunch this week,' Celeste suggested.

Bec nodded. 'Definitely.' She greeted the receptionist before continuing in the opposite direction to Celeste, down a passageway to her office.

❊

Celeste's words, and the comments Max had made about Paul's innocence, played over in Bec's mind all morning. Close to lunchtime doubt got the better of her. What if Paul was innocent and they ended their marriage based on a misunderstanding? She ignored the insistent ringing of her phone and collected her handbag. She needed to speak to Paul; to confront him, without warning, without giving him time to pre-plan his answers.

Bec's heart raced as she manoeuvred her Lexus through the busy traffic of St Kilda Road and headed towards South Yarra. She took a deep breath. This was ridiculous; it was just Paul. She'd dealt with so many feelings of rejection and hurt the previous few months, even if she had been wrong it was hard to imagine moving forward as if none of this had happened.

Chapel Street was thriving with people. Lunchtime was not the best time to have acted on an impulse if she expected a car park. Bec continued towards Paul's office block, debating whether to turn into a side street and park behind the building, when a car indicated it was leaving a spot. It was only twenty metres from the office. She waited for it to pull out onto the street before expertly reverse parking. She switched off the engine and released her seatbelt. Her hand went to open her door then stopped. Paul. He was standing near the curb outside his office, one hand behind his back. He looked young and handsome. His hair was slicked back and his navy-blue suit and crisp white shirt complemented his tanned face.

Bec leaned back in her seat and willed her heart rate to quieten. Six months ago she would never have imagined feeling so nervous

129

watching her husband. But now she was spying on him. He looked like he was waiting for someone or something.

Paul's face lit up, his mouth lifted in a huge grin as a taxi approached. Bec let out a breath, one she hadn't realised she'd been holding. The taxi pulled up in front of Paul and he reached out to open the door, the item he'd been holding behind his back now becoming visible. Pink-and-white roses. A lump lodged firmly in her throat. He was giving someone else her favourite flowers.

She wanted to turn away but couldn't. The scene unfolding in front of her drew her in like a magnet. His delighted grin seemed to grow bigger as he spoke to the passenger in the taxi. She watched as he put the flowers on the roof of the car and extended a hand to help the passenger out. Two long, tanned legs boasting a stunning pair of red Jimmy Choos arrived on the footpath. Chris Jenkins. Paul's face was alight with animated pleasure as he spoke, a sight Bec hadn't seen in months. Her breathing constricted. She tried to take deep breaths but they wouldn't come. Her vision blurred as she watched Paul pull Chris Jenkins towards him in a tight embrace. They clung together before Paul finally pulled away and took the flowers from the roof of the taxi, presenting them to her. Chris's face broke into smile as she put them to her nose and smelled them. She leaned across and kissed Paul lightly on the lips.

Tears rolled down Bec's cheek, her breath coming in short, sharp rasps. She had her answer, had her confirmation that her husband was a liar and a cheat, but seeing it was another thing.

After more discussion and laughter, Paul grabbed the handle of the suitcase, placed a hand on the small of Chris's back and guided her towards the entrance of the office building. Before entering the building, he looked quickly in both directions up and down the street. There was no doubt in Bec's mind – he was guilty.

# CHAPTER THIRTEEN

## *Shauna*

Shauna waited for her mother to open the front door, unable to shake the uneasy feeling that had settled in the pit of her stomach. Her own mother sue her? It was crazy, but, based on Lorraine's erratic behaviours, not all that surprising. While it was unlikely speaking with her mother would make a difference, she'd decided to try and have a conversation before meeting with the lawyer the next day.

Lorraine opened the front door a fraction. 'What do you want?'

'To talk to you. Are you going to let me in?'

'Fine.' Lorraine opened the door wider.

Shauna pushed past and walked down the hallway. Bob rose to his feet as she entered the lounge room.

'Hello, Shauna.'

'Bob.' Damn, he was the last person she wanted as part of this conversation. She turned to Lorraine. 'Can we talk in private please?'

Lorraine folded her arms across her chest. 'No, whatever you plan to say you can say to both of us.'

Shauna was silent for a moment. 'Okay,' she said finally. 'What do I need to say to convince you to withdraw your claim on the money?'

Lorraine's laugh was bitter. 'Nothing. We'll fight until we get our share, won't we, Bob?'

Bob nodded.

Shauna turned to face him. 'Did you put her up to this? What on earth do you need five million dollars for?'

'Why do you need ten million?'

'I don't, but it's my money, not yours.'

'Debatable. Your mum bought the ticket for us.'

Shauna stared at Lorraine. 'What? The ticket was my birthday present.'

Bob laughed. 'Yeah, a present you got because she forgot to buy you one and had to quickly turn something into a gift. If only we'd had a spare bottle of wine, hey, love?'

Lorraine shrugged.

'You're kidding? You forgot my birthday again?'

'So? It's a birthday, big deal. It's hardly the end of the world.'

'You're unbelievable. How can a mother forget her daughter's birthday?'

Lorraine sighed. 'Oh, don't be so melodramatic. Listen to her, would you, Bob?'

'Ridiculous.'

Shauna tried to keep her cool. 'I'm right here you know. So, you think you have a claim to the money, because the ticket was yours and not supposed to be mine?'

'Exactly,' Lorraine said. 'And please note we're only asking for half, we're not expecting the entire winnings, even though the ticket should be ours.'

'My, how generous of you.'

'No need to be sarcastic. Bob and I would have given you half if we'd won.'

Shauna raised her eyebrows. 'Really? I can't quite imagine Bob handing over five million dollars.'

Anger flashed in Bob's eyes. 'You have no idea what I would do, but I can assure you you'll be handing five million over to us.'

'Why don't you save us all this unpleasantness and give us our share,' Lorraine said. 'Not waste a lot of money on lawyers.'

Shauna looked at her mother. 'You went to a lawyer before even speaking to me.'

'I spoke to you. When you gave me the measly one-and-a-half million, I told you I expected half. Your response was to walk out and tell me to return the rest if I wasn't happy. I hardly thought talking to you again was going to make any difference. We spoke to Bob's friend Greg. He's a lawyer, and he said we were being extremely reasonable only asking for half, and he says we have a winnable case.'

Bob put an arm around Lorraine. 'Yeah, Shauna, he reckons we're entitled to the lot.'

Shauna shook her head. 'There's no point discussing this any further.'

'Don't be greedy, Shauna,' Lorraine called. 'You can prevent a lot of ill feeling by doing the right thing.'

Shauna walked out of the house and over to her car with mixed feelings. Sure, she didn't need ten million dollars, but being forced to hand it over to the likes of Bob, no way. The meeting with the lawyer was at ten o'clock the next morning. It couldn't come soon enough.

***

Nervous energy coursed through Shauna as she sat across from Clare Spencer. She still found it hard to believe that her own mother had driven her to organise this meeting with the lawyer. But then again, with Lorraine's changeable personality and extreme behaviours it really shouldn't surprise her.

Clare looked up from the letter Lorraine's lawyer had prepared. She pushed it across the desk to Shauna. 'Your mother has no entitlement to your winnings. She gave you a gift and now that it's worth something she wants a share. I doubt any judge will rule in her favour.'

Shauna let out a breath. 'Even though they say they bought the ticket for themselves?'

'They would need proof. If they'd chosen numbers that were significant to their lives, they might be able to put a case forward. A Quick Pick stuck inside a birthday card doesn't suggest this was any more than a present. Did she discuss sharing the winnings at any time before the draw?'

'She didn't say anything. She handed me an envelope at the end of dinner and wished me a happy birthday. That's all.'

Clare's train of thought appeared to be broken by a tap at her door.

'Sorry to interrupt.' A woman dressed in a beautiful Chanel suit poked her head into Clare's office. She smiled at Shauna, her hazel eyes full of warmth, before turning to Clare. 'I'm desperate to find the Hinkle file. You're not sitting on it, are you?'

'Think I might be, sorry.' Clare got up from the meeting table and walked over to her desk. She rummaged through numerous files before pulling one out. 'Here you go.' She handed it over. 'Actually, Bec, hold on a minute. Can you give a second opinion on a financial issue my client is having? This is Shauna by the way.'

'Of course.' Bec closed the office door and sat down in the chair next to Shauna.

'Shauna, I'd like Bec to give another opinion, make sure I haven't overlooked anything. Are you okay if she does? All conversations are confidential.'

Shauna nodded. 'Fine by me.'

'Good. Now, Bec, we've got an unusual situation. Shauna came into a large sum of money recently and her mother and mother's partner are demanding a fifty-percent share. I'm not aware of any similar cases.' Clare handed Bec the letter Shauna had received.

The colour drained from Bec's face as she read down the page.

'Is everything okay?' Shauna asked.

Bec's eyes widened as she stared at Shauna. 'This is unbelievable.'

'You're telling me,' Shauna said. 'How greedy are they?'

Bec stood up. 'Sorry, Clare can I talk to you for a minute?'

Clare gave Shauna an apologetic smile. 'We'll just be a moment.' Shauna nodded as the two lawyers left the room. She stood up and walked over to the office window, observing the chaos of cars and trams below. She took a deep, calming breath. The other lawyer, Bec, had obviously seen something Clare hadn't. Perhaps it wasn't as black and white as Clare had indicated?

Shauna took her seat as the lawyers re-entered the room. Clare's eyes were wide, as if she'd had a shock.

'Problem?' Shauna asked.

Bec smiled. 'Not at all. I'm sure Clare is right. No one has any legal claim to the money. My guess is they're hoping you'll settle out of court. You'll incur fees if you choose to defend the case.'

Shauna glanced at Clare.

Clare cleared her throat, her face returning to a more normal expression. 'Yes, Bec's right.' She picked up the legal letter from the desk. 'I'd recommend we draft a response to this on your behalf and see whether they choose to take the matter further.'

Shauna glanced from Bec to Clare and back again. Clare appeared to be doing her best to look normal whereas Bec now sported a wide grin and could hardly stand still.

'Are you sure everything's okay?' she asked.

Bec turned to Clare. 'Would you mind if I had a quick word with Shauna, alone?'

'Fine by me.' Clare moved towards the door. 'I'll check if any case precedents exist while you two talk.'

Bec waited for Clare to close the door before turning back to Shauna. She smiled. 'I'm aware there were two other winners when you won your money.'

Shauna nodded. 'That's right. Did you see it on the news?'

'No.' Bec hesitated. 'Unlikely as this is going to sound, I was one of them.'

Shauna's jaw dropped. 'You're kidding?'

Bec grinned. 'Nope, ten million dollars, same as you.'

They sat in silence as Shauna absorbed this information. 'This isn't some kind of stupid joke, is it?'

The corners of Bec's mouth began to twitch. 'Seems like it should be, but no it's not.'

Shauna continued to stare until Bec burst out laughing. 'I'm sorry.' Bec wiped her eyes. 'It's just so ridiculous. I feel like I'm living in some weird daydream and meeting you adds another layer of strange.'

Shauna's eyes locked with Bec's and moments later she began to laugh. Anyone entering the room seeing client and lawyer simultaneously shaking their heads and laughing would think they were mad.

Once their laughter subsided, Shauna moved forward on her chair. 'Tell me your story. When did you find out you'd won?'

Bec explained how Millie had convinced her to buy a ticket, and then the shock she'd experienced as the seven numbers came up.

'You haven't spent any?' Shauna was shaking her head as Bec finished telling her story.

'No, I gave some to a friend and some to Millie once I tracked her down. The rest is hidden in a bank account.'

'Hidden?'

Bec's cheeks flushed red. 'Yes, hidden. Paul, my husband, walked out on me before I bought the ticket. I'm working out whether to divorce him or not. He doesn't know about the money, so yes, it's hidden.'

'That's awful,' Shauna said. 'My dramas seem pretty insignificant compared to yours.'

'I wouldn't say someone claiming five million from you is insignificant.'

'But the most unbelievable thing happened to you and you can't share the news with anyone. Although based on my experience, sharing might be a little overrated.'

Bec smiled. 'Yes, it doesn't sound like it's been a lot of fun for you either. I wonder who the other person is? Maybe we should find out, see how the win has affected them.'

'Perhaps,' Shauna said. She looked at Bec. She wasn't sure if it was the surreal circumstances that had brought them together today, or the knowledge that they had shared the win, but she felt an unusual connection to her. 'This might sound weird,' she said, 'but I feel like we need to celebrate. You're the only other person who totally gets what I'm going through and can really enjoy the moment.'

Bec nodded. 'Don't worry, I feel exactly the same.' She pulled out her card. 'Here are my numbers. Call me and we'll plan a catch-up. Do you think I should try to find the third winner?'

Shauna shrugged. 'I guess there wouldn't be any harm. If we don't like the sound of them we don't need to take it any further.'

Bec nodded. 'Exactly, leave that one with me. I'll see if I can pull some strings.' She stood and made her way to the door of the office. 'I'll get Clare for you so you can finish your meeting. It's been great to meet you.'

Shauna grinned. 'You, too, I'll be in touch.' She shook her head after Bec left the room. What were the odds of meeting one of the other winners? She'd hardly given either of them a thought up until now. It was mind-boggling. Her smile remained in place as she waited for Clare to return.

Back in her office, Shauna sorted through her mail and messages. She was surprised to see a message from Lisa Gentville, a girl she'd gone to high school with and another from Miles Blauchamp, a neighbour from her childhood. How bizarre to receive two messages in the same morning from people she'd not given a thought to in years. She smiled as Josh came into her office.

Josh didn't return her smile. 'Seen this?' He held up a copy of *Empowered She* magazine.

'No, I don't usually read trash mags. Why?'

'I think you'd better read it.' He opened the magazine to an article and handed it to Shauna.

Shauna felt her throat constrict. 'Shit, shit, how did this happen?' She was peering at a photo of her mother under a caption which announced: *Daughter Steals Mother's Lotto Win.*

She quickly scanned the article. It appeared Lorraine had sold her sob story to the magazine.

'It doesn't mention your name at least,' Josh said.

'No, but anyone who knows my mum will know about the lotto win.' Shauna paused. 'I had phone calls last week from this magazine but I never returned them. I honestly assumed they were trying to sell me a subscription.'

'Appears not.'

'It also explains the phone messages I've received this morning,' Shauna said. 'Blasts from the past. They must have seen this and decided I'd be good to hit up for some money. What should I do?'

'Probably nothing. Don't return the calls, don't talk to any magazines or papers and just lay low. Possibly contact your mother and tell her not to give your contact details to anyone.'

Shauna nodded. 'I bet it's not the only story either. She'll be loving the attention. As much as I'd like to kill her right now, there's not a lot I can do other than ignore any phone calls and tell her to shut up in future.'

'Good girl. As my mum always says, when you're served with lemons, make lemonade.'

Shauna narrowed her eyes. 'Are you for real? She says that?'

'Yep, now, shut up and let me buy you a drink.'

'It's only four o'clock.'

'So?'

'So, my work day goes officially until five-thirty, and unofficially until about ten if I want to get this presentation finished.'

'Due tomorrow?'

'No, Friday, but I need to get a headstart.'

Josh walked over and closed the cover on Shauna's computer. 'No you don't. Presentations will wait, life won't. There's a bottle of Gewurztraminer waiting for us.'

Shauna snorted. 'Gewurzt-what-the-fuckier? Are you trying to impress me? Because it's not working.'

'Gewurztraminer is wine, you ignoramus. Next time I'l white wine, okay?'

'Or something a normal person would say, like sav blanc or pinot grigio?'

Josh folded his arms and towered over Shauna. 'Get your stuff, smart-arse, you're coming with me.'

Shauna's tongue rolled over her upper lip. 'Mmm, Mr Dominant, asserting yourself, aren't you?'

Josh pretended to scowl. 'Stop talking. Don't spoil my moment. Now, come on, we're leaving.'

Shauna suppressed a smile, scooped up her bag and followed him out of the office.

# CHAPTER FOURTEEN

## *Frankie*

Frankie slammed the document down on the kitchen table. *The first to know*. What a joke. Tea spilled from her favourite mug and splattered the wall and floor. A week had passed since Tom had sworn nothing was going on with his brothers. The date on this document dated back more than two weeks. She wiped up the tea, took a deep breath, then picked up the phone and dialled Tom's number.

'Hey, beautiful wife.'

Frankie strained to hear Tom over the music and laughter in the background. 'Where are you?'

'At the pub, darls, what's up?'

'Darls? Are you drunk?'

Tom laughed. 'No, just having a beer or two with my brothers to celebrate.'

'Celebrate what?'

Tom hesitated. 'Oh, you know, nothing special. Life being good to us at last.'

'Shouldn't you be at work?'

'Work? No I told them they could keep their job. What's the point of turning up to earn a pittance?'

'You quit?'

'Yep, it was a spur-of-the-moment thing. Rod and Dash both resigned, which motivated me to. We're millionaires. It's ridiculous to continue doing a job I hate.'

'I agree for you, but Rod and Dash? They quit their jobs? Why?'

'Hated Old Man McGregor. Wasn't a good place to work.'

Frankie shook her head. She'd only ever heard good things about Karl McGregor from Rod and Dash. 'Okay. So, what are you all planning to do?' Frankie knew from the documents in front of her exactly what they planned to do, but she wanted to hear it from Tom.

'Let's talk about this when I get home, sweets. I'd better go, it's my shout. I might be a bit late.'

Hope came into the kitchen as Frankie hung up the phone. She smiled at Hope, glad for the distraction. 'Everything okay?'

'No, it's bloody not.' Hope dropped her bag on the floor. She looked ready to explode.

'Hope!'

'What? It's not bloody alright, thanks to you.'

'What are you talking about?'

'You. What did you say to the school about Hamish?'

'Hamish? What, that horrible boy? I didn't say anything.'

Hope stared at Frankie, her anger replaced with surprise. 'Hold on, did you say anything to anyone?'

Frankie nodded. 'Yes, his mother.'

'What?'

'I spoke to his mother, mentioned how badly he had behaved that afternoon towards you. She was even ruder than he was. I didn't say anything to anyone else.'

'You shouldn't have said anything to her. I'm not four. Are you sure you didn't talk to someone else?'

'Of course I'm sure. Calm down and tell me what this is all about.'

Hope picked up her bag. 'It's nothing, don't worry about it.'

Frankie moved towards her daughter. 'No, it's not nothing. You don't come in here all worked up and then tell me nothing's wrong. Tell me what's happened.'

Hope forced a smile. 'Really it's nothing. I got my wires crossed.'

Frankie stared at Hope. Why was it so hard to get a straight answer?

'Well, how are things at school? Is Hamish still hassling you?'

Hope hesitated before opening the fridge, her face now hidden from Frankie. 'Um, no. He's actually been very nice. He apologised for how he'd behaved.'

'Good. So, why did you come in all worked up before?'

'Sorry. It's just, well, I thought he'd been put up to it. The apology, the being nice. It's a relief to know he wasn't forced.'

Frankie smiled. So, Hamish was now being nice to Hope. Perhaps he'd worked out there was an easier way to get her attention. Being a teenager certainly wasn't easy. She wanted to ask more but knew better. Hope had a smile on her face, a vast improvement from the past few months. 'Do you need any help with your homework?'

Hope closed the fridge, her eyes meeting Frankie's. 'No, it's maths, so please stay far, far away.'

Frankie laughed. 'Fair enough. Can I help with anything else?'

'No,' Hope said. 'Except I did want to ask you something. Can I go to a party on Saturday night? Susan Tillie's having a sixteenth.'

'Will her parents be home?'

'Her dad will be, but there might be alcohol. Don't worry, I won't drink any.'

'They're serving alcohol at a sixteenth?'

'Not her dad. Susan's boyfriend is eighteen and he and his mates might bring beer.'

Frankie hesitated. Parties. It wouldn't just be nasty kids they'd need to look out for now. Drugs and alcohol would be the next thing. She trusted Hope, but she also remembered being the same age. Experimenting was all part of growing up. She needed to be able to trust her daughter and that would only be by giving her some freedom and expecting her to do the right thing. 'Okay. Home by midnight, deal?'

Hope threw her arms around Frankie. 'You're the best!' She pulled away. 'The other thing I wanted to ask is whether I could buy some new clothes?'

'What about the shirt I made you?'

'I wore it to Lisa's party, so everyone's seen it. I'd love something new and we can afford it now, can't we?'

Frankie didn't respond.

'Mum?'

Frankie shook herself. Why did she clam up every time the money was brought up? 'Yes, of course we can afford new clothes.'

'But?'

'But, I'm still uneasy about the money. Silly, I know. I'm not sure I'll ever feel it's ours to spend.'

'You found the ticket. We have no way of finding who dropped it. Dad says we've been blessed and should enjoy ourselves.'

Frankie raised an eyebrow. 'Blessed? Interesting, as he's never set foot inside a church. Regardless, spending someone else's fortune doesn't sit right with me.'

'Why don't you put some of the money to good use?'

'What do you mean?'

'Find a charity, somewhere you can make a difference.'

'We've already given some to charity.'

'Yes, but they were handouts to big charities. Why not give money to something you're passionate about? You say the old people always complain they can't get out enough at the retirement village. Buy them a minibus and pay for someone to be employed to drive them.'

Frankie stared at Hope. 'What a wonderful idea. Why didn't I think of doing something for the oldies?'

Hope laughed. 'Because you're too busy hating the fact that we're millionaires and thinking of all the things that might go wrong. You haven't spent enough time thinking of the good money can do.'

Frankie gave Hope a hug. 'You are one extremely wise young woman. How about we go shopping after school on Thursday? I'll give you a budget and you can go nuts, a new wardrobe maybe?'

'Really? I can buy more than one thing?'

Frankie laughed. 'We'll go mad. Tell Fern and she can come, too.'

Hope flung her arms around Frankie again and squeezed her tight. 'Thank you, thank you, thank you.'

Frankie hugged her daughter, unable to shake the feeling of unease as her eyes travelled back to the document on the table.

❧

Frankie allowed Tom to sleep late the next morning. He'd finally arrived home close to midnight and fallen into bed fully clothed, smelling like a brewery.

A little after ten she decided it was time for an explanation. 'Good morning,' Frankie spoke loudly. She couldn't help smiling as she heard the groan from their bed. 'Here, take these.' She passed Tom a glass of water and two paracetamol tablets. 'I need to talk to you.'

Tom dragged himself to a sitting position, washed the tablets down, then sank back into the pillow. 'I'm sorry, hon, I'm not sure what came over me. I won't be out drinking midweek again.'

Frankie sat on the edge of the bed. 'It was a celebration, wasn't it?'

A flicker of concern crossed Tom's face. 'Yes. How did you know?'

If she wasn't so angry, the look on Tom's face would have made Frankie laugh. 'You told me when I spoke to you that you'd quit your jobs and were having a celebration.'

Tom exhaled. 'I forgot you rang.'

'I don't understand how you and your brothers are suddenly best friends, when only a few weeks ago Dash was calling you an arsehole.'

'He was disappointed, he didn't mean anything.'

Frankie slowly shook her head. 'An interesting change of perspective. So, now what? You're brothers, friends and business partners?'

Tom buried his head deeper into the pillow, his eyes focused on the ceiling. 'Who told you?'

Frankie waved the document at him. 'No one. This transfer of ownership of Blue Water Charters to Tom York, Rod York and Dash York gave me a hint.'

Tom glanced briefly at the paperwork. 'Sorry, I was planning to surprise you. Announce the new business once the paperwork was finalised and the boats were ready to show you.'

Frankie crossed her arms. 'Don't lie. You were scared to tell me, weren't you?'

Tom looked sheepish. 'Honestly? Yes. I thought you would try to talk me around and I didn't want to miss out on the opportunity.'

'According to the date on this application it happened over two weeks ago. You've had plenty of time to fill me in.'

Tom pushed his fingers through his hair. 'Yes, I'm sorry. Please trust me, it's a good thing. We want to work together, a real family business.'

'So, Rod and Dash threw in their jobs and invested nearly all the money we gave them in this? Will they have any left over?'

Tom's eyes darted around the room. Finally he spoke, still unable to look at Frankie. 'They should be okay.'

A knot formed in the pit of Frankie's stomach. Had he given them more? 'What aren't you telling me?'

'Can we discuss it later, when I'm feeling a bit better?'

'No. Explain now.'

Tom sighed. 'Okay, so they didn't use their money to buy the business.'

'What do you mean? How can you all own a third if they didn't contribute?'

Tom shrugged.

Frankie's mouth dropped open. 'No. Please tell me you didn't pay the whole lot?'

'You're turning this into a bigger deal than necessary. It was only six hundred grand.'

Frankie stared at Tom. Was he kidding? '*Only six hundred grand?* On top of what we already gave them?' Surely she must have misunderstood him? 'Let me get this straight. Without even consulting me you handed over more than a million dollars to your brothers?'

'No, a third is still mine.'

'So, two hundred and fifty thousand each as a gift and then an additional two hundred thousand each as part of this business?'

Tom nodded.

'Nine hundred thousand dollars! Tom, I can't believe you would do this without first talking to me. When Dash hit us up for money in the botanical gardens you said you wouldn't dream of joining them.'

'Hold on, I said I was disappointed they only came to me when they wanted something, not that I wouldn't go into business with them if I could.'

'Why on earth didn't you buy the business in your name and employ them? You now have two business partners who've invested nothing but are entitled to two-thirds of the profits.'

Tom shrugged. 'They'll be investing a hell of a lot of hard work. Don't underestimate what it takes to make a successful business. Dash was right, being equal partners helps avoid any resentment down the track. If everyone works hard we should all get equally rewarded.'

Frankie sat down, taking a deep breath to calm herself. She spoke quietly. 'Agreeing to share the profit three ways, that would make sense, but instead you've given them an extra two hundred thousand each. If they decide tomorrow to sell up, then you'll get a third of the sale price.'

Tom was silent. 'They won't sell. We're going to turn this into a successful business.'

'Oh, Tom, you should have had a lawyer or an accountant look over this before you agreed to anything.'

'We did. Dash's mate is a lawyer and he checked everything out.'

Frankie threw her hands up in the air. Sometimes she really wondered about Tom. 'Do you really think Dash's mate had your best interests at heart?'

Tom rubbed his head and closed his eyes. After a few moments he opened them. 'Let's go down to the boats later this afternoon, take the girls. I'll show you everything and then you'll know why I'm so pumped about this whole idea. Please come. It's important to me.'

'Okay.' Frankie nodded. 'But I want you to promise me something.'

'What?'

'You don't spend large amounts of money, and by that I mean buying anything that costs more than a thousand dollars, without consulting me first. Either that, or we get the bank to change our account to both sign.'

'I promise,' Tom said. 'Of course I should have told you. This is the most impulsive thing I've ever done.'

Frankie swallowed. She needed to go outside for some air. 'Why don't you get some more sleep,' she said.

Tom grinned. 'Okay, babe. I promise I'll come down showered and not hungover. I can't believe how the money is changing our lives.'

Tom's words played over in Frankie's mind as she left the bedroom and walked back down the stairs. 'Changing our lives,' she muttered. 'It sure bloody is.'

※

Tom looked human again by the time they collected the girls from school. They drove towards St Kilda and the marina.

Fern hadn't stopped talking. 'Can we go out on the boat today?'

'Maybe,' Tom said. 'If Rod or Dash are happy to go, too. Until I get my marine licence we need one of them. Once I've got a licence we can go anytime we want.'

'Rod or Dash? I thought it was going to be the four of us?' Frankie really wasn't in the mood to see Dash.

'I mentioned we were coming down and they insisted on being there. They want to thank you and show you the boats.'

Frankie sat in silence. She would be interested to gauge how grateful Dash was. To Tom's face maybe, but to hers it was always a different story. She was jolted out of her thoughts as Tom pulled into a parking space at the marina.

'Uncle Rod, Uncle Rod!' Fern squealed and jumped out of the car. Frankie watched as Rod engulfed Fern in a gigantic hug and turned and did the same to Hope.

She smiled as Hope squirmed with embarrassment.

'Where's Dash?' Tom asked.

'Working on the boats. I wanted to be out here to greet my favourite girls.' Rod pretended to tickle Fern. She swatted his hand away, telling him she was too old for that. Rod turned to Frankie. Before she had a chance to say anything he had her in a tight bear hug.

Frankie started to laugh when Rod continued to squeeze her. 'Help, I can hardly breathe!'

Rod let her out of the embrace but placed one hand on each of her shoulders, his eyes locked with hers. 'Thank you. What you and Tom are doing is life-altering for me and for Dash. I can't thank you enough and want you to know we will work harder than you could ever imagine to make sure this business is a success.'

Frankie smiled. Rod was genuine, she knew that.

'Come on,' Tom said. 'Enough of the warm-and-fuzzy stuff. Let's go and find the boats.'

Frankie freed herself from Rod and walked with the girls. As they rounded the corner of the building the marina spread out before them.

'Check out these boats,' Fern said as they wove their way along various jetties. 'Who owns them?'

'People with a lot of money,' Hope said.

Frankie couldn't get over the contrast from their lifestyle of only a few weeks ago. They passed some beautiful-looking craft. She could imagine going out in one of those. When Frankie thought of boats she tended to think of the aluminium tinny ones. These were real boats, with cabins, comfortable chairs, kitchen areas and toilet facilities. Wafts of petrol fumes and seaweed mixed in the salty ocean air. The gentle breeze whipped across her face, transporting her back sixteen years. With no money between them and a baby on the way, their honeymoon had consisted of three nights in a tent down on

Melbourne's Mornington Peninsula. As basic as the accommodation had been, Frankie would never forget it. Being five months pregnant at the time had not stopped them from making love at every opportunity. Frankie's cravings for salty foods had been accommodated for with a fish-and-chip shop across the road from the campground. Other than the many hours they spent inside the tent, one of the more memorable events was Tom hiring a small tinny for a romantic sunset cruise. He'd packed soft drinks, chocolates and blankets and off they'd gone. Twenty minutes into their trip the engine had stopped working, a large puff of smoke erupting from it. At this stage petrol fumes had been combined with the stench of rotting seaweed. Within seconds Frankie had been retching over the side. Over an hour later another boat had come past and offered some help. The same smell now brought back fond memories of the honeymoon and a time in their lives when they had many exciting, yet frightening, events ahead of them.

Tom stopped in front of one of the older-looking vessels and Frankie was jolted back to the present. '*Get Reel* is the first of the fleet,' he announced.

'Fleet?' Dash's recognisable snigger echoed from within the boat. 'Not sure if you can refer to two boats as a fleet.' His head appeared from an opening in the deck. 'Hi, girls.' He waved to Hope and Fern. He made no effort to acknowledge Frankie. 'I'm sorting out ropes down here. Will be up in a minute.' He disappeared below.

Tom helped everyone onto the boat and the girls headed inside the cabin.

Rod followed and Frankie overheard him explaining the jobs of the various instruments.

Tom turned to Frankie. 'What do you think?'

'It's older than I imagined.' Having walked past so many luxurious boats, the reality of the fishing charter was a letdown.

'She needs a cosmetic overhaul, that's all. We plan to get this boat out of the water in the next two weeks for maintenance. You'll be blown away at the difference a coat of paint makes. After we sort out storage compartments and a couple of minor repairs, you won't recognise her.'

'What about the other one? How much work is needed?'

Tom pointed to a smaller but more modern boat, with the name *Fish Tales* written in fancy lettering on the side. 'Minimal.' The fishing rods were organised on the back of what appeared to be a very professional set-up. Frankie relaxed. 'That one seems nicer.'

'They both will be when we've finished,' Tom said. 'But *Get Reel* has room to take more people, so making improvements is a priority. I can imagine *Fish Tales* being hired out by one group at a time, whereas with this boat we can charge per person and allow twenty people on at once.'

'Is twenty the limit?'

'No, but the total we take depends on how many of us go out each time. We might get someone on casually if we start getting busy.'

'Come on, show me everything.' Frankie smiled. She knew nothing at all about fishing charters so decided to put her doubts aside and let Tom enjoy his moment. He showed her around the cabin and took her down through the hole in the deck Dash had appeared from. They found him down below sorting ropes and fishing gear.

In the small space, meant for storage, Frankie felt the walls close in. She reached out for the wall to steady herself. The smirk on Dash's face wasn't worth engaging. 'I'm going up on top.'

'On deck, you mean,' Dash called after her. 'Learn the lingo, franks and beans.'

Frankie ignored him, grateful to be back in the fresh air. 'Sorry, not the right space for me.'

Tom squeezed her hand. 'Come with me. Time to visit *Fish Tales*.'

Rod and the girls were already enjoying the more modern of the boats. Fern sat in the captain's chair pretending to drive, while Hope lay back, eyes closed, on one of the bench seats.

Frankie laughed. 'Now, this is more my style.'

'Picture yourself on this one?' Rod asked.

'Definitely. It's newer, cleaner and nicer. I would enjoy a day out on this boat.'

'Don't worry, it will be as nice when it's finished. You wait.'

'Speaking of a trip, shall we motor out?' Tom looked at Rod.

Rod checked his watch. 'Sorry mate, can't. I need to leave in five minutes. Dash might, though.' He called out to Dash before Frankie had the chance to stop him.

Dash jumped down onto the deck and agreed to take them out. After saying their goodbyes to Rod, they untied the boat and motored slowly out of the marina. Tom and the girls had moved to the front of the boat, leaving Frankie at the back, closer to Dash than she would normally choose to be.

Dash opened a can of beer and turned towards her. 'I suppose you realise what a good idea this was now?'

'Wasn't given much of a choice, was I?'

'Yeah, well, it's stupid to sit on millions of dollars when Tom could be doing something like this.'

Frankie looked across to Tom and the girls and lowered her voice. 'A few weeks ago you were happy to blackmail me into getting what you want. Now, you're pretending it's all for the good of your brotherly relationship. Answer something for me. Are you actually interested in having a relationship with Tom, or just using him?'

Dash laughed. 'I think you're accusing me of being a gold-digger. How could you? I treasure my brothers.' He grinned and took a swig of his beer.

Frankie gritted her teeth, unable to respond. She turned and gazed towards the shoreline. He was so arrogant, so disrespectful.

'Don't be like that,' Dash said. 'I'm kidding. This is about family, not money.'

She turned back to face him. 'That's good to hear because you need to get one thing straight. No more money is being made available to the business, or to you. You'll be expected to work hard, and if expenses can't be met, you and Rod will contribute a third each.'

Dash took another swig of beer. 'Is that right? Look, I don't want to cause problems with you. I want to forget everything that happened in the past and not mention it again. We both need to move on.'

Frankie nodded. He wasn't stupid. He had too much to lose to risk upsetting Tom.

'But this is business. You can't start making up conditions on something that's already been agreed. I suggest you read the fine print of the little contract Tom signed. Expenses aren't part of the deal for me or Rod.'

Pressure began building inside Frankie's head. 'Why?'

'The business is responsible for all expenses. In the case of no income the obligation to meet expenses falls to Tom. Ask Tom for the contract. A lawyer drew it up.'

'What, your mate?' she spat.

Dash raised his eyebrows. 'So? He's a lawyer and he's only concerned with our best interests.'

'Your best interests, you mean.' Frankie turned away from Dash. She clenched her fists. How she'd like to wipe the self-satisfied smirk off his face. His offer to forget the past didn't appear to extend to building a good relationship for the future. She looked over at Tom. He was laughing at something Hope had said. Tom was too trusting, too easy to take advantage of.

A week later Tom arrived home to find Frankie at the kitchen table, engrossed in a document.

'What are you reading, hon?'

Frankie jolted upright. 'You scared me.' She folded the letter. 'Nothing important. How was your day? Get a lot done on the boats?' Frankie carefully slid the paper inside her book.

'Great.' He opened the fridge and took out a beer. 'We decided to take a bit of a break so, out into the bay and did some skiing.'

'Skiing?'

'Yeah, Rod bought all the gear last week. Dash came, too.'

'Does the boat go fast enough for skiing?'

'With the new motor she flies. It's not an ideal ski boat, I think Rod's planning to buy a proper one.'

Frankie opened her mouth then closed it. She remained silent.

'You should come next time.'

Frankie nodded.

Tom sipped his beer. 'Is something wrong?'

Frankie pressed her fingers into her palms. 'I'm trying to be supportive of this new business, but you make it hard when you choose a day of skiing over the work you should be doing. I thought the boats still needed a lot of work, so why aren't you working on them?'

'We are. *Get Reel's* repairs to the hull are nearly completed. Once they finish cleaning her she'll be back in the water.'

'What about *Fish Tales*? You still have improvements to the cabin to do. Why isn't this happening?'

Tom's face hardened. 'We took one day off. Don't turn this into a big deal.'

Frankie sighed. Arguments were rolling from one into another at the moment and she didn't feel like instigating the next round.

Tom put a bunch of files on the table before sitting down with a beer. 'Now, you'll be pleased to hear I met with the new lawyer you organised.' Tom had agreed, somewhat reluctantly, to using a different lawyer from Dash's. 'He's looked over the paperwork and Dash's lawyer hasn't done anything dodgy. Every document is as we discussed.'

'Every document says you're putting in all the money and covering every expense, while Dash and Rod retain a third ownership each. That's the problem as far as I'm concerned. They aren't contributing anything, yet they'll receive a third of any profit.'

Tom pulled out a document from his file and handed it to Frankie. 'I agree, so I had him draft an amendment. Both Rod and Dash agreed with the terms.'

Frankie read through the details. 'Dash has agreed to this? He's actually said yes to investing fifty thousand dollars in the business?'

Tom nodded. 'They both did. Their money will go towards the start-up costs and for on-going maintenance. Once this first injection of cash dries up we all agree to contribute another equal amount.'

'Has he signed this?'

'Not yet, his lawyer is reading over the documents, but everything was approved in principle. So, stop worrying about me being taken advantage of.'

'When Dash signs the document and hands over fifty thousand dollars I'll stop worrying.'

'Good. Now, how about you consider joining the business?'

'What do you mean?'

'Delivering leaflets is a waste of time when you can work with us. All sorts of jobs need doing. Organising a new website, business cards, brochures, accounts, answering the phones. There's so much more than just taking out the boats.'

Frankie shook her head. 'Are you crazy? I have no experience, that's why I could never get a job other than delivering leaflets. I wouldn't know where to start.'

'None of us do. We're all learning. Dash knows a bit about the computers and the booking system. He could show you how that all works and then if you still needed help we could get someone else in for more training. Will you do it?'

'How do I continue running the household, looking after the girls?'

'The job would only be part-time, during school hours.'

Frankie bit her lip. She'd found the ticket, surely she should decide what she wanted to do. Working with Dash was hardly an incentive to get involved.

'What's wrong? I thought you'd jump at the chance to be a part of the team from the outset.'

'Then maybe you should have involved me from the outset. You know, before you actually decided to buy the business.'

The vein in Tom's head was beginning to throb. 'I can continue to apologise for that or you could let it go and we could move on. I can't go back in time and change what I did.'

Frankie sighed. 'Yeah, I know. Let's drop it. There's something else I want to talk to you about anyway.'

'Mmm?' Tom took another sip of his beer.

'I want to donate some money to Birkdale.'

'What, the retirement home?'

'Yes, I want to solve their transport problem for them. Provide them with a minibus and driver. So, the donation would need to cover the cost of buying and maintaining a vehicle, or leasing one, and a wage and the running costs.'

Tom looked sceptical. 'That's very generous.'

'We can afford to be generous. Look how generous you've been.'

'Rod and Dash are family. It's hardly the same thing.'

'Well, this is what I want to do. I want to see the money doing some good for someone, and my old ladies are the perfect candidates. I'll talk to Marg, the CEO, first and see if there's a particular way they want it structured.'

'They might prefer you to hand over a lump sum.'

'Maybe, but I want it used my way. The ladies are always complaining about the cost of getting out. Taxis are expensive and many of them don't have any family to take them around. A minibus service will give them back some independence and allow them to plan outings they can look forward to. Are you okay with me going ahead? I don't want to use the money if it's going to cause problems.'

'Like I did?'

The defensive tone in Tom's voice was one Frankie was getting used to hearing since they'd won the money. It seemed he was constantly needing to explain himself, defend what he'd done. They needed to get back to where they were before the win. Openly communicating and making decisions together. She took a deep breath. 'I'm not looking for an argument, I'm looking for a way to embrace the money, see the good it can bring. This is something I believe in. It's not some faceless charity we're just handing money across to, and yes, I want to make sure you're in agreement with me spending the money. It'll be a lot. I want us to make the decision together.'

Tom's face relaxed into a smile. 'You're right, we should make decisions like this together and yes, I think you should do it.' He laughed. 'I should be focusing on your willingness to actually spend some of the money rather than questioning why. Hopefully you'll come around to the idea of the business, too.' He took another sip of his beer then reached across and pulled out the letter Frankie had hidden in the book. 'So, what's this and why are you being secretive?'

'I wasn't being secretive. The letter's from the lotto people. The other two winners met somehow and are asking to meet us. The letter asks if we're happy for our details to be released.'

'Do you want to?'

'Not sure. What do you think?'

Tom considered this for a moment. 'I guess I'd be intrigued to find out how they've used their money. Pick up some good ideas.'

'Mmm, maybe.'

Tom got up from the table. 'But I don't really care if we meet them or not. At this stage, I'd rather you think about the job. Working together would be fantastic.'

Frankie turned her focus back to the letter as Tom left the room. Fantastic? Seeing Dash on a regular basis was something that she could describe in many ways. Fantastic definitely wasn't one of them.

'Frankie, Frankie! Hello!'

Frankie turned to find Sheila Matheson hurrying towards her. She braced herself. What insults would this stupid woman unleash today?

Sheila wiped the sweat from her forehead and smiled. 'I just wanted to say hello. How are you?'

Frankie tried to hide her surprise. They had had one conversation; they were hardly friends. 'I'm fine, thanks. You?'

'Good, all good, but it's you I'm interested in. So?'

Frankie tilted her head to one side. 'I'm sorry, I have no idea what you're asking.'

Sheila pointed at Frankie. 'You, the girls, the car, the move. I'm intrigued. Did someone die and leave you a fortune? I even heard Tom was starting a fishing-charter business?'

Frankie bit the inside of her cheek.

Sheila's eyes searched Frankie's, waiting for a response. Frankie remained silent.

Sheila smiled. 'I'm so happy for you and I wanted to come and tell you. Hope looked beautiful the other night at the party in her new clothes. Logan came home demanding I take her out to buy the same jeans. And you, too, your outfit is so stylish and your hair's lovely. The highlights suit you.'

Frankie touched her hair self-consciously. The t-shirt, jeans and boots she was wearing were what everyone wore. She certainly hadn't thought she'd stand out wearing them. 'I had no idea anyone was paying such close attention to us.'

Sheila leaned towards Frankie. 'I keep my finger on the pulse.'

Frankie tensed. This woman really had no idea. She cleared her throat. 'I'm glad you find us more acceptable.'

Sheila nodded. 'Oh yes, you most certainly are. So, will you tell me the secret to your success? How do you go from a life of rags to owning luxury boats?'

Frankie hesitated before letting her muscles relax, and started to laugh. No doubt Sheila thought she was being supportive rather than rude and offensive. She decided to give her the benefit of the doubt. 'I'm not sure I'd call our clothes rags, and as for the luxury boats they're a new business my husband and his brothers hope to make a success. I hate to disappoint you, but fishing boats are hardly luxurious. The rest, well, I guess I would call it good fortune.'

Sheila clapped her hands together. 'Wonderful, wonderful. I suppose you can stop wasting your time with the leaflets, too?'

'That's where I'm off to now.'

'Oh. What a shame. I wanted to invite you out for coffee. A group of us meet every Tuesday morning. They're all mums from Hope's class. I'm sure you'd love them.'

Frankie doubted that very much. 'Sorry, thanks for the offer, though.'

'Oh, there's Dianne.' Sheila pointed and waved as a woman crossed the courtyard.

Frankie recognised her immediately. Hamish's mother. The woman she'd had a run-in with not long ago. Dianne walked towards Frankie and Sheila, keying something into her phone. She stopped as she reached them, not bothering to look up.

'Frankie,' Sheila said, 'this is Dianne. Dianne, do you know Frankie?'

Dianne glanced up, her face flushing red as recognition dawned. 'Oh yes, sort of.' She put her phone away and gave a hesitant smile. 'Hello.'

Frankie crossed her arms.

Dianne shifted from foot to foot, unable to meet Frankie's gaze. 'I probably owe you an apology. I spoke with my son and I came to realise he and his friends had been a little mean. I think it was supposed to be in jest, but words can be misinterpreted. I'm sorry for being so rude. I believe Hamish apologised to Hope.'

Frankie nodded. 'Thank you. I appreciate how difficult this must be for you.'

'Yes. Things have changed I suppose. Seeing people for their true selves does make a difference.'

Heat coursed through Frankie. 'You don't know me any better today than you did the other week when you called me a loser and a dole bludger.'

Sheila gasped. 'You didn't?'

'She certainly did,' Frankie said. 'I'm intrigued as to why the sudden change in attitude?'

Dianne's face turned an even darker shade of red. 'Well, you. Your situation. You've obviously been making more of an effort than I realised. I was wrong suggesting you were lazy. I hope the new business is a huge success.'

Sheila beamed at the two women. 'Good, all sorted; all friends. Why don't you come, Frankie? The other mums would love you to join us for a coffee.'

'Yes, come with us,' Dianne said.

Frankie marvelled at Dianne and Sheila's eager faces and attempted to calm herself before she spoke. 'Do either of you understand how rude you are?'

'What do you mean?' Sheila asked. 'We were just trying ...'

Frankie put up her hand. 'No, let me finish. You've judged me purely on the assumptions you've made about my life. Neither of you made any attempt to talk to me in the past or include me in coffee mornings. You assumed my financial situation changed recently, and apparently, I now fit into your version of acceptable so you want to be friends. I'm sorry, but I'm not interested. Now, I'd better get on. I need to get to work.' The women's mouths dropped open as Frankie turned on her heel and strode towards the car park.

# CHAPTER FIFTEEN

## *A Lunch Date*

Bec took a deep breath and shook herself. She had nothing to be nervous about. It was only lunch. She smiled across the table at Shauna. Impeccably dressed in a white pencil skirt and jacket, Shauna had come straight from a sales presentation. It had been her suggestion that they meet for a quick drink prior to meeting the other winners. The combination of sunshine and outdoor heaters made the courtyard at Cloud the perfect location for a private lunch.

'I spoke to the woman, Frankie,' Bec said. 'I wonder what they'll be like?'

Shauna nodded towards the restaurant entrance. 'If that's them, I guess we're about to find out.'

Bec glanced in the direction of the door as a couple in their early thirties entered the restaurant. Was it them? The man took the woman's hand and whispered something to her. She looked nervous, her hands smoothing her skirt, while her eyes darted around the restaurant. Bec smiled at Shauna. 'I'll go and check if it's our millionaire friends.' She got up and moved close enough to the couple to hear their conversation.

'Do you think that's them?' The man pointed towards the back of the restaurant.

Bec turned to see who he was pointing at. Two women, both in their early sixties, were deep in conversation. Their designer dresses dripped with expensive jewellery. The one who faced Bec threw her head back and laughed at something her friend said.

'Oh God, why didn't we say no?' Hearing the woman speak, Bec turned her attention back to the couple. The woman looked pale and continued to whisper to her husband. 'They look awful.'

Her husband smiled. 'Don't be silly, they wanted to meet us. I'm sure they're lovely.'

Bec moved behind them. 'No, they're awful, and if you're meeting them I'd run a mile.'

They turned to face her.

'However, if you happen to be Frankie and Tom I'd ditch them. Join us for lunch instead.'

'Bec?' Frankie asked.

'Yes, Bec.' She pretended to curtsey. 'Millionairess.' She then pointed to Shauna, who was waving at them from the courtyard. 'Shauna, millionairess, is over there.'

Frankie glanced at Tom, who started to laugh.

Linking her arm through Frankie's, Bec led them towards their table. 'Come on, let's move away from this stuffy lot and get our celebration underway.'

Shauna threw her arms around Frankie as soon as she was near enough and hugged her tight. 'Even though we're complete strangers, I'm so delighted to meet you both.'

Frankie laughed as she hugged Shauna back. They sat down as a waitress arrived with a bottle of champagne for the table.

'I hope you don't mind,' Bec said. 'I took the liberty of ordering for all of us.'

'Mind?' Tom grinned. 'Is there a better way to mark a new beginning?' He lifted his glass once the drinks had been poured. 'Here's to new friends.'

'Rich friends,' Shauna added. 'Who are loaded, so won't be after any of my fortune.' Laughter erupted as they clinked glasses. 'Come on,' Shauna said, her eyes bright as she faced Frankie and Tom, 'tell us your story. How did you find out you'd won and what have you done so far?'

Tom launched into the story of Frankie finding the ticket and all that had happened since, including the charter business.

'Brilliant,' Bec said. 'Did you give up your job?'

'Yes, I was working as a labourer. We've had a tough ride since having kids. We were only seventeen when Hope was born. Our main focus has always been making ends meet, not a lot else to be honest. My brothers are co-owners of the business.' Tom described Blue Water Charters and his hopes for a successful venture with Rod and Dash.

Bec watched them. Tom's enthusiasm was contagious – contagious for everyone except Frankie. Her face was anything but enthusiastic as Tom spoke. She looked tense and resentful.

Shauna appeared oblivious to Frankie's reaction. 'That's fantastic. You're the sort of people who should win lotto and live happily ever after. Your lives will be changed forever. How about you, Frankie? Are you working with the business, too?'

Frankie shook her head. 'No, I'm leaving the boats to the men. Fishing's not my thing.'

'Not through my lack of trying to convince her otherwise,' Tom said. 'There's the administration side of things, running the office, organising the promotional materials, the website. The list is endless. Frankie would be perfect.'

Frankie glared at her husband. 'Again, not my thing.' She shifted in her chair.

'Becoming a mother at seventeen probably hasn't left you much time to be anything but a mum,' Bec said. 'How many children do you have?'

'Two girls, Hope's fifteen and Fern's thirteen.'

'So, they're at school,' Shauna said. 'Plenty of hours for you to work if you get bored sitting around.'

Tom spoke before Frankie was able to respond. 'Frankie won't get bored. She never stops. If she's not looking after the girls and me, she's delivering leaflets or she's up at the old people's home helping out. I just hoped she might want to be part of the business.'

Shauna coughed, nearly spitting out her drink. 'Leaflets?'

'Let's order,' Bec suggested. She signalled to the waitress that they were ready. While she barely knew Frankie, it wasn't hard to see she was uncomfortable. After they selected their meals she handed the menus back to the waitress and turned to the others. 'Let us tell you a bit about ourselves.'

Bec and Shauna took turns telling Frankie and Tom how they reacted to winning the money and what had happened since. They were shocked to hear Shauna's mother was suing her.

'The only good thing about that is we all met,' Shauna said. 'If I didn't need a lawyer I wouldn't have bumped into Bec. This is meant to be. Perhaps the universe made us win lotto to bring us together.'

Tom laughed. 'Maybe, although I can think of cheaper ways the universe could organise us meeting. Not that I'm complaining, mind you.'

'I'm afraid I'm rather boring at the moment,' Bec said. 'Other than my best friend and a couple of lawyers I work with, I haven't told anybody. I gave my best friend a gift and the woman who convinced me to buy the ticket, but other than that I haven't touched a cent.'

'Boring?' Frankie raised an eyebrow. 'Your story is anything but boring. It sounds like a television drama unfolding. When will you tell your husband?'

'I'm not sure. I'm angry with him for what he's done, and even angrier knowing he will get half. He'll find out when we go through the division of assets.'

'You don't think if he knew you might be able to make things work between you again?' Frankie asked.

'No way. Our problems had nothing to do with money to start with, so it won't solve anything either.'

'Not even for your boys?' Tom asked. 'Wouldn't you try for their sake?'

Bec turned her attention to Tom. 'Imagine finding out Frankie was having an affair and she left you for him. How would you feel?'

Tom nodded. 'Fair point. I'd be devastated.'

'You can't imagine until you're in this position. Even now I'm not sure what I'm doing except trying to protect myself and the boys from getting hurt further.'

'How awful,' Frankie said. 'I hope we're never in your position. I'm sorry you have to go through such a tough time.'

Bec smiled. She could see Frankie genuinely meant what she said.

'Main course is served.' The waitress hovered behind Bec's chair with their meals. Tom's phone beeped as she placed their plates down.

He read the message. 'Damn.'

Frankie touched his arm. 'What's wrong?'

'I should be down at the marina. *Get Reel's* ready to be re-floated. I need to check that all of the final improvements have been made.'

'Go,' Frankie said. 'You can't leave this up to Rod or Dash. Most of the improvements were done under your instructions.'

'You're right, but my lunch will be wasted.'

Bec turned to the waitress. 'Could we get this meal to go please?'

The waitress removed the plate and returned moments later with a container for Tom.

Bec and Shauna stood to hug Tom as he said his goodbyes. Anyone watching would have assumed they were old friends, not people who'd met less than an hour ago. He kissed Frankie and headed out to the car park.

'Nice guy you've got there,' Shauna said.

Frankie nodded. 'He is.' She pushed her food around her plate with a fork then cleared her throat. 'I was wondering, are either of you worried about the money ruining your lives?'

'What do you mean?' Bec said.

Frankie put down her fork. 'I did a lot of research after we won. There are so many stories of people not only losing all the money after winning, but then going bankrupt. Along the way their friendships, family relations and marriages appear to be destroyed. I'm paranoid this is going to happen to us.'

Shauna laughed. 'God, I should be worried, not you. My mother's already suing me and an article she appeared in has people from our past calling, I assume to beg for money.'

Frankie stared at Shauna. 'And you're laughing?'

'What else can I do? Hopefully, my mother will come to her senses at some point. I'm in discussions with an accountant and financial planner as to how I look after the rest. There's no way I'd let it ruin my life.'

'Good,' Frankie said. 'We all need advice. You, too, Bec. Once you've told your husband and worked out what you're doing, your first stop should be to see an expert.'

Bec smiled. 'Absolutely. I will. It seems like you and Tom have really thought through how best to use the money. You've invested, given gifts and bought a business. I'm impressed.'

Frankie blushed. 'I think we had the most need to change out of the three of us. It's allowed us to really improve our lives. You and Shauna have good jobs and were probably financially stable before your wins.'

'You're lucky to have such a motivated husband,' Shauna said. 'I imagine he'll do well with his new venture.'

'Mmm,' Frankie replied. 'Let's hope.'

'If you don't mind me saying,' Bec began, 'you don't seem very enthusiastic. Are you unhappy with Tom's choice of business?'

Frankie seemed to be considering her answer as she sipped her drink. 'The problem is I wasn't given a choice. What Tom neglected to mention was he went ahead and bought the business without any discussion with me until it was too late to back out. He also paid one hundred percent, yet his brothers both own a third each. So no, in answer to your question, I'm not enthusiastic.'

'You're kidding?' Shauna said. 'He bought a business without checking you were okay with the idea?'

'Yep, after having already given them two hundred and fifty thousand dollars each, also with little discussion.'

'God, I'd kill Paul in those circumstances,' Bec said. 'Is Tom close with his brothers? Is that why he thought it would be okay?'

'No, and that's my main problem. They haven't been close for years. In fact his younger brother, Dash, couldn't give a toss about any of us, other than our money. Rod's okay, but Dash is using Tom outright. Tom's so keen for a good relationship with them and to be one big happy family he'll do almost anything. Dash won't put in the work required to justify his ownership. Time will tell. It's still early days, but my prediction is things are unlikely to end well.'

'You never know,' Bec said. 'The brother might surprise you. Having your own business and some money after many tough years might change him, give him something he's passionate about and enjoys.'

Frankie sighed. 'I'll be surprised if that happens. You'd have to meet him to understand how arrogant he is.'

Shauna nodded. 'And you, Frankie? Surely you're not going to continue with the leaflets?'

'I've already given my notice. I'd hate to deprive someone else who needs the money. I'm just waiting for my route to be taken over.'

'Tom said you did things for an old people's home,' Bec said. 'What do you do for them?'

Frankie explained about the computer and sewing work she did at the retirement village.

'So, you're trained in computers?' Shauna asked.

'I wouldn't say trained exactly,' Frankie said. 'I took some courses at the library to learn to use email, the internet and basic wordprocessing. I learned to touch-type in Year Nine at school which has come in handy. The old ladies like to dictate emails for me to send, in between telling me their life stories.'

'What about sewing?' Shauna said.

'How do you mean?'

'Do you enjoy sewing?'

'Yes, I love it, particularly making clothes.'

Shauna nodded. 'It seems pretty straightforward. Either use your

166

computer skills and go into business with your husband, or open a shop and make clothes or teach others to. You could turn it into a charity even.'

Frankie's fingers tapped on the tabletop. She gave Shauna a glassy stare. 'Why are you so keen for me to be doing something? My life doesn't affect you. Maybe I'm happy just enjoying our new financial freedom. We don't all have to be workaholics.'

Shauna's cheeks flushed red. 'Oh God, sorry! The recruiter in me rears her ugly head once again. I've spent too much time trying to fit people into the right job, so when I see someone wasting their time I feel obligated to try to help. Ignore me, I'm sorry.'

Frankie's eyes narrowed. 'You think I'm wasting my time?'

Shauna's hand flew to her mouth. 'Oh jeez, are both feet down my throat yet?'

Frankie's smile didn't reach her eyes. 'I'm intrigued. Why, in your opinion, am I wasting my time?'

Shauna took a sip of her drink. 'Okay, well, if you're asking. You've been given a chance to do something with your life. You've gone from having to scrape by to being able to do anything you want. You'll get bored doing nothing. You can keep visiting your old ladies, but you could make a difference if you chose to. You've got the funds to start up something new, something meaningful. Sorry, I'm, just being honest.'

Bec felt her own neck and face growing hot. What was wrong with Shauna? Frankie's life was really none of her business. Couldn't she see that? She appeared to be the most insensitive female on the planet. 'Tell us about your girls, Frankie.'

Bec's desperate attempt to change the subject brought a genuine smile from Frankie. 'Hope's in Year Ten and Fern's in Year Seven.' Frankie pulled out a photo and passed it to Bec.

Bec looked at the photo. 'They're gorgeous.'

'Wow, Hope should be a model,' Shauna said. 'Give her a few highlights and some new clothes, the result would be stunning.'

167

'She already is stunning,' Frankie said.

Shauna rolled her eyes. 'Don't get defensive, I agree with you. I meant if she was given a more modern look agents would be falling at her feet.'

'She'd hate modelling. She's pretty comfortable with who she is.' Shauna snorted.

'What now? Don't tell me you have an opinion about my daughter, whom you've never met?'

'My guess is she's a lovely girl who wants to make sure she doesn't hurt your feelings. You haven't been able to afford much up until now. Homemade or hand-me-down clothes are fine, even pretty cool when you choose to wear them, but Hope would hate it. We were all teenagers once. Girls are bitchy. You don't want to stand out and you need to fit in. Anything that makes you different is used against you. Hope might tell you she's happy because she's a good kid. You won millions of dollars. Surely a new wardrobe isn't unreasonable?'

Frankie stared at Shauna. 'What is your problem?'

Shauna frowned. 'I don't understand.'

'In the couple of hours you've known me you're an expert on my life.'

'Frankie, this unlikely opportunity has been handed to you and yet you seem content living your old life. That would be fine if your old life was perfect, but from what Tom described it was anything but.'

'We've moved, we've furnished a house, we've bought a business. This is hardly my old life.'

'That's all great, but I'm talking about personal development. You're still exactly where you were before the win, and, if that photo's current, you're forcing your girls to retain an identity which screams poor. I don't quite understand, that's all.' Shauna stood up. 'I'll be back in a tick.'

Bec and Frankie watched as Shauna walked towards the ladies.

Bec waited until Shauna was out of hearing. 'Are you okay? This hasn't exactly turned out as I had planned. Ignore Shauna. Hope and

168

Fern are beautiful and your life is for you to live how you choose.'

Frankie smiled. 'God, she's so outspoken. Don't tell her, but that's an old photo. We had a massive shopping spree a couple of weeks ago and all have more new clothes than we could ever wear. Hope's even had a proper haircut and highlights.'

Bec laughed. 'Why don't you want Shauna to know?'

'I'm not used to having anyone talk so directly to me. I wonder what else she'll come out with. It's refreshing in a horribly confronting way. It beats talking behind my back.' Frankie told Bec about the women from school.

'Good for you, putting them in their place.'

Shauna sat back down. 'Who did you put in their place?' Bec retold Frankie's story.

Shauna cracked her knuckles. 'The bitches. I've a good mind to go and give them a piece of my mind.'

Frankie's mouth dropped open and then she started to laugh.

'What? What did I say?'

'You're so intense. One minute you're telling me everything that is wrong with me and the next you're ready to defend my honour. You're a mystery.'

'No, I wasn't telling you what was wrong with your life, I was suggesting ways to improve it. We're in a position to make our lives better, and you owe yourself the opportunity to do that. Your girls will grow up and be out of the house soon and then you'll find your life isn't stimulating enough. Why not set something up now? I could get you a job in a heartbeat, although your husband's business is the obvious place for you.'

'Mmm, maybe,' Frankie said. 'Now, let's change the subject, talk about you. What are you going to do about your mother?'

The three women sat and talked for another half hour before Bec checked her watch and declared that time was up. 'School pick-up calls. I'd love to catch up again soon. Dinner perhaps?'

Shauna stood up. 'Absolutely. Leave it with me and I'll organise something for a couple of weeks' time.'

The women all hugged each other as they said their goodbyes.

'I feel like you're old friends, not people I only just met,' Bec said.

'It's so strange,' Shauna said. 'I guess they say extreme circumstances bring people together, create lifelong bonds.'

'I always assume they're talking about disasters when they say extreme circumstances,' Frankie said.

Shauna laughed. 'You've got to admit, our reason for meeting is pretty extreme.'

'Sure is,' Bec said. 'Let's just hope our extreme circumstances have a happy ending and don't all end in disaster.'

# CHAPTER SIXTEEN

## *Bec*

Bec looked out of the lounge-room window for the tenth time. She checked her watch – where the hell was he? So much for the relaxing bath she'd planned to have before her date with George. At this rate she'd be lucky to even have time to get changed.

'Mum, is Dad here yet?' Alex dropped his bag by the front door and came over to Bec.

'No, sweetie, he's running late.'

'But he said he'd be here two hours ago. Maybe he's not coming.'

'I'll try to ring him again.' Bec dialled Paul's number, which connected directly to his voicemail. She didn't bother to leave a message; her seven other missed calls would show up when he finally turned on his phone.

'I'm hungry.' Will came into the room and bounced his bottom on the couch. 'I don't want to go to Daddy's apartment tonight. It's too late. I need food and my own bed.'

Bec looked at the two boys. 'Okay, into the kitchen with you. We'll stay here tonight. You can go to Daddy's another night.'

'Yay!' Will yelled.

'Sorry, sweetheart.' Bec ruffled the top of Alex's hair. 'I'm sure there's a good explanation as to why he's late.'

Alex shook his head. 'He probably forgot about us. He doesn't care very much now that he's moved out. At least it means I don't have to be apart from Earl.'

A lump formed in Bec's throat. 'Don't be silly. He'd never forget you guys. He'll call soon, but for tonight I'll make you and Will an omelette. Pop your bag back upstairs and wash up.'

Alex nodded and went up to his room while Bec started on dinner. She yanked open the fridge, ready to kill Paul. Her date with George was at eight, but there was no way she could go now. She would have to cancel. She quickly mixed together the ingredients for the omelettes and heated up the pan. Once the boys were eating, she excused herself and went upstairs to ring George.

George immediately suggested he come to her instead. 'I can wait until the boys are asleep if you'd prefer I didn't meet them yet. It's been too long. I really miss you.'

Bec felt herself waiver. It had been over three weeks since their last date ended prematurely at the hospital. George had gone to Bali for business two days later and had only just arrived back in Australia. But running the risk of the boys meeting him wasn't something she was ready for. 'Not tonight, sorry. How about I ring you tomorrow and we make plans for another night?'

George's disappointment was obvious, but not enough to sway Bec to change her mind. She still had mixed feelings about where this might be leading. 'Thank you again for the flowers,' she said. Another beautiful arrangement of roses stood on the dresser in front of her. 'They're magnificent.'

'Hopefully, they make up for our last date and my absence. Hospitals mixed with ex-wives are hardly at the top of the romance list. The business trip was especially bad timing, too.' George sighed. 'So, I guess I'll have to think sweet thoughts of you tonight and wait to hear from you to plan our next date.'

After saying their goodbyes, Bec hung up, a little relieved that the issue of sex was once again delayed, and went back downstairs. Just after eight, with the boys in bed, she poured herself a glass of wine. She was beginning to get worried. As angry as she had been earlier, Paul was not usually unreliable.

172

At ten o'clock a taxi pulled into the driveway. A door opened and closed and then the taxi reversed back into the road and drove off. Bec got up and switched on the outside light. Peering through the window, she watched Paul weave his way up the path.

She flung open the front door and glared at him.

'Bec daarling! Slorry I'm late. Are the boys awake?'

'For God's sake keep your voice down and get inside.' Bec grabbed Paul by the arm to prevent him from stumbling.

'What's swrong, swith you?' Paul swayed to and fro.

'You're drunk. Now, come in.' Bec guided him to the kitchen, where she pushed him into a chair and flicked the switch on the kettle. 'I'll make you some coffee.'

'Slanks, daarlin'.'

Bec managed to slop half the coffee on the bench before slamming the mug down in front of Paul. It was unlike him to write himself off like this. She went upstairs and got some pillows and a blanket and took them into the lounge room. After making up the sofa bed, she came back to find him slouched across the table, coffee mug gripped in one hand, his head resting on the other arm, fast asleep. She untangled the mug from his grip, poked him to wake up and then half dragged, half carried him to the couch. He fell face first into the cushions and was snoring within seconds. Bec threw the blanket over him and left a bucket by his side before she headed upstairs to bed.

The sounds of retching from the downstairs toilet woke Bec early the next morning. She went downstairs and into the kitchen. She filled a large glass with water and two paracetamol tablets, and took them through to the lounge, where she found Paul collapsed on the couch.

'Should I bother asking how you are?'

He groaned, holding his head in his hands. 'Awful, thanks. What am I doing here?'

'You tell me. You arrived around five hours late last night, absolutely trashed. The boys' night was ruined, my night was ruined.'

'Oh shit, I'm so sorry, I'll apologise to Alex and Will as soon as they wake up. God, I'm an arsehole.'

Bec stood over Paul, hands on her hips. 'And?'

'And what?'

'Any other apologies?'

Paul hung his head. 'Yes, sorry, I should have called earlier and gone back to the apartment, not here.'

'Fine, go and have a shower and brush your teeth before the boys wake up. You reek.'

Paul gave her a weak smile. 'I don't deserve you being nice.'

'This isn't me being nice, this is me protecting my boys from more disappointment. They'll be up soon so get organised. Some of your clothes are still in the bedroom, so put something clean on.'

Twenty minutes later Paul, smelling fresh, came into the kitchen.

Bec leaned against the bench, sipping her coffee. 'So? What happened?'

Paul sat down on one of the bar stools. 'Honestly, nothing much to tell. I went out for lunch with a new client and we just got a bit carried away. I definitely can't keep up these days. I had no idea of the time and completely forgot about the boys. I'm so sorry.'

'You'll need to grovel. I'd suggest you come up with a better story for them and don't tell them you forgot them.'

'Don't worry, I'm not that stupid. Thanks for letting me stay.'

'You didn't give me an option.'

Paul raised an eyebrow. 'Did I ruin your plans?'

'Yes, but I'll reschedule.'

'What did you do? Sneak him out when I arrived?'

'Who?'

'The guy you're seeing.'

'Not that it's any of your business, but no. I was going out for dinner, so I cancelled.'

A flash of relief crossed over Paul's face. 'Is it serious?'

Bec turned away from Paul and opened the pantry. 'I'm not having this discussion with you.'

'The flowers in the bedroom are pretty impressive.'

'Paul, would you stop? It has nothing to do with you.' Bec's stomach tightened. It was none of his business. He had absolutely no right to discuss George with her.

'Yes, it does.'

'How do you figure that?'

'First because you're my wife, and second because any affair you have impacts my children.'

Bec laughed. 'Affair, good one. I don't think *affair* is the right word when we're separated and getting a divorce. However, if I slept with someone while we were still married and living under the same roof, then you'd be correct. You know, like what you did.'

Paul crossed his arms. 'You just moved on without looking back, didn't you? No proper discussion, nothing. If you care at all about our nine-year marriage and children you might like to hear my side of the story, ideally before you commit to this other guy. My affair is all in your head.'

Bec glared at him. *In her head*, yeah, right. She'd seen them together. She was not the bad guy here and she wasn't going to let him bully her into thinking she was in the wrong.

Paul continued, his eyes cold. 'Whereas yours appears to be happening right here in our bed. Now, I'm going upstairs to apologise.'

Bec continued to get breakfast ready as Paul stormed off to talk to the boys. She swung open the fridge in search of the milk. *All in her head.* God, he had some nerve. Should she confront him? Tell him she'd seen him and Chris together? She hadn't imagined it or all of the nights away, the lies, the fitness regime, the perfume-covered shirt. Interesting that now she was seeing someone else he was suddenly keen to discuss their marriage. She slammed the fridge shut. As far she was concerned there was nothing left to talk about.

175

# Chapter Seventeen

## *Shauna*

Shauna made her way to reception and held up the message Jenni had left on her desk. 'Who's Don Rice?'

'I'm not sure,' Jenni said. 'He's rung at least five times and every time I ask him for more information he says it's personal.'

Shauna scrunched up the message. 'Never heard of him. Another gold-digger no doubt. Now, where are those letters for Tonacoal?'

'Sorry, the printer's jammed. Troy's fixing it. Is five minutes okay?'

'Yes, fine.'

Jenni poked her head into Shauna's office a few moments later. 'Shauna?'

Shauna looked up. 'What? Have you got the letters?'

'No, it's this Don Rice guy. He's in reception. He wants to talk to you. Says he's happy to wait all day if necessary.'

'Really?' Shauna sighed. 'Fine, tell him I'll meet him briefly in about ten minutes. I'm not rushing out for a stranger.' Shauna sat down at her desk wondering who Don Rice was. She did a quick search on LinkedIn. Sixteen matches didn't help her. She replied to a few emails, and after ten minutes had passed, went out to reception.

A man in his early sixties stood up the moment he saw her. He visibly drew in his breath as he scrutinised her appearance.

Shauna hesitated before approaching him. He was familiar. She couldn't quite place him, but she knew him from somewhere. She held out her hand. 'Don, I'm Shauna, how can I help you?'

176

Don took her hand in his. He didn't speak. His eyes searched hers.

A feeling of unease settled over Shauna. She pulled her hand back, crossed her arms and waited for him to speak.

'Sorry,' Don said. 'Do you remember me?'

Shauna shook her head, the unease growing in the pit of her stomach. 'Should I?'

'I hoped you might.' He looked around the reception area. 'Would it be possible for us to go somewhere more private to talk?'

Shauna hesitated.

'Are you sure you don't recognise me?' Don said. 'At all?'

Shauna couldn't shake the feeling of familiarity but struggled to place Don. There was a warmth in his eyes that stopped her from dismissing him completely. 'Okay, come down to my office.' She led Don past the conference room and into her office.

'Impressive view. You've done very well.'

Shauna sat down and motioned to one of the visitor's chairs.

Don sat and locked eyes with Shauna. 'I'm not sure there's any good way to announce this, so I'll just say it outright. I'm your father, Shauna.'

Shauna drew in a breath. There was no way she could have anticipated this. She stared at Don. He looked nothing like the man her mother had described as her father. 'What are you talking about? My father's name is Lucas Jones. He has fair hair, not dark and he looks nothing like you.'

Don shook his head. 'No, I'm your father. Your mother has done everything possible to keep you away from me, including changing her surname and my name by the sounds of it.'

'My father walked out on us when I was four and never attempted to make contact again. My mother didn't need to keep him away.' Every muscle in Shauna's body was wound as tight as a spring. She couldn't believe the nerve of this guy.

Don took his head in his hands, shaking it to and fro. 'Oh God, is that the story she's told you?'

'Story? No, I'm telling you what happened.'

Sadness clouded Don's face. 'I suggest we get Lorraine in here and all discuss the events of thirty years ago. How I came home from work to find you both gone without any trace. I spent the next two years trying to track you down. I only gave up when the police convinced me you were probably both out of the country with false identities. Not to say I stopped looking, though. I kept in contact with her friends and her mother and rang them every week for over ten years, hoping to get some information of your whereabouts.'

Shauna froze. This couldn't be true. Her mother would hardly win mother of the year, but she wouldn't have lied to her so consistently about something this important, would she? Also, her grandmother was dead; he could hardly have rung her every week for ten years.

'You don't believe me, do you?'

'No.'

Don pulled out his wallet and took out some photos. 'Familiar?' He passed them to Shauna. Shauna recognised the first photo of herself and her mother when she was about six months old. In the second Shauna guessed she was two. She held an ice-cream in one hand and the other held hands with a younger version of Don.

She looked up at Don. 'Okay, this is definitely you, I get that, but this is crazy. Why would my mother go to such extreme lengths to hide from you? And how did you find me now?'

Don sighed. 'She did it to hurt me. Things were strained between us. I wanted us to meet with a counsellor. She thought I was rejecting her. Instead of a rational discussion about getting help to fix our marriage, she threatened me. I honestly thought she wouldn't go through with her threats. But then it was too late. She took you and left. She destroyed the most important thing to me, my relationship with you. I don't know what she's like now, Shauna, but I realised once she was gone that she was mentally unstable. She needed help and I failed to realise this until it was too late. There were so many behaviours she exhibited that in hindsight I realised were more than her just being moody. She had a problem that needed help. To answer your question on how I found you, I saw a picture of Lorraine in an article in one of my wife's magazines. I nearly stopped breathing. A private investigator helped track her down from the information we had and he was able to find you quite easily.'

Shauna got up from her desk and fanned her face. 'I need some water. Be back in a minute.' She left the room and went straight to the staff kitchen. Thankfully it was empty. Could this man really be her father? If there was any truth to his story then her mother … She couldn't finish the thought. She filled a cup with water and gulped it down. She refilled it as the door to the kitchen opened.

'Hey, you.'

She turned at the sound of Josh's voice. His smile turned to a frown as soon as her eyes met his. 'What's wrong?' He moved across the kitchen and took her arm. 'You're white, and you're shaking, come and sit down.' Shauna put down her cup and allowed him to lead her to a couch.

'What's happened?'

Shauna swallowed. 'There's a man in my office. He's claiming to be my dad.'

'What?'

'He saw the magazine article about my mum, and had a private investigator track me down. He's been looking for me for thirty years, apparently.'

Josh's jaw clenched. 'I'll bet. What a coincidence an article about winning lotto got his attention. Let me deal with him. I'll get rid of him for you.'

'No don't, not yet. He's got photos of me and him when I was a baby and if his story is real then my mother needs to be run out of town, not him.' Shauna repeated what Don had told her.

Josh nodded. 'I agree you need to speak to your mother, but what do you want to do about the guy in your office? Should I ask him to leave? You look like you're in shock.'

Shauna ran her hands through her hair. 'No, I will, but come with me.'

Josh followed Shauna back to her office, where she introduced him to Don. He stood to the side while Shauna spoke to Don.

'I need some time to digest all of this. Can you leave me your details and I'll call you to meet up again?'

Don reached inside his jacket pocket and pulled out a card. He took out a pen and scribbled something on the back. 'Here are my numbers. Ring me as soon as you're ready to talk. I understand this is a huge shock, but when I saw the article it was one of the best moments in my life. To think I have an opportunity to reconnect with you. I've dreamed about this day for so long.' Tears glistened in Don's eyes as he passed his card across the desk.

Shauna felt a lump rising in her throat. This man could really be her father. She watched as Josh led him out of her office.

Josh disappeared for a few moments before returning on his own. He sat down across from Shauna. 'How are you doing? Need a drink?'

She checked her watch and smiled. 'It's not even twelve o'clock, but the answer is yes.'

Josh jumped up. 'Come on, let's go for an early lunch. I'll get Jenni to cancel the rest of our days.'

'Really?'

'Definitely. This is one massive shock. A relaxing afternoon is probably the best strategy before approaching your mother, which I assume you plan to do next?'

Shauna picked up her bag and followed Josh out of her office to the reception area. 'I can't believe any of this. Don Rice is either a gold-digging liar, or I have the worst mother in existence.'

Josh pressed the button for the lift. 'Unfortunately, I don't think you'll be playing happy families with both of them. Come on, you can sort out how you feel while we numb the shock with a shot or two.'

❧

Josh grinned as Shauna downed her third vodka and slammed the empty shot glass onto the bar. He put his empty glass next to hers. 'Feeling any better?'

Shauna returned his smile. 'Heaps, although I might not thank you tomorrow.'

'Why don't we end the shots and grab a bottle of wine? Go outside and enjoy the view.'

Shauna followed Josh to an outside table. The beautiful blue sky that greeted them contrasted with the icy wind that whipped the city streets. A reminder that they were heading into another Melbourne winter. Chester's prime position, overlooking the Yarra River and Southbank, ensured it was full of city workers every night by five, unwinding with drinks and spectacular views. Shauna took a seat, closest to the outdoor heater, grateful it was the middle of the day and only a handful of people were scattered around the beer garden.

Josh sat across from Shauna and poured them both a glass of wine. 'What's your gut feeling telling you? Do you think he's telling the truth, that he is your father?'

Shauna hesitated. There was a part of her that very much wanted him to be her father. 'I don't know. Part of me hopes he is. I'd have one parent in my life I could possibly depend on. It would kill any hope of salvaging a relationship with my mother, though. It'd be the final nail in that coffin.'

Josh nodded. 'Although, she might have had good reasons for what she did.'

'Stealing me away from him would be pretty hard to forgive. She'd want to have a good story.'

'Maybe she has.'

Shauna stared at the man sitting in front of her. He was always so positive. Always willing to give the benefit of the doubt. In her world, that only led to disappointment. He must have had a pretty easy life. Her face flushed with heat. Josh knew so much about her – the problems the lotto win had caused with her mother, her father reappearing – and she realised she knew very little about him. 'You see the good in everyone,' she said. 'Tell me, what's your real story?'

Josh shrugged. 'I don't know, I like to think people are decent. Hope they are at least. As for a story, not sure I really have one.'

'What about your family?'

'Oh, you know, usual stuff, Mum, Dad, brother and a sister. All pretty close.'

'And?'

'And what?'

'Where do they live? What do they do? How often do you catch up? How old are your brother and sister? What was your childhood like?'

'God, you don't really want answers to all of those questions, do you? I'd rather talk about you.'

Shauna's eyes narrowed. 'Why?'

'Why? Because I find you interesting.'

'Not good enough. I hardly know a thing about you. You told me next to nothing when we last had dinner.'

Josh sighed. 'Fine, I'm the eldest, Kevin's thirty-four and Kayla's thirty-seven. We have dinner with my folks every month. You have to be overseas or dying to miss dinner. I meet the Ks, as I like to call them, every now and then for lunch or a drink. That enough?'

'No,' Shauna said. 'Where did you go to school?'

Josh took a sip of his wine. 'Scotch.'

Shauna raised an eyebrow. 'Scotch?'

'Yes, Scotch.'

'So, are you all networked in with the Old Boys' club?' Shauna was surprised when Josh flushed.

'I keep in touch with a few guys, but I left twenty years ago. School seems like a distant memory.'

'Did your brother go to Scotch?'

'Yep.'

'And Kayla?'

'She rebelled. Started at MLC but ended up dropping out in Year Eleven. She worked and earned some money before taking off to Europe. She was gone for three years. When she got back she started working in real estate much to my dad's horror.'

'What's wrong with real estate?'

'Nothing at all, as long as you're buying it, according to my dad.'

Shauna stroked her wineglass, thinking about Josh's family.

'Why are you so quiet all of a sudden?' Josh asked.

'Just thinking.'

Josh raised his eyebrows. 'And?'

Shauna met his eyes. 'I'm making the assumption from what you've told me that your family is pretty well off?'

'My parents are. My dad's been pretty successful. Kevin works with my dad, but that wasn't really an option for Kayla or me.'

'Why not?'

'I had a falling out with my dad when I left high school. He was trying to control my life, have me do the university course he wanted, work part-time in one of his businesses and basically become a clone of him. I wasn't interested. I wanted to do my own thing. I was eighteen and finally could become independent and he wasn't happy about it.'

'Really? My mother couldn't wait for me to leave home; practically pushed me out the door at eighteen. What happened, what did you do?'

'I moved out and went to uni to do a marketing degree. He disowned me for three years and made sure I knew I was cut off from any financial help. It suited me. I didn't want to be indebted to him, so I worked my way through uni and got a job as soon as I graduated.'

'He must have respected you for doing that?'

Josh laughed. 'You don't know my dad. He's a successful guy who's used to people jumping when he says "jump". He probably never factored in kids who would have their own minds. When I'd been working for about a year, he contacted me and invited me to one of our Sunday dinners. Kayla reckons Mum threatened him and forced him to make peace. He's still never forgiven me for not joining the business, but we can at least sit around a table together and enjoy a meal.'

'He must be proud of you now. You've got a great job and you earn good money.'

Josh smiled. 'Mum is. Dad's not so impressed. If I owned I-People maybe he'd feel differently.'

Anger welled up inside Shauna. How could a father not be proud of a son like Josh? He was intelligent, hardworking and honourable. 'He sounds like an arsehole.'

Josh laughed. 'I've probably made him sound worse than he is. He's actually a nice guy overall, he just doesn't really understand why I want to be independent, be successful in my own right. He's built up quite a business empire and Mum says he's disappointed that he can't share his success with me.'

'Empire?'

Josh nodded. 'Yeah, like I said, he's done okay.'

'So have you.'

'Not quite in the same league as my father, but I do okay. Does my financial position matter to you?'

Shauna smiled. 'No, why would it?'

Josh refilled their wineglasses, his eyes not leaving her face. 'Okay, you need to give me a clue. I have no idea why you're smiling. I'm glad mind you, especially as we're here to drown your sorrows. What's going on?'

'Nothing, it's just nice to finally learn about you and your life.' Shauna sipped her wine. 'Tell me more. Have you travelled?'

Josh launched into stories of his adventures in Thailand and America. Shauna was aware of her body relaxing and her smile widening as she listened to his soothing voice. She didn't plan to explain herself. Explain why, in the midst of Don Rice's revelations and the possibility of her mother having lied to her all of her life, that she suddenly couldn't stop smiling. If anything, it would probably make Josh angry to hear that it had taken her this long to realise exactly how attractive he was.

❁

Twenty-four hours later, Shauna sat on Lorraine's front verandah, waiting for her mother to return. She'd taken the advice Josh had given her when he dropped her home the night before. She'd not rushed over demanding answers first thing that morning as she had planned. Instead, she'd gone for a run to clear her slightly fuzzy head and enjoyed a leisurely brunch poring over the day's newspapers. She'd let her mind wander back to the previous afternoon. They'd been sensible, ordered food and stopped drinking after the first bottle of wine. She didn't need a huge hangover to complicate the discussion she was about to have.

Forty-five minutes after she arrived, her mother's car turned into the driveway. Lorraine climbed out, opened the boot and removed at least eleven or twelve shopping bags.

'Been on a spending spree?' Shauna called.

Lorraine flinched. She grasped the bags, slammed the boot and walked up the front stairs, her face contorted with anger. 'What are you doing here?'

'Waiting to speak to you.'

'Unless you're delivering a large cheque I'm not interested.'

Shauna shook her head slowly. 'No, Mother, this visit is not about money. We need to talk.'

Lorraine crossed her arms. 'Until the money's resolved I'm not talking to you.'

Shauna inhaled, her fists clenched. 'This isn't a choice. I'm here to discuss Don Rice. I assume the name rings a bell?'

Lorraine's eyes widened.

'Yes, Mother, Don Rice. I had a visit from him yesterday. You've got some explaining to do.'

Lorraine's hands trembled as she fumbled in her bag for her keys. She opened the front door and Shauna followed her down the hallway to the kitchen. Lorraine still hadn't spoken. She opened the fridge, pulled out a bottle of wine and poured herself a glass.

'Well? Are you going to say anything at all?'

'Wine?' Lorraine held up the bottle.

'No, I don't want a drink, I'm here for answers. Why have you lied to me for thirty years?'

Lorraine gulped down half the glass. 'What did he tell you?'

'He told me you threatened to leave him many times and how one day he came home to discover it wasn't an empty threat. You'd disappeared into thin air.'

'Anything else?'

'No, why? Is there more?'

Lorraine's eyes narrowed. 'A lot more. I'm not talking about this now. Come back another day. This is such a shock. In fact, I think I'd better sit down.' She walked into the lounge.

Shauna followed. 'No way, you can't avoid this one. You let me believe my father didn't want kids, couldn't handle parenting and was a selfish bastard. The man I met yesterday grieved for years because he lost his child. He would give anything to get that time back again.'

'How did he find you?' Lorraine interrupted.

'He saw *your* magazine article.'

'Great. He knows you won lotto.'

'Is money all you think about?'

'Of course not, but he does. He'll be after a share. He couldn't care less about you, any more than he did thirty years ago. Ten million dollars, however, that's another matter. He's a charmer, believe him and you'll be handing over your winnings within a matter of days.'

'So, he'll charm it out of me rather than sue me?'

Lorraine waved her hand dismissively. 'Fine, give him a few million if that's going to make you happy. Your decision.'

Shauna's body tensed. She could hear Josh's words. *Try to be calm, have an adult conversation with her.* But it was almost impossible. 'This is not about money. You owe me an explanation and some answers. Why did you leave my father and then lie for all of these years?'

Lorraine threw up her hands. 'You really want to know? Fine. Undo all the work I've done protecting you.'

Shauna waited.

'Shauna, he was violent. We had one too many arguments over money. I spent too much feeding us, clothing you, which didn't leave enough for him to drink or gamble away. After yet another black eye and split lip, I decided to get out before you got hurt. I was terrified if he found me we'd both be in trouble, so I disappeared. Moved to Melbourne, changed our surname and maintained a low profile. I wasn't in touch with my mother anymore and the few friends in Brisbane had kept their distance once they realised he was knocking me around. Nothing like supportive friends.' Lorraine refilled her wineglass and gulped another mouthful. 'Now, you know the real story.'

Shauna's stomach churned. The bitterness in Lorraine's voice was real. 'Why not tell me this before? Why lie about him not wanting me and him moving away from us?'

Lorraine shrugged. 'He was an abusive alcoholic and gambler. I couldn't risk him getting his hands on you. I was on edge for years worried he might find us.'

Shauna was reeling. It was hard to believe that the man who stood in her office was either of these things. He was fit, his face glowed of health. But then, thirty years had passed. He'd had plenty of time to clean up his act and change. 'Why didn't you speak to his mother, my grandmother?' Shauna said. 'He said she was devastated.'

'No point. She was a controlling bitch. Wouldn't believe a bad thing about her darling son. I had to get you away from both of them.'

Shauna's mind was racing. To think her mother had gone through all of this and never said anything. If it really had pushed Lorraine to the edge it certainly helped explain some of her mother's unpredictable behaviour. She went to the kitchen, grabbed a glass and returned. She filled her glass and took a large swig. 'I wish you'd told me this years ago.'

Lorraine sighed. 'What good would it have done?'

'Given me a better understanding of you for starters. I'm so sorry you went through such an awful time.'

'You can show me your appreciation by not going near him again. He's bad news. I guarantee the money is the drawcard.'

'I'm beginning to wish I'd never won the bloody money. It's caused so many problems.'

Lorraine's eyes hardened. 'You can fix two problems instantly. Give me my half and stay away from Don Rice.'

Shauna stood up. 'Jesus, even during a revelation like this money is still the only thing on your mind. I'm going. I don't want another argument. I just wanted to learn more about Don Rice. Now, I know.'

'Yes, you do. If he contacts you again tell him to go away and don't believe a word he says.'

Shauna nodded. For once she agreed with her mother on something. 'I'm going to head off. I've got a lot to think about.'

Lorraine didn't get out of her chair. Her hand shook as she took another sip of her wine. 'Just be careful, Shauna. That man practically ruined me. I don't want the same to happen to you.'

Hot tears stung Shauna's eyes as she drove away. Her mother's story was unthinkable. Shauna didn't remember being four. She didn't remember leaving her father or Brisbane. Her childhood memories were of being in the way, of being told she was a nuisance. Of watching her mother with different men; men who were always more important than her. Why did a woman who'd done so much to protect her then spend the subsequent years withholding her love? It didn't make sense, but then Lorraine never had.

Shauna wiped her tears as she manoeuvred the Mercedes out into traffic. Regardless of her mother's motivations, she could take one thing away from tonight. She now had two parents in her life, neither interested in anything but her money.

# CHAPTER EIGHTEEN

## *Frankie*

The blare of the television and the raised voices of Mavis and Betty made it easy for Frankie to track down the old ladies. A heated discussion over which of *The Voice's* contestants should move to the next round was taking place.

Frankie stood in the doorway of Mavis's room and cleared her throat.

The old ladies turned immediately, their faces breaking into wide smiles. Mavis picked up the remote and turned off the television. 'Frankie dear, we weren't expecting you today. What a wonderful surprise. We haven't seen you in weeks. Is everything alright? Are you okay?'

Frankie returned her smile. 'I'm fine, I hope you got my messages.'

Mavis nodded. 'Yes, we did, dear, it was so nice of you to ring and let us know you weren't coming. We've had another young girl help us with our emails while you were away.'

Betty moved closer to Frankie. 'Just between us, you could teach her a thing or two.'

Frankie laughed. 'I'm sure she's doing her best to help. Now, what can I do for you today?'

Mavis glanced at her watch and exchanged a worried looked with Betty. 'I'm sorry, dear, but we have to attend a special meeting in a few minutes. All of the residents have been asked to gather in the rec hall for an announcement.'

'Perhaps you could come with us?' Betty said. 'Then if you have time afterwards we could discuss the Twitterbook program.'

'I'd love to come. A cuppa and a biscuit would be rather lovely.' Unbeknown to Mavis or Betty, Frankie knew exactly what the meeting was about. She had visited Marg, the CEO a week earlier, delivering a very large cheque and the conditions for which it was to be used.

Frankie noticed the women scrutinising her. Mavis was the first to speak. 'There's something different about you today, dear. Don't take this the wrong way, but you look wonderful.'

'Yes,' Betty added. 'Your lovely haircut and those beautiful clothes, and I don't know, you seem different. Doesn't she, Mavis?'

'Yes, more confident or something. Has something happened, dear?'

Frankie laughed and linked her arms through the two old ladies'. 'Come on, let's find that cup of tea. Your imaginations are far too active.'

Groups of residents were already gathered when they entered the rec hall. They took a seat as Marg motioned for everyone to sit down so she could make her announcement.

Gasps went up around the room as the residents were informed that an anonymous donor had provided enough money to purchase a minibus for the centre. A driver would be employed and a regular schedule set up for outings to the shopping centre, theatre and other destinations agreed upon by the travel committee.

'Travel committee?' Mavis asked. 'What exactly is that?'

'We'll need to elect a committee to help create the schedules and plan outings,' Marg said. 'We'll discuss how nominations can be placed this week.'

'Who donated the money?' one of the men asked.

'As much as I'd like to tell you, so we could thank them, they've asked to remain anonymous. I can confirm, however, that this is an ongoing service. There are plenty of funds dedicated to ensure the service runs for at least the next fifty years.'

Another round of gasps could be heard.

'In addition, the donor has sent in a special afternoon tea, including champagne for the occasion.' As Marg finished talking a group of waiters walked into the room, some carrying trays of drinks, others finger food. A cheer went up; this was unheard of.

Mavis turned to Frankie, her face beaming with excitement. 'Frankie dear, what a day to choose to come and visit. Have some bubbles, won't you.' She took two glasses from a nearby waiter.

'Thank you, I think I will.' Frankie accepted the glass.

'What a wonderful gift,' Betty said. 'I wonder who on earth would be so generous? Do you know, dear?'

'No idea,' Frankie said. 'How about a toast though, to new adventures and lots of outings.'

'Hear, hear.' Mavis and Betty clinked their glasses with Frankie.

'So, tell us, dear, what have you been doing? How are your little family?'

Frankie spent the next hour enjoying afternoon tea with the ladies. She told them their luck had taken a turn for the better and Tom had been able to join his brothers in a business venture. She downplayed it, saying it was a new start and they'd see how it went. She then answered their many questions about the girls and listened to their own updates of their children and grandchildren. A little after five she excused herself, saying she really must get going.

Mavis and Betty hugged her tightly. 'Look after yourself, dear,' Betty said. 'And make sure you come and visit again soon.'

Frankie promised she would and walked out of the retirement village, her heart feeling incredibly full. She had experienced a wonderful afternoon, seeing the looks of surprise and delight on the faces of the residents. There had even been a few tears from those without family who rarely got out and now would be able to. Frankie crossed her fingers as she walked towards her car. She could only hope that this feeling would stay with her and help her through the next day.

Frankie straightened her skirt and pushed opened the office door of Blue Water Charters. It was her first day as office manager; she could hardly believe she was doing this. Tom's delight when she'd agreed to work in the family business had given her the confidence to start. Time to put her anger and resentments behind her and get involved. It would also give her the opportunity to keep an eye on Dash.

Frankie smiled as she thought of Shauna's surprise when she had rung her a week after the lunch, to thank her for helping Frankie make such a big decision. Shauna's directness, while confronting at the time, had made Frankie think about her future.

She planned to do her best to be pleasant to Dash. Hopefully, he would be out on the boats most of the time and their interaction, beyond the initial training he was to give her, would be limited. She plastered a smile on her face and walked into the small office.

Dash stood up as soon as she arrived. 'About time. I'm going out, just look after the phones, okay?'

Nausea swept over Frankie. As much as she didn't want to spend time with him, she needed training. 'Dash, I have no idea what to do.'

'If you'd come in earlier I would've shown you, but I'm too busy now, so we'll try again tomorrow. Get here at eight, not nine.' Dash pulled on his jacket and stepped towards Frankie and the door.

Frankie put her hands up. 'Hold on a minute. The hours I agreed to are nine to two-thirty. My work fits in around school.'

Dash snorted. 'No one listened to my opinion. The girls are old enough to take care of themselves, aren't they?'

Frankie forced herself to remain calm. 'That's not the point. The agreement is I work three days a week from nine until two-thirty. You can't change this on day one.'

'If you want training you'll need to be here at eight. Now, can you move? I've gotta go.' Dash pushed passed Frankie and out the door.

Frankie's heart sank as she stood in the empty office. This was hardly the start she needed. She walked over to the desk and picked up the phone. She needed to speak to Tom.

Tom and Rod were out on *Fish Tales* for the day with four American businessmen. Tom calmed her down. 'Don't worry, I'll sort out things later. Just poke around, read the files the previous owner left and make yourself as familiar with everything as possible.'

'What if someone rings? I don't know how much to quote or any information to give them.'

'No need to. Take messages, I'll call them tonight.'

Frankie felt a sense of relief as she hung up. Tom had complete confidence in her managing the office. She slung her coat over the back of the chair and sat down at the desk. The small square-shaped room had enough space for two desks, some filing cabinets and a few chairs. The kitchen and bathroom were shared with the neighbouring bait shop. The sterile, sparsely furnished office was hardly inviting.

The computer in front of Frankie showed movie-screening times at the Dendy Theatre. Surely Dash hadn't rushed off to go to the movies? Would there even be one on this early?

She was relieved to find the phone was the same as the one at home. She could handle incoming calls without needing to learn a phone system. Frankie dug through the drawers and found herself a notepad and pen.

On top of two of the filing cabinets sat three in-trays. A large diary sat in the bottom one. Frankie read through the various bookings. As she flicked forward in the book she noted they only had confirmed business for the next three weeks. So much for the business purchase including all future bookings.

After familiarising herself with the diary, Frankie got organised sorting out the office. It was filthy and poorly laid out. She pushed open the door to the shared bathroom and kitchen and found a cupboard containing cleaning materials. Grabbing disinfectant, cloths and the vacuum cleaner, she got to work.

An hour and a half later every corner and surface of the office gleamed. With the floor and rug vacuumed, Frankie made a mental note to bring in the mop and bucket from home the next morning. She rearranged the furniture so the desk had two visitors' chairs in front of it. She earmarked the far corner for small couches and a coffee table to give people somewhere comfortable to wait if she was busy with other customers. The walls also needed livening up. Frankie wondered what Tom would think of taking and framing some photos of the boats, perhaps a successful catch and smiling faces of happy clients?

With the cleaning and rearranging completed, Frankie decided to make herself a coffee. As she waited for the kettle to boil, the door from the bait shop opened and a man, who Frankie assumed must be at least in his seventies, came in. His deeply tanned skin was wrinkled like tough leather, but the muscles bulging from the cuff of his polo shirt suggested he had the fitness of a much younger man. He stopped when he saw Frankie. He rubbed his white beard and then held up his finger, indicating for her not to speak. 'I've got it,' he said. 'You're the magic coffee fairy here to deliver my mid-morning brew?'

Frankie laughed and put out her hand. 'Frankie York, new office manager next door.'

'Ah,' the older man said. 'Good, those boys need someone to whip them into shape.' He took Frankie's hand and shook it warmly. 'Josiah Jacobs.'

Frankie smiled and turned back to her coffee making. 'I'm happy to make you a drink. How does this all work? Do we share the tea and coffee or do we have our own?'

'The previous owner and I shared, but I'm happy to do separate supplies, too. Whatever suits you.'

'How about I come and visit you tomorrow and we work it out.'

'I'll look forward to it.' Josiah took the coffee Frankie had made for him. 'Thanks for the brew, much appreciated. I'd better get back to the bait business. Lunchtime rush will be here soon.'

'Lunchtime rush?'

Josiah winked. 'You'd be surprised at how many people sit on the pier with their lunch and a rod. I do small bait packs for them, even offer them use of the fridge if they catch anything they can't take back to work.'

The image of men in suits, sitting on the jetty fishing stayed with Frankie as she took her own coffee through to the office and sat down.

The phone rang as she opened the top drawer, ready to tackle the drop file. Her stomach instantly contracted. She shook herself. It was a phone call for goodness' sake. She picked up the phone. 'Hello, I mean, good morning, Blue Water Charters.'

'Frankie, it's Shauna.'

'Oh, thank God,' Frankie exhaled. 'You're the first person to ring since I've been here. I have no idea what I'm doing.'

'What do you mean no idea? I thought you were being trained today?'

'I was, but Dash is playing his power games with me and took off the minute I got here. Told me I was late even though I arrived fifteen minutes early.'

Shauna was silent.

'Are you still there?'

'Yes, sorry, just thinking. Tell me what you've worked out so far.'

Frankie told Shauna of her basic discoveries and the cleaning and rearranging of the office. 'Hopefully, Tom or Rod will be able to bring me up to speed tomorrow. I'm guessing Dash is going to enjoy making this as difficult as possible.'

'Mmm, I think you might be right. Now, I'd better go. I just rang to wish you all the best for a great first day. How about we catch up for lunch later in the week, and you can fill me in.'

Frankie grinned as she hung up. Who would have thought she'd find herself gravitating towards the outspoken woman who had given her enough ammunition at lunch to hate, not like her?

❀

195

The next morning Frankie decided to call Dash's bluff and arrived at the office at quarter to eight. Tom had returned home late the previous night and was booked again by the American businessmen from lunchtime. Frankie insisted he sleep in. She was perfectly capable of dealing with Dash.

An hour later there was still no sign of him. Frustrated, Frankie rang his phone, which clicked through to voicemail. She looked around, wondering where to start. A coffee seemed like a good idea. She got up and let herself into the shared kitchen.

As she was pouring her drink, Frankie heard the office door open and a familiar female voice call hello.

'Shauna?' Frankie went back into the office to find Shauna carrying a huge vase full of lilies, accompanied by a young woman. 'What on earth are you doing here?'

'Visiting you, and bringing you these of course.' Shauna kissed Frankie and handed her the flowers. 'Happy job? Happy new start, happy new life! I'm not sure which, perhaps all?'

Frankie was touched. 'They're beautiful, thank you.'

'You're welcome. Now, this is your real present.' She pushed the young woman in front of Frankie. 'Meet Makenna Finch.' Makenna smiled at Frankie. 'She's an administrative whiz. Makenna is yours for the next two days. She's here to train you, set up systems for you and will ensure you're running this office like clockwork. She'll also be available to you via phone at any time after she has finished, and of course, in an emergency, willing to come back in and help. Sound good?'

Frankie stared open-mouthed at Shauna. 'I'm not sure what to say. Why would you organise this?'

'Because this business should be able to be run in a streamlined manner. Whether this brother of Tom's has any clue or not is irrelevant. This is your baby, so let's make it yours. Learn from an expert. Use this week to implement Makenna's systems, next week to get on top of it all and then the following week I'm sending you Ryan Drysdale. He specialises in small business advertising and promotion. He'll help you map out the next six months' marketing campaigns.'

Frankie continued to stare at Shauna.

'Makenna will also test your computer skills and decide if you require extra training. Once she reports back I'll work out who to send in next.'

A soft giggle escaped from Makenna. 'I'm sorry,' she said. 'I don't think I've ever seen what I think my grandfather terms a stunned mullet before. You might need to give Frankie a shake.'

Frankie closed her mouth. 'Shauna, thank you, I'm blown away, but this is far too generous of you.'

'Don't be silly, I'm responsible, partially anyway, for pushing you into this job. I want to see you enjoy your work and turn this into a profitable business.' Shauna checked her watch. 'Now, I'd better go, I've got to be back at the office in twenty minutes.' She turned to Makenna. 'Call me if you find any areas you feel could use extra help.'

Makenna nodded.

'Good luck!' Shauna gave Frankie a quick hug and hurried out of the office.

Makenna smiled at Frankie once Shauna had gone. 'She's a bit of a whirlwind.'

Frankie laughed. 'Yes, she sure is. Thank you so much for agreeing to do this.'

'No need to thank me. Thank Shauna, she's paying good money. We'll get you up to speed in no time.' Makenna squeezed Frankie's arm. 'You are going to surprise yourself, I promise.' She put her bag down on the desk, pulled up a chair and sat down in front of the computer. She patted the seat next to her, 'Come on, let's get started.'

Frankie swallowed, a nervous smile on her lips as she took her place next to Makenna. This was happening. She was going to learn business management from an expert, not her condescending brother-in-law.

❋

Ten days passed and Frankie felt like she'd been doing the job for years. Tom joked she must have had a similar role in a past life. Frankie knew that it was Makenna, not a past life, who she needed to thank.

Makenna's employment had been extended by two days until Frankie was completely comfortable and on top of things. The booking system worked, the drop files had been cleaned out, and a proper filing system had been implemented. Much of the previous owner's paperwork was filed directly into the bin. The documents that appeared important were read and kept. Not only did Makenna bring Frankie up to speed with the basics of the computer, but she trained her in the accounts work she would need to do. The booking system linked to a website one of Makenna's contacts had been employed to create for the business. Blue Water Charters had a sleek, professional feel. Makenna didn't stop there. The office furniture had all been replaced with modern, attractive items. The small lounge area Frankie had envisaged was complete with a couch, two comfortable chairs and a coffee table, which would house promotional brochures. A small coffee machine finished off the welcoming environment.

As they'd worked through the files of paperwork, Makenna had unearthed a problem with the accounts. Dash had entered a number of transactions into the ledgers with no invoices to back them up. While the details he'd entered sounded like legitimate expenses, that he was unable to produce one invoice had rung alarm bells with both Makenna and Frankie. Frankie had scheduled a meeting with Tom and Rod and the three of them now sat in the new lounge area discussing the matter.

Frankie bit her tongue as Tom was quick to defend Dash. 'Come on, Frankie, do you need to constantly stir the pot with Dash? He's authorised to spend money, we all are. We've needed a ton of equipment and repairs. There's nothing dodgy about what he's doing.'

Frankie tried to stay calm. 'Fine, then tell me why it's impossible for him to provide one invoice?' She held up a bank statement. 'We have fifteen unaccounted expenses totalling thirty-nine thousand dollars. That's fifteen missing invoices. This is in addition to twelve other payments totalling sixty-two thousand dollars.' She handed each of them a printed sheet. 'I've listed here every item the sixty-two thousand dollars was used for. The business name is in the second column and the detail of the equipment or repair is in column three.'

Rod rubbed his forehead. 'What's the point of this? The sixty-two thousand dollars shows our purchases so far.'

'Yes, I'm making it clear in order to stay on top of things. The point of this is to ask you whether an additional thirty-nine thousand dollars of legitimate expenses have been made. If yes, where are the items and where are the invoices? If no, we have a problem.'

Frankie stared at the men, waiting for a response.

They sat in silence for a few minutes and looked through the expenses Frankie had listed.

Rod slammed his page down on the coffee table. 'Shit, this is pretty thorough. We understood the initial outlay to be around sixty grand, which this is just over. Thirty-nine thousand is a lot to spend without knowledge or receipts. I can't think of any big expenses, can you, Tom?'

'Not big expenses,' Frankie said. 'Fifteen expenses add up to the thirty-nine thousand.'

Tom glanced at Frankie then looked away. He picked up the papers. 'Leave this with me, I'll talk to Dash. Looking at some of the items, he might have pre-ordered. Some of the items are for services, too, which have quite likely been carried out on the boats. I'm sure he'll be able to contact the suppliers and organise invoices.'

'That's not the only problem.'

Tom sighed. 'What now?'

'Dash still hasn't contributed his fifty thousand dollars. The money was due two weeks ago, when Rod paid his.'

Tom wrung his hands. 'We've discussed this already. His money is tied up in an investment.'

'Oh, come on, he can break an investment easily enough.'

'He'll get penalised if he does. There's no point losing money unnecessarily when the business is cashed up.'

Frankie held up the bank statements and waved them at Tom. 'It won't be cashed up for much longer.'

'He said he'll receive the money at the end of the month. That's only two weeks away.'

'Fine, I'll chase him up then.'

'Don't antagonise him, hon, this is supposed to be a family business, bringing us all closer, not driving a wedge between us.'

The pleading in Tom's eyes prevented Frankie from saying more. She knew Tom was sick of hearing her complaining about how rude and condescending she found Dash. Every time Dash set a foot inside the office, an argument started between the two of them. He was a master at creating a hostile work environment. Frankie stood and moved back to her desk. 'Okay, I'll do my best to be lovely to Dash.'

Tom smiled. 'We'd better head off. I'll see you tonight.' He gave Frankie a quick kiss then slapped Rod on the back. 'Come on, mate, let's get ready for tomorrow, our first double booking. It's going to be a big day.'

Frankie watched from the office window as Tom and Rod walked towards the boats. Her gut churned as they laughed and chatted. Tom had managed to dismiss her findings, for now. If he wasn't worried yet, everything in her gut told her he soon would be.

※

'Got yourself a good man there.' Frankie looked up from her computer to see Josiah standing in the doorway of the kitchen, arm outstretched with a coffee mug. 'A real family man.'

She got up, accepting the coffee. From what Tom had told her he had only had a brief conversation with Josiah. 'Come and sit down.' She led him to the new sitting area. 'What makes you think Tom's a real family man?'

Josiah tapped his nose. 'Instinct.' He smiled. 'And big ears. The walls are so thin between our offices it's impossible not to hear conversations, especially raised voices.'

'Raised voices?'

'Yes. I'm speaking out of turn here, I know that, but I also think you should know Tom's not taking Dash's side. He knows how badly he's behaving towards you.'

Frankie's face flushed with heat. 'Oh? He certainly doesn't give me that impression.'

Josiah sighed. 'Don't be embarrassed, love. If I knew him better I'd give him a swift kick up the behind. He's been on at Dash nearly every afternoon after you leave, to be professional and stop the games with you.'

'Really? What does Dash say?'

'Says he's being nice and you constantly stir up trouble.'

Frankie's grip tightened on her coffee cup. The nerve of Dash. 'That's not the case at all, he …'

Josiah held up a hand. 'No need to tell me, I hear the way he speaks to you. His behaviour's appalling. Said so myself to him, I did.'

Frankie was taken by surprise. 'You spoke to Dash?'

'Yes, just yesterday, in fact. Told him if I heard him raise his voice again I'd be in here with my gutting knife.' Josiah laughed. 'Should've seen his face. Didn't know whether to believe me or not.'

'Shame Tom doesn't realise what a troublemaker he is.'

Josiah sipped his coffee. 'Oh, he does, don't you worry about that. Your husband is a good man. He's doing his very best to get that rotten brother of his to wake up and make a go of this opportunity. Reminds me of myself. Wants to fix a problem before admitting there is one. Give him some time, he'll realise it's an impossible task with that one.'

Frankie sipped her coffee. Josiah's words resonated with her. So, Tom did believe her and was trying to improve the work environment. Why on earth hadn't he told her? Although Josiah was right, Tom would definitely try to make peace between everyone in his own way. 'Thanks for telling me, Josiah.'

Josiah winked. 'Hopefully Tom will turn him around, or better still realise he's a lost cause.'

Frankie nodded. 'That would be nice, but unfortunately, I think there'll be bigger issues to come. The problem is no longer just about behaviour, there appears to be a lot of money missing. With any luck, it'll be accounted for.'

Josiah stood up. 'I hope so for all your sakes. Now, better be getting on, done my interfering for the day.' He winked again as he walked back into the shared kitchen, leaving Frankie deep in thought.

Frankie remained deep in thought as she drove home. She parked in the garage and walked through the internal access. Loud voices greeted her. She walked into the kitchen to find Hope and Fern arguing. They stopped as soon as they saw her.

'What's going on?'

'Fern wants to tell her friends we won lotto,' Hope said. 'I'm trying to explain why we don't want anyone knowing.'

Frankie put her bag on the bench and turned to Fern. 'I thought you understood. I know it's exciting, but if people know they'll start asking for money.'

'My friends wouldn't ask,' Fern said.

Frankie pulled her close. 'I know, darling, but people spread stories very quickly. Your friends would tell their parents, they'd tell other people and before we know it we'd have a line of people outside the door begging for money. It's best if we keep this to ourselves.'

'But people are talking anyway,' Fern said.

'What do you mean?' Frankie looked at Hope, who didn't meet her eyes.

'When I was at Cecilia's house the other day, I heard her mum talking to Jessica's mum. They were laughing, saying maybe Daddy robbed a bank, or someone really rich must have died. They weren't being very nice.'

Frankie hugged Fern even tighter. 'Don't worry about what people are saying. They're curious, but they'll lose interest in us pretty quickly.'

Frankie turned to Hope. 'Are you hearing the same kinds of things?'

'I did a few weeks ago. I told a couple of people that you and Dad were shrewd investors and it had paid off. They must have believed me as no one has asked since.'

Frankie laughed. 'Obviously, no one thought to question what we were using to make these investments with. Good for you, I wouldn't normally condone lying, but in this case you've handled it perfectly. Fern, if anyone asks you again, just tell them the same. That's the story we'll all stick to, okay?'

Fern nodded. Frankie could see she wasn't happy at having to keep this secret but knew she would.

'Now, tell me what else is happening at school? Hope?'

Hope shrugged. 'Nothing out of the ordinary. Lots of work.'

'What about Hamish and his friends?'

Hope blushed. 'The teasing's stopped, you don't need to worry.'

'Is he staying away from you?'

Hope picked up an apple from the fruit bowl. 'He's not annoying me if that's what you're asking.'

'So, you're friends now?'

Hope polished the apple against her shirt. 'Sort of. He's actually quite nice when you get to know him.'

'Just be careful, won't you. You've seen how cruel he can be.'

Hope refused to meet Frankie's eyes. 'Okay, now, I'd better finish my homework. Come on, Fern, I'll help you with your maths if you like.'

Fern followed Hope out of the kitchen, leaving Frankie to consider their discussion. She hoped Fern would be able to resist the urge to tell her friends about the win. As for Hope blushing at the mention of

Hamish, now that was a turnaround. The moody, sullen teenager of late had been replaced with a happier, more confident girl. No doubt that had something to do with the new and improved Hamish. Frankie couldn't help smiling as she thought of how horrified Tom would be.

# Chapter Nineteen

## A Night Out

Bec felt like she'd been transported to a French bistro as she soaked up the ambience of Deliceux. French-themed posters lined the walls and laughter and music reverberated from the giant white chandelier, an impressive centrepiece. 'I love this music,' Bec said. 'Do you know who it is?'

Frankie shook her head. 'Someone French, I would guess.'

Bec laughed. 'I worked that bit out.'

'French Indie music according to this.' Frankie pointed to the menu.

'Well, whoever they are they're lovely.' Bec stared at Frankie. 'As are you. I still can't believe all of this has been going on since we first met. Our lunch was only a few weeks ago yet you're quite different, you're glowing. Shauna won't recognise you either when she gets here.'

Frankie's face turned red with the praise. 'My life is hardly recognisable. I love being in control of something important. I thought Tom and the girls were all I needed to be satisfied. Shauna's fast-track training was incredible. I've gone from knowing nothing to running the place in a matter of weeks. I'm still a bit slow with some things, but the basics are covered and overall the systems are working.'

'Basics?' Bec snorted. 'I'd hardly call coming up with a brilliant marketing idea the basics.'

Frankie's mouth dropped open. 'How did you hear about my idea?'

Bec laughed as Frankie's face turned an even darker shade of red.

'Shauna told me. She couldn't help herself when she rang to organise this dinner. She's so proud of you. Now, come on, give me the details.'

Frankie outlined her idea to contact large corporate organisations with an offer of an unusual venue for a meeting or networking opportunity. 'Not all businesspeople like golf, which seems to be the standard recreational thing they do. I thought fishing charters would be good, as all you need to do is turn up. The rest is organised for you.'

'Fantastic idea.' Bec was impressed. 'Any great ideas to promote the service yet?'

'A brochure is being printed right now, and we've had a woman in the office the past week ringing organisations and talking to the secretaries of CEOs. She's secured seven bookings and generated a lot of interest. I've also spoken to a catering company who will do the food for each charter at a good price. We order the day before and they deliver early morning.'

Bec pulled out her card. 'Sounds like everything's falling into place. Pass this on to your salesperson and get her to ring me. I'll put her through to our CEO's assistant. I'd say she'd be interested. It'd be good for some team building amongst the staff.'

'Thanks.'

Bec leaned towards Frankie. 'Don't take this the wrong way, but I can't believe you've managed to do so much in such a short space of time. Not long ago you were delivering brochures to people's letterboxes. Now, you're designing and printing them for your own business.'

Frankie laughed. 'Don't give me too much credit. My involvement was the idea. Ryan, the marketing guru, wrote the copy for the brochure and had a graphic designer lay it all out. I just gave approval.'

'You've discovered the secret to running a business. You don't need to do everything yourself. Do what you're good at and employ the services of an expert for things you aren't familiar with.'

'Shauna's taught me that. Her contacts and generosity are unbelievable. She seems able to provide top-level experts in everything.'

'My ears are burning.'

Bec and Frankie swung around, delighted to find Shauna grinning at them.

'Sorry I'm late, a few dramas to deal with.'

'Nothing serious, I hope?' Bec noticed the dark rings under Shauna's eyes. She'd done her best to conceal them with her makeup, but they were still noticeable.

'Nothing a few drinks won't fix.' Shauna smiled as a waiter arrived with a bottle of Veuve. 'What are we celebrating tonight?'

'Actually, more of a thankyou,' Frankie said. 'You hardly know me, yet you've helped change my life.'

Shauna waved her hands dismissively. 'God, no need for thanks. You're in a unique position of being given the opportunity to turn your life around. Not that there was anything wrong with your previous life, of course.'

Bec smiled. Shauna appeared to have developed some tact during the past few weeks. 'Frankie was telling me about the business and the marketing initiative. Sounds remarkable.'

'So far so good, except for Tom's shit of a brother.' Shauna's eyes met Frankie's. 'Sorted him out yet?'

A vein in Frankie's forehead began to twitch. 'Not yet.' She turned to Bec and lowered her voice. 'Close to forty thousand dollars of expenses are unaccounted for.'

Bec sucked in her breath. 'And he's responsible?'

Frankie nodded. 'I'm sure he is. Tom's trying to convince me they're legitimate expenses, yet he can't find any invoices. He's kidding himself.'

'Why would Tom believe him if there are no invoices?' Bec asked. 'Have they received the goods?'

'Most of it appears to be for services and items that supposedly have been pre-ordered for installation at some future date.'

Bec raised an eyebrow. 'Really? And Tom's not suspicious?'

'You'd have to meet Dash to understand. He can charm the pants off anyone. He's manipulative and a liar. He'll do anything he can to get his own way. Blackmail is a specialty. He's not just an arsehole, he's a professional arsehole.'

'He sounds awful,' Bec said. 'What do you mean by blackmail? Has he blackmailed you?'

'He's tried.'

'With what?' Shauna asked. 'I can't imagine you've ever done anything wrong.'

Frankie hesitated, her eyes fixed on her drink. Finally she spoke. 'There's something I haven't told anyone.' Frankie kept her eyes down. 'He attacked me and then decided he could blackmail me.'

'What?' A shiver ran down Bec's spine.

'Arsehole. I'll fucking kill him.' Shauna looked like she was about to get up and go in search of Dash.

Her reaction brought a smile to Frankie's lips. She put a hand on Shauna's arm. 'Thank you, but don't worry, this happened over a year ago and I don't think he'd try it again. He was drunk and to be honest scared me more than anything. Luckily a friend of his walked in and pulled him off me, before anything actually happened.'

'Jesus! And you never told Tom, did you?' Shauna said. 'Because if you had told him, there's no way the arsehole would be part of the business. You must tell him.'

Frankie picked up her glass and sipped her drink. 'No, I made a promise to Tom's mum that I'd look after her boys, make sure they remained close. If I told Tom, their relationship would be over forever.'

'So what?' Shauna said. 'He attacked you. You shouldn't have to spend time with him, let alone work with him. I'm sure Tom's mum wouldn't expect you to keep this secret. How did he blackmail you?'

'Before we won the money he had the idea for the boat business and wanted us to go into debt to help him finance it. He threatened to tell Tom that I'd come on to him and wanted to sleep with him, if I didn't support the business idea. His friend who walked in on us was going to back up his story.'

Bec was shaking her head. 'Even though he pulled Dash off you?'

'Yep, I assume he was being bribed.'

'But Tom wouldn't believe him, Frankie. He knows you wouldn't do anything like that.' Shauna threw back the rest of her drink, slamming the glass onto the table. 'I want to kill the bastard.'

'I was worried it would plant a seed of doubt for Tom, especially if Dash's friend said it happened,' Frankie said. 'I just wanted the whole situation to disappear.'

Bec squeezed Frankie's hand. 'I don't blame you. I remember you telling us Tom's parents died in a car crash? When did you make the promise to his mum?'

'She didn't die straightaway. She was alive for about twenty hours after the crash. We all had a brief chance to speak to her. The doctors thought she might pull through, but with what she said to me she knew she wasn't going to.'

'Still, I don't think she'd expect you to honour your promise after what he did,' Bec said.

'Tom was devastated when his parents died. I don't want to be responsible for breaking up the rest of his family.'

'You wouldn't be,' Bec said. 'Dash would, wouldn't he, Shauna?'

Shauna's mouth was set in a firm line. 'I'd say he's going to break up the family anyway if he's been ripping off the business.'

Frankie nodded. 'Yes, so there's no need to tell Tom, if that happens.'

'What if it doesn't?' Shauna asked. 'What if Dash turns out to be above board, or he manipulates the situation to look like he is. Are you going to tell Tom then?'

'No. He won't ever try anything again. He couldn't risk Tom cutting him out of the business. Anyway, let's not talk about him, I don't want him to ruin the night.'

Shauna sighed. 'Okay, enough about the arsehole brother, for now. But other people getting wind you've won is the downside to winning lotto, isn't it?'

Bec was surprised at the bitterness in Shauna's voice. 'Problems?'

Shauna told the women about her father contacting her and her subsequent conversation with Lorraine. 'Turns out I'm the lucky owner of two money-sucking parents. I actually thought for a moment that my mother telling me the truth might bring us closer. But no, five minutes later she's still demanding money.'

'Are you sure your dad is only after money?' Frankie asked. 'You don't think on some level he wants a relationship with you?'

'He was an abusive alcoholic with a gambling problem, who my mother had to flee from when I was four to protect me. She gave up her friends and her family to make sure we were safe. Even if he is reformed, I could never forgive him.'

'Your poor mother,' Frankie said. 'I hate to imagine what she's been through.'

Sadness clouded Shauna's face. 'I probably should give her half of the money and move on. Maybe then we would have a decent relationship.'

'I wouldn't rush into anything,' Bec said. 'Keep the two issues separate. The amount you offered her is generous enough.'

Shauna raised an eyebrow. 'Less sympathetic than I would expect from you?'

'Sorry, don't mean to be, the lawyer's coming out in me. Every story has two sides and I'm one of those people who likes to learn both sides before I make a decision. Might not change my stance, but at least I made a choice based on the facts.'

Shauna nodded, her lips slowly forming a smile. 'So, you sat down with the ex-husband and listened to his side of the story?'

'Touché.' Bec raised her glass. 'My theory works better with other people and their problems. My own stuff is harder to consider objectively, especially when I'm dealing with a complete bastard.' She gulped down her drink and refilled their glasses.

'So, things aren't any better?' Frankie asked.

'He forgot to come and collect the kids a few weeks back. Finally turned up five hours late trashed. Passed out and spent the morning vomiting. He then had a go at me for seeing someone.'

Frankie and Shauna exchanged a glance. 'Seeing someone?' Shauna tapped the table. 'Details please?'

The women chatted for hours over more drinks and dinner.

'How long ago did we meet?' Bec laughed as the waiter cleared their dessert dishes. 'Five minutes? This connection is so strange. Who would have thought winning ten million dollars would come with the added bonus of two new friends. I wonder if we would have met otherwise?'

'You would never have met me,' Frankie said. 'A poor housewife delivering leaflets on the other side of town? I doubt we'd share much in common. Still, whether the money is responsible or not, I love that we've met. In fact, you both should come out for the day on one of the boats. Bring kids and boyfriends if you want?'

Bec laughed. 'Kids? Yes. Boyfriend who is secret from kids? No. We'd love to be included. How about you, Shauna?'

'Count me in.'

Bec tilted her head to one side. 'And will you be inviting someone?'

Shauna blushed. 'Maybe. He's just a friend though, so don't start getting the wrong idea.'

Frankie clapped her hands together. 'Fantastic, the more the merrier. Let's pencil it in for Saturday in three weeks' time. I'll check with Tom the boats aren't booked, and I'll text you.'

Frankie caught the smile that passed between Bec and Shauna. 'What?'

'Text us,' Shauna laughed. 'You've embraced the twenty-first century so quickly.'

Frankie pulled a face. 'You can't run a business without email or an *iPhone* now, can you?' It was a perfect imitation of Shauna's voice.

'Oh God, did I say that?'

Frankie and Bec laughed.

Shauna signalled to the waiter as he passed their table that they were ready for the bill. 'Let's get the bill then head down the road for a nightcap,' she said. 'We'll regret this decision tomorrow, but I'm having such a good time I don't want tonight to end.'

# CHAPTER TWENTY

## *Bec*

Bec groaned, opened one eye and shut it again. A family of caterpillars seemed to have taken up residence in her mouth. If her pounding head was anything to go by, it appeared they were redecorating, too. She heard footsteps on the stairs and buried herself under the doona. She could kill Paul. She didn't want the boys seeing her so hungover. This was his weekend. They weren't supposed to be home until the next afternoon. Bec ignored the gentle tap on the door. If she didn't respond, maybe he'd just go away.

'Bec, it's me, are you awake?'

Hearing Jess's voice, Bec threw off the covers and muttered something indistinguishable.

The door swung open and Jess laughed. 'Jesus, you look terrible. Good night?'

Bec groaned.

'Here, drink this.' Jess handed her a glass of water from the bedside table. 'I'll go and make some coffee. Although, by the looks of it you need a head transplant, not coffee. I'll try to find one.' Jess's laughter became muffled as she went back downstairs.

Bec semi-registered that she didn't remember inviting Jess over, so wondered what she was doing in her house so early. The key she'd given her was supposed to be for emergencies. She glanced at the clock. Five past one – okay not so early. She hauled herself out of bed, pulled on her robe and shuffled down the stairs to the kitchen. Her eyes glanced to Earl who was in the corner, hunched over his bowl crunching biscuits as if he hadn't eaten in a month.

'I fed him,' Jess said. 'Assumed the cat's breakfast wasn't your highest priority this morning.'

Bec flopped onto one of the stools at the kitchen bench. 'Thanks. Alex would kill me if he knew I'd forgotten about poor old Earl.' Jess put a coffee in front of her, but all she could do was lay her head against the cool marble benchtop.

'Poor old Earl?' Jess said. 'Methinks you are warming to the cute four-legged creature.'

Bec groaned in response.

'You poor love, bad or terrible?'

'Worse. If we'd stopped at the restaurant I'd probably be okay, but another two bottles between us at Chester's afterwards clenched the hangover deal. I bet the others are feeling rotten, too, especially Frankie. I doubt she's drunk so much in her entire life.'

'When am I going to meet these new friends of yours? Should I be jealous?'

Bec lifted her eyes to Jess's, relieved to be met by a twinkle in her friend's eye. 'It's only the second time we've been out. It's like I've known them for years though. Of course you can meet them. I'll organise something.'

'I'm kidding, I'm just not used to so many changes in your life.'

'Don't worry, you'll always be my closest friend whether you like it or not. Not to be rude, but what are you doing here?'

Jess rolled her eyes. 'Um, not to be rude to you either; however, I imagine our twelve-thirty reservation at Blakes has been given to someone else by now.'

Bec hid her face in her hands. 'Oh God, I'm so sorry. I've been looking forward to lunch all week.'

'That's okay and I know exactly what we need to do to get you moving. Finish your coffee and go and have a shower. Put some workout clothes on.'

214

Bec's horrified face reduced Jess to fits of laughter.

'Workout clothes? You're kidding?'

'Only a walk, okay? It'll clear your head and the destination will do wonders for you.'

Bec was sceptical.

'No arguments. Imagine what it's taken for me to get this afternoon off. I'll be repaying Max with sexual favours for weeks, so get your arse into gear. You're not ruining my freedom.'

Bec took a sip of her coffee and dragged herself off the stool. 'Ten minutes, okay?'

'Deal, I'll get some water bottles ready.'

Thirty minutes later Bec reappeared. 'Sorry.'

'It's alright, you appear to be half human. Come on.'

Bec followed Jess out to the driveway, stopping in front of a new, racing red Range Rover. She whistled. 'Wow, when did you get this?'

'Yesterday.' Jess unlocked the doors and looked across at Bec. 'It's okay, isn't it?'

'Better than okay. The car's beautiful. I love the colour.'

'I didn't mean the car, I meant are you okay with us spending some of the money?'

'The money's yours. You should do whatever you choose.'

'I know, but it feels weird when you haven't spent any and Paul hasn't been told. We paid off our mortgage as well.'

Bec climbed into the passenger seat. 'It is strange. To be honest once the initial excitement wore off, the money has become nothing more than figures in a bank account. I'll tell Paul soon.' Bec sighed. 'Who would believe bad timing could exist in relation to winning lotto?'

Jess patted her friend's knee. 'You and Paul need to sit down and map out what's going to happen moving forward. As much as you want to punish him, resolving the situation is a priority.'

'I don't recall you being so wise. After the fuzzy caterpillars move out of my body, and I enjoy a good night's sleep, I'll give it some brain

215

space. Now where are we off to, Dawson's Park?'

Jess backed her new car out of the driveway. 'No, somewhere else today. We're likely to bump into our families at the park.'

'Oh?'

'Max and the kids are spending the day with Paul and the boys. I think they were taking the scooters and a barbecue. Sorry.'

'It's okay. I never thought Max would side with me.'

'It's not a case of him siding with anyone. The main problem is he believes Paul. Paul is adamant he didn't have an affair.'

Bec ran a hand through her hair. 'Pity Max wasn't with me when I saw them together. He wouldn't be so trusting of Paul, then. Have we caused problems for you two?'

'Minor issue, but enough that we've agreed for me to catch up with you and Max to see Paul. We aren't sharing information with each other to make sure nothing gets passed back and forth.'

Bec groaned. 'I'm so sorry, I had no idea. Divorce sucks. Until it's official, I probably won't believe it's happening. Not having sorted out anything with Paul properly doesn't help. I should take Celeste's advice and book a mediation session.'

'Maybe, but try talking to him first. Tell him everything. Decide what you want moving forward, and talk to him.'

'How do you mean?'

'Well, the kids for a start. What's your ideal custody arrangement and what is realistic with both of your work schedules? The house, are you planning to sell and re-buy? The contents, the things you've bought together containing sentimental value, who gets what? Plan the detail and then there's a starting point at least.'

Bec was deep in thought when Jess pulled into the beach car park.

'Come on, let's go for a walk along the coast path.' Jess jumped out. 'Perfect, cool and breezy, should help clear your head.'

An hour later Bec learned the ulterior motive of Jess's destination. 'I can't believe I'm actually doing this.' Bec held up the vodka and lemonade placed in front of her.

'Come on, hair of the dog.' Jess raised her own glass. 'Here's to making plans and moving on.'

Bec took a tentative sip. 'Okay, that's good, but don't let me have too many.' She gazed out to the ocean. 'How's this view?' The waves lapped the shore only metres from where they sat, separated by a path that a constant flow of walkers and bike riders were using. Seagulls harassed those brave enough to picnic with their fish and chips, and plenty of beachgoers relaxed on the sand with books, footballs and fishing rods. It was an unseasonably warm winter's day and people were taking advantage of it.

'The whole of Melbourne is probably out soaking up the sun, or at least those fine specimens.' Jess craned her neck to check out the shirtless guys playing football further down the beach. As she turned back to face Bec someone caught her eye. 'Hey, isn't that George?'

'Where?'

'Over by the drinks van. He looks like he's with those two girls.'

'Shit, shit, shit, that's his daughter.' Bec rummaged frantically through her bag looking for her sunglasses.

Jess laughed. 'They're on your head.'

Bec pulled them down to hide her eyes.

'You look fine.'

'Hopefully he won't see us. Shit, too late.' Bec raised her hand to wave back to George, who had spotted her. She plastered a huge smile on her face as he approached.

'Bec, what a surprise. I thought you had the kids today?'

'Change of plan. You remember Jess, don't you?'

George put his hand out to shake Jess's. 'Of course I do, Bec's lovely friend. And how are you?'

'I'm great, thanks,' Jess said. 'Do you live around here?'

'No, South Yarra. Natalie, my daughter, lives in Elwood. I meet her occasionally for a walk and if I'm being generous, an ice-cream.' He grinned. 'Although from what I gather, she'd prefer to be sitting here having drinks with you. She's eighteen, but I'm not comfortable

217

with her drinking; she's still my little girl.' He turned back to Bec. 'So, a change of plans? You should have called. Can I take you to dinner?'

Bec shook her head apologetically. 'Sorry, I've been neglecting my friends of late and promised Jess this afternoon and tonight.'

George smiled. 'Never come between a woman and her best friend. How about lunch tomorrow instead?'

'I'd love to.'

'Leave me to plan something and I'll text you tonight. Alright?'

Bec nodded. 'Of course.'

George's eyes twinkled as he looked from Bec to Jess. 'Wonderful, what a nice surprise. I was so disappointed when I thought I wouldn't see you again this weekend. Now, I'll leave you beautiful ladies to your drinks.' He leaned in and gave Bec a quick kiss on the lips. 'Tomorrow, gorgeous.' He turned and winked at Jess. 'Lovely to see you again.'

They watched as George returned to Natalie and her friend. The kiss he'd given Bec hadn't gone unnoticed, and heat rushed to her face as the girls teased him. George laughed and waved to Bec.

'Wow,' Jess said. 'He's quite a guy. So, what's the plan for this dinner you've supposedly promised me? I might hold you to it, you know.'

'Sorry, I wasn't comfortable about seeing him this weekend. I'm not sure I'm ready to sleep with him. Physically yes, mentally no.'

'So, avoid dinner and avoid bed?'

'Something like that.'

'Is lunch much safer?'

Bec sighed. 'No, but I can cancel more easily via text than face to face. Seems I'm a bit gutless. He's been away for work again the past couple of weeks so we've only chatted by phone. I haven't had to actually make a decision about what I'm going to do.'

'Why can't you tell him you're not ready?'

'He knows as well as I do that every fibre in my body is tingling when he's near and I'm definitely ready. If I could stop my brain from saying no, I'd take him right now, on the beach.'

Jess laughed. 'In front of all these people? Including his daughter?'

'Yep, you'd better believe I would.'

They both burst out laughing.

Bec played with the straw in her drink. 'Okay, so not right here, but you get the idea.'

Jess put her hand on Bec's. 'Say no to lunch, meet with Paul and try to sort some things out. Then you'll be free to move on. If that involves enjoying yourself with George you should. I'm happy to mind Alex and Will for a few hours.'

'No, you've done enough. I'll talk to Paul tomorrow when he brings back the kids. You're right, we need to sort things out. I'll invite him for dinner. Try to set things on the right path for an amicable – if they exist – divorce. The boys will be thrilled and we can chat afterwards once they're in bed.'

'Good girl,' Jess said.

'But if I'm going through with this, we'd better get more drinks.' Bec drained the rest of her glass. 'Another?'

❖

Bec knew she needed to come clean with George. She wasn't ready to take their relationship further, but instead of telling him directly, she'd sent him a text using the kids as an excuse to cancel their lunch date. It was now close to four, and she expected them home any minute.

She was putting the final toppings on the pizzas when she heard Paul's car in the driveway. She rushed out, eager to see the boys.

Will raced up the driveway and threw himself into her arms. She laughed as he hugged her like he hadn't seen her for a month. Alex played it cool, getting out casually and saying something to Paul she didn't quite catch. He wandered up towards Bec and at the last second couldn't help himself and ran to her. She hugged them both tight, only letting go when Paul, his mouth set in a hard line, approached them with their bags.

Bec stood up and gave Paul a bright smile. 'How did you go?'

Paul's facial expression didn't change. 'Fine. I need to talk to you, when would be convenient?'

'Pizza's about to go in the oven if you'd like to stay?'

'Go on, Dad,' Will urged. 'It'll be like old times.'

A vein in Paul's neck throbbed as he ruffled Will's hair. 'Sorry, mate, can't today, but we'll work something out for another time, okay?'

'Oh.' Will walked towards the house, his head down.

Bec put her hand on Paul's arm. 'I'd like you to stay. We should get arrangements worked out between us so we're not always angry and avoiding each other.'

Paul shook Bec's hand away. 'A bit late for that, don't you think?'

'No, it's exactly the right time. We'll have to talk at some stage, and without a lawyer involved would be better.'

Paul stared at the ground. Finally he raised his head, his eyes boring into Bec's. 'Oh, there'll be lawyers involved, mark my words. I'll take you for every cent I can.'

Bec took a step backward. He'd practically spat the words at her. So much for a nice, amicable chat. 'What do you mean? Everything of mine is yours and vice versa. Other than custody, the material stuff will be split down the middle.'

Paul looked over to where Will stood in the doorway. He lowered his voice to an angry whisper. 'How about we have this discussion when little ears can't listen and get upset.'

'Yes, good idea.' Paul's outburst had completely thrown Bec. 'Why don't you come back just before eight, I'll make sure the boys are in bed early.'

'Fine.' Paul walked over to Will and gave him a hug. He called out goodbye to Alex, and without looking at Bec got into his car and backed out of the driveway.

Bec stared after him. This was a whole new level of anger she hadn't been prepared for. In her mind they would have a civilised discussion, agree on a custody arrangement, and she would give him the good news about the lotto money. They would part as friends and continue a reasonable relationship. What fairytale had she been living in?

❦

Paul arrived at five to eight. Bec opened the front door and ushered him into the lounge room. She decided to try the friendly approach once again. 'Would you like a drink?'

'No, I want answers not a fucking drink.' Paul kicked at the couch before taking a seat in one of the armchairs.

Bec felt an uneasiness unfold in her stomach. 'Are you angry about George?'

'George? Who the fuck is George?' A look of distaste came over Paul's face as recognition dawned. 'Oh, the flower guy, the one you're seeing. No I don't give a fuck, screw who you want.'

Bec's heart began to race. Something had happened. They'd had some intense arguments and screaming matches prior to Paul leaving, but she'd never seen him like this. 'Calm down and stop swearing, would you. Why are you so angry?'

Paul's hands gripped the arms of the chair, his knuckles white. 'Guess how many reasons I have to be pissed at you?' He waited.

Bec didn't respond.

'I'd say about ten million, wouldn't you?'

Bec's voice was hardly a whisper. 'Oh. You know.'

'Yes, I bloody well know. How could you keep winning ten million dollars to yourself? Am I some sort of monster?' Misery replaced the look of anger on Paul's face. He sighed, as if defeated.

Bec couldn't bear to look at him. She didn't answer. Instead, she went into the kitchen to pour herself a drink. Her iPhone vibrated on the bench as she walked past. Six missed calls and two texts from Jess. The phone had been switched to silent. Bit late for the warning. She poured a large glass of wine and went back into the lounge. She sat across from Paul.

'So?' Paul appeared to be a little calmer.

221

Bec gulped a mouthful of wine. 'So, I bought a ticket and won a share of a mega draw. We're officially millionaires. Before you ask, I was planning to tell you tonight, when I invited you for pizza, but I guess Max beat me to it.'

'He's a bad liar. Putting our friends in such an awkward position was incredibly unfair.'

'Let's not get into that. What matters is you found out.'

'How convenient. You were going to tell me the same night I coincidentally found out. Yeah, right.'

Bec stood up, her self-imposed calm evaporating. 'Why don't you just shut up? I didn't tell you because what you've done to our family is despicable. Our boys are hurting. Did you even register Will's disappointment tonight? They won't ever recover. When they're older and find out our marriage broke up because you were screwing around, how do you think they'll react? Other than giving gifts to Max and Jess and the old lady who convinced me to buy the ticket, every cent is still in the bank.' Bec got up and went to the office nook. She opened a desk drawer and pulled out an envelope. She walked back to Paul and threw it at him. 'Look in there if you don't believe me. It shows two transactions.'

Paul opened the envelope and withdrew the account statement. 'Eight and a half million, plus a few thousand dollars in interest?'

'Yes, I gave Jess and Max a million. They wouldn't accept more. They're our friends and I only bought the ticket as a result of Jess's generosity and an old lady's persuasiveness. I gave the old lady, Millie, five hundred thousand as a thankyou. Without them we would never have won the money so I hope you're not going to have a problem with me giving them a share.'

'No, my problem is you hiding this from me since the first week I moved out.'

Bec threw her hands up in the air. 'Your double standards amaze me. Fine for you to keep secrets, lead a double life, but me having a secret from you is the end of the world.'

Paul stood up. 'How on earth did we get to this point? This isn't getting us anywhere. In answer to your question earlier tonight, no I don't think we'd gain anything from discussing the details ourselves. You haven't listened to anything I've told you about the affair you're hell-bent on accusing me of having, so why would discussing this be any different? We definitely need lawyers involved. I'll be seeing one tomorrow to make sure this account is frozen.'

'What? That's ridiculous. All of the money is there.'

Paul tossed the paperwork back at Bec. 'This proves I can't trust you. Regardless of our situation, if I'd won I would have been straight around here to celebrate. Instead of using the money as an opportunity to save our marriage, you chose to use it as a weapon against me. I don't even recognise who you are anymore. All I can say is if I'd met this version of you eleven years ago, we'd both be living very different lives right now.'

Bec wasn't given an opportunity to respond. Paul walked out of the lounge, opened the front door and headed towards his car.

※

Jess took deep breaths in an effort to calm down. 'Oh my God, I'm so sorry, please forgive us. I tried to ring to warn you, but you didn't answer your mobile or the home phone. Where were you?'

Bec opened the front door wider to let Jess in. She ushered her into the lounge room.

'Listening to Paul rant and rave about what a terrible person I am.'

Jess groaned. 'I'm so, so sorry. Bloody Max and his big mouth. He's in such a happy place having paid off the mortgage and being able to buy a few new things, he forgot and talked on and on about them. Paul of course asked how we'd managed to do this. Max went all weird and funny, looking at me for help. I wanted to lie, but I froze. In the end Max told him a friend who'd won lotto had given us a million dollars.' Jess rubbed her hands over her face. 'Watching his reaction was horrible. He was so thrilled for us I started sobbing.'

'So, you told him?'

'I kind of had to. My reaction was ridiculous if our story had been true.'

'But it was true, a friend who won lotto did give you the money.'

Jess sighed. 'Technically maybe, but we weren't being honest with him. Lying for the short period we did has left him pretty pissed with us.'

'Why, what did he do?'

'Initially when he found out you were the friend he was ecstatic. He jumped up and down like a looney. Max thinks he went into shock, started telling us everything he wanted to do. Saying the house would be paid off and the kids would have their pick of schools and uni with the fees paid up front. Then he talked nonstop about the trip he'd take you on through Europe and America.'

Bec smiled. 'He said those things?'

'Yes, but suddenly he stopped talking, looked really strangely at us and then went berserk. He only calmed down when, well ...' Jess's face flushed red. '... when I made him.'

'Made him? What do you mean, made him?'

'That doesn't matter. What matters is we are so sorry.'

Bec shook her head. 'You've nothing to be sorry for. This is all my fault. I never should have kept the money secret. What did he say while he was going berserk?'

'He ranted and raved for a while about how you hid this from him, about how much you must hate him. How much he wished he could rewind the clock six months to before the night he left. How he wanted to make the marriage work, but seeing you keep this secret made him realise you didn't want the same.' Jess squeezed Bec's arm. 'Sorry, you did ask.'

Bec gave a tight smile. 'No, I'm glad you told me. Anything else?'

'Not about you. After he finished he moved on to Max and me and how he would never be able to trust us again.'

224

'I'm so sorry.'

'No, we're responsible, too. We took the gift knowing we had to be discreet. I agree with Max, we should have waited until Paul knew and agreed to give us the money, and not accepted it earlier.'

'Paul wants you to have the money. It was the only part he was happy with.'

'I'm glad, but it's more about honouring our friendship. We didn't do a very good job with him.'

Bec sat down next to Jess. 'The finger should be pointed at me, not you and Max. I messed this one up all by myself.'

'Don't beat yourself up. He's given you good reason.'

'Yes, but ten million dollars is rather a lot of money not to mention. My motive to piss him off was a success. So, why aren't I jumping up and down?'

Jess took Bec's hand. 'Because you're a decent person who isn't used to dishing out revenge. Sounds good in theory, but unless you can turn off your emotions it never works.'

'Mmm, I'm not sure what I'm doing. Looking for every distraction available to avoid dealing with Paul and the separation probably.'

'Go and talk to him. You need to talk to each other.'

'No point. You should have seen him.' Bec shivered. 'In eleven years and a zillion arguments, he's never been this cold or angry.'

'So, what next?'

'Apparently I'll be hearing from his lawyer.'

'You should try again. The passion in his voice and face as he talked about the places he wanted you both to visit tells me how much he still loves you. The disappointment was so real when he snapped back to present day.'

A lump formed in Bec's throat. 'Half of me feels guilty, but the sensible half keeps reminding me why we are in this situation. I admit I did the wrong thing with the money, but I'm not the bad guy. Suddenly he thinks his slate's wiped clean because in his eyes this is worse.'

Jess nodded. 'Bec, you need to talk to him, not about the lotto win, but about the problems before. If both of you stopped being so stubborn you might hear what each other has to say.'

Bec got up off the couch, ready to go and switch the kettle on. 'I'll ignore the stubborn comment this time, but after last night I can guarantee a discussion with Paul is never going to happen, not without his lawyer present.'

# CHAPTER TWENTY-ONE

## *Shauna*

'Don Rice calling for you, Shauna.' Jenni announced through the intercom.

Shauna hesitated. Two weeks had passed since her discussion with Lorraine, and she had ignored a multitude of messages from Don already. He was persistent, probably desperate to get his hands on her money.

She picked up the phone. 'What do you want?' She was met by silence. 'Hello?'

Don cleared his throat. 'Sorry. Your greeting threw me.'

'Surely you realised once I spoke with my mother I wouldn't want anything to do with you?'

Silence again.

'Are you there?'

Don sighed. 'I don't know why I expected her to tell you the truth this time. What did she say?'

'She started with your drinking problem, gambling problem and the fact that you're a wife basher. I can hardly blame her for leaving you. Now, I'm busy. Don't contact me again, and no way am I giving you any money, so maintain some dignity and don't ask.'

Josh's head appeared around Shauna's office door as she put down the phone. His smile disappeared the moment he saw her face. 'Everything okay?'

Shauna spoke through pursed lips. 'Bad day.'

'Can I do anything to help?'

Shauna shook herself and forced herself to smile. 'Not unless you have the power to find me a new set of parents and erase my memory of the real two.'

'Did you speak with your father?'

'Yes, that was him. I told him in no uncertain terms to leave me alone.'

'How did he react?'

'He didn't get a chance, I hung up.'

'Good, hopefully he listened and you won't be bothered by him again. Now, come on, I'll buy you lunch.'

This time Shauna managed a genuine smile, collected her bag and followed Josh down to the reception area.

'Feel like sushi?' Josh asked. 'Sushi Zone's supposed to be pretty good.'

The lift opened and before Shauna had the chance to answer, Don Rice stepped out.

Shauna took a step backwards. 'Are you kidding me? What are you doing here?'

Josh held the lift door open. 'Mate, Shauna asked you to stay away. I suggest you get yourself back down to the street and disappear.'

Don shook his head. 'Hold on, please give me a chance to talk. I need to defend myself. Unfortunately, your mother has chosen to lie to you again. I was outside the building when I rang. I'd been hoping to take you to lunch. I can't walk away until you hear the whole story. If you want me to stay out of your life after you learn the truth, I will.'

Josh turned to Shauna. 'Your call.'

Shauna's face was strained. 'Okay, five minutes. Come to my office.'

Relief flickered in Don's eyes.

'Why don't you join us?' Shauna said to Josh. 'We can go out for lunch as soon as he leaves.'

They filed back to Shauna's office. Josh pulled the door shut before taking a seat next to Don.

'Shauna, everything Lorraine has told you is lies. I need you to believe me. I never touched her. Nor have I ever had a drinking problem or any interest in gambling. She was hurt and angry at me. We were having problems. The writing was on the wall for our relationship, but she wouldn't admit there were any issues. Her mood swings were so erratic I never knew where I stood. Appearances were however too important for her. She couldn't stand the thought of her friends finding out we had split up, or worse, the embarrassment of them discovering I'd left her. She threatened me many times, saying if I was serious about splitting up she'd ensure I'd never see you again.'

'And you didn't believe her?'

'No, I'd spoken to a lawyer and been assured I would gain a share of custody. Probably not full custody, but at least fifty percent. He said not to worry until we got to court. Neither of us anticipated her disappearing act.'

Shauna rubbed her jaw. 'Why should I believe any of this? You seem as bad as each other.'

'I can prove my story. I contacted the police when I couldn't find her. They had you both on a missing-persons list.'

Shauna snorted. 'Hardly proves anything. She hasn't denied disappearing.'

'Give me a chance to prove I'm telling the truth. Please, you've got nothing to lose.'

'Just ten million dollars.'

Don flinched as the accusation left Shauna's lips. 'I'm not after your money. I'm quite comfortable in my own right. I'm after a chance to get to know you.'

Shauna stood up. 'Fine, get your proof. Show me you're a decent person and my mother is a compulsive liar and we'll talk.' She pointed towards the office door. 'If I don't believe what you've got to say I want you gone, for good.'

'Okay, I'll be in touch in a day or two.' Don's eyes didn't leave Shauna's. 'Once I prove this to you I hope you'll change your mind.'

Shauna sat down again as Don left the office. She turned to face Josh. 'What do you think?'

'Hard to tell. He seemed pretty genuine, but if he's a con artist after your winnings he would do. Wait until he comes up with some proof.'

'I can't imagine how he'll prove anything to me except we'll find out what lengths someone is willing to go to for money.'

'Do you have his card?'

Shauna opened her business-card holder and flicked through it. She pulled out Don's card and held it up.

'Mind if I take it and do some digging? Check out Don the businessman?'

'Thanks, I'd love you to.' Shauna passed the card over to Josh. 'He's got a small vitamin business from what he told me. If they're in debt we'll have our answer quickly.'

Josh glanced up. 'Is he a doctor, too?'

'I don't think so, why?'

'The name of the company is D.R. Supplements. Might just be using his initials in a clever way.' Josh placed Don's card in his pocket. 'Leave it with me. Now, come on, my stomach is still demanding sushi.'

Two days later Shauna and Josh sat in a cafe following a presentation to a new client. Shauna had remained a hundred percent focused on the client during their meeting; however, her mind now was miles away. She took a bite of her sandwich. 'He says he's got proof and wants to see me at two o'clock. Do you want to come?'

Josh didn't need to ask Shauna who she was talking about. 'Of course, if you'd like me to. I'll admit I'm quite intrigued.'

'The information your accountant uncovered proves he's unlikely to be after the money, so I'd say it guarantees to be interesting.'

Josh nodded. 'Maybe he implied he had a small vitamin company to downplay his success?'

Josh's research had uncovered that D.R. Supplements was Australia's largest exporter of vitamins and supplements. Don had grown their annual sales to one hundred and thirty-three million dollars in the twenty-six years since he had established the business.

'Maybe,' Shauna said.

'What are you going to do if he's been telling the truth?'

'About him or my mum?'

'Both?'

Shauna let out a deep sigh. 'God knows. With him, easy, begin a relationship. With Mum, a different story altogether. I don't even want to think about her for now.'

'Fair enough. I'll get us a coffee and then we should head back to the office if you're meeting with him at two.'

'No, I agreed to go to his office in Carlton. He has something to show me that he'd prefer to do there. It's only about five minutes from here.'

Shauna and Josh pulled up in a taxi outside D.R. Supplements a few minutes before two. Josh raised an eyebrow. 'Small business, huh?'

The building in front of them was massive. The signage suggested the entire complex belonged to Don's company.

Josh squeezed Shauna's hand. 'Come on, let's go in and listen to what he has to say.'

A pretty woman in her mid-twenties leaped up from a couch the moment they walked in and rushed over to greet them. 'Hello, you must be Shauna, it's wonderful to meet you. I'm Rose, Don's ...' She hesitated. '... I guess assistant.'

Shauna shook Rose's hand and returned the warm smile. She introduced Josh and then took a moment to survey the impressive foyer area. The only indication they were in a place of business was a long reception desk. The remainder of the space housed a meandering mixture of greenery and water features. 'This is beautiful.'

Rose nodded. 'Don wanted to create a relaxing and natural work area. He told the designer his vision was for a space as much like a creek and forest as possible. The couches are probably the only thing out of place in a forest, but he insisted on having them strategically placed around the area so you can meet by one of the water features without anyone being able to overhear your conversation.'

'He's certainly created an impression,' Josh said. 'The running water might be a bit too relaxing for getting any work done.'

Rose laughed, an infectious high-pitched sound. 'Don't worry, we get plenty of work done. With a boss like Don you can't help it.'

Shauna raised an eyebrow. 'Bit of a tyrant, is he?'

Rose's hand flew to her mouth. 'Oh gosh, no, he's too relaxed if anything. Don't tell him I said that. I'm supposed to be impressing you. No, he's a great boss. He's created such an inspired workplace and team, no one wants to disappoint him. I'm not sure how much you know about the company. Don started from nothing. He works harder than anyone but is the first to acknowledge and reward our hard work. Ask any of the staff; everyone loves working here.'

Shauna smiled at Rose's dedication and obvious respect for Don. 'You don't need to impress us, so don't worry.'

'Yes, but ...' Rose stopped. 'Enough of me talking, I'd better take you up to him. He's probably still fussing over which coffee to serve.' Rose took Shauna's arm and whispered conspiratorially. 'Don't tell him I told you, but he's a bit nervous. He brought in four ties this morning for fashion advice.'

Shauna was touched. Her own nerves had been pushed aside when she believed her money was the attraction, but now she could feel them resurfacing.

Rose led them up a beautiful hand-carved staircase to the second floor. The sounds of laughter drifted from a meeting room. The office furniture resembled nothing like their own modern workplace. Beautifully carved desks, with a similar feel to the staircase, were scattered throughout the space, separated by plants. The cabinets, bookshelves and other furniture appeared to be handmade, with intricate designs featured on each piece. At the far end of the area a

232

water feature, the height of the ceiling, could easily be mistaken for a real waterfall.

Josh whistled. 'It's breathtaking.'

'Glad you think so.' Don's smooth voice spoke from behind them.

They turned to face him. Josh reached out to shake his extended hand.

'Thank you both for coming.' His eyes met Shauna's. 'I'm thrilled you've come.' He turned to Rose. 'Thank you, I'll look after our guests.'

Rose smiled and surprised Shauna by squeezing Don's arm as she walked past.

'Come this way. There's someone I want you to meet.'

They followed Don into his office. It was large and inviting. His desk faced a window that overlooked a beautiful garden on the same level. The rest of the office was dominated by a couch area. Four couches surrounded an enormous coffee table. An older woman sat perched on the edge of one of the couches. She stood up as they entered the room. The moment Shauna made eye contact the old lady burst into tears.

Don rushed over to her. 'Come on, Mum, you promised you wouldn't do this.' He offered her a tissue.

Shauna's hand flew to her mouth.

Josh rested an arm on her shoulder. 'You okay?'

Shauna nodded and moved towards Don and his mother. 'Shauna this is Madeline, your grandmother.'

Shauna looked at Don in surprise. 'Madeline? But Madeline's Mum's mum?'

The older woman blew her nose, a small sob escaping. 'Yes, Lorraine is my daughter.'

'I thought you were dead.'

Madeline wiped her eyes. 'She told you I was dead?'

Shauna nodded. There was no need to ask for proof of who Madeline was; she was looking at an older version of her own mother.

'I'm sorry to shock you,' Don said. 'But Madeline is the one person

233

I know can convince you my story is true. Why don't you come and sit down and I'll organise some coffee.'

Shauna sat on the couch across from Madeline. She realised Josh hadn't followed her. She turned to find he'd remained standing at the door.

His eyes searched hers. 'Would you like me to wait for you downstairs?'

'No, of course not. Come over and sit down. Meet my grandma.'

Madeline smiled at Shauna through her tears. 'This is the happiest day of my life. The pain Don and I suffered when you disappeared was unbearable. I still find it hard to believe Lorraine would do something so awful to us.'

'But ...' Shauna hesitated, looking at Don.

Don picked up on Shauna's hesitancy. 'Why don't I show Josh the amazing roof garden while you two chat.'

Josh stood up and followed Don.

Don stopped as they reached the door. 'Please ask Madeline any question you have. I've nothing to hide.'

Shauna nodded and watched as he guided Josh out to the garden. They closed the door behind them.

Shauna and Madeline stared at each other. Finally Madeline spoke. 'He's a good man, believe me. The biggest mistake he ever made was getting involved with my Lorraine. You're the only thing he doesn't regret from their relationship.'

'But the story she told me?'

'About the violence, alcohol and gambling?'

'Yes, why would she lie? Are you sure nothing ever happened?'

Madeline sighed. 'No, it did happen, but not with Don. She's described my husband, her father.'

'How awful. I'm sorry.'

'Yes, it was awful. Unfortunately, I never realised Lorraine suffered so much. I thought she was too young to be affected. He died when she was seven. In many ways it was a blessing for all of us.'

Tears welled in Shauna's eyes. This was all so overwhelming and this one fact explained so much about her mother.

'Oh, my dear girl.' Madeline moved next to Shauna. She took her hand. 'Lorraine has no excuse for what she did to you or to any of us. Stealing a child away is a despicable act. She gave up her family and friendships purely to hurt Don. I never imagined she would turn her back on me, rob me of my granddaughter, any more than Don thought she would do it to him. She had created a fantasy world in Brisbane. Boasted to her friends about the wonderful life she had, her devoted husband and perfect existence. When everything was on the brink of crashing down she disappeared. Looking back I realise that when she had you her behaviour changed dramatically. She went from being fun-loving and happy to suddenly having bouts of intense anger. She wasn't rational in her thoughts. I really just thought she was overtired from having a baby and then a toddler. It was only after she disappeared that I realised there was a lot more to her behaviour.'

'She disappeared just like that? No note, nothing?'

'No. In thirty years she never contacted me.'

Shauna tried to process this information.

Madeline got up and retrieved a photo album from Don's desk. She handed it to Shauna. 'Have a look.'

She opened the first page to a photo of herself as a baby, only a few hours old, being held by Madeline.

'I was dying to see you,' Madeline said. 'It was one of the happiest days of my life.'

As she turned the pages Shauna was greeted by more photos of herself as a baby, each time being held by Madeline. Occasionally Don or Lorraine appeared in the pictures, but this was predominantly an album about her and Madeline. The last photo showed Shauna on her fourth birthday sitting on Madeline's lap, a fluffy toy monkey in her arms.

'I remember that monkey. I loved him so much.' He was the one toy Shauna remembered from her early childhood. She realised he was probably one of the few toys her mother had allowed her to bring when they left.

Madeline smiled as Shauna turned the pages. Following the photos were birthday cards, one for every birthday right up to her last one.

'Even though there was nowhere to send the cards I still needed to write them. I've thought of you and your mother every day for thirty years.'

Shauna blinked her eyes, trying to contain her tears. 'This is beautiful.'

'You keep the book, dear.'

'Oh no, I couldn't.' Shauna passed the book to Madeline.

Madeline pressed it back on her. 'No, please keep it, remind yourself how much we've always loved you. I'm hoping I'll get to enjoy the real you now.'

Shauna reopened the album. After the last birthday card Madeline had stuck in a series of newspaper articles. The first nine or ten reported Lorraine's disappearance with her small daughter. Following these was a newspaper history of Don's success. Shauna didn't read them but turned the pages to reveal years of information on the success of D.R. Supplements, the charitable contributions the company made, and the opportunities given to young people. The last article had a picture which showed Don standing outside D.R. Supplements, his arm around a woman in her late fifties and three young adults crouching in front of them.

'Don's wife and children.' Madeline answered before Shauna had a chance to ask.

Shauna looked closer and then back at Madeline. 'Rose?'

'Yes, love, she's Don's youngest. She's twenty, Patrick is twenty-two and Liliana is twenty-five. Don met Sandy three years after you and Lorraine disappeared. A second chance at happiness.'

Shauna fell silent.

Madeline joined her in silence for a few minutes before speaking. 'Are you okay, love?'

'I'm not really sure. A brother and two sisters I have no knowledge of. How could she do this to me?'

Madeline drew Shauna to her and rubbed her back. The gentle rub transported Shauna back thirty-one years to when she was three. She had been frightened by her mother screaming at her father and leaped into Madeline's arms the moment she'd arrived to babysit. Madeline had comforted her exactly the same way. The simple gesture of rubbing Shauna's back brought back so many memories. A single tear rolled down her cheek, followed by another and another. They continued to flow as Madeline held her and rubbed her back. After a few minutes she finally pulled away and took the tissues her grandmother offered.

'I'm sorry.' She tried to pull herself together. 'I've no idea where all of that came from.'

'Don't be silly. This is a huge shock. I blubbered like a baby when Don told me he found you. He was terrified you wouldn't believe him. He's not after your money, which you probably already gathered.' She gestured to the magnificent offices surrounding them. 'He's done well for himself.'

'What about his wife and kids? Are they going to be okay with all of this?'

Madeline chuckled. 'If Rose had been allowed her way this morning you would have been greeted with a brass band and huge celebration. Don almost made her stay home for the day so she wouldn't go over the top. Patrick isn't contactable, he's serving in Afghanistan, and Lili, I think you'll find she's as receptive as Rose.'

'And Sandy?'

'You'll see for yourself. Don't forget you aren't a secret or surprise to any of them. They all knew you existed and Don always talked about you.'

'This is all so hard to take in. Mum told me we had no living relatives. Now, I have a grandma, siblings and a father.'

Madeline laughed. 'I hope you'll get used to us quickly so we can enjoy each other. I insist you and your lovely young man come to my little cottage for dinner on Friday night. You can fill me in on the last thirty years. Sound good?'

'I'd love to, but not Josh. We work together, he's only a friend.'

'Oh,' Madeline raised her eyes in surprise, 'I assumed boyfriend. He's obviously in love with you.'

'What?' Shauna started to laugh. 'I can assure you we're just friends and you only saw him for about thirty seconds.'

Madeline tapped her nose. 'I may be old and decrepit, but I'm not blind, my girl. You mark my words, when you have the time to open your heart you'll see what I mean. For now though, we had better let them come back in.'

Shauna remained on the couch as Madeline walked over to the garden doors and called out to Don. There was so much to take in. Don, a new family, what her mother had done. And now Madeline suggesting Josh was in love with her? She dismissed the suggestion. They got along as friends, even flirted at times, but she wasn't going there again with a work colleague. She couldn't.

Don's face flooded with relief as Madeline whispered something in his ear.

Shauna stood up as he approached her. 'I believe you.'

A huge smile spread over Don's face and he moved towards Shauna and hugged her tight. She stiffened in his arms.

He let go immediately. 'Oh, I'm sorry.'

Shauna laughed. 'It's okay, you're my dad, I'm going to have to get used to the situation, that's all.'

The office door opened and Rose stuck her head in. 'Sorry, Don, you're needed for an urgent call. I know you asked not to be interrupted but this is an emergency.'

'Come in, you silly girl,' Madeline said. She turned to Shauna. 'You've just heard Rose's code talk for, Daddy let me meet my sister properly.' They all laughed while Rose grinned and shrugged her shoulders.

A little after four, Shauna told them she and Josh must go as they still had work to do. Rose had bombarded her with every fact she could possibly think of about Don and her other siblings. Rose's enthusiasm and love for her father were contagious. Shauna found herself smiling and laughing.

She was quiet in the short taxi ride back to the office. Josh took her hand. 'You okay?'

Shauna smiled at him. 'Sorry, I'm in my own little world here. I'm fine, a bit overwhelmed, but fine. Thank you so much for coming.'

'I'm glad you asked me.'

'My grandma invited you to dinner on Friday night. She assumed we're an item. I told her we were just friends, but I'm not sure she believed me. Sorry.'

Josh stroked her hand. 'Don't apologise and let's not disappoint Madeline. I'd love to come if you'd like me to.' Josh's eyes searched Shauna's for an answer.

She nodded. 'I'd love you to.'

❈

The taxi dropped Shauna and Josh at Madeline's a little before six. 'She's old.' Shauna laughed. 'We'll probably be eating by six-thirty and she'll be in bed by eight.'

Josh whistled as they opened the gate to Madeline's garden. Madeline's description of her house as a little cottage certainly underplayed the beautifully restored terrace house. The front garden boasted a glorious display of winter roses. Pale and dark pinks dominated with a spatter of white.

The door opened and they were met by Madeline's huge smile. Shauna debated whether to follow her urge to hug her. The decision was made for her as Madeline embraced her and practically squeezed the breath from her. Josh enjoyed the same warm welcome and laughed when Madeline eventually let go.

Madeline glanced towards the house and lowered her voice. 'I'm

239

sorry about the next hour. A select few people heard about our dinner and demanded an invitation. I refused as this is my night with you, but Rose manipulated me quite craftily and they all arrived ten minutes ago for drinks. I hope you don't mind?'

Shauna smiled, her stomach flip-flopping. 'Doesn't sound like we were going to be given a choice. Don't worry, it's probably better to be thrown in the deep end. When you say a few people, who do you mean?'

'Don, Sandy, Rose, Lilliana and Graeme, Lilliana's husband.'

The door opened and Rose poked her head out. 'There you are, Grandma, we wondered where you got to.' She grinned. 'Hi, Shauna. Hi, Josh.'

Madeline waved Rose back inside and motioned for Shauna and Josh to follow. 'You watch yourself, Rose Rice or you'll be leaving early.'

'Rose Rice,' Josh mouthed. A small smile played on Shauna's lips.

The long passage of Madeline's cottage opened up into a large open-plan kitchen and lounge. Five sets of eyes stared at Shauna as she entered the room. Don was immediately at her side. 'Let me introduce everyone,' he said. 'This is my wife, Sandy.'

Sandy shook Shauna's hand warmly. 'You can call me Mum.' She laughed at Shauna's horrified face. 'I'm joking. I'm so pleased we finally get to meet you. You've been an important member of our family in memory and spirit since the day I met Don. It's wonderful to finally have you in person.'

Shauna felt herself relax a little, instantly liking this funny, quirky woman.

'Now this is Lilliana, my eldest daughter.' Don's faced turned beetroot red. 'Sorry, my second eldest.'

Shauna smiled. 'This is going to take all of us some getting used to. I'm sure Lilliana has always been referred to as your eldest. You'd hardly be wanting to explain to every man and his dog what had happened to me.' Shauna stepped towards Lilliana with her hand out.

Lilliana showed less enthusiasm than the others. She limply shook Shauna's hand before introducing her husband, Graeme.

'What do you drink, Shauna?' Rose was busy opening a bottle of sparkling wine.

'Anything,' Shauna said. 'A big glass of anything please, I'm a nervous wreck.'

Rose's laugh was infectious, helping Shauna relax further.

Graeme handed Josh a beer. 'This might be more up your alley, mate. Who do you barrack for? Please don't tell me Collingwood?'

Josh accepted the beer and started talking football with Graeme. Shauna caught his eye about ten minutes into Graeme's predictions for the game to be played later that night.

He winked and flashed her a smile.

Madeline busied herself in the kitchen, which allowed Don and the girls to monopolise Shauna.

'Can I ask a question?' Shauna lowered her voice and moved closer to her father and Sandy. 'I'm intrigued. Madeline's not related yet you'd think she was head of your family.'

Sandy smiled. 'She may as well be. When I met Don he introduced me to his mother, Madeline. It took a few months before I realised his own parents had passed on and she was his mother-in-law. The girls love calling her Gran, and we wouldn't have it any other way. Although she almost did.'

'What do you mean?'

'When Don asked me to marry him she suggested she should move on. She believed she represented his past, a past full of hurt. Thankfully we convinced her otherwise. We would have been lost without her.'

'And me without them,' Madeline interrupted. 'Sorry my ears are burning over here.'

'One big, happy family,' Lilliana said. Shauna couldn't miss the hint of sarcasm in her voice and noticed the warning look Sandy gave her daughter.

The rest of the hour flew past. Everyone had questions and Shauna found herself laughing in the end when Madeline rang a little bell asking for silence. 'Enough. Seven o'clock, time for you to be on your way.'

'Oh,' Rose pouted. 'Can't we stay for dinner?'

Madeline handed Rose her jacket. 'Out now, missy.'

Rose was the first to hug Shauna. 'Any chance we could meet for lunch one day this week, or a drink after work?'

'I'd love to.' Shauna dug into her bag and gave Rose her card. 'Give me a ring or send me a text with what suits you.' She turned to Lilliana. 'Join us if you'd like.'

'Another time perhaps.' Lilliana picked up her handbag. 'I'm too busy at the moment. Come on, Graeme.' She removed a beer from his hand, leaving it half-drunk on the kitchen bench. 'Time to go.' Graeme gave a little wave to Shauna, thanked Madeline and followed Lilliana. Don and Sandy remained behind to say their goodbyes.

Sandy hugged Shauna. 'Don't worry about Lili, she's not as prickly as she's making out, she'll get used to the idea of you soon enough.'

Shauna hugged Sandy back and turned to her father.

He smiled. 'Thanks for putting up with us invading your space tonight. Everyone is so curious, I hope you don't mind.'

'No, I've loved meeting them.'

'Could we have dinner soon, the two of us?'

'Of course.'

'How about Sunday night or early next week?'

'Sunday's good.'

'Shall I pick you up?'

'No, text me the details and I'll meet you,' Shauna said.

Madeline shooed them down the passage to the front door, leaving Shauna and Josh on their own.

Shauna exhaled. 'Phew, ambush over. Sorry you got stuck with Graeme, was he okay?'

'If you like beer and football, yes.' Josh moved to the couch next to Shauna. 'He's a nice guy. How about you, approve of your instant family?'

'They're lovely, perhaps with the exception of Lilliana. She didn't seem too happy about my appearance.'

Madeline walked back into the room, apologising as she did. 'What a relief they've gone. I didn't mean you to face an entourage tonight. They mean well, but Rose is so excitable she's exhausting. Can I get either of you another drink?'

'Let me organise them,' Josh said. 'You come and sit down. You've been running around ever since we got here.'

Madeline didn't argue. 'What a lovely young man you are.'

Josh returned with three glasses of wine.

'Oh, would you prefer a beer, dear? I'm sure you'll find more in the fridge.'

'No, this suits me much better. Here's to two beautiful women.' He raised his glass.

Shauna sipped her wine and refocused on Madeline. 'Tell me about Lilliana. She didn't exactly seem pleased to be reunited with a long-lost half-sister.'

'Don't you worry, dear. She needs to get used to the idea.'

'Sandy said the same. What's her issue? As you said yourself, my existence wasn't a secret.'

Madeline paused, appearing to be searching for the right words. 'No, you were never a secret, which is why being reunited with you is so wonderful. However, I think Lilliana's preference may have been that you were a secret. She's always struggled with hearing about you.'

'Do you think she wished Shauna never existed?' Josh asked.

'I'd hate to upset you, but quite likely. Sorry, love.' Madeline's eyes were full of concern.

Shauna waved her hand dismissively. 'Don't worry, I'd much prefer to know what I'm dealing with.'

'Yes, let me fill you in a bit more. Your mother disappeared with you, and three years later Don met Sandy in Melbourne on a business trip. He moved to Melbourne within a month of meeting her. Sandy accepted he had a daughter and hoped, like we all did, that one day you would be found. Every Christmas Don bought you a present, just in case. On your birthday, not only did he organise a gift, but he made a cake. This continued once Don's children were born. As they got older, both Patrick and Rose joined in. They would make you cards, or sometimes they would buy a present or a unique candle for your cake.'

Shauna stared at her grandmother. She swallowed. 'But Lilliana?'

'She was jealous. Her siblings have always been close, but Lili pretty much kept to herself. She hated such a fuss being made of you and often complained that it wasn't fair. She convinced herself that no one cared about her birthday.'

'Her birthday wasn't celebrated?'

'They were over the top if anything. Still she believed you were more important to Don than her. I talked to her many times to no avail. Both Don and Sandy tried too, but nothing changed her attitude. We all decided to accept we couldn't change her and at the same time continued to mark your birthday.'

'What about Sandy? I'm not even her child.'

'The way she embraced you is one of the many reasons Don fell in love with her. She has one of the kindest, most generous spirits you'll ever find. Look how she not only accepted me, but welcomed me as a family member and gran to her own children. She insisted I move down from Brisbane to be near them. Never did she show any signs of being jealous of you or Lorraine. She shared your father's sadness and lessened the pain for him.'

Shauna tried to digest all of this. 'How ironic that while my birthday was celebrated by a loving family every year, my own mother forgot half the time. The lotto ticket was a present because once again she'd forgotten. If she'd remembered and gone shopping, I certainly wouldn't be sitting here right now.'

'So, after thirty years we finally owe her a thankyou.' Madeline smiled. 'Does she know you're with me tonight?'

Shauna shook her head. 'No, I haven't spoken to her about the lies she's told. I'm not sure what to say to her. I thought I'd deal with one thing at a time, get to meet all of you first.'

'Good idea.'

'What about you?' Josh asked. 'Are you planning to see her?'

Shauna looked at Madeline. 'Will you? I hadn't even thought about your relationship with her.'

Madeline took another sip of her wine. 'I would like to see Lorraine. After everything she's done she'll always be my daughter. However, I'm not sure I can forgive her. For now, I'll enjoy you and think about Lorraine later.'

Shauna nodded. 'I don't know if I can forgive her either, but she's still my mother.'

'Yes, she is, dear. Come on.' Madeline pulled herself up from the couch. 'Sit down at the table and I'll serve dinner. You must be starving.' She took Josh's arm. 'A growing lad, like you.'

Josh laughed. 'At thirty-nine I'm probably not a growing lad, but yes I'd love to eat. My stomach is rumbling. The smells coming from your oven are mouth-watering.'

As they sat down to dinner Shauna tried to focus her attention on Madeline and Josh, but her thoughts were invaded with images of her mother and the unpleasant confrontation to come.

❁

After saying goodnight to Madeline, Josh suggested they take a walk along the Southbank Promenade. It was past eleven and the cafes and bars were packed. Music, laughter and glorious cooking smells surrounded them.

'Your grandmother is an amazing lady.'

'She is,' Shauna agreed. 'It's hard to believe my mother is related to her.' She stopped next to a crowd of people and held her breath as a street performer juggled with fire.

245

Josh took her hand and squeezed it. 'Look on the positive side. You now know who your father is and the people who make up your family. It's no longer just you and your mum.'

A cheer went up from the crowd as the juggler managed to juggle five fire sticks. Shauna smiled. She turned to face Josh, her hand still entwined with his. 'You always know the right thing to say, don't you?'

Josh took her other hand. 'Not always, but you're lucky and I want to make sure you focus on what's good.'

'I think I'm focusing on it right now.' Shauna's eyes locked with Josh's. He was right, she was incredibly lucky. Lucky to be here with him. He had the most generous heart of any man she'd met.

Josh pulled Shauna to him. She felt a shiver go through her as their bodies melded together. Lifting her chin, he searched her eyes with his own. She knew what he was asking and to answer his unspoken question, Shauna lifted her mouth to meet his.

# CHAPTER TWENTY-TWO

## *Frankie*

Frankie manoeuvred the car into the driveway, her mind still at the office. For the first time since she'd started with Blue Water Charters, Dash had been pleasant to her. This turnaround in behaviour made her suspicious and anxious.

Dash had arrived at work to find Frankie involved in a job for the accountant. She'd been asked to send through copies of the original purchase documents for the business. The accountant needed information relating to their lease on the marina berths. When Frankie pulled out the documents she read them to make sure she understood everything. The figures, however, didn't match up to what Tom had told her, and what the bank statements showed.

She had been told the purchase price of the business had been four hundred and fifty thousand dollars, of which Tom had contributed another one hundred and fifty thousand to cover start-up expenses. The document signed by Tom, Rod and Dash showed the business being purchased for only three hundred and twenty thousand dollars. When she'd rung to check whether the document was correct, Tom assured her she must be looking at the wrong copy and to contact Dash's lawyer for the current one. He couldn't explain why the document was signed by all of them, but insisted it was a mistake.

Dash arrived at the office just as Frankie had placed the call to his lawyer.

'Why are you calling Johnnie?' he demanded.

'I need a copy of the original purchase document for the accountant, I can't seem to find the final one,' Frankie said. 'Why? Problem?'

Dash hesitated. 'Um, no, I guess not. Next time tell me and I'll call him for you.'

'No need, you'll be doing my job and I'm sure you've got a million other things to do.'

Dash smiled. 'Thanks, you're right, lots to get on with.'

Johnnie Drowl was unexpectedly friendly when Frankie rang. She wasn't sure why she assumed he wouldn't be. His association with Dash had her automatically thinking the worst of him. As good as his word, he emailed through a copy of the signed agreement and offered to send her a hard copy. The figures on the document confirmed the purchase price of four hundred and fifty thousand.

'Got everything you need?' Dash asked.

'Yes, I think so.'

'Let me know if I can help you with anything. By the way I should get the funds from the term deposit at the end of next week. The bank has delayed things. No idea why. You know banks, such a pain.'

Frankie gave a tight-lipped smile. 'Tom will be pleased.'

'You know, Frankie,' Dash said, 'I'm quite happy to take the accounts work back from you, lighten your workload. I see how much you're doing and it's an awful lot. I could help.'

Frankie stared at Dash. Did he honestly believe she was stupid? 'Thanks, but I've finally got my head around the processes and it makes sense for one person to manage the admin. I appreciate your offer, though.'

Dash stood up. Frankie half expected him to get angry, demand she hand over the accounts and stop snooping about, but instead he flashed her another smile. 'You're doing a fantastic job. I know I can be a bit hard to work with and that's going to change. I'll show you how much I respect the contribution you're making. And, you know that other business, the stuff that shouldn't have happened.'

Frankie nodded.

'Well, I'm sorry, truly sorry. Nothing like that will ever happen again. Now, I'd better get out to *Fish Tales*, got some cleaning to do before tomorrow.'

Frankie watched as Dash strode out of the office towards the boat. She would have laughed at the insincerity of his speech if she wasn't so worried as to what he was up to.

❊

Frankie tried to rid her mind of all thoughts of Dash as she arrived home. The girls were helping themselves to afternoon tea.

Frankie hugged them and sat down to join them. 'So, what's happening?'

Fern quickly launched into an account of her day while Hope remained silent, nibbling on an apple.

'Everything okay?' Frankie asked.

Hope nodded. 'Yes, just a small problem.'

'It's about a boy,' Fern said.

Hope shot her a deadly look.

'Okay, Fern, let Hope explain what's happened.'

Fern poked out her tongue at Hope. 'Fine, I'll go, I need to ring Sally anyway, tell her about Hope's boy trouble.'

Once Fern was gone, Frankie turned to Hope. 'What's going on?' She suddenly had a flashback to sixteen years earlier, sitting in her own parents' kitchen about to tell them they were going to be grandparents. She inhaled. Hope had never even mentioned a boy. Surely she couldn't be pregnant?

'I have to do my science project with a boy.'

Frankie exhaled and began to laugh. 'Oh, thank God.'

Hope narrowed her eyes. 'What did you think I was going to say?'

Frankie shook her head. 'Nothing. Now explain why this is a problem.'

Hope blushed. 'The boy's Hamish.'

Frankie hid her smile. 'Is that an issue? I'm sure you could ask to change partners.'

Hope's eyes dropped to the floor. 'I don't want to. I want to do it with him. I just didn't know how you or Dad would feel about it after the way he behaved.'

'But that's all behind you now, isn't it?'

Hope looked up at Frankie. 'Definitely, he apologised. I think he was just trying to get my attention.'

'Well, he certainly managed to get all of our attention. Okay, so you like him and have to do an assignment with him. Any other worries?'

'No, I just wanted you to understand and not make a big deal when he comes over.'

'He's coming over?'

'Yes, in about half an hour. I thought you'd prefer we work here.'

Frankie smiled. 'Of course, and I promise I won't be too horrible to him.'

Alarm flashed across Hope's face. 'Mum, you can't be horrible at all. He's scared of coming over. You need to be nice. He's worried Dad will shoot him.'

Frankie laughed. 'Okay, I'll behave and I'll talk to Dad, too. How's that?'

Hope got up and hugged her. 'You're the best. Thanks. I'd better go and get ready, I mean get my books ready.'

Frankie felt a gentle tug on her heart as Hope's face flushed red. Her little girl really liked this boy. It was bound to happen; after all Hope was nearly sixteen. Frankie thought back to the talk she'd had with Hope about a year ago. Hope had squirmed at the very thought of contraception, and at that time Frankie had known she had nothing to worry about. Now, even though she knew she could trust Hope, this wasn't something she was ready for.

❧

Frankie let Tom relax with a beer before mentioning that Hamish was upstairs working with Hope. She had to stop herself from laughing out loud at his reaction.

He leaped up from the kitchen stool. 'What? He's in our house? Why didn't you tell me? I've got a few things I'd like to say to the little shit.'

Frankie pulled him back down next to her. 'Leave them. They're working on a homework assignment together. Hope can handle him, and I hate to tell you, but I think she quite likes him.'

Tom put his head in his hands. 'Oh no.'

Frankie laughed. 'Are you upset because it's Hamish or because it's a boy?'

Tom lifted his head. 'A boy, my little girl likes a boy.'

'Tom, she'll be sixteen soon. Think about what we were doing at sixteen.'

'That's why I'm worried. I don't want to be a grandparent just yet.'

Frankie shuddered. 'God, no! Imagine how our parents must have freaked out.'

Tom nodded. A knock on the kitchen door interrupted them.

Hamish appeared in the doorway. 'Excuse me, Mr York, Mrs York, could I talk to you please?'

Frankie noticed a slight tremble to his voice. 'Of course, Hamish, come in.'

Hamish walked towards them, his eyes focused nervously on Tom. Tom moved off the stool and stood, arms crossed, jaw set in a firm line.

'Sir,' he began and then stopped, clearing his throat. 'Sir, I want to apologise.'

'Go on.' Tom's expression remained unmoved.

'The things I said to Hope and to you and Mrs York, I didn't mean them. I'm very sorry.'

Tom nodded. 'Tell me, why would you tease someone who's financially less fortunate than yourself?'

Hamish couldn't meet Tom's eyes. He shifted from foot to foot, staring at the leg of the bar stool.

Tom raised his voice. 'I said why would you—'

Hamish locked eyes with Tom, cutting him off mid-sentence. 'I heard you, sir. I like Hope, I've always liked Hope, but she wouldn't talk to me. As stupid as this sounds, I guess I was trying to get her to notice me.'

Tom exchanged a look with Frankie. She could tell that this was not the answer he'd expected. Frankie gave him a little smile.

Hamish watched the silent exchange. 'I want you to know I will never treat Hope badly again. I wanted to ask your permission to take her out on a date.'

'A date? You're asking us?' Frankie said.

Hamish's face turned a darker shade of red. 'Hope said she couldn't go out with me unless I explained myself to you and asked permission.'

Frankie noticed the corners of Tom's mouth start to twitch; he forced his face to retain a fierce look. 'Damn right, too.' Tom's eyes bored into Hamish's. Frankie had to give the boy credit; he didn't flinch.

'I'll tell you what,' Tom said. 'If Hope agrees you can take her out, but on the weekend during the daytime. Treat her with respect or you'll be having a chat with me.' Tom rubbed his hand against his clenched fist. 'Do you understand?'

Hamish nodded. 'Yes, sir.'

They waited until Hamish left the kitchen, listening to his footsteps on the stairs. Frankie burst out laughing. 'Wow, you're sexy when you're playing mean dad.'

'Think he got the message?'

'How could he not? He'll be too scared to hold her hand.'

Tom took a swig of his beer. 'Good. That was my intention.'

'You should give him some credit. Talking to us took courage.'

Tom sighed and sat back down at the counter. 'Doesn't change the fact that I still don't like him.'

Frankie raised her eyebrows at him. 'Would it make any difference who it was?'

Tom looked sheepish. 'Probably not.'

'Another beer?'

'Thanks, babe.'

Frankie fetched another beer for Tom and one for herself. She had a feeling she was going to need it. Discussions with Tom about Dash rarely ended well. She passed Tom his beer. 'I got the lawyer to send through the purchase document today. You were right, I was looking at the wrong document.'

'Good.' Tom opened his beer his eyes fixed on her. 'Why are you looking so concerned still?'

'Because Dash talked to me like a human being. In fact, he went out of his way to be friendly.'

Tom laughed. 'What? Why would that make you concerned? I told you he'd come round.'

Frankie shook her head. 'I'm sorry, but I'm sure he's up to something. He told me his money would be paid at the end of next week, and he told me I was doing a fantastic job. On top of that, he offered to take over the accounts work to lighten my load. That's what concerns me.'

Tom stared at Frankie. 'I don't believe this, he's bending over backwards and you still find a problem with him.'

'If Dash makes his fifty-grand contribution to the business, produces the invoices for the thirty-nine thousand, and then continues to treat me nicely, I'll change my opinion about him. For the moment his behaviour rings alarm bells. I know you want to play happy families, but I think you're being taken advantage of. You can't ignore this. If he's done nothing wrong then he's got nothing to cover up.'

Tom sighed. 'What do you believe he's covering up?'

'Other than the missing invoices, my gut tells me there's a bigger issue with the purchase price of the business. It doesn't make any sense to find a document showing the purchase as so much less.'

'What are you going to do?'

Frankie chewed on her bottom lip. 'I'm not sure at the moment. I might chat with Bec tomorrow out on the boat, see if she has an opinion. Don't be mad at me, I'm not doing any of this to deliberately cause problems.'

Tom took her hand. 'I know. And I know the outstanding invoices are a huge issue. I'm not ignoring them, just hoping he'll prove you wrong. He's promised we'll get them at the end of next week.'

Frankie nodded. 'I've rung a couple of the companies that show up on the bank statement, they've never heard of Blue Water Charters or Dash York.'

'Really?'

'Really.'

The nerve in Tom's cheek began to twitch. 'So much for my idea of a family business. Speak to Bec, see what else is going on and we'll make a decision from there. Hopefully in the meantime, he'll surprise us and produce the invoices.'

Frankie nodded. 'Hopefully, but if anything he's been doing isn't legit he has to go.'

Tom rubbed his forehead. 'Let's hope it doesn't come to that.' He pushed the beer away. 'I'm going for a run. I need to clear my mind.'

A lump rose in Frankie's throat as she watched Tom leave the room. His body was slumped, defeated. He had been so sure the money would finally give him the chance to fix his relationship with Dash. She hated that she was the one trying to end it for him.

# CHAPTER TWENTY-THREE

## *Out on the Boat*

The dishes rattled the next morning as Frankie slammed the dishwasher shut. 'He's not coming. These are my friends and I want to enjoy a day out. I put up with Dash's arrogance and indifference during the week, not on the weekend. Call him now and tell him no.' Frankie was furious. She had been looking forward to taking Bec and Shauna out on the boat since they last had dinner, and she couldn't believe Tom had invited Dash.

'I only asked him for an extra hand to help out. With the four kids it's going to be a lot of work. I thought it might be another chance for him to show you that he can be a decent guy.'

Frankie shook her head. 'Like I said last night, if he pays his money and produces the invoices I'll consider giving him a second chance, not before. Today is an opportunity to head out on the water and stop at one of those wonderful secret coves you keep going on about for a picnic. Today is not about Dash.'

Tom threw up his hands. 'Fine, I'll call him.'

Frankie took a deep breath as Tom left the room.

The girls came into the kitchen as she put the drinks into an esky. Hope grabbed a banana from the fruit bowl and plonked herself down on a stool.

'Ready to head out?' Frankie asked.

'Do we have to?' Hope asked. 'Going out with little boys for the day isn't my idea of fun.'

'Sorry, but yes, you're coming. These are my friends and I want us all to have a fun day out together. Treat the boys like little brothers. Who knows, you might like them. Now, is your homework done?'

'Some,' Hope said. 'I'll do the rest tomorrow.' She smiled. 'The new computer makes it so much quicker. The old one took ages to do anything.'

'That's great, hon. Now, come on, help me out with these, would you?' Frankie handed Hope a bag. 'We'd better get going.'

The girls loaded up the car and Tom came out as they finished. 'You ready?' Frankie asked.

'Yes, but I only got Dash's voicemail. I'll let him know at the marina.'

Frankie gritted her teeth. 'Make sure you do. Now, let's go or we'll be late.'

Twenty minutes later they were loading the bags of food and esky of drinks onto *Fish Tales*. Frankie looked up, delighted to see Shauna strolling hand in hand with a tall, handsome man. A genuine smile lit up his face as he spoke to Shauna. Frankie climbed back onto the pier and waited for them to reach the boat. She hugged Shauna and stuck her hand out and introduced herself to Josh. 'Come on board, Tom's down below with Hope and Fern.'

'He's gorgeous,' she whispered to Shauna as they climbed down to the deck.

Shauna's face flushed.

Frankie called out to Tom and he and the girls poked their heads up from the hull to say hello.

'Oh wonderful,' Fern said. The shouts of little boys drifted down the pier. 'Brat alert.'

'Fern!'

'Okay, Mum, I'll try to be big-sisterly.'

256

Frankie waved to Bec, and the boys came running over to the boat. She helped them down, introducing herself as she did. Bec followed closely behind, calling out to them. 'Alex, Will, listen to everything Tom says, okay. He's the captain and that means he's the boss.' Alex turned and saluted, while Will walked with Tom to the front of the boat. Bec smiled as he fitted him with a small life jacket and got another ready for Alex.

'No risks today.' Frankie smiled.

'Hey, this is lovely.'

Frankie felt her heart swell with pride as Bec admired *Fish Tales*. 'She's more modern than I imagined.'

'A lot of hard work and money,' Tom called out.

'And some,' Dash said. He jumped down onto the deck. 'Sorry I'm late, everyone. I'll get us underway for our departure in a few minutes.'

Frankie turned to Tom mouthing 'now' as she pointed at his back.

Tom nodded before going to talk to Dash.

'Is this the arsehole brother?' Shauna spoke in a lowered voice. 'Got a gutting knife? I could put it to good use.'

'Sure is, and he's not coming out with us today. Watch out, here he comes.'

Dash stormed past them and scowled at Frankie. 'Make your bloody mind up, would you? You get me out here on a Saturday and now you don't need me. What the fuck is wrong with you?'

'Keep your voice down, Bec's got young kids here,' Frankie said.

'You don't make life easy, Frankie. I'm trying to be nice to you during the week and you thank me by stuffing up my Saturday. The biggest mistake was ever allowing you to be part of the business.'

Frankie kept her mouth clamped firmly shut, determined not to have an argument in front of her friends. She was the biggest mistake? That was rich. As for *allowing* her to be part of the business she and Tom had financed, God, he had a cheek.

Dash kicked the side of the boat. 'I hope you all have a disastrous day out.' He took off down the jetty without looking back.

'Pleasant guy,' Josh said. 'I imagine he helps create a unique work environment?'

'That's one description,' Frankie said. 'I'm sorry about his little outburst. Tom and I had a miscommunication and he was asked to come. He had every right to be annoyed.'

'But not speak to you like that,' Bec said. 'With your friends here and the children.'

Frankie sighed. 'Let's forget about him. I'd certainly like to.'

Tom untied the boat and they set out into Port Phillip Bay. The idea was to go to one of the good fishing areas Tom had found and let the kids fish, before motoring to Ricketts Point for a picnic and a chance to explore the rock pools.

'Your girls are beautiful, Frankie,' Shauna said. 'Hope really should think about modelling. Look at those cheekbones, she's stunning.'

Frankie examined her daughters as if she was looking at them with fresh eyes. She felt her heart contract when she realised how much Hope had matured in the past six months. Shauna was right. She was no longer her little girl, she was a young woman and a very beautiful one at that. She carried herself with an air of confidence. Frankie wondered when she'd developed that? 'It's hard to believe she'll be sixteen soon.'

'Has she got a boyfriend? Boys must be asking her out all the time.'

'Ironically, the boy who was teasing her a few months ago asked our permission to take her out last night.'

'What?'

Frankie laughed at Shauna's shocked expression. 'Yep. Apparently he's always liked her, just had a funny way of showing it. Thank God that's sorted out. Hope transformed into some kind of teenage alien for a month or two, and I was worried there was a major problem. Turned out it was just a boy. It's not much fun being a teenager, or the mum of one.' Frankie looked to the front of the boat. 'Tom's slowing down. I'd better give him some help with the fishing rods and get the kids set up.'

'I'll do it,' Josh said. 'You stay and talk. I haven't fished in years.'

The three women sat down as Josh moved towards Tom and the boys. They could hear Will's high-pitched chatter as Josh said something to him.

'The boys are so excited,' Bec said. 'They've never been fishing. They'll probably wet their pants if they catch something.'

Shauna and Frankie laughed.

'So, spill.' Frankie pointed towards Josh's back. 'Boyfriend or friend?'

Shauna avoided Frankie's eyes. 'Um, boyfriend.'

'What? You told us not to get any ideas and you were only bringing a friend.'

'I'd convinced myself he was only a friend back then. I didn't want to muddy the waters with anything else and possibly risk losing our friendship. But, my extremely wise grandma planted a few seeds in my head, made sure Josh was involved in some pretty heavy family stuff, and it seems it's woken me up to the fact that it's a risk I'm willing to take.'

'That's fantastic,' Bec said. 'Now, who's this grandma, your dad's mum?'

Shauna filled them in on everything that had been happening.

'What an amazing story,' Frankie said. 'How wonderful for you to discover you're part of this new family you didn't know existed, or at least didn't know were alive. How about your mum?'

'Yet to be tackled. I keep putting her off. She's too hard. Instead of taking any responsibility she'll become the victim. The fact that Don has done well financially will be the first problem, add in her own mother living comfortably as a member of Don's family, and there you have the icing on the cake. I probably should give her the money she wants to make sure she doesn't cause issues for Don and Sandy.'

'Don't,' Bec said. 'She's done enough to hurt you. If you did she might still go after Don or her mother anyway. She won't be entitled to any money at all.'

'Even though they were married?'

'He probably filed for divorce before he started the company. With her as a missing person, the court would have acted on her behalf and granted the divorce. He couldn't remarry otherwise. She has no entitlement to anything.'

Shauna nodded. 'Thanks, that's good to know. Now, let's change the subject. My mother is the one thing I don't want to talk about.'

Frankie squeezed Shauna's arm before turning to Bec. 'Got any more capacity for handing out legal advice?'

Concern clouded Bec's eyes. 'Of course, what's going on?'

'This business with Dash. I might need some help.'

'Explain to me what's happened.'

Frankie did. 'I also think he's done something dodgy in the original purchase documents for the business.'

'What do you think is dodgy?'

Frankie went on to explain the two documents with the lesser purchase price. 'It had all their genuine signatures on it, yet they all say it must be an error.'

'Did you contact Dash's lawyer?' Bec asked.

'Yes, and he sent through an identical document with the right purchase price.'

'What does the bank account show? Did you think to check?'

'Four hundred and fifty thousand was transferred to the lawyer, who supposedly paid the seller. The document I have worries me though. Why have they all signed it? I wouldn't be surprised if it's real and the one showing four hundred and fifty thousand is fake. Dash is so unscrupulous he probably did some deal with his lawyer.'

Bec nodded. 'Why don't you come in on Monday and bring everything with you? I'll represent you and call Dash's lawyer for further information if it's required. I'll also call the seller's lawyer and check what documents they have and ask to see copies.'

'Would you mind?'

'Of course not, I'd love to.'

Frankie smiled and put her arms around Bec and Shauna. 'You two are my business angels. First Shauna with all her expertise and now my own personal lawyer. I hope I'll be able to repay you both.'

'You already are. Take a look at my kids,' Bec said. 'They're having a ball. You'd think they'd known Tom and Josh forever.'

Frankie and Shauna agreed as they watched Tom help Alex bait his hook, and Josh show Will how to slowly reel in his line. 'Mummy, Mummy,' Will squealed. 'I caught a fish!'

The women went over to cheer as Will, with the help of Josh, reeled in a snapper longer than his arm. Bec got out her phone to take a photo.

Will was jumping up and down, while Alex cast out his line, determined to catch one, too. Will's catch had even sparked interest for Fern and Hope, who were getting their own rods rigged up, arguing over who was going to catch the next fish.

'How are things going with you?' Shauna asked. 'Any progress with your ex?'

'Don't even ask.'

'Bad?'

Bec nodded. 'He found out about the money and went ballistic. I got a call from his lawyer on Thursday wanting to schedule a meeting between us, and advise he would be presenting documents to the court to get our bank accounts frozen.'

'Why?'

'So I can't give away the lotto money. Paul doesn't trust me. Ironic, of course. The unfaithful not able to trust.'

'I'm sorry. If I can do anything, ring me. Not sure exactly what, but even meeting for drinks might help.'

'Count me in on that, too.' Frankie squeezed Bec's arm.

'Thanks, I appreciate the offer,' Bec said. 'Hey check out Josh, he's a natural.'

Shauna smiled as Josh high-fived Will and the little boy flung himself into his arms for a hug.

After returning the hug Josh untangled himself from Will. 'Come on, little matey, let's catch ourselves another.'

'He's good with him, isn't he?' Shauna said.

'Definitely father material,' Bec said. 'Catch of the day.'

Shauna laughed. 'Ooh, bad line.'

'Sorry, couldn't stop myself, but he might be a keeper.' Bec went to help Alex untangle a knot in his fishing line, leaving Frankie and Shauna to sit back and watch Josh enjoy his time with Will.

A smile played on Frankie's lips as she saw Josh wink at Shauna. Her friend blushed, her cheeks giving her a glow that Frankie hadn't seen before. The no-nonsense businesswoman had a softer side, one that Frankie was getting to know and love.

# CHAPTER TWENTY-FOUR

## *Frankie*

Tom shook his head as Frankie prepared the files to take to her meeting with Bec. 'Do you really think this is necessary? He says he's got the invoices, and the fifty thousand was transferred over the weekend. He's living up to what he promised.'

Frankie bit her tongue, determined not to start another fight. She closed the filing cabinet. 'The fifty thousand isn't in the account this morning, but it's not just about that. I need to learn everything about the business and get to the bottom of the discrepancy with the purchase documents. I find Dash's lawyer difficult to get information from. This way someone I respect and understand can explain the details.'

'As long as you're not on a witch hunt to show up Dash.'

'I don't need a witch hunt to show him up. Look, if everything is in order then we can move on. I need an explanation in non-lawyer talk.'

Tom laughed. 'What? You think a lawyer is the right person to do that?'

'Perhaps not normally, but Bec's going to answer my questions no matter how stupid they might sound.' Frankie put her arm on Tom's. 'I'm hoping everything is above board, too. As much as I find Dash difficult I'm not out to ruin him. I just want to make sure that he's not being dishonest.'

Tom nodded. 'Okay, now I'd better get out on the boat.' He rubbed his hands together. 'Another corporate group to cater for this afternoon.' He leaned over and kissed Frankie. 'I'm proud of you. The way you've taken to all of this office stuff and these fantastic marketing ideas you're having. This was probably always your forte. Still wish you hadn't picked up the ticket?' Tom winked at Frankie and walked out towards the boats.

Frankie checked her watch – enough time for a coffee before going to see Bec. She went through to the shared kitchen to find Josiah already making one.

'Was about to bring this to you, Frankie. Thought I'd wait until you'd finished talking to your husband.'

'You're very kind.'

Josiah tugged at his beard. 'More problems with the brother?'

'Yes, I think we have some much bigger issues to worry about, other than his rude behaviour.'

'Do you mind if I speak out of turn, again?'

Frankie's eyes widened. 'Of course not.'

'Always trust your gut. Don't be swayed by anyone else. Something doesn't feel right, trust your instincts.'

'We've certainly got ourselves into a difficult situation.'

Josiah tapped his stomach. 'Your gut is usually always right. Don't let up until you have proof.'

'I'm worried that Tom's relationship with his brother will be irreparable if I'm right.'

'Probably for the best. I've seen plenty of con men in my time, and he fits the description. Hopefully we're both wrong about him. Now, enough from me, none of my business.'

Frankie watched Josiah collect his coffee from the bench. 'Thank you, I appreciate your support.'

Josiah winked and walked towards his shop. He stopped at the door. 'You're a good egg, so I keep my eye out for you. It's the bad eggs we need out of our lives.'

Frankie nodded in agreement as he disappeared into his shop.

Visiting Bec in her work environment revealed another layer of Bec's personality to Frankie.

'Okay, I'm ready to call Stuart Carbine,' Bec said, after they'd read over and discussed the documents. 'He's the lawyer for Lawrence Wilde, the guy who sold Tom the business to start with. We should be able to get some answers from him.'

The authority in Bec's voice as she spoke had Frankie sitting up, back straight, focused on every word. She wondered if Bec's manner would have the same effect on Stuart Carbine.

She listened attentively to Bec's side of the conversation, wishing she could hear the other lawyer talk. She held her breath when Bec put down the phone.

Bec shuffled her papers together before making eye contact with Frankie. 'You were right, these contracts are definitely not the originals. Someone's tampered with them.'

'Tampered?'

Bec nodded. 'Dash's crooked lawyer must have helped orchestrate this. Carbine's going to email some documents through in a minute.'

Frankie groaned. 'How bad is it?'

'Carbine confirmed the business was sold to Tom for three hundred and twenty thousand dollars. Included were the boats, equipment, marina lease and goodwill of the company. Carbine's documents show his client received no other payment.'

'Yet our documents show the purchase at four hundred and fifty thousand, a one-hundred-and-thirty-thousand-dollar discrepancy.'

Bec nodded. 'Yes, so we need to find out exactly where the money went. Give me a few days to get the information together and then we'll call a meeting and invite Dash and his lawyer to come along. In the meantime, we should sit down with Tom and Rod and bring them up to speed. I'll give them some suggestions for retrieving the funds, and dealing with Dash.'

'I want him gone.'

'I doubt there'll be any difficulty showing them what their brother has been up to. I think Dash's days in the family business are numbered.'

'The news being delivered by you will have more impact than from me. I'm sure Tom believes I'm out to get Dash at every possible opportunity, so he chooses to ignore me.'

'He'd be an idiot to ignore this information. Now, let me do some more digging and then we'll organise the meetings.'

Frankie smiled. 'Bec, I can't thank you enough for your help.'

'No need, I'm glad to help, give the little bastard what he deserves.'

Frankie laughed. 'Well said. Now, is there time in your busy schedule for me to buy you lunch?'

Bec didn't need to be convinced. She grabbed her bag and led Frankie out of the office.

Frankie looked at the clock on the office wall. It was already past two. The meeting with Bec, followed by lunch, had taken up most of the day. She collected her glass and coffee mug from her desk and took them into the kitchen. After washing them, she did a quick tidy-up of the shared area and walked back into the office, ready to gather her things and lock up. She froze. Dash was sitting at her desk. 'I didn't realise you were coming in this afternoon. Do you need something?'

Dash's eyes locked with Frankie's. 'Need something? Yes, you could say I do.'

Frankie waited.

Dash got to his feet and walked towards her. 'So, I had a call from my lawyer today. Wants to see me.' He sat down on the corner of the desk nearest to where Frankie stood. 'Know anything about that?'

Frankie remained silent.

'What's the matter, cat got your tongue?' Dash slammed his hands down on the desk.

Frankie jumped.

'I hear you've got a lawyer snooping around, asking all sorts of questions. What's the matter with you? I haven't done anything wrong.'

'Who said you had? My lawyer is helping me understand the business and explain a few things.'

'Like what?'

Frankie's body straightened. She wasn't going to let Dash intimidate her. 'Like why two documents showing different purchase prices exist. Unless you can perhaps explain this one to me?'

Dash's eyes narrowed. He stood up and moved closer to Frankie. 'If you know what's good for you, you'll call your lawyer and tell her you've made a mistake.'

Frankie's heartbeat raced. Dash was standing so close she could feel his breath on her face. 'If you've done nothing wrong, my lawyer will just help me sort out the correct paperwork. It's no big deal.'

'No big deal?' Dash grasped Frankie's arm and squeezed it. 'You think destroying this opportunity for me is no big deal? The paperwork won't add up. We both know that.' His grip tightened. 'Now, I said call off your lawyer.'

Frankie felt her body begin to tremble under Dash's grip. She tried to pull her arm free. 'Let go.'

Dash's eyes remained locked with Frankie's. 'I'll let go when you promise to call off your lawyer and not mention any of this to Tom. We can add it to our stash of secrets.'

'No, you'll let go now.' Josiah's deep voice boomed across the room. He strode over to Dash, grabbed him by the shoulder and pulled him off Frankie. 'Are you okay?' he asked her.

She nodded, rubbing her elbow.

Josiah turned to face Dash. 'I suggest you leave. Now.'

Dash folded his arms and stared at Josiah. 'Really. Well, guess what ol' timer, this is my business, so I suggest you get out before I call the cops.'

Josiah stepped towards Dash and grabbed his arm. 'I said get out.'

Dash tried to shake him off, but Josiah retained a tight grip and led him towards the door.

'Go!' Josiah pushed Dash firmly out the door.

Dash turned back towards Josiah. 'You'd better watch yourself, old man.'

Josiah shut the door and turned back to Frankie. 'You okay, love?'

Frankie sat down at her desk, her body still trembling. 'Thank you so much. I'm not sure what he would have done if you hadn't stopped him.'

'Probably nothing. He's a coward, trying to scare you into doing what he wanted. Do you want me to ring the police, or Tom?'

Frankie shook her head. 'No, neither. He's gone and I'm not hurt, a bit shaken up but not hurt.'

'You are going to tell Tom, aren't you?'

Tell Tom? Frankie knew she should tell him, but she hated to think of how he might react. He'd probably want to kill Dash.

Josiah came over and sat opposite her. 'You can't let him get away with this.'

Tears welled in Frankie's eyes. 'It's not him I care about. It's Tom. He's going to be upset enough when it's confirmed Dash has stolen money from the business. Add this to it and I hate to imagine what he'd do.'

Josiah nodded. 'He'll give Dash exactly what he deserves, I should think.'

'Yes, and end up in jail himself. I honestly think he'd go crazy. I really don't want to find out. He'll be devastated if he finds out Dash has threatened me. Let's leave it. My lawyer will sort things out in the next few days and then he should be out of the business. If for some reason he's not, then I'll have a chat to Tom.'

Josiah nodded again. 'Okay, I'll go along with you, but I think it's a mistake. If you were my wife I'd want the chance to knock his block off.'

Frankie smiled. 'With you looking out for me I think I'll be fine.'

268

She glanced at the clock. 'I'd better go, the girls will be wondering where I am. Thank you again.' She leaned over and kissed him on the cheek.

Josiah's face flushed. 'No worries, love. You take care of yourself and if he comes anywhere near you again let me know.'

'Will do.' Frankie let herself out of the office and hurried over to her car, grateful there was no sign of Dash.

Frankie's stomach churned as she sat in the conference room with Tom and Rod, waiting for Dash and his lawyer to arrive.

'Don't worry, this won't take too long.' Bec handed Frankie a glass of water.

Frankie gave Bec a weak smile. She wasn't convinced Dash would even turn up after what had happened earlier in the week.

Moments later the conference door opened and a short, bald man, wearing an expensive suit and thick gold chains around his neck walked in. Dash followed closely.

Frankie gasped. Dash's face was bruised, his left eye was black and half closed, and his arm was in plaster.

'Jesus, what happened to you?' Tom asked.

'Your bitch wife can probably answer that,' Dash said.

'Hey,' Rod said. 'Watch your mouth.'

Tom turned to Frankie, his forehead creased in confusion.

Her thoughts instantly flashed to Josiah. It must have been him, but surely he wouldn't go this far? Frankie shrugged. 'I've got no idea what he's talking about.'

Dash snorted.

'Enough,' Bec said. 'We have other important issues to discuss. Please take a seat.'

Once Dash and his lawyer were seated, Bec presented the proof she had that they had conspired to steal from the business.

Bec folded her arms and leaned back in her chair. 'So, Councillor Drowl, or shall I call you Johnnie? Is there anything you'd like to say in your defence?'

Dash's lawyer peered over the rim of his glasses, his mouth twisted in an ugly fashion. 'You can't prove anything.'

Bec laughed, throwing a copy of the documents at him. 'Interesting defence. I knew you were a crooked lawyer, but I didn't realise your skills were so bad.'

Johnnie got to his feet. 'Come on,' he said to Dash. 'Let's not waste our time with this.'

As they reached the door, Bec slammed her hands down on the table. 'Come back and sit down.' She glared at Johnnie and Dash until they both retook their seats. 'Now, you will listen to me. Don't speak until I instruct you to.'

Johnnie rolled his eyes in disgust but kept his mouth shut.

'*"You can't prove anything"* appears to be your defence. Terrible defence when I can prove you forged purchase documents for a business which robbed my client of one hundred and thirty thousand dollars. I can prove you took close to forty thousand dollars out of the company for personal expenses. I can prove you did not meet your part of the agreement and invest in the company.'

'Fine,' Johnnie said. 'Let's assume you can provide evidence to all of this, what are you planning to do?'

'I've advised my clients to take this to court. The outcome I predict is you will be struck off and never work as a lawyer again, and your client can look forward to jail time in addition to repaying all of this money and legal costs.'

Frankie was satisfied to see the colour drain from Johnnie's cheeks. Dash was staring down at the table, unable to meet his brothers' eyes. The cockiness had vanished.

'If that's the plan then why are we here?' Johnnie asked. 'Is there a particular reason for this meeting?'

Bec nodded. 'Yes. As I said I advised my clients on the path I believe they should go down. However, my clients, against my advice, are willing to consider settling out of court.'

'On what terms?'

'Your client will sign over his ownership of Blue Water Charters to Tom York with no future involvement in the business.'

'Anything else?'

'Your client will also agree to document the exact amount of money he has taken from the company and with whose help. This information will remain on file and if your client ever tries to contact my clients, or their children, you both will be taken to court.'

'Are you finished?'

Bec stood up. 'I'll give you five minutes to agree to these terms and your client will need to remain behind to complete the document. You may be present if you wish.'

Frankie, Tom and Rod stood and followed Bec out of the meeting room to her office.

'Relax,' Bec pointed to her couches. 'You don't need to go back in again, I'll sort out the details.'

'Do you think he'll agree?' Tom asked.

'Tom, he's got no choice,' Bec said. 'His lawyer can't fight this unless he wants to lose his licence to practise and go to jail. Your offer is incredibly generous. Mr Crooked Lawyer in there is well aware of this.' Bec left the group and went back to the meeting room to present the document Dash needed to sign.

Tom sighed. 'Not exactly the best start to our family business. I can't believe he'd steal money from us so blatantly.'

'His method wasn't very smart,' Frankie said. 'Still, better we found out now rather than a year or two down the track. Who knows how much he would have helped himself to.'

'No doubt the whole lot,' Rod said. 'Bec's right, Frankie. Your agreement to settle out of court is more than he deserves.'

'Don't thank me. Like you I'm sad he didn't use the money and the business as an opportunity for a better life and a closer family.'

Rod hauled himself up off the couch. 'Let's not waste any more time talking about him. Come on, let me take you both out for lunch.'

Tom looked up from the loose thread on the carpet he had been staring at. 'What's the occasion?'

'We should thank Frankie for looking out for us and the company and enjoy the launch of a real family business. The one where all the partners care about each other and want to work together. We've had a bit of a false start, that's all.'

Tom nodded slowly. 'You're right. Putting this behind us is a way to move forward. Okay, let's celebrate the future of Blue Water Charters.'

'And celebrate being rid of Dash and his scheming,' Rod said.

Frankie knew she would be the first to drink to that.

Frankie curled her hand around Tom's and pulled the doona over the two of them. 'How are you feeling?'

'Right now?' Tom rolled over onto his side, his fingers stroking Frankie's stomach.

Frankie smiled. 'No, the stupid grin on your face tells me how relaxed and content you are right at this second. I meant about Dash.'

Tom flopped back onto the pillows. 'Oh, him. I'll probably never understand why he did what he did, but I know that it's his loss, not ours.'

Frankie lay next to Tom and watched the rhythmic rise and fall of his chest. She knew it would take some time for him to accept that his relationship with Dash was over. She, however, wasn't going to deny the relief she felt. She'd used the excuse that she needed to collect some paperwork on the way home, in order to stop in and see Josiah. She needed to check that he was okay. He'd grinned and flexed his knuckles when he saw her. 'Hurt? Dash? Really?' was all he'd said. 'Know nothing about it, love.' She'd kissed him on the cheek, watching him blush, and raced home to join Tom.

Frankie stretched. 'I hate to tell you, but we'd better get up. The girls will be home soon.'

Tom groaned. 'You can't do those wicked things to me and expect me to function afterwards. I need sleep.'

Frankie picked up a pillow and whacked him. 'Ten minutes, and then I want to talk to you about something.'

'Deal.' Tom rolled over. By the time Frankie had put her clothes on and was walking out of the bedroom, she could hear his gentle snores.

An hour later, Tom made an appearance in the kitchen, dressed but groggy-eyed. He opened the fridge. 'Where are the girls?'

'Hope rang to say she was going to a friend's house to study and Fern is across the road. Apparently, she's made a new friend at number thirty.'

Tom took a swig out of the milk carton and winked at Frankie. 'Back to bed?'

'Sorry, as irresistible as you are, I want to talk to you about the money.'

'What money?'

'The lotto money. I'd like to give it away.'

Tom dropped the milk carton onto the bench. 'What?'

Frankie laughed. 'You should see your face. Not all of it. I want to leave us comfortably off, but we don't need ten million dollars. Let's work out who we can help. Look at the oldies. The minibus has given them so much independence and enjoyment already.'

Tom nodded. 'Okay, so how much would we keep?'

'We still need to buy a house, and we want to have enough for the girls' uni fees, plus enough to live on. I'd also want to keep a bit extra for our future, just in case. So, I was thinking three million?'

Tom's face relaxed. 'Thank God, I thought you were going to suggest we move back to Poor Street again.'

'No, but from day one my gut told me something bad would happen with the money, and the situation with Dash proves my gut right. Shauna and Bec are having as many problems. It's damaging relationships for them, too. Let's unburden ourselves. Help people.'

Tom came around the kitchen island and took Frankie's hand. 'You are such a good person. I'm so glad I knocked you up as a teenager.'

Frankie laughed. 'Mr Romance.'

'No, I mean it. You probably would've gone off to uni and moved on from me otherwise. I never would have found someone as generous or as loving. I'm a lucky man.' Tom pulled Frankie close to him.

'You're happy with my idea?'

'As long as we keep enough to retain our millionaire status, I'm fine.'

Frankie smiled. 'I think I'm pretty lucky, too, Mr York.'

Tom leaned forward and kissed her. His hand ran down the back of her dress and rested on her bottom. 'Any chance of showing me how lucky?'

Frankie felt Tom harden against her. She took his hand and led him back to their bedroom, locking the door behind them.

# CHAPTER TWENTY-FIVE

## *Bec*

Bec watched the lift doors close and turned back towards her office. Hopefully she would never have to engage with Tom's brother or his slimy lawyer again. She was pleased to be able to help Frankie and Tom.

'You're looking smug.' Bec turned to find Celeste smiling at her.

'Sorry?'

'You look like the cat who got the cream or whatever the stupid saying is. Win a case?'

'Yes, for a friend. The good guys winning always gives me a buzz, assuming I'm representing them.'

Celeste laughed.

'Actually, I was going to come and talk to you later. Paul's lawyer called and they want to schedule a meeting. Can I give you the details and get you to speak with them? Make sure they realise I'm not representing myself?'

'Of course. So, the two of you weren't able to sort things out?'

Bec shook her head. 'No, the lotto money complicated everything. Quick summary: he found out from friends, not me, and hit the roof. The last time I had contact with him he was screaming about taking me to the cleaners.'

'Oh, another textbook case.' Celeste gave her a grim smile. 'Leave everything with me. I'll organise a meeting and we'll go from there.'

'Thanks, I'll forward the email to you now.' Bec walked back to her office and opened her computer. She forwarded the email to Celeste as a new email arrived from Paul. She hesitated before opening it, expecting another awful attack. Instead, a picture of a white flag appeared. Paul's message read: *Please meet me at our spot at Dawson's Park on Wednesday week at three, I'm in Sydney until then. Jess has offered to pick up the kids. I hope you will come.*

Bec picked up the phone and called Jess.

'All I know is he's had a change of heart and thinks talking through lawyers is ridiculous. He wants to meet you at some special spot in Dawson's Park to talk. He wouldn't tell me any more, other than asking if I can pick up the boys.'

'He put a white flag on the message.'

'Maybe he's trying to call a truce or at least apologise. He did suggest to me he behaved like a spoilt brat the other night. He didn't use those exact words, but I helped him fill in the blanks. Now, send him an email back saying you'll go. Don't over-think anything. Listen to him. You need to go with an open mind, so I suggest you head down to the supermarket and buy yourself one.'

'What the hell is that supposed to mean?'

Jess laughed. 'It means you make decisions about things too quickly and then won't allow any further discussion on the matter. Sometimes you should consider listening to the other person. You might be pleasantly surprised.'

Bec was silent for a few moments. 'I do that?'

'Perhaps not in your lawyerly life, but in your personal life, yes, sorry, lovely, you do. Give him a chance. Remember he was your best friend for eleven years and is a wonderful father. Don't throw away something so precious without at least listening to him.'

'Sounds like you know a lot more than you're letting on.'

'My lips are sealed.'

Bec hung up from Jess and re-read Paul's email. She typed a quick message agreeing to meet him and pressed 'send'.

Making arrangements to meet Paul and discuss their way forward gave Bec a boost. She needed to get her emotions back on track; remove the uncertainty that had clouded her mind for the past few weeks. Part of removing uncertainties included George. She agreed to another date. As mixed as her feelings were towards him, avoidance wasn't the solution.

As the waitress refilled their wineglasses and removed their empty plates, George reached across the table and took Bec's hand in his. 'Your beautiful eyes are troubled.'

Bec couldn't hold his gaze. She stared at her hands, the laughter and music of the busy restaurant filling her silence. This gorgeous man was so gentle, so kind. He didn't deserve this. 'I'm sorry.' Her well-planned speech went straight out the window. She had agonised for hours over what she would say, and now couldn't remember anything.

George sighed and continued to stroke her hand. 'I think you're trying to tell me we were never meant to be.'

Bec nodded. 'You're a wonderful man, but as much as I want to be ready, I'm not.'

'No, I'm afraid you're still in love with your husband, and of course you should resolve those feelings and your marriage.'

Bec met his gaze. 'I don't know about being in love with him, but I do need to sort things out so we can move forward on an amicable level. The divorce itself will just be a formality if we work out the details between us.'

George shook his head. 'I'm sorry, gorgeous, but divorce is never a formality and is rarely amicable. I hope you can achieve this, but remember you can't control the other person's feelings. That's what generally makes divorce less than amicable. You both believe you're right and find agreeing with the other person difficult.'

'Hopefully we'll rise above that for the sake of the kids.'

George continued to hold Bec's hand. He was quiet for a few

moments. Eventually he spoke. 'Part of me doesn't want to have this discussion, but the decent part of me knows I should. You need to consider your feelings for your husband. Forget what he's done for a moment. Think back over your entire relationship. Before you got married, once you had children. Other than this one indiscretion, have you ever hated him like you say you do now?'

Bec didn't need much time to think. 'No, this affair and Paul moving out is the first time we've had problems. We've had a close relationship all along. Even when the kids were born my mother insisted on babysitting every week so we could spend time as a couple, make sure we didn't lose our connection.' Bec thought of her mother, realising this was the longest period her parents had ever been away for. It was actually a relief that they were away. As well-meaning as her mother was, if she had any idea of what was going on she'd be trying to push Bec and Paul back together regardless of the circumstances.

'So, you're ending the entire marriage to someone you love very much because he's slipped up once.'

Bec snatched her hand back. 'An affair is a pretty big slip-up.'

'Yes, but can you find it in your heart to forgive him and see where that takes you?'

'You sound like Jess. She's all for me forgiving him and going on as if it never happened.'

'I'm not suggesting you move on as if it never happened. I'm suggesting you get in touch with your feelings. Don't block them all out. Don't leave it until it's too late because you're too stubborn to admit this is hard. It's easy to put up a protective wall around ourselves hoping they can't hurt us even more than they have.'

'Speaking from experience?'

George gave a wry smile. 'Unfortunately yes. The one thing I did learn from my divorce was I gave in too easily. I thought I'd get less hurt if I accepted it was over. I was wrong. I grieved for a long time and it was almost worse than if she'd died. If she'd died there would have been nothing I could have done, but she hadn't and I was too cold and dismissed our marriage purely for self-preservation. I didn't think I could handle being hurt again. What I didn't realise was how much the finality of divorce would hurt.'

Bec thought about George's words. He was right. She definitely closed up when things went wrong in relationships. She put her lawyer hat on and saw everything in black and white, right and wrong. She detached emotionally. If she was honest with herself, she had done this with Paul. She wasn't sure that feeling the raw hurt was going to help in this situation; she didn't think she could get past forgiving an affair, no matter how hard she tried.

Bec smiled. 'You're a beautiful man. This is not the conversation I expected tonight.'

'What did you expect?' George laughed. 'I would convince you to end your marriage and come to bed with me?'

Bec blushed. 'Maybe.'

George winked. 'I'm not saying I still won't try. Our bodies deserve one opportunity if nothing else.'

Bec laughed. 'I couldn't agree more, but I will say no. I've got a lot to think about.'

'Shall we call it a night? Stop me from trying to ravish you?'

'That might be a sensible idea.'

'A sensible idea to ravish, or a sensible idea to call it a night?'

Bec signalled to the waiter. 'Let's get the bill, shall we? As lovely as you are I'm not sure I can trust you, or myself.'

They left the restaurant hand in hand. George waved down a taxi. Bec turned to him to say goodbye, but was silenced by a passionate kiss. He whispered in her ear. 'Be happy.'

Bec felt a lump rise in her throat as she pulled away and opened the taxi door. She climbed in and looked over her shoulder. 'Thank you.'

George's eyes crinkled into a smile. 'Bye, gorgeous lady. Just remember where I am if you ever need me.'

Bec waved a final goodbye as the taxi moved out into the road, ready to take her home.

# CHAPTER TWENTY-SIX

## *Shauna*

The soft murmurs of other diners and gentle sounds of a grand piano brought a smile to Shauna's lips as she and Josh crossed the restaurant floor to their table. The candlelit table was tucked in the corner, perfectly suited for a quiet, romantic dinner. Shauna hugged her arms around herself, loving the care that Josh had put into booking this evening.

'At last,' Josh said, once they were seated. He reached across the table and stroked Shauna's hand. 'At last I get you to myself.'

Shauna curled her fingers around his. 'I'm sorry. My life has suddenly become crazy.'

'No need to apologise. It's not every day you're reunited with your long-lost father and discover a new brother, sisters and a stepmother.'

Shauna smiled. 'Don't forget a grandma, too.'

'I'm hardly going to forget her, am I? Dinner at Madeline's is a night I'll always remember.' Josh winked.

Shauna blushed thinking about the overwhelming first kiss she and Josh had shared at Southbank. Tentative at first, it had become more passionate, unlocking feelings for Josh she hadn't been aware were so deep.

Josh continued to stroke her hand. 'How are things going with Don?'

'He's fascinating. I hate that I've missed so much time with him. He would have been such a good father.'

'He still can be.'

'Of course, but I'm thinking of my teenage years. Those years were spent avoiding a bunch of men my mother traipsed through the house. None of them lasted more than a few months. They were also pretty horrible, a good way to be put off men.'

'I'm sorry she did that to you. What about Rose and Lilliana?'

'I'm having lunch with Rose on Friday and I'll leave Lilliana for now. She's taking the whole thing pretty hard. None of this is either of our fault. If she wants a relationship with me, fine. And if she chooses not to, I'll understand.'

Josh nodded. 'I'm glad everything is working out. At least the lotto win brought someone good into your life, someone who wasn't after your money.'

'Definitely not after my money.' She leaned closer to Josh, her voice low. 'You won't believe this, but he's bought property for all of his kids since his business became successful.'

'Even you?'

'Yes, he's organising for the titles to be transferred into my name this week. Four houses. He purchased two of them in South Melbourne over twenty years ago, one in Ascot Vale and one in Richmond. Imagine what they're worth now? Crazy, isn't it?'

'How do you mean?'

'For anyone else this would be life-changing, but with the lotto money they simply add more property to my assets.'

Josh shook his head. 'No, you're wrong, this is still life-changing. The houses are further proof of how much Don has always loved you.'

Shauna smiled. Trust Josh to point out something even better about her father. 'True. The other thing he showed me, which blew me away, was years of birthday cards and gifts. He has an enormous attic in his house full of the cards and some of the presents he bought for me over the last thirty years.'

'Only some? What happened to the rest of them?'

'He gave away the toys and children's books, anything I would have outgrown. Mind you, he photographed every present and put a photo in the card. He kept the adult presents. First editions of books, paintings and lots of jewellery.' Shauna fiddled with the diamond pendant on the necklace she was wearing. 'This is my present from this year.'

Josh smiled. 'Beautiful, like you.' He leaned across the table and kissed Shauna lightly on the lips.

Shauna kissed him back before pulling away. 'I haven't told you what happened today.'

'What?'

'My lawyer, the one who works with Bec, rang. Mum's dropped the case for the money.'

'You're kidding. Why?'

'I don't know. I'm going to go and see her tomorrow. I imagine she's trying to make up for lying to me for so long about my father. I'm not going to forgive her, but it's unheard of to see her show some sign of regret. This is definitely a first.'

Josh's fingers entwined with Shauna's. 'See, I told you she might come good.'

'I don't know about good, but it's certainly unexpected behaviour. It might just be a new tactic; guess I'll find out soon enough.'

Josh leaned across the table again. 'I can't help myself,' he said, drawing Shauna towards him.

The moment was spoilt by their waiter clearing his throat.

Josh sat back and rolled his eyes.

'Your drinks, sir.' He placed two glasses on the table, pouring a small amount of wine into Josh's. 'Would you like to try the wine?'

'No, it'll be fine.' They watched as he filled both glasses before returning to the bar.

Josh leaned back towards Shauna. 'Now, where was I?'

'About to order, if this is anything to go by.' Shauna laughed and pointed at the waitress standing next to the table.

'I give up.' Josh slumped in his chair. 'Actually, no I don't. Listen,' he said to the waitress, 'I'll double your tip if you go away. I'll call you over when we're ready to order.' She disappeared and Josh resumed his position. He kissed Shauna, gently parting her lips with his tongue. The warmth of his mouth had her melt in towards him. She lost all sense of time, or where she was, until the crash of glasses breaking in the bar area brought her back to reality.

They pulled apart, Josh's frustration mirroring her own. 'This restaurant isn't the right place for us tonight. What do you think?'

'Perhaps it's the right place for dinner, but not the right time for other things? Maybe we should get the order right; eat first, other things later.' Shauna ran her tongue over her top lip.

This was too much for Josh. He stood up, threw fifty dollars in the middle of the table and grabbed her hand. 'Come on, we'll eat later.'

Shauna didn't object. She let Josh lead her out of the restaurant and into a nearby taxi. She heard him give the driver his address, before losing herself in another passionate kiss. They arrived at Josh's apartment building and Shauna found herself blushing as her eyes met those of the taxi driver in the rear-vision mirror. Josh paid the driver, jumped out and ran around to open Shauna's door. He put one arm around her and guided her to the lifts. He stopped as the lift arrived and searched her eyes with his. 'Are you sure you're ready for this? Really ready?'

'Ready? Are you kidding? You're about to find out exactly how ready I am.' Shauna dragged Josh into the lift, leaving him in no doubt at all about exactly how ready she was.

Shauna's body still tingled as the taxi drove from Josh's house to her mother's the next morning. She smiled, thinking about the passionate night they'd had. She had only had a few hours' sleep, yet was full of energy. In a short space of time she'd grown closer to Josh than she ever would have imagined. He was so easy to be around, seemed to intuitively understand what she needed, and how to make her relax. A warm glow surrounded her. Their night together had her ready to face anything Lorraine might be about to throw at her.

Shauna paid the taxi driver and walked up the driveway towards the house. She drew in a deep breath before knocking on the front door. She was going to do her best to remain calm and not get drawn into Lorraine's petty arguments or guilt trips. Moments later the door opened and a stranger faced Shauna.

'Can I help you?'

Shauna took a step backwards. 'Oh. Is Lorraine home?'

'She is, but she's not seeing anyone at the moment. Can I take a message and get her to call you?'

'Excuse me, but who are you?'

'I'm Wendy and I'm afraid I'll need to ask you the same.'

'I'm Shauna, Lorraine's daughter. Now, let me in please, I'd like to talk to my mother.' Shauna pushed past Wendy.

'Shauna, wait.'

Shauna stopped and turned back to face Wendy.

'Has your mother been in contact with you during the past few weeks?'

'No, why?'

'I must warn you she hasn't been well and you might get a bit of a shock.'

'What's wrong with her?'

'She can tell you. Please keep in mind she tires easily.'

'Are you a friend?'

'No, I'm from Blue Cross. Your mother's in the lounge. I'm sure she'll be happy you're here.'

Shauna hurried down the hallway. Blue Cross? What was going on? She stopped. Lorraine lay on the couch, pillows propped around her, a warm blanket covering her body. Her face was pale and drawn and she'd lost an enormous amount of weight.

'Hello, Shauna.' Lorraine spoke in a weary voice, void of any of her usual sarcasm. 'I wasn't expecting you.'

'Mum, what on earth's going on? You look terrible.'

'Thanks, I'd say the same to you, but firstly it wouldn't be true and also I wouldn't like to offend you. I've been a bit sick, not my usual self.'

'What kind of sick?'

Lorraine patted the edge of the couch. 'Come and sit down and I'll fill you in.'

Shauna moved closer and sat down. Lorraine was behaving out of character. Usually, when she had a head cold she'd call it the flu and insist Shauna bring her meals. It was unheard of for Lorraine to be ill and not deliver a list of demands.

'So, a few weeks ago, actually the day after you were here, I had a little incident.'

'Incident?'

'Yes, I slipped in the shower and hit my head pretty hard. Luckily Bob was with me so he called an ambulance.'

'An ambulance? The injury was that serious?'

Lorraine nodded. 'I was unconscious and dripping with blood. Bob had no idea what to do so he rang the ambulance. The next thing I found myself in hospital. They said I was out of it for about six hours. I had the biggest headache when I did come to.'

'Why didn't you call me?'

'After our last conversation I wasn't sure you'd want to know.'

'Of course I would. What happens now? Do you rest up for a while?'

Lorraine patted Shauna's hand. 'Wait, there's more. They ran CT scans and all sorts of tests in the hospital to make sure I hadn't done any internal damage.'

'And?'

Lorraine took a deep breath. 'And they found a large tumour pressing on my brain.'

A lump formed in Shauna's throat, restricting her breathing. She gasped. 'What? Can they operate?'

Lorraine forced a smile. 'Afraid not, the cancer is already in the final stages. Untreatable.'

'They can't do anything at all?'

'No, other than give me some pills to keep me comfortable until the end and supply help like Wendy to keep me in my own home as long as possible.'

Tears streamed down Shauna's cheeks as she stared at Lorraine. 'I can't believe you didn't call me.'

'Oh, darl.' Lorraine gave a little laugh and patted Shauna's hand. 'Selfish right up to the end I am. I didn't want you getting all upset and sad. I'm the cause of enough sadness in your life, believe me.'

'Nothing should have stopped you calling me at a time like this.'

'What's done is done. You're not even aware of some of the horrible things I'm responsible for.'

'You mean Don and the lies you told?'

Surprise flashed in Lorraine's eyes. 'You know? I hoped he'd be long gone by now. You get your stubbornness from him. I take it he wouldn't go without a fight?'

Shauna gave a little smile. 'I always thought I got my stubbornness from you.'

'From both of us, that's why you're so bloody stubborn. Now you know what a horrible thing I did to you and to your father all those years ago. To be honest, when I look back the only reason I can give you, and it's not a very good one, for what I did was that I was scared, actually terrified more to the point. We had a good relationship, your father and I, but I found myself sabotaging it at every opportunity. I pushed him away on one hand and threatened him on the other. I couldn't help, or seem to stop what I was doing. At times I felt like I had no control at all over my own thoughts or actions. Don kept trying to work out what was wrong, why I was doing what I was doing and in the end I couldn't stand it. Rather than getting help, which I probably needed, I took you and disappeared. There was a part of me that truly believed Don would turn out to be like my father and I couldn't live through that again.' Lorraine sighed. 'But in reality, Don was nothing like my father. He probably would have made an excellent husband and father, if only I'd let him. I'm not sure I have energy right now to tell you about my own childhood. Another day, perhaps.'

'Someone else already has.'

'Who?'

'I met Madeline, your mother.'

Lorraine pulled herself up to sitting. 'What? How did you meet her? I thought she'd be dead by now.'

'No, she remained part of Don's family and he used her to help convince me he was telling the truth. She's wonderful.'

Lorraine nodded.

Wendy came into the room. 'Lorraine, I think you should rest, you're looking tired.' She smiled at Shauna. 'Could you finish this conversation later?'

'Yes,' Shauna said. 'I'll stay, so when you're ready to head off I can organise a meal and spend the night. Do you normally sleep here?'

'No,' Wendy said, 'I come in for four hours a day. Lorraine doesn't need full-time care yet, although we may need to increase the hours soon. Why don't we help her into bed and I'll show you what needs to be done regarding meals and medication.'

Wendy helped Lorraine off the couch and down the passageway to her bedroom. She returned to the kitchen moments later where Shauna was rummaging through the fridge.

'You won't find anything enticing, I'm afraid,' Wendy said. 'Everything's bland. Lots of easy-to-swallow foods.'

Shauna shut the fridge and turned to face Wendy. 'Is the cancer definitely untreatable? I can afford to send her anywhere in the world, to any surgeon.'

Wendy's face was full of sympathy. 'Unfortunately we're too late. The cancer has progressed beyond help. It may have gone undetected if not for the accident. This is unusual, but happens when people aren't showing any symptoms.'

Shauna sat down at the kitchen table next to Wendy.

'This is a huge shock for you and I'm sorry. I tried to convince your mother to ring you when she first came home, but she wouldn't. I honestly think she was hoping you would find out after she'd gone.'

'Surely she wanted to say goodbye?'

'She's spent hours writing letters, I assume to you and other people explaining and, from what she's told me, apologising for things she's done. She wanted to save you from the pain that comes from watching someone die.'

'A selfless act.' Shauna gave a small laugh. 'So unlike my mother.' Tears started rolling down her cheeks. Wendy put an arm around her, but Shauna gently shrugged her off and wiped her eyes. She was embarrassed to be so emotional in front of a stranger.

Wendy busied herself and made tea, handing Shauna a cup. 'Here you go. Can I ring someone to pop over and keep you company?'

Shauna thought of Josh. They had plans to catch up for drinks later. 'Thank you, but I'll be okay. Why don't you head off. I'll stay until Mum wakes up.'

'Be aware she may sleep for hours. The medication is strong.'

Shauna waited until Wendy left before bursting into tears. She'd planned to confront her mother; she'd spent hours planning what she would say, wondering if she would ever forgive her for taking her away from her father. Everything seemed so insignificant now.

Shauna called Josh and explained the situation. He offered to come and be with her, but she needed to be alone. She needed time to digest everything.

Three hours later Shauna heard a bump in Lorraine's room. She went in. The bed was empty and she could hear her mother in the ensuite. She waited until she came out.

'Oh, are you still here, darl? I thought you'd be home by now.'

'I wanted to check you'd be okay by yourself. I can stay the night.'

'Don't be silly, you go. You can come back and visit me again another day.' Lorraine shuffled back to the bed and slowly climbed in.

'Where's Bob? Is he helping out?'

Lorraine laughed. 'I didn't realise Bob could move so fast. The day after I was given the diagnosis, he high-tailed it out of the hospital never to be seen again.'

'What? The bastard! I thought you two were in love.'

'In hindsight, I think my bank account was the real object of his love. Once I found out the cancer was untreatable, I told him I was dropping the lawsuit. He was furious.' She smiled. 'It seems having cancer, and no financial prospects, made me less desirable to him.'

'Didn't he think you'd leave him money in your will?'

'No, I told him a long time ago my will was one thing I would never change, and was also the reason I wouldn't get remarried or live with a man again. I wouldn't let someone have a claim on your inheritance. It's not much, but I do own the house. I've been a bad enough mother, I wouldn't add that to the list.'

'Really? Even though I don't need it?'

'Yes, I know it's hard to believe but it is true.'

Shauna smiled. 'You seem so different. Do you even care about Bob?'

Lorraine sighed. 'Yes and no. He's a disappointment, but that's all. I've had time to think. A lot of time to reflect on the things I've done badly and how self-centred I've been. You may not believe this, but I think since leaving Don and moving to Melbourne all those years ago, I went into a kind of self-preservation mode. There are so many things I wish I could change. The men, my relationship with you, the—'

Shauna cut her off. 'The only thing I want to change right now is your diagnosis. Are you sure there's no specialist in America? Or that guy in Sydney? He's always on the TV? He performs miracles all the time. We've got the money, we can afford anyone and anything.'

Lorraine shook her head. 'He's already seen my test results and even he agreed with the diagnosis. As hard and as horrible as this sounds, we have to accept there's no cure; we certainly can't buy one.'

'Did the doctors tell you how long you have?'

'A matter of weeks. They said six, maybe eight.'

Shauna recoiled with shock. 'Only six or eight weeks?'

Lorraine pulled her close and hugged her. 'Afraid so, and they gave me that information three weeks ago.'

'Oh shit.'

'Yep, oh shit alright. Now, let's change the subject. Tell me about Don and Madeline. On a scale of one to ten how much do they hate me?'

A little before ten, Shauna rang Madeline's doorbell, grateful that she had somewhere to go after leaving her mother's. Shauna took one look at her grandmother and burst into tears. Madeline guided Shauna into the house and down to the lounge room. It took fifteen minutes for the tears to subside and Shauna to be able to tell Madeline what had happened. It was harder than Shauna had imagined. Madeline's eyes welled with tears as Shauna explained the situation.

'She was a different person. Considerate, selfless, together, not like she normally is at all.'

'Death is a funny thing.' Madeline's voice was distant. 'People handle death in their own way. Sometimes it brings out the best in them. Robert, your grandfather, he died when Lorraine was only seven. You wouldn't find a more selfish man than he was, but during the last three months of his life I didn't recognise him. He became selfless, worried about me, worried about Lorraine. The abuse stopped. If only he'd been like that all along.'

'That's how I feel about Mum. She's now a person I'd love to be around, but we only have a few weeks at the most. It's not fair.'

'I know, love, I know.'

'I dreaded going to her house today. I was planning to confront her for the lies she'd told me about my father. I also wanted to tell her how successful Don has been, about his family and about you. Before she got sick she would have hit the roof, made up some other story to get out of her lies, and most likely rushed over and demanded a share of his money. Instead, she can't apologise enough for her own behaviour and was genuinely happy when I told her about Don's success.'

Sadness washed over Madeline's face. 'All too late.'

Shauna yawned. Her eyes felt like they had sand in them. She couldn't remember the last time she'd cried so much.

Madeline stood. 'It's after midnight, love. Would you like to stay here tonight? You're exhausted.'

'Thanks, I think I will.' Shauna got up off the couch and hugged Madeline. 'I'm so sorry to drop this on you, but I thought you had a right to know. She didn't ask me to tell you, in fact quite the opposite. Mum's written letters to you and Don, which I'm supposed to deliver after she's gone. I don't agree with her. I think you should be given the opportunity to speak to her while she's still alive.'

Shauna searched Madeline's face for a reaction, but the face that stared back was vacant.

Madeline showed Shauna to the spare room and offered her some pyjamas and a toothbrush. Shauna hugged her grandmother again before saying goodnight.

When she awoke the next morning, Shauna found Madeline asleep in the armchair in the lounge. Shauna tiptoed into the kitchen.

The smell of fresh coffee woke Madeline and she came into the kitchen as Shauna poured two large mugs.

'Perfect,' Madeline said. 'Exactly what I need.'

'Did you get much sleep?'

'A bit. It was daylight by the time I must have drifted off. I'd like to visit your mother, perhaps this afternoon.'

Shauna smiled. 'I hoped you would. Should I pre-warn her?'

'Yes, I want her to be prepared. You go over first. Tell her I'm coming.'

Shauna stared at Madeline for a moment. 'You won't be too hard on her, will you?'

'Shauna! She stole you away from your father and the family who loved you. No contact for thirty years. Do you think I should just ignore that?'

'Of course not, but she's dying. We shouldn't upset her too much.'

Madeline smiled. 'Don't you worry, love, we'll sort things out. Things need to be said. She may have things she needs to say, too. We'll both say our piece and move on. How does that sound?'

'Terrifying.'

Madeline patted her arm and sipped her coffee. 'I'm going to finish this, shower and refresh myself. Why don't you do the same?'

'No,' Shauna said. 'I think I'll go home. I'm still in clothes from two days ago.'

She blushed as Madeline raised a knowing eyebrow.

'I'll get some fresh clothes and do a few things before going back to Mum's. I'll ring you this afternoon, okay?'

'Of course.'

Shauna watched as her grandmother walked towards her room. Her shoulders sagged. Her body seemed to have aged ten years overnight.

Shauna hugged the phone to her. Just hearing Josh's voice gave her a much-needed boost.

'Are you sure you don't want me to come over and give you a hand, keep you company, bring you food, anything?'

'No. I need to do this myself today,' she told him. 'Thank you though. You're being so lovely.'

'Hey, I'm always lovely, you're realising this much later than most people do. Usually people realise it as soon as they meet me. That Josh Richardson, they say, he's so lovely. I get sick of hearing it they say it so often.'

Shauna laughed and spoke with Josh for a few more minutes before ending the call to have a shower.

A little before twelve Shauna pulled up outside Lorraine's house. She'd been playing over in her mind some of the things she wanted to say to her mother. She was instantly jolted from her thoughts at the sight of an ambulance parked in the driveway. She jumped out of the Mercedes and raced towards the house.

A paramedic met her at the door.

She caught her breath and searched the paramedic's face for news. 'What's going on?'

The paramedic didn't get a chance to respond. A voice called out from inside.

'Shauna, I'll fill you in.' Wendy met her at the front door.

'Why didn't you call me?'

'Calm down, I was about to.' Wendy guided Shauna back out to the driveway. 'I arrived fifteen minutes ago and your mother was finding it difficult to breathe. I called for an ambulance. I needed to make arrangements before I rang you. The ambulance only just arrived.'

At that moment Lorraine was wheeled out on a stretcher.

Shauna took her hand. 'Mum, I'm here. I'll come to the hospital with you.'

Lorraine squeezed Shauna's hand, her eyes shut.

The paramedic turned to Shauna. 'Why don't you meet us there. That way you'll have your car for later?'

'How long do you think she'll be in hospital?'

The paramedic's eyes filled with sympathy.

Wendy took her arm. 'I think this might be her final journey. She's gone down so rapidly. I'm afraid it'll only be a matter of days. Hopefully the doctor can tell you otherwise when you get to the hospital, but you should prepare yourself for the worst. I'm sorry.'

Shauna stared at Wendy. How could this be happening so quickly? She thought she had weeks. She pulled herself together. 'Okay, so do I need to take anything?'

'No, we've had her bag packed for a couple of weeks now. I added the few things Lorraine told me she'd need when the time did come.'

'She had her bag packed?'

'Yes, she was realistic about everything. Didn't want to be a bother, she kept telling me. She's a remarkable lady, your mother.'

Shauna thanked Wendy and climbed back into her car, ready to follow the ambulance.

An hour later Lorraine was resting comfortably in a private room at St Vincent's Hospital. The doctor had been in to examine her and confirmed what Wendy had suspected. She was into her final days or perhaps even hours. Shauna had rung Madeline to tell her the news and expected Madeline to arrive at any moment. Shauna felt her own eyes drifting shut when there was a gentle tap on the door and Madeline looked in. Shauna went over to greet her. 'She's still asleep. She hasn't woken up since they brought her in. They gave her a sedative.'

Madeline stood in the entrance of the doorway staring at Lorraine. Shauna could only imagine what her grandmother must be thinking. Lorraine would have been twenty-nine the last time Madeline had seen her – young, healthy, so full of life. Now, she was thin, her skin sallow, cheeks hollow. A terrible way for anyone to remember their daughter.

Shauna's eyes filled with tears. 'Are you okay?'

Madeline nodded. A sad smile on her lips. 'Yes of course, love. Why don't you go and get yourself a snack, or take a walk.'

'I didn't get a chance to tell her you were coming.'

'That's okay. We'll be fine. You head off and refresh yourself. You have a long night ahead.'

Shauna turned back as she walked out of the room to see Madeline wipe a tear from the corner of her eye.

Thirty minutes later Shauna looked in to find Lorraine's bed tilted upright, and Lorraine and Madeline deep in hushed conversation. 'Everything okay?' she asked from the doorway.

Madeline looked up. 'All good, dear. We need a bit longer if you don't mind.'

Shauna decided to go and find a coffee. When she returned Madeline was quietly closing the door. 'She's sleeping,' she whispered. 'Come down here and we'll talk.' Shauna followed Madeline down the corridor to a waiting area. It was empty so they sat down.

Madeline's pale face suggested the visit had been difficult.

'Are you okay?'

Madeline smiled. 'Yes, I'm fine but exhausted. We had a good chat.' Madeline patted Shauna's leg. 'I'll fill you in another time, love. I'm drained. I'll call a taxi and go home, but I'll be back in the morning. What are you going to do? The nurse said she'd probably be asleep for a few hours.'

'I'll stay. I haven't spoken to her properly since she was admitted.'

Madeline hugged Shauna. 'Call me if you need anything or think I should come back in.'

Madeline gave her a final wave as the lift door shut and Shauna turned and slowly walked towards her mother's room.

The room was bathed in moonlight by the time Lorraine opened her eyes. The day had been a blur for Shauna, and for the past four hours, since Madeline had left, she'd sat next to her mother's bed. She was caught up in her own thoughts. Regardless of the arguments and problems their relationship had suffered, she'd realised she would miss her mother terribly.

'Hey, darl, what are you still doing here?' Lorraine managed a weak smile.

Shauna put down the magazine she had been flicking through. 'I had no other plans, so I thought I'd stay. Do you need a drink?' Shauna reached for the cup of water.

'No, just sit me up, can you?'

Shauna pressed the buttons on the bed until Lorraine was raised to a sitting position.

'Thanks, love.'

'How are you feeling?'

'Honestly?'

'Yes.'

Lorraine gave a little laugh. 'Like I'll be meeting my maker sooner than expected.'

'God, don't say that.'

Lorraine took Shauna's hand. 'I'm sorry, but we need to face facts. I don't think I have much longer.'

'You seem a lot better right now.'

'Must be the drugs. They're giving me a new lease on life.'

'How was Grandma's visit?'

Lorraine smiled. 'Grandma, that has a nice ring to it. Her visit was weird, horrible and lovely. She's a hell of a woman. Make sure you become part of her life, won't you.'

'I think I already am. Did she forgive you?'

A range of emotions played over Lorraine's face, sadness being the final one to settle.

'Sorry, it's none of my business.'

'Don't be sorry, of course it is. You're the main part in this and what I did.' Lorraine considered her answer. 'I'm not sure about forgiveness, but we've made a kind of peace with each other. We talked for a long time. I think she needed me to realise the extent of how much I hurt both her and Don, but also wanted me to understand that she's never stopped loving me and never will. She also wanted me to know how sorry she was that she hadn't realised that I was suffering at the time, that I needed help and she feels that she failed me not getting me that help.' A tear escaped from Lorraine's eye. 'Like I said, she's a hell of a woman.'

Shauna handed her a tissue. 'I wish you'd realised this years ago.'

'Me, too, but I'm also realistic. I would never have stopped and looked at myself and the hurt I've caused without some kind of huge wake-up call. It doesn't get much bigger than this. My biggest regret though is not listening to Don and even you in your adult years. You both suggested that I might need some help and I dismissed you. Perhaps you were right, perhaps things might have been different.'

She managed a weak smile. 'Now, tell me something sensational, something to take my mind off this. How's that guy you're seeing? Anything serious?'

They spent the next two hours chatting quietly. Shauna told her mother about Josh, about her job and the wonderful friendship she had developed with Bec and Frankie. She spoke more about her current life in those two hours than she had done in the previous two years. Close to midnight Shauna noticed how quiet Lorraine had become.

'Are you okay? Do you need to sleep?'

Lorraine could only nod. Her eyelids sagged heavily and the colour she'd had earlier drained from her face.

Shauna lowered the bed, leaned down and kissed her.

Lorraine spoke softly. 'I love you, and if you do nothing else just remember this one thing. I love you more than I've ever loved anything; and I'm sorry.' Lorraine tried to smile but the effort was too much and her eyes closed.

A large tear fell from the corner of Shauna's eye; it would only be a matter of time now. She sat next to her mother's bed until the early hours of the morning when she stopped breathing. The doctor came to confirm that her mother was gone. Shauna remained next to her, not knowing what to do. After some time a hand rested gently on her shoulder. She turned to see Josh's kind, concerned face looking at her.

'How did you ...? I mean how did you know?'

Josh didn't answer, he just pulled Shauna up out of her chair and held her tight. 'I'm so sorry.' He spoke softly in her ear. The unexpected kindness opened the floodgates for Shauna. One tear followed another as she buried her face in Josh's chest.

# CHAPTER TWENTY-SEVEN

## *The Funeral*

Shauna was pleasantly surprised by the turnout for her mother's funeral and wake. People were gathered in the Dragonfly room of Grey's Funeral Home. Now that the service was complete, they were being served finger food and wine. The presence of Bec, Frankie and Tom was comforting. She walked over to where her small group of friends had gathered. 'Thank you so much for coming.'

'Don't be silly, we wanted to be here for you,' Bec said. 'How are you doing?'

Shauna forced a smile. 'Okay. Everything's been a bit of a shock. I'm not sure if it's hit me yet.'

Bec nodded. 'Promise you'll ring us when it does. That will be the perfect opportunity to visit you with an expensive bottle of wine.'

This time Shauna's smile was genuine. 'Any excuse for a drink.'

'Josh is popular,' Frankie said. Shauna looked across to where Josh was talking to a group of women.

'Does he know those people?' Frankie asked.

'No,' Shauna said, unable to hide her amusement. 'Although he'll have had intimate conversations with everyone in the room by the time we leave. He's a special man. He helped me organise every detail of the funeral.'

'You did your mum proud,' Tom said. 'Now, I might do Josh a favour and go and rescue him.' The women watched as Tom headed towards Josh.

Shauna's gaze fixed on Bec. 'How are things with you? How's the boyfriend and the husband?'

'Boyfriend's no longer and husband's unresolved. I'm going to chat with him on Wednesday and sort a few things out.'

'To get back together?' Frankie asked.

'No, but I hope we can move forward as friends. We've got the kids to think of. I'm hoping he wants the same.'

'I hope so, too,' Shauna said. 'And what happened with Tom's brother? Did you sort him out for Frankie?'

Frankie spoke up before Bec had a chance to answer. 'She sure did. You should see her in action. Dash is gone forever.'

Shauna grinned. 'That's fantastic news.'

'I need to thank you two,' Frankie said. 'If you hadn't pushed me into changing my life and getting involved with the business, Dash might have stolen a lot more. Bec saw to him and his nasty little lawyer.'

'Little ferret, you mean,' Bec said. 'Shauna, he was disgusting. The sort of man you can only imagine will be single for life. He didn't possess one redeeming quality. In fact, he oozed repulsiveness and I couldn't stand the sight of him.'

Frankie started to giggle. 'You were so professional during it all, I had no idea you were thinking those thoughts.' Her hand flew up to her mouth. 'Sorry, I shouldn't be laughing, not at your mother's funeral.'

'Laughter is good for the soul, my dear.' The women turned to find the kind eyes of an older lady smiling at them. She took Shauna's hand. 'So, are you going to introduce me to your friends?'

'Of course.' Shauna nodded. 'Grandma, meet Bec and Frankie. Ladies, this is my mystery grandmother.'

'We're sorry for your loss, Mrs Budd,' Frankie said.

'Thank you, dear. Call me Madeline though. It was a lovely service, wasn't it.'

'Yes, although small,' Shauna said. 'Mum didn't have many friends, well not that I knew of anyway.'

Madeline squeezed Shauna's hand. 'Lorraine found it hard to maintain friendships. Even as a little girl she'd present herself one way but there'd be something very different bubbling under the surface. As people got to know her she'd ultimately push them away. That's why I never realised how much her father's actions and behaviour affected her. I think having her own child triggered emotions she was incapable of dealing with. She was jealous of sharing you, jealous of having to share Don, terrified Don might turn into her own father. If she'd accepted the help Don tried to get her thirty years ago, we'd all be in a different situation today.'

'Mmm.' Shauna was deep in thought. She looked across to where Don was talking to two men. 'Can you believe my father came today? Not every man would be so forgiving.'

'He loved her very much once.' Madeline's eyes became distant. Shauna wondered what memories she was reliving. 'She had problems he couldn't find solutions for, and he's always blamed himself that he didn't do more to help her. In spite of what she did, I'm sure a part of him still loved her. If nothing else she gave him you, something he'll always be thankful for, as will I.'

Shauna's eyes misted over. She took the tissue Frankie offered.

Over the next hour the few guests in attendance began to leave. As the last guest departed, strong arms slid around Shauna's waist. She turned to face Josh. 'You've been wonderful.' She tugged him close. Josh lifted Shauna's chin up so he could look into her eyes. 'You know why I've been like that, don't you?'

'Because you're the nicest guy alive?'

Josh smiled. 'One valid reason of course, but no, a more important reason. I love you. I am completely in love with you.' Shauna wasn't given a chance to respond. Josh leaned forward, his lips meeting hers.

# CHAPTER TWENTY-EIGHT

## *Bec*

Lively chatter filtered throughout the cafe, the coffee machine hissed and steamed, and the counter, boasting a corrugated-iron front, groaned under the weight of elbows, breakfast plates and newspapers. Bec and Jess were tucked away at a corner table, offering them privacy and a perfect spot for people watching.

'How did you find this place?' Bec asked as a waitress set down their coffees.

'Max came here the other week,' Jess said. 'Apparently, they opened about a year ago, but being tucked away we'd never noticed it before.'

Bec's eyes continued exploring the Rustic Cafe. 'Who would have believed you could make exposed brick and heavy wooden beams work so well? Just look at that gorgeous fireplace. This place might be hidden away, but for a Sunday it's packed. We were lucky to get a seat.'

'So, how was the funeral?' Jess asked.

Bec smiled. 'Lovely. Josh, Shauna's boyfriend, helped her put together a beautiful service and wake.'

Jess emptied a sugar packet into her coffee. 'Did many attend?' She looked up, waiting for Bec's response. 'Bec?'

Bec's eyes were firmly fixed on a woman waiting in line to order takeaway coffee.

'Bec?' Jess shook her arm. 'Are you okay?'

Bec picked up a menu and hid her face. 'No. It's her, it's the woman.'

'Who? Not ...'

'Yes, Chris bloody Jenkins.'

Jess pulled the menu away from Bec, her eyes dark with fury. 'Why on earth are you hiding? I should be holding you down, stopping you from killing the bitch, not watching you hide. I mean it, Bec. She deserves a huge serve from you.'

Bec gave a weak smile. Jess's head would spin around any second if she got any more worked up.

'And anyway, she's ugly. Your definition of gorgeous is severely skewed.'

This comment had Bec laugh outright. 'Thanks, you've jolted me back to human status. You're right, she is ugly, in a kind of Angelina Jolie way.'

'Okay, so she's not exactly hideous, but she's still a bitch.'

Bec couldn't help staring at Chris. The woman who'd ruined her marriage. She should get up and flatten her. The barista placed two coffees down on the counter just as another woman came in through the front door. She walked up to Chris, draping her arm casually over her shoulders. Chris turned to her and smiled. The woman leaned closer and kissed Chris on the lips. She then moved back as she waited for Chris to pay for the coffees. The woman's hand caressed Chris's back before coming to a rest on the back of her jeans.

Bec stared at Jess. 'Did that just happen?'

Jess's eyes widened. 'Yep.' She lowered her voice. 'And I think she's seen you.'

Bec felt her stomach churn as Chris walked towards her. What had she just witnessed?

'Hello, Bec, lovely to see you.' Chris's voice trembled as she spoke. She smiled at Jess.

'Hi.' Bec's mind was racing. What was going on?

'So,' Chris said. 'My friend ...' She motioned to the woman still standing at the counter. 'My friend thought you might have noticed us ordering coffee.'

Bec nodded.

Chris's face flushed red. 'This is awkward. I'll just say it. Vicki is my fiancée, and while I'm generally open about my sexuality, I've chosen to be discreet at work. Paul knows and a couple of the other staff, but I'd appreciate if you would keep this to yourself.'

'You and Vicki?'

'Yes.' Chris's jaw set in a hard line. 'No need to look so shocked.'

Bec continued to stare at Chris. 'No, no you've misunderstood, it's you, you and Paul.'

'What about me and Paul?'

Bec couldn't speak. How had she got this so wrong?

Jess spoke for her. 'Bec is under the impression that her husband has been having an affair, with you.'

Chris's eyes widened. 'What? I told you nothing was going on the day you phoned me.'

'No you didn't, you laughed at me.'

Chris's hand flew to her mouth. 'Oh no, I'm so sorry. I laughed because of the ridiculousness of it. I spoke to Paul later and he assured me he'd explained to you that we were just colleagues. I actually assumed he would have told you about Vicki at that point.' Chris's face filled with concern. 'You and Paul, are things okay between you?'

Bec shook her head. 'He moved out months ago. Jesus.' She buried her head in her hands. 'I've really made a mess of this.' Her mind raced. Hold on, she'd seen them together with her own eyes. She looked up. 'I saw you and Paul. It was a while back now. You arrived in a taxi at the offices on Chapel Street. Paul was waiting, with roses, for you. You certainly looked like you were together then.'

Chris covered her mouth with her hand. 'Oh, no. Bec, why didn't you say something? You've totally misinterpreted the situation. Paul met me down at the taxi to congratulate me. I'd told him on a phone call the night before about my engagement to Vicki. You're right, he was lovely, gave me a beautiful flower arrangement. In fact, he said he'd chosen them because they were your favourite.'

Bec's head was spinning. Paul didn't have an affair with Chris.

Maria, what about Maria and her letter? 'Can I ask you something?'

Chris nodded.

'Do you know why Maria Upworth left the company?'

Chris's brow crinkled. 'Maria? She was dismissed. I'm not sure of the details. A sexual harassment issue, I believe, which the company dealt with through mediation.' Chris leaned closer to Bec and Jess and lowered her voice. 'Between you and me, I heard she was a nutter. She propositioned some of the clients, and when they said no, she contacted their wives and told them she'd slept with their husbands. She wasn't good for business.'

Bec tried to stretch her legs out under the table; they'd tensed so much they were beginning to hurt. A dull thudding had begun in her head and waves of nausea seeped through her body.

Chris looked at her strangely. The reality of the situation was apparently becoming clear to her. 'She didn't say she'd slept with Paul, did she?'

Bec nodded.

'Shit. Oh shit. So, you believed her and then didn't believe me?'

Bec nodded, unable to speak. Months and months of hating Paul for something he hadn't done.

Chris's face turned a ghostly white. 'I'm so sorry, Bec. Look, I'll leave you alone. It sounds like I've done enough. But please, if I can do anything to help, explain anything to Paul, contact me.' She passed Bec her card before retreating to the counter and her fiancée.

Jess's hand rested on Bec's arm. 'Are you okay?'

Bec raised her eyes to meet Jess's. 'What have I done?'

'You were wrong. Thank goodness, you were wrong.' Jess smiled. 'This is a good thing, a great thing. Paul didn't lie and he didn't cheat on you. All the questions you've been asking yourself about what you did to make him have an affair have been answered. You did nothing.'

'Nothing?' Bec could hardly utter the word. 'Nothing? I've not trusted my husband and pushed him to a point where he felt his only option was to leave. I ruined our marriage! It wasn't Paul, it was me.'

304

Three days after bumping into Chris at the Rustic Cafe, Bec found she couldn't calm the bundle of nerves in her stomach as she changed out of her gardening clothes to go and meet Paul. The past three days, plus the two hours she had spent digging and planting a new flowerbed, had given her plenty of time to go over what she needed to say.

At five to three she pulled into an empty space next to Paul's car at Dawson's Park. She got out and wound her way down the main walking track, until she got to the old hollowed-out tree she and Paul had carved their initials on many years before. The faint outline of their initials could still be seen. She walked off the track through the thick trees. How Paul had ever discovered this place still left her wondering. The undergrowth was thick and, other than Paul's recent tracks, it didn't look like anyone had been through here for a long while. Bec tried to remember the last time she and Paul had visited. Three, maybe four years ago? She pushed her way past overhanging vines, and finally found the clearing. The water sparkled from the small lake and Bec smiled at the lone pelican cruising in the warm sunshine.

'Hi.' Paul stepped out from the trees where he had been waiting for her, holding a single white rose.

Bec took a step backwards. 'What's this for?'

'Peace offering. I'm sorry about my reaction to the lotto win. I'm sorry about everything. Thanks for coming. We need to talk. Do you feel like afternoon tea?'

Bec looked over to the picnic rug and hamper Paul had set up on *their* spot. 'You don't think this will be a bit weird?'

'Weird? What, afternoon tea?'

'No!' Bec laughed. 'I meant the location of the rug.'

Paul smiled. 'I thought I'd try to lighten the moment.'

'Well, it certainly does.' She followed Paul over and sat down. 'How was Sydney?'

'I didn't go to Sydney.'

'But you said in your email you were in Sydney.'

Paul pushed his hand through his hair. 'I took some time out. I needed to think. Jess said a few things the night I found out about the money that made me angry, but also made me realise I've been acting like an idiot.'

'Jess?'

'Yes, I'm surprised she didn't tell you.'

'She said very little.'

Paul grinned. 'Did she tell you she hit me?'

Bec gasped. 'What! Jess? No way.'

'She did. Slapped me right across the face. Said she was sick of having to listen to me rave on like a lunatic about you and the money, and I assume she was trying to bring me to my senses.'

'Did she?'

Paul smiled. 'Not at the time. I ended our friendship and stormed out of their place.'

Bec raised an eyebrow. 'I can't believe she didn't mention any of this.'

'Don't worry, I went back the next day and apologised. Then I took off. Went up to the Murray River, bought a tent and a hammock. It gave me time to think. Work out what I want.'

Bec nodded. She couldn't believe all of this had gone on and Jess had kept it to herself. 'Before you tell me what you've decided, I need to say something.'

Paul looked her directly in the eye. 'No, let me have my say first. I need you to hear it before you say anything.' He took a deep breath. 'I want to fix us. I hate what's happening. I hate the kids being affected and us not talking. I'd like to sort things out between us and get back together.'

Bec didn't respond, she just looked at Paul in disbelief. He wanted to get back together. He was willing to put everything she'd put him through behind them and start again. A tear escaped from her eye.

Paul dug a clean handkerchief from his pocket and handed it to Bec. 'Don't cry. I know this is hard. Have you moved on already?'

Bec wiped her eyes. 'Moved on? You mean George?'

'Yes.'

'No. I ended my friendship with him. I'm not crying because I've moved on, I'm crying because of what I've done. I spoke to Chris Jenkins on Sunday. I know you didn't have an affair. I know that my nagging and bitching, as you called it months ago, drove you away.' Tears were now running down Bec's face. 'What have I done to us?'

Paul reached out and pulled Bec to him, stroking her hair. 'Oh, thank God.' He pulled away so he could smile at her. 'To be fair, I'm not sure I helped the situation. I never gave you the real explanation for why I did all of the late nights and trips to Sydney. Why I felt the need to buy new suits and work out every day. I hoped moving out might give you a shock, make you realise how much you loved me and we needed to work on things. Instead you seemed to embrace the idea of divorce immediately.'

Bec nodded. 'So, what was the real reason behind your behaviour? I thought you were having a midlife crisis.'

'I needed to change and the promotion forced me to. I'm not sure about it being a midlife crisis, but I definitely started reflecting on things. I was looking for motivation to become more successful. I'd let myself go, grown fat and lazy and the first meeting in Sydney made me realise others had noticed.' Paul's face darkened as he relived the memory. 'Their thirty-year-old top advertising executive, dressed in his Armani suit, tanned and looking like a triathlete got to me. I overheard him in the men's toilets talking to another guy. Laughing at me.'

'Why, what did they say?'

'Something along the lines of me being a joke. That management must have something wrong with them to give the promotion to a big fat loser. The other guy agreed. I assume he did anyway by the laughter, and then suggested I'd be dead from a heart attack pretty soon so the promotion would be up for grabs again.'

Bec's hand flew up to her mouth. 'Oh no, why didn't you tell me?'

'I was embarrassed. I figured you probably considered me a fat loser, too. I got back on the plane after the first meeting with them and decided to make some changes. I joined the gym the same afternoon.'

'But you let me think you were having an affair! Why didn't you explain then?'

'I did tell you I wasn't having an affair.'

'Not with any real conviction. Half the time you'd just snap at me or say don't be stupid. You never explained what had happened.'

Paul rubbed his hands over his cheeks. 'Yes, I know I didn't. I think I kind of liked the assumption I might be desirable enough for someone to want to have an affair with me. To start with I thought you were kidding, but then we started fighting all the time. It didn't matter what I did or said, you were angry. I didn't think it was the only problem anymore.'

'Of course it was, it was the root of all the problems. I didn't trust you and resented every night you spent away. Not trusting you manifested into snapping at you, nagging. I couldn't help it, I hated you for doing this to us, or what I thought you were doing at least.'

Paul shook his head. 'Jesus, we've really made a mess of this, haven't we?'

Bec nodded. 'I can't believe we've let this go on for months. Bloody hell, I started seeing someone.'

'You've got to know how much that ate me up. Another man with you to start with is bad enough, but also around the boys. It made me realise if we did split up not only would I lose you, but someone else could become a big part of my boys' lives. I couldn't share them.'

'They never met George. In fact, they don't know he exists. If it helps at all, I didn't sleep with him.'

The relief on Paul's face brought more tears to Bec's eyes. She realised in that moment how much he still loved her.

Paul opened up the picnic basket and pulled out two glasses and a bottle of Moët.

Bec raised an eyebrow.

'I was hoping this afternoon would be a celebration. Don't worry, if you'd stormed off or pushed me into the lake I'd have drunk it all to commiserate. Instead, I get to share this with my beautiful wife.' Paul poured them both a glass. 'Here's to starting again. To trust and love.'

Bec leaned over and kissed Paul. She was overcome by an incredible sense of lightness. All of the hurt and unhappiness she had been bottling up for months left her. 'This really is our magical place, isn't it?' Bec thought of the many wonderful times she and Paul had escaped here in the past.

Paul took her hand and wove his fingers in amongst hers. 'That's for sure. This is a place for starting new chapters in our life. For all those times, today is probably the most special one for me.'

Bec smiled at him, her eyes twinkling. 'Really? I remember a moment about eight years ago you might consider more special.'

'Mmm.' Paul looked at her wickedly. 'My memory's a bit hazy, perhaps you could remind me.'

Bec put her champagne flute on a rock and turned to face her husband. She slowly unbuttoned her shirt and lowered her voice. 'Bring back any memories?'

Paul nodded and took Bec in his arms. She knew at that moment that the feelings she had developed for George, whilst real, were nothing in comparison to what she felt for her husband. Lost in Paul's kisses, tears mixed with joy and relief filled Bec's eyes. A surge of desire flooded her as Paul pushed her down gently on the picnic rug; a rug he'd placed in the same spot they'd conceived Alex eight years before.

# CHAPTER TWENTY-NINE

## *Six Months Later*

The sun's soft glow, as it slowly disappeared behind the hills, threw a beautiful light on the garden and wedding guests. The waterfall and majestic weeping willows provided a stunning backdrop for the ceremony, and now, sounds of laughter and music filled the air. Fairy lights, strung through the trees, added to the magic of the day.

Frankie and Bec stood together and admired the beautiful setting. 'Oh my God, I think I'm going to cry, again.'

Bec put her arm around Frankie and passed her a tissue. 'I agree. I don't think I've been to a more superb wedding. She's so in love with him. Did you see her face?'

Frankie dabbed her eyes. 'It's like a fairytale. Being walked down the aisle by her long-lost father to marry such a gorgeous man. And she was crying. So much for the hard-nosed businesswoman.'

'Oh, I think she's still pretty hard-nosed.' Josh came up behind the women and put his arms around their shoulders. 'I was lucky to find the softer side to her, too.'

'Congratulations.' Frankie kissed Josh on the cheek. 'We're so happy for you.'

'Thank you.' Josh beamed. 'Did you see my stunning wife by the way? Here she comes now.' Josh held out his hand, which Shauna took and glided towards the group.

'Simply lovely.' Frankie continued to dab at her tears. 'The most magnificent wedding I've ever been to.'

'Thank you,' Shauna said.

Bec threw up her hands. 'That's it?'

'What do you mean?'

'No smart-arse remark to add? Who are you?'

'Ah.' Josh winked. 'Marriage, it's softened her already.'

Shauna slapped Josh's arm. 'Shut up, you. You'll remember this wedding night for all the wrong reasons if you're not careful.'

'Seriously,' Bec said. 'You're dazzling and the service was perfect. Your sisters are striking, too.'

'Two sisters for bridesmaids; how unbelievable. And did you see my aunt?' Shauna pointed to a woman deep in conversation with her father. She was so like Shauna it was uncanny.

'Oh my God.' Bec laughed. 'Incredible. Imagine if you'd bumped into her in the street before reconnecting with your dad. At least you know what you'll look like in forty years.'

'She's really lovely, actually,' Josh said. 'Hopefully, my beautiful wife will be as gorgeous when she's in her seventies.'

They continued to stare at Shauna's Aunt Sharon until Frankie broke the silence. 'Who's the guy in the suit talking to Hope?'

'Patrick, my brother,' Shauna said. 'He came back from Afghanistan so he could be here today. I finally met my little brother, and check him out, he's gorgeous. Mmm, Patrick and Hope are very cute together.'

'She's only sixteen,' Frankie said.

'He's only twenty-two.' Shauna grinned at Frankie's horrified face. 'Okay, perhaps a bit too old for her. She looks beautiful by the way. I love her hair.' At that moment, Hope looked over towards Frankie and gave her a little wave. 'And her dress.'

'It seems that all the boys at school agree with you. Her phone never stops ringing.'

Shauna fanned her face. 'Oh my God, you mean you allowed a haircut, new clothes and a phone?'

Frankie blushed. 'Yes okay, point made. Now, be quiet.'

'Hey, this is my wedding, I can say what I like.' Her smile faded.

'On a more serious note, how are things with the business? Any news of the brother?'

'Not recently,' Frankie said. 'Although he didn't just disappear as we hoped. A couple of months ago he contacted Tom and tried to convince him I'd set him up and that it was all a big mistake. Of course he was after more money.'

'What did Tom do?' Bec asked.

Frankie blushed. 'The summary of their meeting was Tom flattened him. Dash made the mistake of referring to the night he'd tried to force himself on me. I guess he was going to suggest that I'd wanted it, but Tom didn't give him the chance. He was so upset when he came home. I should have told him when it happened. I was ashamed though. Of course Tom believed my version of that night. He won't allow Dash near any of us ever again.'

'Good,' Shauna said. 'And remember you had absolutely nothing to be ashamed of. I'm just glad that Tom made sure he realised that. Your old fisherman friend gave him a small taste of what he deserved but in my opinion it wasn't enough. Now, that's enough about him. We have many reasons to celebrate and never seeing the brother again is definitely one of them.'

She turned to Josh. 'Sweet husband, would you mind finding a waiter and getting us some drinks please?'

Josh kissed Shauna and went in search of the waiter.

'He's the happiest man alive right now,' Frankie said.

'Who wouldn't be,' Bec said. 'Married to an intelligent, funny, sexy, rich woman. He's also the luckiest man alive.'

Shauna nodded. 'He is and at least he's not marrying me for my money.'

Bec raised an eyebrow. 'Oh?'

'Turns out our Josh was hiding a secret of his own. See that guy over there?' Shauna pointed to a silver-haired man who had just thrown back his head and was roaring with laughter at something someone said. 'He's Josh's dad, Lloyd Richardson.'

Bec sucked in her breath. 'What, the billionaire? You're kidding. How come you didn't tell us before?'

'I only found out when we had a family dinner so that my dad and grandmother could meet his family. Turned out he and Dad had done business together in the past.'

'How did Josh explain?'

'He never denied having money. Ages ago he told me about his family and how successful his dad was. He made it very clear that he'd lived independently since he left home at eighteen and refused any handouts or help. He just didn't let on who they were or the extent of the family empire. He wanted to make sure I loved him for who he was. He's never used the family's position to benefit him, always done things on his own terms, but he can't deny the fact that he has a rather large trust fund and a ridiculous inheritance to accept one day. Our lotto win pales in comparison. Mind you, he'll probably donate the lot to charity. He's adamant about making it on his own. Anyway, I'd better stop, he's coming back.'

Josh returned with the drinks. 'I've just been chatting with Paul. He's a decent guy, Bec.'

'He is,' she agreed.

'So, things are good with you two?' Frankie asked.

'Incredible,' Bec said. 'I feel like I'm on a second honeymoon. There's something to be said for almost breaking up. Especially when you're starting life again with millions of dollars in the bank. Amazing what that can do to jazz up a marriage.'

Shauna waved her hand dismissively. 'Just the norm for Josh and me, millionaires before we were married, we won't know any different.'

Bec swatted Shauna on the arm. 'Listen to you would you? You'll turn into one of those stuck-up rich cows if you keep talking like that.'

'What? Like you, with your fancy designer house and these jewels you're flaunting today?' Shauna touched the beautiful diamond necklace Bec was wearing. 'Where's the maid and the Rolls?'

Bec laughed. 'Hey, I'm still a working mother. Paul threw in his job, not me. Although I'm not saying no to the regular games of golf on the Peninsula, or the occasional winery lunch we seem to be managing while the boys are at school.'

'Sounds wonderful,' Frankie said. 'When will the house be ready?'

'They're saying another two months. I can't wait. It's pretty special.'

'Looks like your house will be the next big celebration,' Shauna said.

'What will?' Tom joined the group, putting his arm around Frankie.

'Bec and Paul's housewarming,' Frankie said. 'It should be ready in a couple of months.'

'A party to look forward to,' Tom said. 'Hopefully you'll still be up for a late night,' he said to Frankie. 'Have you told them yet?'

'Told us what?' Bec demanded.

Frankie patted her stomach. 'We'll be introducing someone new in about five months.'

Shauna threw her arms around Frankie and Tom. 'That's such brilliant news!'

Frankie struggled out of Shauna's grip and laughed. 'Let's just say it's been an unexpected but welcome surprise.'

'Do you know what you're having?' Bec asked.

Tom rubbed Frankie's stomach. 'Can I tell them?'

Frankie laughed. 'You'll burst if I say no, so you might as well.'

'A boy. Can you believe we're having a boy? I was sure we'd have another girl.'

Josh raised his glass. 'This calls for a toast. To Frankie, Tom and Tom junior.'

They all raised their glasses and toasted the new arrival.

Frankie turned to Shauna, a gleam in her eye. 'You two will need to get a move on. Tom junior here is going to want a playmate.'

Shauna laughed. 'Don't hold your breath. Imagine me as a mum? I'd be a nightmare. Now, let's check what this band is doing and get some dancing underway.' Shauna dragged Josh towards the dance floor. Frankie and Tom followed closely.

'Want to dance, Mr Hutton?' Bec tugged Paul towards her.

He kissed her.

'Mmm, what was that for?'

'Just thinking how lucky I am. A beautiful wife, two awesome boys, good friends, freedom to do whatever we like. I'm scared it's a dream.'

'Don't be scared,' Bec said. 'Just thank God we woke up from the nightmare.'

'Yes, let's just live happily ever after.'

'Sounds good to me.' Bec allowed Paul to guide her to the dance floor.

Josh stood in front of Shauna in the early hours of the next morning. The wedding guests had all been farewelled and finally he was able to undress his wife. 'You don't really believe you'd make a terrible mother, do you?'

Shauna placed a hand on her belly. 'No, I just wanted to put them off the scent. Couldn't upstage Frankie's news now, could I? Trump her with a wedding and a pregnancy; it was her moment, not mine.'

Josh laughed. 'Wow, you're a big softie, aren't you? Where's the ball-breaker gone?'

Shauna slipped her hand inside Josh's pants and took a firm grip. 'She's still here, and don't you get the wrong idea now.'

Josh groaned. 'Hey, be careful, you might want more babies after this one. Although from memory, I think this is what got us into the baby situation.'

Shauna parted her lips. 'You may be right, Mr Richardson. Now, it's time to forget about these wanton women you've been knocking up and make slow, romantic love to your wife.'

Josh drew Shauna towards him and kissed her. He didn't need to be told twice.

# ALSO BY LOUISE GUY

## *Everyday Lies*

For Emma and Lucie, the art of lying appears all too easy . . .

Emma Wilson has it all. Beauty, wealth, and a loving and successful husband. But appearances can be deceptive. Bored and restless, her need for more fuels a dangerous craving; one she intends to keep hidden. Against her husband's wishes and trapped in a deep web of lies, Emma returns to the family and hometown she left seventeen years earlier. Here, her lies magnify, threatening to destroy her marriage and all she holds dear.

Widowed and struggling financially and emotionally, Lucie Andrews is pushed to her limits. Delayed grief combined with an obstinate five-year-old drive her to rash decisions and reckless behaviour, the consequences of which she is determined to keep secret. For Lucie, the most damaging lies are not the ones she tells others, but those she tells herself.

Thrown together by circumstance, will friendship be strong enough for Emma and Lucie to survive the fallout from their lies, or will the fragile threads of their lives continue to unravel?

WWW.LOUISEGUY.COM

# DID YOU ENJOY THE STORY?

I do hope you enjoyed *Fortunate Friends*. If you did, I would be very appreciative if you could take a few minutes to leave an honest review on Amazon (www.amazon.com.au), Goodreads (www.goodreads. com) or your favourite book retailer's website. I'd love to hear your feedback too, so please get in touch via: **www.louiseguy.com**

# ACKNOWLEDGEMENTS

I'd like to send a sincere thank you to the many wonderful people in my life who continue to encourage and support each step of my writing journey. Having friends and family who are not only interested, but love to talk writing and reading is a dream come true.

A very special thank you to Ray for your constant encouragement, support and enthusiasm for my writing, coupled with your willingness to read early drafts and proof-read final drafts.

To the early readers of *Fortunate Friends:* Judy, Maggie, Sarah and Tracy, thank you for the invaluable feedback provided at various stages of the manuscript development.

Thank you to Louise Cusack for her manuscript assessment many moons ago when this story was known as *Lucky Numbers.*

To Alexandra Nahlous, thank you for your knowledge and expertise in editing this story.

To Bonnie Wilson, thank you for your proof-reading services.

A huge thank you to my wonderful writing friends: Claire, Laila, Linda, Robyn and Sueanne for your input to this manuscript. Your *final eyes* after the proof-reading stage were invaluable, as is your friendship.

And lastly, to all the wonderful readers who continue to read, comment, review and message me about my books, an enormous thank you. Your enthusiasm and support is incredibly uplifting.

Made in the USA
San Bernardino, CA
08 April 2018